ALL
the
MONEY
in the
WORLD

ALL
the
MONEY
in the
WORLD

ROBERT ANTHONY SIEGEL

RANDOM HOUSE NEW YORK

Library of Congress Cataloging-in-Publication Data is available

ISBN 0-679-44832-2

Random House website address: http://www.randomhouse.com/

Printed in the United States of America on acid-free paper

2 4 6 8 9 7 5 3

First Edition

TO MY FAMILY,
AND TO KAREN

It was worse than a crime, it was a blunder.

—Otto von Bismarck, as quoted by Richard Nixon

ALL
the
MONEY
in the
WORLD

1

CASH IS AN ACCEPTABLE FORM
OF PAYMENT

Louis Glasser was a man of large appetites, and on mornings like this one, when he didn't have to appear in court, he treated himself to a second breakfast at his desk. He began with half a grapefruit, digging politely with his plastic spoon; but when he came to the omelette, the buttered bialy, the home fries, there was no pretending anymore—his attack was savage. Slivers of egg speckled the sky-blue Egyptian cotton that covered his barrel stomach, and butter dribbled over his hand-painted Italian necktie. Reaching over for the egg cream, he glanced up at Henry Auerbach, who sat slumped in the armchair opposite. "You sure you don't want anything?"

Auerbach, dyspeptic pornographer and Glasser client for more than a decade, shook his head no. "I can't eat, Lou. My stomach's in knots. I can't hold anything down." He had reason to be upset: two daughters in college, a mortgage, and a failing business, and now obscenity charges worth a good three years in prison.

"How about a poached egg? I could order one up for you."

Auerbach tugged at his straggly goatee as if he meant to tear it out. There was something primitive in the fury with which he mourned his own misfortune. "All I eat are Tums."

"I've got Maalox if you want."

"Forget it, I'm past help."

This may have been truer than Auerbach realized. The day before, Glasser had called the prosecutor assigned to Auerbach's case, an assistant district attorney by the name of Michael Kean. Glasser had dealt with Kean in the past and knew him to be decent—a slight man in his mid-thirties, with pictures of his kids hanging on the office wall and the look of a worrier about his pouchy, wrinkled eyes.

Over the phone, Glasser had appealed to the A.D.A.'s sense of fairness. "The case is a piece of shit, Mike. This is a porno film we're talking about—a waste of a jail cell."

"Christ, don't you think I know that?" Kean had his own reasons for being unhappy, of course; Auerbach was a hard-luck assignment, not the kind of thing to help a young A.D.A. win advancement. "Maybe he wants to take a plea and help me out. I've got six robberies stacked up and no time for this crap."

"The guy's fifty-three, with high blood pressure and bleeding ulcers. Jail will kill him."

A rustle of papers, the *ka-chunk* of a stapler. "Then he shouldn't be making obscene movies, right?"

Glasser sighed. The movie in question was called *Butt Mitzvah*, and that gave a fair indication of the problem they faced. The Lubavitcher rabbi had denounced the film in a speech in Crown Heights, and three members of the City Council had called for prosecution—all of which would have been excellent publicity if picketing hadn't forced the film out of circulation.

"The movie's gone," said Glasser. "The theaters won't touch it, and the production company is broke. The whole thing's over and done with already."

Kean lowered his voice. "We're heading into an election year, Lou. You know these things take on a life of their own." It was 1987, and 1988 was already promising to be a tough contest.

But Glasser wouldn't let him get away so easily. He had seen the family photos on the prosecutor's walls and knew just how to squeeze him. "He's got two daughters in college, Mike, two lovely girls."

"Stop it," said Kean. "Don't—"

"I've known them since they were in diapers. One's pre-med and the other plays the piano like you wouldn't believe."

There was a moment of silence on the other end, followed by a tired exhalation. When Kean spoke again his voice had that tone so common to people working in the criminal justice system, a blend of frustration and annoyance and something darker—regret. "I don't like it either, but there's nothing I can do. Give me a call when you're ready to talk about the plea."

Looking over his desk at Auerbach now, Glasser was afraid the pornographer wouldn't be able to withstand the pressure of a trial. Doom-ridden at the best of times, Auerbach looked wild-eyed now, as if he expected the floor to drop out from under him. Glasser wanted to reassure him without masking the seriousness of the situation, but it was a hard balance to strike. "You have nothing to worry about, Henry. Not yet, anyway."

"Except the money you owe us." This was Glasser's partner, Jerry Feldman, seated on the black leather couch by the wall. The firm's second in command, Feldman was obligated to bring up the question of money.

More than a decade younger than his senior partner, Feldman was almost as heavy, a boyish-looking man of forty-five with a head of curly black hair and a wounded, smart-alecky face. Once a frail, asthmatic kid, Feldman had grown up certain that mold, dust, pollen could kill him. He had gone from school straight home every day, where in the twilight of a pristine room his mother had fortified him with bowls of soup, boiled vegetables, whole roast chickens. Thirty years later, the result was a cunning, garrulous lawyer, with a child's love of trickery and schemes.

Feldman said, "Good legal representation doesn't come cheap."

Auerbach's eyes were closed, and he was massaging his temples with the tips of his fingers. "Give it to me easy, please, Jerry. I'm not feeling good."

Glasser hid himself behind the remains of his bialy. After almost thirty years in the practice of law, he was still uncomfortable negotiating fees, and his big brown eyes looked over at Auerbach with delicate concern, almost apologetic for his partner's strong-arm tactics.

"We want to get started on motions," Feldman was saying, "but you know how it is, we can't do that without some money down."

"How much?" Auerbach's eyelids trembled.

"Seven thousand now. More if we go to trial."

The pornographer's eyes sprang open, two huge wet orbs incandescent with misery, appealing to Glasser. "I've got a daughter at Bennington, Lou, and another at Smith. For chrissake, do you know what those tuitions are like?"

"I know," mumbled Glasser, his mouth full of bialy. He was a famous soft touch, and there was no telling what stupid thing he might say if he could speak freely. Tell Auerbach to forget about the fee? Offer him a loan? He took a long drag of the egg cream instead.

"I'll miss the payments for next semester and they'll have to drop out of school. I'm going to lose my house and my business too. I'll be bankrupt before I'm in jail."

"You're not going to jail," said Glasser. "Probably not."

"Not if you pay your lawyers," added Feldman.

A look of shrewdness entered Auerbach's face then, not erasing the panic there but merging with it. "I can give you three thousand —cash." He lifted a beat-up leather satchel that had been resting by his chair, put it on the paper-strewn desk.

Glasser spent a tense moment staring at the bag. Three thousand was not seven, and in collecting fees the idea was to get as much as possible up front. Once he went down as the attorney of record, he would be legally committed to the case, unable to quit unless excused by the judge; and with a client like Auerbach, there was a good chance the retainer would be all they'd ever see.

But Glasser could not keep himself from reaching. There was money in that bag, and he felt the impatience of a little boy faced with a present, a present that must be opened *now*. His hands squeezed the old satchel, feeling a hint of what lay inside, blocky and dense. "Cash is an acceptable form of payment," he said.

Feldman threw him an angry look. "Let's consider this a first installment."

But it was too late. Auerbach was no longer listening, and Glasser had the bag open and was lifting out little rubber-banded packets of money. The packets were about half an inch thick, made up of old ones and fives, the bills worn soft as cloth, dark with the grime of countless fingers. They gave off a damp papery smell, tinged with the scent of leather from the satchel and all the wallets and purses that had come before.

"Now isn't that something?" said Glasser.

Even Auerbach looked rapt, his face a complicated mixture of pride and pain. One hand massaged his temple gently. "I made that," he said softly. "I made it a dollar at a time."

Feldman pushed himself up from the couch, unable to resist the lure of those bills. He and Glasser began counting—running the money through their fingers, muttering numbers to themselves in a private reverie. Three thousand dollars was not a lot of money to them; but they made ten dollars with the same delight as ten thousand, reveling in the sheer pleasure of the act.

When the counting was finished and the money back in the bag, Glasser beamed over at Auerbach. "You sure you don't want anything, Henry? Some coffee?"

The pornographer was standing now, looking frail in an old pair of baggy jeans and a lumberjack shirt, worn colorless at the elbows. "I've got to pick up my wife at her aerobics class." He hesitated a moment. "Listen, I need a lawyer for Reuben too." Reuben was his assistant, an NYU film student who moonlighted as his chauffeur, cameraman, and sidekick. "You know, somebody good but not too expensive. I feel like I owe the kid."

Glasser nodded sympathetically. "I've got just the man. I'll give him a call and get back to you."

"Thank you, Lou. I know you're going to save me."

They all said this, but it touched Glasser every time. "I'm going to try. Now go home and stop worrying."

With Auerbach gone and the door to Glasser's office shut, Feldman began to complain. "I thought you were going to let me negotiate the fee."

"I thought so too." Aware there was little he could offer in his own defense, Glasser began slurping the last of his egg cream.

"We'll never get the rest now. He'll string us along till the case is finished."

"He didn't have the money, Jerry. Just look at him, dressed in *schmattas*." Glasser picked up the phone, hoping to close the discussion. "Listen, I'm sending the other case to Petruccio, so we'll get a third of that too." A single practitioner with offices in the same building, Rocco Petruccio got their excess business in exchange for a one-third referral fee.

"We would've had that anyway," said Feldman, unappeased. He looked like he wanted to say something more, but Petruccio's voice came over the line just then, much to Glasser's relief.

"Lou! How the hell are you?" A longtime favorite with Glasser, Petruccio was something of a criminal court character. Five feet tall in elevator shoes and a black toupee, he dressed with systematic verve, color-coordinating socks, tie, pocket square—even smoking Nat Sherman cigarettes in colors to match, their gold filters pincered between his teeth.

"I've got a case for you," said Glasser, scooping a forkful of home fries. "The guy's a co-defendant with one of our clients."

Glasser explained the background while Petruccio took some notes. Rocco had a thriving practice, but it occupied the bottom of the criminal status hierarchy: pickpockets, cat burglars, and most especially prostitutes, whom he handled like a wholesaler, giving the pimps discounts for volume. Glasser would run into him in night court after the police had made a sweep, negotiating bail for twenty or thirty women at a time, their pimps standing in a line in the back of the courtroom, waiting for their release. It was a weekly occurrence: Rocco surrounded by these women in their shiny hip boots, hot pants, and lingerie, top-heavy with fanciful beehive wigs in pink or silver. Exhausted from their wait in the holding pens, strung out and glassy-eyed, barely able to follow the proceedings, the women swayed above him like weird palm trees.

As always, Petruccio was floridly grateful for the referral. "You're the king, Lou. I mean it, the king." And then, business concluded, his voice dropped conspiratorially. "Listen, I bet you haven't heard the news." A compulsive backslapper and joke teller, Rocco prided himself on being in the know. And his sources really were very good. He was careful to make friends everywhere, especially among those who counted—secretaries in the D.A.'s Office, clerks and bailiffs in the court building. "You know Ray O'Donnel, right?"

Glasser knew him only slightly. O'Donnel was a hotshot trial lawyer with a lot of big Mafia clients and a nose for publicity—an abrasive, arrogant man with a bulbous forehead and the chesty strut of a petty dictator. He dated starlets, his name was in the gossip columns, and he was invariably quoted in any newspaper article about a gangland shooting. Skimming TV channels the other night, Glasser had seen him on a news show, commenting on the killing of a Mafia chieftain. "What about him?"

Petruccio's voice was smoky, flavored by a dark, giddy pleasure. "The word is that he's under investigation by the Feds." He meant the U.S. Attorney's Office. "It looks like they've turned one of his clients."

"One of his own clients?" Glasser was genuinely shocked. The attorney-client relationship is based on trust, and it engenders a strange and powerful intimacy. Glasser picked out the clothing his clients wore in court, brought them fresh underwear if they were in jail. He diagnosed their physical ailments, patched their emotional wounds, advised them on their marital problems. Killers had cried on his shoulder, and he had comforted them in his arms.

"It would never have happened in the old days," he said to Petruccio. "The old sense of loyalty is gone."

"The clients are the same, Lou, it's the Feds that've changed. They'd rather hang lawyers than criminals now, it gets them better headlines."

"What do they have on him?"

"What do they need? When word gets out that his phone's been bugged, he won't have a client left anyway."

This was true, of course; it was enough that O'Donnel was under investigation; the clients would all desert him now. "That's why I always stay away from Mafia cases," said Glasser. "They're bound to get you in trouble."

"Who knows what it was? Maybe they just got tired of watching him brag on TV."

Off the phone, Glasser told Feldman about Ray O'Donnel. "Do you think it's true?" he asked, picking at the leftover home fries with his plastic fork.

Feldman was seated in the chair vacated by Auerbach, browsing through a copy of the *Law Journal*. "It's the climate these days. Here, look at this." He held the newspaper up for Glasser to see, pointing to one of the columns. "It says here that Morty Elfenbein just got indicted for money laundering. You remember Morty Elfenbein?"

Morty Elfenbein had had an office in that very building for more than a decade, and Glasser had seen him nearly every day, in the elevator or the halls of the court building, at a nearby table in the deli at lunchtime. A grayish, slouch-shouldered man in a baggy suit, with a cigarette dangling from the corner of his enormous mouth, he had moved with a pot-bellied, hangdog sort of elegance, walking down Broadway as if he were on his way to a funeral. Glasser remembered him stopping at the magazine stand in the lobby to buy lottery tickets—not one, but four or five at a time.

And then suddenly he was gone. Glasser might not even have noticed had not Petruccio called to tell him, but then he made a special trip to Elfenbein's floor and saw for himself: a rectangular discoloration and four screw holes in the wooden door where Elfenbein's shingle had once hung.

"But why him?" Glasser reached for the pack of cigarettes by his coffee cup, lit one, and blew a contemplative plume of smoke. "Elfenbein was no big cheese, not like O'Donnel."

Feldman began folding up the *Law Journal* very carefully, smoothing it down with the flat of his hand. He was as meticulous as Glasser was sloppy, and his own office was spotless, the desk clear of papers. "You know, I saw him on the street a few weeks ago. His hair had gone completely white."

"Did you speak to him?"

Feldman looked surprised by the question. "Nah, I hid behind a newspaper stand. I guess I didn't know what to say."

Glasser took a long drag on his cigarette, blowing the smoke out of his nose. The image of Elfenbein shambling down the street, his hair gone prematurely white, stuck with him uncomfortably. In the highly competitive world of criminal law, success was valued above all else. People like Elfenbein became the subject of gossip for a little while—clucked over, pitied in a condescending sort of way. But that was it. After the novelty was gone, they were expected to pack up and disappear—quickly. Acquaintances avoided them on the street, old colleagues neglected to return their phone calls. Even sweet-natured, portly Feldman crouched behind a newsstand.

What must it feel like, thought Glasser, to see your friends ducking into doorways, pretending not to see you? He recalled Elfenbein in one of his ill-fitting suits, looking over a lottery ticket with all the solemnity of a rabbi reading Torah. Had he known that disaster was on the way? Never a big earner, he couldn't have had very much in the bank. What was he living on now? How was he paying his lawyers? Glasser was an impulsively generous man, and if Elfenbein had been standing right there, by his desk, he would have handed him Auerbach's satchel of money without a moment's hesitation.

But Elfenbein wasn't there, and the money was already earmarked for something else. Glasser looked at his watch, dropped his cigarette in the remains of his home fries, then reached for the leather bag. "Listen," he said to Feldman, "let me take my share right now." He began pulling out bundles of money, stacking them on the desk like bricks—fifteen packets equaling fifteen hundred dollars.

"What's up?"

"The kid's coming at noon, and I've got to buy him a suit for his interview. That Japanese thing."

Glasser's son, Jason, was twenty-two, a senior at Harvard and a source of concern for the entire office. Graduating in June, he refused to apply to law school, refused to sign up for the big corporate interviews held on campus—declined, in fact, to do anything that might impart some kind of shape to his future and relieve a father's worry. Instead, he was trying for an academic fellowship offering a year's study in Japan. In the opinion of Glasser & Feldman, it was little more than a joy ride.

"Geisha girls," scoffed Feldman.

Glasser could only shrug. "Beats working, I guess." But in reality he was troubled. The kid seemed wholly unprepared for the harsher aspects of life, the rough-and-tumble in which his father specialized. At some point this would cause pain, and the thought of Jason in pain made the lawyer nearly frantic. The only solution—the only relief—was to make sure the boy got exactly what he wanted. If Jason wanted Japan, Glasser would do everything he could to get it for him, starting with a new suit for the interview. He picked up the phone and buzzed Rainbow, asking her to come in.

"Get him a haircut too," said Feldman. "And tell him to shave that peach fuzz off his face."

"I know, I know."

The situation was familiar. Four years before, the whole office had been mobilized to help with Jason's college applications, as if getting him into Harvard were a big case to be won at all costs. Glasser read drafts of the essays, then passed them on to Feldman for comment, who conferred on particularly sticky questions with the associates and even the paralegals. Rainbow edited them for spelling and grammar, then typed them up on heavy bond paper bought specially for the purpose. The boy was relegated to Glasser's couch, furiously rewriting, or trying to argue for his version of a particular paragraph against the combined forces of the two lawyers.

Rainbow's heavy, squarish frame appeared in the doorway, a pencil and pad in one hand, some files tucked under her arm. "You rang, master?"

"We've had a visit from Mr. Green," said Glasser, using the office slang for money. He held up the satchel like a fisherman displaying a prize fish.

"Auerbach cough up?" She tucked the pencil behind one ear, then walked over to take the bag from Glasser's hand.

Rainbow: the hippie name had almost fit once, fifteen years before—apt in its sheer goofiness. She had been in her twenties then, a scatterbrained ex-client in tie-dyed dresses and rectangular blue sunglasses, three arrests and a drug problem already behind her. But the office had brought out her practical side, and over the years she'd grown increasingly stolid, even matronly, graying black hair pulled back in a long ponytail, an image of what her mother in Detroit must have been.

"Jerry put the squeeze on him," said Glasser. "It was a sight to see."

Feldman looked annoyed at this. "We would've gotten double if you'd kept your mouth shut."

"It's cash. Everybody gets a discount for cash." Glasser had grown up during the Depression, the era of bank failures, and still kept a childlike faith in the feel of real dollar bills.

"You want me to put this in the firm account?" asked Rainbow.

"Safe-deposit box." This was the usual procedure with cash, when they didn't just split it on the spot. Though they sometimes disagreed about collection, the partners were happily united in their dislike for the tax man.

The phone began to ring, and Rainbow went all the way around the desk to get it, Glasser watching her with a mixture of interest and trepidation. A compulsive promise-maker, he did not dare answer his own phone. There were too many people he had to avoid: creditors, salesmen, angry judges, anxious clients who called five and six times a day.

"It's Brian Brianson," said Rainbow, passing the phone. "He's been arrested."

"Arrested?" Glasser's large delicate face registered something very much like shock. Brian Brianson was his oldest and most important client, a major marijuana dealer with a network of distributors all over the East Coast. Brianson's friends and employees created a constant stream of work for the firm of Glasser & Feldman, yet Brianson himself hadn't been arrested in over seventeen years.

Glasser put the receiver to his ear. "Brian, are you okay?"

The pot smuggler's voice sounded shaky over the wire. "I'm not okay, I'm definitely not okay. I told them I'm claustrophobic, but they wouldn't listen." His laugh came out strangled into a sob. "Sorry, man, I'm a little freaky right now. If they put me in one of those cells, I'll die."

"Just stay calm. Tell me where you are."

"I'm in MCC." Manhattan Correctional Center, the federal jail on Park Row.

"Did they take you over to the U.S. Attorney's Office yet?"

"Yeah, but I told them I needed to talk to you first."

"Good, you did the right thing. Don't say anything to anyone, understand? Let me find out what's going on."

"I'm not a kid, Lou." He was in fact in his late thirties, but his voice quivered. Brianson had been a teenager when they first met, a runaway with long greasy hair and tattered bell-bottoms, hustling loose joints among the hippies in Washington Square Park. Glasser had watched the boy transform himself from a street urchin living in abandoned buildings to a merchant prince of the marijuana trade, a millionaire many times over. Yet the original boyishness remained, a peculiar tangle of vulnerability and bravado.

"Listen to me, Brian, this is important. The phones are bugged in there, so don't make any more calls, and don't talk to the other prisoners. You can't trust them."

"Get me out of here, Lou. *Please.*"

"We'll be there in five minutes. You just sit tight, okay?"

"I love you, man." It was a child's wail, disconcerting in its nakedness.

"I love you too."

Glasser hung up, sinking back into his chair. Surprise was absurd, he knew, and yet he found himself stunned; after so many years without an arrest, Brianson had come to seem almost invulnerable, the one fixed point in a shifting landscape of clients and cases.

Feldman rose to his feet. A federal case involving Brianson was worth a hundred times the contents of Auerbach's little bag, and the prospect made him positively gleeful, his round face shining with excitement. "Let me negotiate the fee, that's all I ask."

But Glasser's mind was taken up with the enormity of the event. The situation was complicated, much more complicated than Feldman knew, and it would have to be handled with the utmost care. He rose, absentmindedly brushed the breakfast crumbs from his lap. "Let's get over there before he starts talking to the walls."

"Wait," said Rainbow. "What about Jason?"

"Jason?" He had forgotten all about his appointment with his son. He checked his watch, then looked down at the packets of bills resting on his desk, money for the boy's clothing. Alterations would take a few days, and the interview was next week; there was no time to lose. "Tell you what," he said to Feldman, "you go down there, hold Brian's hand for a little while—"

"He wants you."

"Tell him I had to go to court. I'll be there in an hour, right after I get the kid a suit." A delay would be useful in any case, a chance to clear his head and start thinking things out.

Feldman ran from the room, Rainbow following behind with Auerbach's satchel. Alone for the first time that morning, Glasser leaned back and lit a cigarette, waiting for Jason to arrive. Brianson's arrest would mean a big fat fee, and Glasser had already begun to share his partner's excitement. A good payday was just the thing he needed right now; he could pay off some of his credit cards, make up the late payment on his Jaguar, put something toward the bank loan that was coming due.

But underneath the anticipation he still felt a twinge of unease, enough to make him search through the remains of his breakfast, looking for something to snack on. Nothing was left but a lump of home fries, his last cigarette butt stuck upright in the middle. He pulled a piece of potato from the edge of the pile, dusted it for tobacco ash, and popped it in his mouth.

2

DON'T TELL YOUR FATHER

Jason Glasser arrived at his father's office still buoyant from his morning flight. He was a senior, he was going to graduate, he was going to Japan, and to get there he was going to have an interview for the Kiyomoto-Tate Fellowship—an interview so important that it involved unusual and exciting preparations, including missing his haiku seminar and racing to New York, summoned by his father to buy a new suit.

Much of the plane ride had been spent discussing haberdashery with the man next to him, an older gentleman on his way back from a commemorative coin convention in Medford. "Shakespeare, Lindbergh, outstanding Czech-Americans, that sort of thing," the man had said. But his sartorial advice had been frankly dull. "The Japanese wear baggy blue suits, I know because I sell to them. They like the Beatles coins—Ringo's the big one—and Great Moments in Science. Newton, Copernicus, Pasteur." The pink face with its fringe of silver hair had turned kindly then, looking at Jason through smudged bifocals. "Trust me and get yourself a really baggy blue suit."

"What excellent advice," Jason had said, instantly dismissing the idea. He had no intention of outfitting himself in the coin dealer's drab camouflage, had in fact already decided on buying himself something truly wonderful, something like the black-and-white check that Brian Brianson wore. Where had Brianson gotten that? Bergdorf's? Saks? Jason had spoken to him on the phone the other night, but had forgotten to ask. Instead they'd made a date for sushi that evening. Surrounded by the low murmur of Japanese voices, Jason would show off the new suit his father had bought him and tell Brian about the K-T Fellowship. It was Brian, after all, who had given him his first taste of the Orient: a puff of Thai stick in the bathroom at Ratner's Dairy Restaurant, circa 1975. Jason had been ten.

But Jason's giddy mood received a jolt at Glasser & Feldman. The atmosphere was not good—dark and excited all at once. He had barely walked through the door before his father hustled him out and down in the elevator, no word about where they were going. On the street he was left to follow as best he could as the elder Glasser barreled through the lunchtime crowds, crossing against lights and weaving between stopped cars.

"What's the rush?" asked Jason, though this was in fact an age-old scenario. As a little kid he had learned to grab onto his father's belt whenever there was walking involved, so as not to be left behind. Even so, father-son outings had usually ended with him in the lost-and-found, glumly playing hearts with cops or park rangers or department-store personnel till his father came to claim him.

"Something happen?" he asked now, dodging around a woman with a stroller. He was familiar with his father's crises, had been ministering to them since he was old enough to talk.

"No." Glasser walked with his head down and shoulders hunched, a dark, hunted look around the eyes.

"Credit cards?"

"No."

"Car loan?"

A dismissive wave of the hand. "I've got to go to MCC after this."

"Yeah? Who got busted?"

His father's only response was to pick up the pace. Glasser turned in on White Street, went through a door, and bounded up a long flight of stairs, straight into Piffleman's. Jason followed behind.

Piffleman's was a sort of bargain basement for the well-to-do lawyers that worked in the neighborhood, a big loft space with bare wooden floors and a high tin ceiling, divided up by racks of clothes. The store had a strangely reverential hush: footsteps, some talk, the tinkling of hangers—all muffled by a forest of jackets and pants. The salesmen walked about silently, their Orthodox beards and yarmulkes giving them a solemn, almost scholarly air.

His father beckoned to a salesman, the same two-fingered gesture he used to hail a cab. The man came over, and though they did not greet each other, he and Glasser seemed familiar. "Harvard," said Glasser, putting a hand on the salesman's shoulder. "Fellowship interview."

"Something Ivy," the salesman murmured. "Blue blazer, rep tie." He himself was dressed in oatmeal tweed, a sort of English Country Squire getup that went surprisingly well with his vigorous dark beard and black skullcap.

Glasser shook his head. "That's the way every kid walks through the door. I want to give him the edge before he sits down." He gestured to his own suit, charcoal gray with a pinstripe, the material glossy and thick. "He needs something like this, something that makes a statement."

"Like his father," the salesman said. "Say no more."

Jason listened in horror. *No,* he wanted to scream, *Not like his father, not!* But Glasser was already striding like a great buffalo alongside the salesman, a look of single-minded determination in his eyes. Jason had no idea what had happened to set him off, but he knew him in this kind of implacable mood, knew his ruthless need to do good, to give and arrange and take care of, to make sure no mistakes were made. In pursuit of his son's best interests no deviation would be tolerated. All opposition would be crushed— including Jason's own.

The salesman led them down a long aisle, past row after row of slumbering gabardines and glen plaids, straight to what must have been the most lawyerly pinstripe in the entire shop: heavily padded in the chest and shoulders, double-vented to allow for an enormous lawyerly ass. Impressive in its way, like a cruise ship or a giant Cadillac, but weighty, stifling. A suit of armor.

"There you go," said Glasser, feeling the sleeve. "We have something here."

"I don't know," said Jason. "I was thinking maybe something a little sportier."

"Sportier?" His father's look was incredulous.

"You know that suit Brian has, with the black-and-white checks? Isn't that Italian or something?"

Glasser made a face. "You'll look like a chessboard." And then he turned to the salesman for affirmation. "What do you think?"

The salesman arched an eyebrow. "You know what they say, Think Yiddish, dress British."

"Exactly. This is British tailoring, it tells them who you are."

"I'm not British," said Jason.

His father gave him a dark, ominous stare. "You can't go in there looking like a riverboat gambler. I'm not going to let you wreck your chances like that."

"You make it sound like the clothes are all that matters."

"Here, just try this on, see if it fits."

"It doesn't." This was nothing more than a delaying tactic, however, and Jason knew it. There was no resisting his father's desperation to do right. He sparred for a few minutes more, but in the end he gave in and left for the changing room, pinstripes in hand. When he returned they stood him on a little round dais, surrounded on three sides by full-length mirrors. An elderly, hunchbacked tailor crouched at his feet, measuring cuffs for the pants, and Jason stared at his shiny black yarmulke as he worked, too annoyed to look in the mirror.

"Look at you," said Glasser, pacing now. "You could argue before the Supreme Court in that suit. You could sell me the Brooklyn Bridge."

"I'm not selling anything to anyone," Jason growled. He sensed what was on the way—another lecture about law school.

Glasser stopped and turned to the salesman. "He doesn't know what it's really like out there. He didn't have to grow up on the streets. He flies in from Boston so his rich daddy can buy him an eight-hundred-dollar suit."

The salesman shook his head sadly. "He doesn't know how lucky he is." His tone had turned disgusted, as if the subject were juvenile delinquency and Jason's good fortune in avoiding jail.

Jason understood the implication. Spoiled and bookish, a Harvard boy, he could never be as tough as those fabled heroes from his father's boyhood on the Lower East Side, men like Cousin Herman, who conquered in wholesale meats, or Harry Susman from Seward Park High, now a giant in industrial tiling. Or his father, of course. "Just admit it," Jason said now, looking into the mirror at the elder Glasser's multiple reflections. "You're angry about law school. That's what this is about."

"Well, what's wrong with law school?"

"Can you see us in practice together, Glasser & Son?"

"You have to do *something*, don't you? Or do you want to be a professor?"

"I'm going to be the first Jewish emperor of Japan."

"It's not a joke, Jason. Don't get me wrong, studying in Japan is a wonderful thing. But the vacation can't last forever."

"Vacation? Is that what you think I do?" Jason started to turn around, breaking the pose inflicted on him by the hunchbacked tailor, who was still down by his feet, pinning up the second cuff.

"Don't moof," the tailor said, slapping him hard on the calf. "Your fadder's tryink to teach you sometink."

Too surprised to protest, Jason turned back to the mirrors. He could see three images of his father, all of them waving their fingers at him.

"Money isn't everything, Jason, but without it you're in trouble, you're vulnerable, people push you around. I've been poor and I know."

"Don't start that stuff again."

"Just listen to me. The world can be a pretty rough place. A little money is like a good lock on the door. It's protection from the bad things that can happen."

"I guarantee you I'll never be a burden."

His father's eyes looked deeply pained. "That's not what I meant."

Predictably enough, this last exchange set off a final rampage of buying, short but intense. Jason got back into his jeans and followed as the elder Glasser picked out shirts, ties, a pair of glossy black wingtips, piling them up by the cash register. The expression on his face was wounded and grim, as if he were arguing a case he knew he had to lose. Afterward, while the salesman calculated the bill, he turned visibly anxious, as he usually did when it was time to settle up. He drummed on the counter for a while, only to head back into the racks to pick out another tie. For him, the antidote to paying was always more buying.

Jason staggered off in the opposite direction. To be saddled with all that expensive clothing now felt like a terrible burden, the full weight of his father strapped to his back. His father's tyrannical love, his fear of doom, his hurt brown eyes—they were strangling the breath out of him, like a silk tie pulled tighter and tighter.

Enclosed in a nearby row of sports coats, he peeked through a gap in the hangers and saw their salesman talking to the gray-bearded old fellow who operated the cash register. What about them? Did they look at him and see a spoiled rich kid? A weak-minded egghead coddled and bullied by his father? A Harvard boy?

"That man," Jason heard the old guy say, his eyes darting after Glasser. "No credit."

The salesman simply nodded in response, then finished adding up the numbers on their bill.

Jason knew that his father wasn't so quick about paying his debts. He loved to buy but hated to pay, and the past-due notices collected in piles, while the rubber checks bounced like Spaldeens. Jason had seen him write these checks out while snickering to himself, taking obvious pleasure in his own mischief. "That one should bounce till it hits the roof!" He had watched his father scrawl DECEASED RETURN TO SENDER on unopened bills and pop them back in the mail.

But his father always paid eventually—with interest and penalties, as Jason's mother liked to point out.

Watching from between the coats, he saw his father come back with another tie. "Add this on," said Glasser, scrutinizing the bill. Jason held his breath, hoping he would not say, Put it on my tab, Chief, or any of the old movie-ish things he usually said. But this time Glasser started to pull money out of his coat pocket—rubber-banded bundles of cash, one after another, like clowns pouring from a circus car. And when that pocket was empty he switched to the other one. The old guy and the salesman watched the pile build, then started to count. Even with the two of them, it took a while.

"Um," said the salesman, finally stacking the last bundle on top of the others. "Tax is fifty-nine dollars."

"I'm paying cash," said Glasser.

"We've still got to collect the tax. They watch us closely."

"Oh, come on." Glasser made his typical gesture of impatience, the heel of his palm against his forehead. "This is cash. Cash. Do you know the meaning of cash?"

"Counselor, I know the meaning of IRS."

Glasser reached into one of his suit pockets and pulled out yet another bundle of bills, slapping it on the counter as if trying to swat a fly. The salesman took off the rubber band, counted the money, then returned some of the dollars to Glasser. "Death and taxes," he said. "Alterations by Friday."

Glasser looked tired, distracted. "Where's the little emperor? I've got to get out of here and make some money."

Back on the street a moment later, Glasser left Jason in the lurch once again as they racewalked toward the federal jail on Park Row. When he spoke it was over his shoulder, in the form of an afterthought, though Jason understood it was anything but that; his father's most important communications usually came in this off-the-cuff manner. "Brian got arrested this morning. Feldman's waiting with him at MCC."

Upset by the news, Jason accompanied him the half dozen blocks to MCC. The jail was faced with the same café au lait–colored stone as the U.S. Attorney's Office next door, and at first glance the entrance looked corporate—tinted glass doors with big chrome handles, like the entrance to IBM. It looked a lot more comfortable than the filthy city jail a few blocks west, the Tombs, where prisoners stuck their heads through the open windows, yelling down to friends on the sidewalk.

Yet security was obviously tight. A guard stood on the corner wearing blue fatigues and shiny black boots, a bullet-proof vest fat as a life preserver. In his arms he cradled a shotgun of some kind, surprisingly thick and stubby—a hunter's weapon shortened for use against human beings.

"Can I go in with you?" asked Jason.

"To see Brian? No." The answer was curt, and Jason could see that his father's mind had already moved on to the next thing, Brian's case, leaving him behind. "I'm late," Glasser said, and hurried through the door.

Jason was ten years old when he first met Brian, in the summer of 1975. Back then the clients were hoarse, drawling voices on the phone, asking for his father, calling him "little Lou"—grown-ups too important to be interested in a kid's name. His father brought them home for dinner without warning, and his mother treated them with polite dismay, as if they were large, overenthusiastic dogs threatening to track up the furniture. Of course, this only increased their standing in Jason's eyes. They seemed like movie stars to him, boy-men in sunglasses and purple velvet boots. He categorized them according to their facial hair, which they cultivated in exotic patterns—a soul patch beneath the lower lip, long as a billy goat's beard, or muttonchops growing like giant caterpillars—or by the jail time they faced, about which his father always muttered the next day, over breakfast. And when his father got up and left with them after dinner—"To discuss some things"—he felt they were leaving for a world made of a different color. He listened to the door slam, and a dark jealousy surged through him.

But Brian was different. Brian knew Jason's name from the very first moment they met. By way of greeting he showed the boy a complicated handshake, his big hand swallowing Jason's little one in a series of slaps and grips that made them both laugh. And he was a polymath of the kind that took real pleasure in delighting a child. Over dinner he explained the history of the fork—an eighteenth-century innovation—and described Henry VIII eating chops with his hands and wiping his fingers on the jester's head. He noted the origin of the napkin in the neckerchief, and detailed how the first restaurant was invented in Paris, when a nobleman's servants started selling leftovers from the mansion's kitchen door—"Take away, man."

Dazzled, sated, Jason didn't mind so much when the conversation finally shifted to adult business. He watched how his father listened to Brian—not in his usual distracted way, playing with a spoon or searching through the scraps of paper he pulled from his pocket, but really listening, his eyes trained on Brian's face, attentive and present, as he so rarely listened to Jason himself. From that moment, the boy believed in the pot dealer. Brian was the door into that other world of bright colors and important events, the world where the clients were, the world in which his father moved like a king.

From Jason's point of view it was only natural that Brian should come to the house again, take him out for ice cream and movies— movies his parents wouldn't have allowed him to see. Afterward, they went on long treks through the East Village, the dealer towering beside him, all boot and leg, peering through blue granny glasses and swinging a walking stick. As they strolled, the conversation moved from Jason's teachers and school friends to the many exotic places Brian had visited—Syria, Lebanon, Afghanistan, India. But the topic it always returned to was Glasser. Brian had questions mostly, of the quirkiest sort. What kind of hair pomade did Glasser use? What kind of razor? Did he have brothers or sisters? Not wanting to disappoint, the boy gave long, elaborate answers, making up what he didn't know.

But these walks were only a form of courtship, really; looking back on it, the true start of their friendship came later, on the day Brian took him to lunch at Ratner's. Ratner's was a kosher restaurant on the Lower East Side, much favored by Jason's father; Jason had in fact been there with the elder Glasser once or twice before. The decor had a vaguely aquatic theme, forlorn as an old Miami Beach hotel. The lights were dim, the walls blue, and strips of floor-to-ceiling mirror batted the shadows back and forth. The tables were populated by portly old Jewish men in groups of twos and threes, big dishes of whitefish and chopped herring sitting in front of them. They seemed to mix eating with a kind of silent argumentation, as if long partnership in discount menswear or wholesale upholstery made actual speech unnecessary.

On his previous visits, Jason had been completely anonymous, a little Jewish boy with his big-bellied father, arrived to sample the gefilte fish. But Brian stood out wonderfully and created a stir. The other diners lifted their heads, and Jason saw their pouchy eyes drooping with disapproval. Old guys in Sansabelt double knits and polyester shirts, how could they possibly appreciate Brian? Brian wore jeans and lizard-skin cowboy boots. He moved down the aisle with a slow antelope's gait, leather bag slung over one shoulder and that ever-present walking stick in his hand, lightly prodding the carpet.

Some of that glamour rubbed off on the boy. Though he was dressed in nothing but his usual, Jason tingled with privileged knowledge, secrets the other diners could never guess. He knew, for example, that Brian's walking stick was really a gun. Brian had shown him how the barrel inside the shaft held a single shotgun shell, full of bird shot small as peppercorns. The thing was pure Brian: stylish and impractical, reeking of Sherlock Holmes and the curio shop—closer to a dangerous toy than a deadly weapon.

They took a spot at the very back of the long room, one of a cluster of empty tables that offered some privacy. Brian propped his walking stick against the wall, then claimed a chair facing the entrance. "Sit here," he said, tapping the chair next to him. "You should always face the door, so you can see who's coming."

"Who's coming?"

"Some friends of mine." He smiled faintly, rubbing his chin. "Always make sure you're the first to arrive, little man, so you can stake out the high ground. Preparation is everything in this business." He put two cigarettes in his mouth, lit them both, and handed one to Jason—a ritual they had developed over the weeks of walking. "Now tell me the truth, is he wearing the bracelet I got him? The big silver one?"

Jason put the cigarette in his mouth and took a short timid puff, the best he could manage without making himself cough. "He" was, of course, his father, and the bracelet was a heavy Navaho affair studded with chunks of turquoise big as walnuts. "I heard him say to Mom that he can't close it."

"Can't close it? What does that mean?"

"You know, that thing with a hook—" He meant the clasp. "He says it doesn't work right."

"Well, why didn't he tell me? Christ, I'd get it fixed for him." With that, Brian's face went through a series of very private changes, from perplexed to offended and then angry, ending in a strangely wounded look. For the first time Jason sensed that the dealer's connection to his father was different from his own—darker, more complicated. But he could not put this feeling into words, and then it was gone, leaving only a shadow of discomfort. "Sorry," he said, putting his cigarette down in the ashtray.

"*You* didn't do anything." But the dealer still had that wounded look in the dark hollows under his eyes. He glanced at his watch, an enormous golden thing with three or four smaller dials inside the bigger one, the same style as the elder Glasser's. "We've got a little time. Come on." He stood up and grabbed his bag.

Jason followed him through a passage and up a couple of stairs into what turned out to be the bathroom, a damp narrow closet in black tile, with a drippy sink, a urinal, and a single stall. "Anyone here?" called Brian, though they were obviously alone. "Good." He rammed shut the bolt on the bathroom door. "I think we need to cool out."

He reached into his shoulder bag and took out a stubby little earthenware pipe, examined the contents of the bowl, then put it in his mouth and lit it with his lighter. He drew in deeply, a deft, practiced motion that seemed to involve his whole body, and when he breathed out finally a new smell filled the room, pungent and peppery. His eyes were watery as he looked at Jason. "You want some?"

A shiver of nervousness moved through the boy's legs. "I don't know." But he didn't resist when Brian put the end of the pipe stem to his lips.

"Just breathe in and hold it down, you know, like you're going to swim underwater." And then the dealer touched the long fingerlike flame of the lighter to the bowl.

Jason did as instructed. The smoke was sharp and hot, and though he swallowed it down like a pill it came up again almost immediately in a sputtering cough. The second time went better, though. His chest expanded like a balloon and then slowly deflated, blowing a little jet of gray smoke out his mouth.

"Now, that's a toke," said Brian.

Back at the table, Jason felt as if he'd hidden the most powerful of secrets inside his very chest—part of him now, like a second, beating heart. He looked over at the other diners with grave condescension, wondering if they could sense the difference in him. "Am I stoned?" he asked Brian hopefully.

"Sure you're stoned. You're baked." Brian had lost the wounded look under his eyes; he talked in an easy drawl, his voice sounding strangely distant, though he was only inches away. "Lou is just so great, you know, like a bodhisattva, always helping people, giving all the time. You don't know how lucky you are. If he'd been my dad, I'd never have left home."

Jason's tongue felt thick. "What was wrong with your dad?"

"My dad had us down on our knees, praying all day. Thank you, Lord, for this, thank you, Lord, for that. I just wanted to get up off my knees."

"Don't you miss him?"

Brian looked amused. "By the time I left I was living in the garage. He wouldn't let me in the house anymore. I got tired of sleeping next to the snowblower."

Jason laughed, though he actually felt sad. It seemed like a terrible thing to live without parents, without a father, terrible but thrilling too, like falling through empty space—and then a moment later he had lost the thought completely. Time was moving in funny ways now, drifting to the side and then suddenly darting ahead, like a toy boat seized by the current. He felt like he was floating on a raft in a pool, ricocheting gently off the walls, returning to the place he had left. Brian talked on, a murmurous voice farther and farther away.

The friends came finally. One had a grizzled beard and a graying ponytail, large tinted sunglasses that covered most of the upper half of his big sunburned face. Brian called him Petie. The other was younger, with shaggy brown hair sticking out from under his baseball cap, and dark round eyes. His name was Groover. Groover carried a leather satchel, which he placed under his chair when he sat down.

"Who's this?" asked Petie, aiming his glasses at Jason. He looked like an oncoming bus.

"My associate, man. Jason Glasser."

"Lou Glasser's kid?" Recognition but not friendliness.

Brian shrugged with an offhanded pride that pleased Jason immensely. "I'm trying to give him an education, you know, something he can't get in school."

The conversation drifted away from the boy then, became wholly the property of the adults, and their low voices had the gentle, distanced fascination of surf hitting the beach. The waiter came, and then came again with their food, and except for those two brief interruptions Brian, Petie, and Groover continued at their inscrutable work, some kind of weaving of meanings that Jason could not understand. Only very slowly did he sense that something was wrong, that the men were unhappy with one another, and that their pleasantries were a substitute for something else that they did not want to say directly.

"How's the gefilte fish?" asked Brian, spooning sour cream into his borscht—little icebergs in a sea of red.

Groover nodded. "Good, man. You want to try?"

"Nah, I'm a strict vegetarian. No meat, no fish."

Groover kept nodding, earnest and boyish. He wore a dark wooden cross around his neck, hanging from a string of beads, and he fingered it as he talked. "Far out."

Whatever their problem was, it didn't seem very important compared to the food. Jason gobbled his cherry blintzes, letting the sour cream soothe his burnt throat. The blintzes were fabulous; sweet and buttery, with a hint of the smoky residue left in his mouth by the pot.

Across the table, Petie applied himself to a bowl of bananas and sour cream, remixing the contents thoroughly before each new spoonful. He wasn't tall but wide, with a bull neck and heavy chest peeking out from a black tank top. Curly gray hair covered his pink shoulders.

Brian slurped some borscht. "Petie, man, tell me what's going on."

There was a pause filled by the sounds of eating, and then Petie spoke, still delicately mixing his bananas. "I was hoping you'd tell me that."

"If I don't get paid soon I'm going to start charging you interest, man."

Petie looked up from his bowl. "You shorted us, Brian. I told you I wouldn't pay for what I didn't get."

"You know my reputation—I don't do business that way."

"Groover weighed the product, man."

"Almost a hundred pounds short," said Groover, nodding slowly. "It was a real bummer, man, 'cause we'd presold everything already."

"We had to buy a hundred pounds locally, just to meet our obligations," said Petie. "We got gouged on the price and the quality was shit."

"Seeds and stems," sniffed Groover, with a connoisseur's disdain.

"Well, somebody on your end is skimming, and that's not my problem," said Brian. "You asked for five hundred and I got it to you, with a lot of fucking trouble. I had to make other people wait in line."

Petie leaned his big torso across the table. "If we can't depend on you for a fair count, Brian, we can hook up with somebody else."

"There *is* nobody else, Petie, not at this volume."

"I can think of one or two."

Brian shook his head, as if disgusted by the comment. The conversation died away for a while, replaced once again by the clinking of spoons and forks—Brian munching a roll, Petie furiously mixing his bananas and sour cream. But the sounds were different now, loud and jangly, and Jason sat upright, watchful.

Brian finally spoke. "So what's the bag for then?" He meant the big leather satchel under Groover's chair.

Groover fingered his wooden cross. "It's the bread we owe you, man."

"Minus the money for the hundred we never got," said Petie. "And the hundred we had to buy."

Suddenly Brian exploded to his feet, almost upending the flimsy table. "Motherfucker!" he yelled, as the plates clattered around them. A second later Petie was up too, half Brian's height but twice his bulk, a thick forefinger stabbing into his chest from across the table. "Scumbag!" he bellowed back.

Jason recoiled in shock. The two men were screaming at each other—none of it intelligible as anything but noise, a roar like a jet engine. He put his hands over his ears, but the fight seemed to be taking place in his head, filling it to bursting, and he could not dampen the sound. He glanced around the dining room and saw the old men at the other tables staring at him with sour curiosity, jaws arrested in midchew. The disdain he'd felt for them was gone now; he wanted to be one of them, yearned to be taken under their familiar grandfatherly protection. But they made no move toward him, and he did not know how to ask for their help.

His own table was now a tiny island of chaos. Petie had Brian by the shirt and was shaking him with his two heavy fists, while Groover fumbled for the bag under his chair, making ready to run. Silverware and dishes clattered to the floor, and a glass of water splashed into Jason's lap, propelling him to his feet. *Do something,* he thought, and lunged for Brian's walking stick, still propped against the wall. He didn't really intend to use it—he didn't intend anything at all—just grabbed for it like a drowning man grabs for a rope. Only it was much heavier than he'd expected, and longer, and in swinging it around he lost his balance, tripped, and began to fall. The walking stick went flying. From the carpet he heard a hard smack and then a terrible boom, and then, a second later, glass shattering.

"I didn't do it!" he screamed. But he needn't have bothered, because no one was paying him any attention. The customers were running for the door now, old men in half-crouch, pushing one another down the aisle. Looking around, he saw things in discrete snapshots, whole pictures absorbed in a second's time: the place where the mirror used to be, now a brown strip of bare wall, speck-led with bird shot; glass shards piled on the table underneath, shin-ing like ice in the sun.

I did this, he said to himself, and felt not fear but a momentary sense of awe at the possibilities within him.

The next thing he knew he was running through the kitchen on wobbly legs. An arm was around his shoulders—Brian's arm—half guiding him, half carrying him through this alien terrain of bright light and aluminum counters, giant pots and pans hanging on hooks from the ceiling. Brian was loaded down with a jumble of stuff—the walking stick, his bag, Groover's bag—and he was laughing. "Don't tell your father," he said.

3

———⊗⊗⊗———

THE COAT OFF HIS BACK

If he had been free to choose, Brian Brianson would have been a Taoist immortal. Occasionally he would get stoned and wander the Oriental wing of the Metropolitan Museum of Art, staring happily at Chinese brush paintings almost a thousand years old. The immortals were easy to recognize in these paintings: chubby, laughing men in flowing robes, seated on a mountaintop and contemplating a chessboard, untroubled by the world of pain and confusion spread out in the valley below. In the valley, ordinary people develop cancer, go bankrupt, get divorced, embezzle money to pay the bookie. But the immortals sip their little cups of rice wine and laugh. They are free of the disease of the valley, that burden of passionate, contradictory selfhood; so free that they aren't even troubled by sympathy for those below. They do not yearn to be good or bad, do not care if they win or lose. They play chess for the pleasure of playing, unconcerned with the outcome, and therefore always win.

Brian aspired to this level of detachment but could not quite reach it. It was one thing to achieve the serenity of a Taoist immortal while stoned in the Met, and quite another to do so while sitting in bare feet and pajamas in the U.S. Attorney's Office. To be fair, he had already been through quite a lot that morning. At five A.M. a posse of DEA agents had broken down the door to his town house with a battering ram, and then run up the stairs to his bedroom on the second floor, howling like Apaches—no, like little boys *playing* Apaches. A chronic insomniac, he had taken a couple of Halcions just a few hours before, and the noise had reached him only very dimly, intermixing with his troubled dreams. The agents had had to shake him awake in fact, so he could watch them ransacking the place. He had stood in a corner for nearly two hours, handcuffed, while they slit open the upholstery on his Biedermeier furniture, pulled up his antique Persian carpets, smashed a late Ch'ing incense holder—all with a barbaric pleasure in destruction that had left him trembling.

And now he was seated in a cramped little office on Park Place, a very self-satisfied DEA agent in the chair to his left, an assistant U.S. attorney behind the desk in front. The air was overheated and stale, and his throat felt dry enough to crack. He glanced with real fellow-feeling at the spindly avocado plant withering on the radiator, then wiped the sweat from his face with a silken pajama sleeve—both arms raised together, as his wrists were still cuffed.

The assistant U.S. attorney was a young woman in her early thirties, and though it was barely seven A.M. she was in her work clothes, a white blouse and severe woolen jacket with big padded shoulders. She had dark hair pulled back in a bun, intelligent dark eyes, a pale office pallor—but he was too nervous to look at her whole.

"You know the name Randy Schotts, don't you?" she asked him. It was a matter-of-fact, businesslike voice, neither hostile nor friendly.

"I want my lawyer," he told her, which was certainly true; he would have given everything he owned to have Louis Glasser's reassuring bulk seated beside him.

The request was ignored. Instead she began reading aloud from the pad in front of her. "Randy Schotts, arrested May twelfth, nineteen seventy, sale of LSD to a federal agent . . . jumped bail on June fifteenth . . . at-large these seventeen years." She looked at him, careful to hold his gaze. "That's you, isn't it?"

Brian felt a deep emptiness opening inside his chest. He had lived as Brian Brianson for the last seventeen years, and on the rare occasions when he recalled that earlier self, Randy Schotts, it was with bewilderment bordering on pain. Runaway, street urchin, nickel and dimer: that sad lost boy was best left where he was, forgotten in the past. "I said I want my lawyer."

The prosecutor began flipping pages on her pad, evidently searching for something. "Forget about your lawyer for a few minutes. I just want you to know how much trouble you've got."

With that she began reading from her notes, a long litany of facts and figures about his operation. She named a dozen boats and planes he used for transport, recited a list of landing sites in the Carolinas, Louisiana, Texas. For the first time he began to understand the immensity of what was happening to him, began to feel the profundity of his loss. Linton Beach, Merryweather, Harper's Cove: some of his happiest moments had been spent in those lonely, barren places, listening to the surf hit the rocks, waiting for the telltale engine sputter—a shipment about to arrive. He had built his business from nothing, had given it seventeen painstaking, devoted years. It was wife, child, family to him, but for some reason he had never realized how deeply he loved it till he heard it profaned in this way, its deepest secrets mouthed by a stranger.

The prosecutor looked up from her pad. "We have a half dozen high-quality informants, wiretaps, money transfers, a first-rate paper trail. We can get you on at least fourteen counts of import and sale over the last decade."

The DEA agent to his left turned to face him now. He was a menacing presence, thickset and fleshy, with a face like a rare roast beef. "In other words, you're fucked."

The prosecutor nodded, frowned, took a thoughtful sip from the coffee mug beside her. "We are definitely talking about life without parole."

Life without parole. The words left him too stunned to protest. He listened instead as they began reciting a kind of two-part fugue on the theme of punishment and suffering, detailing the charges they would load on—"Just for fun," said the agent—and then the living conditions he would find in a maximum-security facility like the one in Marion, Illinois. "Built underground," said the prosecutor. "Like a bunker. Not a window in the place."

"And the *food*," said the agent, chuckling merrily. "They feed you this space-age shit the Bureau of Prisons invented. Nutriloaf. Ever had it? No? It's gray and tastes like a sweatsock."

Brian understood that this was all an act, designed to scare him, but knowing this didn't matter because the fear it engendered was real, a creature inside his body, squeezing the air from his lungs. "I want my lawyer," he said, and was dismayed to hear his voice break.

This seemed to trigger something. "Fuck your goddamn lawyer!" roared the agent, pounding his armrest in a fury. "Fuck him! He can't do shit for you! Only we can!" He was on his feet then, screaming in Brian's face, spraying saliva, gesticulating wildly. As far as Brian could make out, it was all threats and curses, but he wasn't hearing the words anymore so much as feeling them deep in the pit of his stomach, like punches.

"Stop it," sputtered the dealer, "stop," and then leaning far back in his seat, trying to get away: "Well, what do you want from me then?"

He hadn't meant this the way it sounded, had meant only that he'd had enough and wanted to be left alone. But the agent fell immediately silent, eased his big body back into his chair, and the prosecutor leaned forward over her desk, looking earnestly at Brian with her dark eyes. "We can help you, Randy. But only if you're willing to help yourself."

"*You've* got the key," said the agent, and his voice was hoarse after all the yelling. "You've got the key to the cell. But you've got to turn it yourself. No one can do it for you."

"We want to help you," said the prosecutor. "But you have to let us."

"Let us help you," said the agent, his big round face full of soulful exhortation.

"Cooperate," said the prosecutor.

Cooperate? Cooperate in the destruction of everything he'd worked to build over the last seventeen years? Turn in friends, partners, customers? What he wanted to do was bury his face in his hands and hide, wish this nightmare away. He wanted to get up and slam his chair over the DEA agent's meaty shoulders; to jump across the desk and wring the prosecutor's gently curving neck; to flee through miraculously open doors, down magically empty hall-ways.

Instead, he took her business card.

I t was past ten when they led him over the footbridge to MCC, nearly two when he got downstairs for his attorney visit. Drained by then, he had to fight to suppress the emotion in his voice, afraid that it would scorch the two lawyers who had come to see him. "You've got to get me out of here," he told Glasser. "I'm going nuts, man, I'm freaking out."

Glasser was half sitting on the little Formica table, a blurry halo of light illuminating his large sensitive face, the big brown eyes. "We'll put in a bail application," he said.

This didn't seem like much of an answer. "I'm suffocating, I can't breathe."

"What did they ask you?"

Brian began pacing back and forth, though it was only a single stride between walls. "They have a lot, Lou, a hell of a lot. They stopped a boat off North Carolina carrying a ton of grass, they have the captain and crew, and they've got those morons from Long Island, Groover and Petie. And they've got Leon."

Leon was Brian's accountant, a gray-bearded and pot-bellied ex-hippie with pens in the pocket of his Mr. Natural T-shirt, a scuffed Samsonite briefcase dangling from one hand.

"Are you sure about Leon?" asked Glasser, looking grave.

"They have bank accounts, credit-card numbers. That sort of thing could only come from him."

The lawyer gave a long, thoughtful sigh. He had a large reper-toire of inarticulate sounds conveying sympathy and understand-ing, deep expertise in solving human troubles. "Well, it's just the beginning, we'll know more soon."

"They're talking about life."

"They always talk big."

Staring into Glasser's face, with its look of professional concern, it came to Brian that the world was *not* in fact divided between Taoist immortals and poor blighted humanity. The real division was between those who are in trouble and those who are not. A drowning man will do anything to stay afloat; he will rip the life vest off the poor unfortunate dog-paddling beside him. But what could Glasser know about that? The lawyer was safely ensconced in his little dinghy, making his soothing *hmmms* and *ahhhs* while watching the ugly struggle in the water. For a moment, just a moment, Brian wished he could somehow reach up and drag Glasser over the side—even if it meant they both would drown.

"They're interested in cutting a deal," he said, trying to control himself.

"Okay, I'll give her a call and see what she's offering."

"I won't take anything less than a complete walk." He meant no jail time.

From life in prison to a complete walk: this was a little unrealistic, it seemed; Glasser had replied with one of his noncommittal *hmmm*s. Later, back on the cellblock, Brian lay on his bunk, overcome with a loneliness so powerful it became a form of clearsightedness, as if he were observing himself from miles above. He knew this feeling from other times in his life, moments of decision when everything had abruptly changed for him. He had experienced it the day he ran away from home, a sixteen-year-old kid with twenty-nine dollars in his pocket, walking along the interstate at dawn. He had felt it the night he decided to jump bail too, skipping out on the LSD charge. Unable to sleep, he'd called Glasser around one in the morning and arranged to meet him at a diner on Twenty-eighth and Third, ostensibly to say good-bye. Of course he'd had other, half-formed motives as well, vague expectations of assistance, a little money perhaps, a suggestion as to where to go. But he'd found out that lawyers don't take unnecessary risks; they stay safely within the rules of their guild—even Glasser, who smoked in elevators and collected parking tickets, who gleefully cheated the IRS. Glasser gave him some free advice and sent him on his way.

This time would be much the same, obviously. The lawyer would stick his hands in his pockets, muttering about rules and procedures, motions and hearings, while Brian grew moldy in jail. Waiting for Glasser to save him was nothing but a trap, he decided, a form of slow creeping death; if he wanted out, he'd have to do it himself. And so he began piecing together the elements of a deal for the Feds. One by one he added possibilities to an imaginary scale, watching the needle tip toward freedom. There were the thirty or so people who worked for him directly, a rotating crew of truckers, fishermen, and small-plane pilots, plus the grunts recruited locally to load and unload the bales—small fry, but possibly worth something as a group. More valuable were the middlemen who bought from him, people like Petie and Groover, many of whom moved millions of dollars of cannabis a year. And then there were his own sources in Jamaica and Mexico, and the large domestic growers he dealt with in northern California. These, he knew, were the most valuable chips he had to play.

He threw his suppliers on the scale, but just as quickly pulled them off. Without suppliers there was no product to sell, and without selling there was no business, and without his beloved business there was no point to freedom. He had the money to retire, if Leon hadn't already traded it to the Feds, but at thirty-eight years of age, the thought was horrifying, a blankness like death. What he needed was something else to put on the scale, something heavy enough to tip the needle to freedom and yet allow him to keep even just a piece of the business. With one or two of his suppliers he could start all over again, rebuild what had been destroyed.

And then it came to him, brilliant and terrible, with all the allure of the supposedly unthinkable: Lou, he thought. Give them Lou. Make them take Lou instead of me.

Lou instead of me. He lay motionless on his bunk, too stunned to move. The idea was fascinating in its utter strangeness, like a sideshow freak glimpsed through the bars of a cage. And yet he had to admit that it seemed familiar to him also, as if he had secretly considered it before or even dreamed it. There was a dark logic to the proposition, an undertow that began pulling him forward, off his bunk, and down the corridor to the pay phone, his heart pounding with each step. His fingers trembled as he reached into the pocket of the jumpsuit they had given him in place of his pajamas, took out the business card the prosecutor had slipped into his hand. He read her name, twice, three times: Anna, Anna Freeburg.

An hour later he was back in that little room, munching greasy lo mein from the take-out carton, negotiating a preliminary deal for himself between mouthfuls. He was starving and couldn't eat or talk fast enough, even as his heart banged like a piston inside his chest. Periodically he would break out into sudden sharp laughter. Where did this manic glee come from? He felt like a sky diver, a trapeze artist flying through the air—held aloft by his own brave cunning, his will to survive. "You want the top guy, Anna—may I call you Anna?" He flashed her a smile, then filled his mouth with lo mein till he could barely mumble. "Well, I'll give you the head of the whole thing, the boss."

For the first time he found the courage to look at her closely, and what he saw was far less imposing than what he had imagined. He noted the heavy circles under her eyes, the unwashed hair pulled back in a bun, her nails bitten down to the quick. She's been working on this case around the clock, he told himself, she's ready for a big score, the bigger the better. If I tell her she's struck gold, she'll believe me.

"We've got the boss already," she said to him now. "*You*. What we want are your suppliers."

"Of course, the suppliers, of course. Every last one." With his plastic fork trailing noodles he waved the issue aside. "But I have a boss too, a man I work for, and I'll give him to you in exchange for a free ride. Complete immunity."

"A free ride?" She laughed, obviously a little tickled by his cheek. "Who is this kingpin of yours, Randy?"

"It's my lawyer, Anna, Louis Glasser."

"Your *lawyer*."

He could see she was interested. In his experience, most prosecutors looked at defense lawyers as just another kind of criminal anyway. "Anna, Louis Glasser is the biggest marijuana dealer on the East Coast."

"And how do you expect me to believe that?"

"Check the court record on my LSD arrest. Who do you think my lawyer was?"

"Glasser?"

"That's right."

"He's been representing a fugitive for the last seventeen years?"

"He needs me, I'm his right-hand man." Brian felt a tremendous surge of energy move through his body, the power to become whatever he needed to be, to say whatever he needed to say. He was a salesman, a great salesman, and this would be the most brilliant sale of his life. "But don't stop there. Take a look who represented Leon LaRosa on his bust in New Jersey last summer."

"Glasser?"

"Of course. I can name ten different people he's represented in the last three or four years alone, all of them connected, all part of our operation."

The method was to sprinkle fact among the fictions; even a schoolboy knew that much. She would check the court records and see that each of his assertions was true. In fact, a lot of what he went on to tell her *was* true: their midnight meetings in the McDonald's on Broadway; their trips in Glasser's private plane; the weekend barbecues at Leon's house out in Montclair. But then he gave it all a twist, a ninety-degree turn: Glasser discussing tonnage and transport problems as he downed his second Big Mac; Glasser talking about delinquent accounts while flying over the Jersey marshes; Glasser yelling about a late shipment from the raft in Leon's pool.

Freeburg shook out her writing hand, cramped from note-taking. "I'm willing to look into it, Randy, but if it doesn't pan out you're in a shitload of trouble. You can't just dick us around."

He smiled in return, attuned to the excitement hidden in her voice. If she didn't quite believe him yet, she was at least willing to be convinced, and that was enough to get him out of MCC. Indeed, when Freeburg wrote up the complaint—the government's outline of its case—the dealer was conveniently transformed into a minor player, his name appearing only twice, one of twenty-seven crowding the text. She put in a word with the magistrate too, and at the arraignment the next day he was let out on bond, in spite of the fact that he was an ex-fugitive, an obvious bail risk. Glasser, poor fool, thought it was his legal genius that had done the trick.

After his release he spent his days at the U.S. Attorney's Office, talking into a tape recorder about Glasser and three dozen other former associates, mapping out more than a decade of labyrinthine pot deals. At night he went home to smoke a joint and plan the next day's testimony. As the hour grew late these private sessions devolved into arguments about Glasser, Brian supplying both sides of the debate in his head. He was concerned not with the right or wrong of his actions, he told himself, so much as the *why*, the meaning of what he had done. It was strictly business, he insisted, nothing personal, though at other times he admitted it was truly, deeply personal, as defining an event as when he ran away from home. He loved Glasser, he needed him—and he had sacrificed him. There was something heroic and grand in the act, something larger than life, like the wolf that gnaws off its own leg to escape the wolf trap. What iron willpower it had taken to betray his closest friend, what cruel vitality! He felt reborn into a new stage of life, but also half-dead with the effort, as if he had clawed his way out of the birth canal into fresh air and sunlight, greasy with blood.

Nevertheless, it came as a blow when Freeburg began pushing him to fire Lou. She pointed out the obvious, that he couldn't be represented by a man he was helping to indict. Conflict of interest, she called it, and a threat to the case they were building against Glasser. Brian was unimpressed by this logic, but the prosecutor was adamant, and he soon ran out of excuses; after some stalling he called Glasser and arranged a meeting at the McDonald's on Broadway.

It took two Valiums to pry himself out of the house and two more to keep himself seated as the cab sped downtown. His secret hope was that he'd end up too high to do the job; barring that, he thought maybe he'd be able to do it without noticing. In the cab he tried rehearsing what he had to say: Sorry, Lou, I've decided to get a new lawyer . . . retain different counsel . . . try something new. Sorry. Those were the lines Freeburg had given him, and he knew he had to be careful not to add anything more—anything more revealing.

It was nearly midnight, and the McDonald's was empty except for Glasser and Feldman at a table in back, by a planter of bright pink plastic flowers. There were life-size cutouts of Ronald McDonald on the wall, red candy striping on the tables and chairs. Muzak floated from unseen speakers—an instrumental version of "Penny Lane," gluey with strings.

"Aren't you hungry?" asked Glasser. He had a burger in his hand and was surrounded by wrappers.

The dealer lurched into a seat. The Valiums had taken hold, but instead of helping they made him feel maudlin and stupid, doomed to slip up and reveal himself. His only hope was to fire Glasser quickly and then escape. "Lou—"

"Are you feeling all right?"

Brian tried to smile. "You know me, I'm like a rock." Now that the moment was here he found it impossible to say the necessary words, could only circle around them. "What horseshit, huh? I should've quit the business years ago. I wish I had."

"Times have changed," said Glasser, evidently in a melancholy mood himself. "The game isn't played the same anymore. It's gotten uglier."

Feldman nodded his agreement. "This Freeburg's a perfect example of the problem. Smart but nasty, like a pit bull. Always trying to bite."

"The young ones are like that now," said Glasser. "Defense lawyers are the enemy to them."

The lawyers talked on, munching burgers and fries, until the tension became too much for Brian to bare. He hunched forward, forcing himself to speak. "Listen, I'm afraid I've got some bad news. I'm going to have to get another lawyer."

"Another lawyer?" Glasser put down his burger. "What are you talking about?"

The lawyer's eyes were large with incipient hurt, and Brian found himself too pained to look. He and Glasser had worked together for two decades, had lived through Randy Schotts and Brian Brianson, through poverty and wealth. Glasser had been like a father to him—as much of a father as a runaway could possibly stand. It wasn't an easy bond to break.

Suddenly he found himself adding something he hadn't meant to say. "The word is you're under investigation, man. The Feds are watching you."

This had a predictable effect. There was a moment of silence, all three of them sitting absolutely still. Brian watched Glasser's eyes flicker over to Feldman and then back again.

"Where did you hear this?" asked the lawyer. His voice was anxious and small.

"Rumor. Going around."

"It's bullshit."

Brian shrugged, hoping he hadn't gone too far. "I hope so, man, but in the meantime I have to think of myself. Maybe when this thing blows over, we'll get back together, you know. But for now—"

Mercifully, there was no need to continue. Glasser stood up, in a hurry to get out. His movements were controlled but his hands were shaking, and he dropped his cigarette lighter not once but twice, bending each time to pick it up. "Lies," said the lawyer. "Somebody's been telling you lies—" There was a quiver in his voice.

Feldman was up too. "Brian, I'm going to chase down these rumors. I'm going to prove to you it's nothing but bullshit."

The smuggler remained seated, staring into his lap. He had done what he had to, and he had added a warning too—little more than a gesture, perhaps, but *something* nevertheless. If it did the lawyer no practical good it at least helped to ease his own conscience to know that in the final moment he had acted magnanimously. For now, surrounded by crumpled burger wrappers and stray french fries, the truth of his situation was flooding in upon him: without Glasser he was completely alone.

Out on the street, the partners headed up Broadway, moving too fast for men of their bulk. "Do you think it's true?" asked Feldman, panting.

"It can't be."

"A rumor like that could ruin us, Lou. The clients would all cut and run."

"Don't you think I know that?" Glasser stopped to lean against a lamppost, pressed his forehead to the cold gritty metal. "Listen, there's something I've been meaning to tell you. I was the lawyer on that LSD case."

"The Schotts thing?"

"Believe me, I never knew Brianson was the same as Schotts." They were two blocks up from the McDonald's, but Glasser looked back, as if afraid the smuggler might come after them. "Schotts was a nickel bagger. I represented him that once, and he jumped bail before we got to trial. I never gave him another thought, and then Brianson walked in five, six years later, loaded with money. There was no way for me to know it was the same guy."

"So when did you find out?"

"Just like you—last week at the arraignment. My heart almost stopped."

"Why didn't you say something?"

"I don't know, I meant to, but there were so many things happening—Jason's interview, the motions for Auerbach." He looked Feldman in the eye. "I haven't done anything wrong, Jerry."

Feldman nodded. "If you didn't know about it, you didn't do anything wrong."

"I didn't do anything wrong."

Feldman stood beside him, nervously looking up and down the empty sidewalk. "Do you think there's a connection? You and this Schotts case and—the rumor?"

"There's no connection. There's no investigation. It's just paranoid bullshit."

"Then why would he fire us like that?"

"He was doped to the gills, you saw how high he was."

"We can't afford to lose him, Lou."

This was true, of course. On top of everything else, Brianson was still their most important client. Glasser closed his eyes for a moment, trying to still the spinning in his head. "Leave it to me, I know how to handle him."

Louis Glasser first met Randy Schotts in 1966, through a marijuana smuggler named Howie Silverman. Silverman was Glasser's most important client in those years, the first real break he'd gotten in private practice. Before representing the pot importer, Glasser had subsisted on scraps, drunk driving and disorderly conduct cases, strays he picked up in the halls of the criminal court building. Through Silverman's contacts he gained access to the burgeoning hippie market: the white, middle-class college kids who were then getting arrested in droves. Judged by his standard in later years, these were small cases—possession of marijuana or LSD, little or no jail time for a first offender—but they were bigger than anything he'd known before, and the sheer volume of work made it lucrative.

On this particular day, late in the fall of that year, Howie and his entourage filled the tiny waiting room outside Glasser's private office. Silverman's escort was made up of four whippetlike kids, thin and delicately boned, stooped slightly forward—overtall teenagers confused by their own sudden height. They were errand boys, really, carrying packages, running messages that couldn't be given over the phone; and though their numbers changed constantly there was a certain generic look to them: wide-eyed and strangely earnest, grateful to be near what they took to be the center of the hippie world. Standing behind their leader, hands in their pockets, they swayed like cattails in the breeze, shy Mona Lisa smiles on their lips.

Silverman himself stood front and center. Dressed in a floor-length sheepskin coat and velvet pants, he had blond hair down to his waist, a Vandyke beard, silver rings on all ten fingers. He claimed to have met Dylan, partied with the Stones, shared a joint with Janis Joplin; and though Glasser tended to doubt these stories, there was no denying the powerful aura Howie radiated, a loose-limbed, giddy confidence that made recklessness seem princely.

"Just got back from Mexico, Lou." He was sunburned and beaming, his voice a sticky marijuana drawl, elongated like a strand of taffy. "Craziest thing happened coming back over the border into Texas. We stopped at customs, and the pigs started to tap down the van for compartments." He meant the false bottom in which he stored the pot for transport, fifty or sixty kilos at a time. "I nearly shat on myself, man."

Glasser was sipping his coffee in the doorway because there wasn't enough space for him in the tiny room. The big offices of later years were yet to come; in 1966 the waiting area was barely ten by ten. "What do you expect with hair like that? They pull you right out of the line."

Howie didn't stop to consider this obvious fact. "It's fucking amazing they didn't find it, man. I mean, how stupid can they get?"

Glasser took another sip of coffee. He'd worked till one or two in the morning every day that week, and he was feeling light-headed, floaty with exhaustion. "Keep playing Russian roulette and you're going to get burnt, Howie." And then he began to laugh at his own admonition. The truth was he liked Silverman's recklessness, the air of danger it brought into the office.

Howie laughed along with him. "You're beginning to sound like my old man, Lou."

Glasser had met Howie's father once, a second-generation furrier in a dark suit and hat, with a gray beard and large bewildered eyes, two heads shorter than his only son. Since the Silverman family was Orthodox the three of them had eaten blintzes in a kosher restaurant down the street, Howie in bell-bottoms and some kind of flowing Indian top, an egret among jowly, gray-suited rhinoceroses.

"Get yourself a hat," said Glasser. "Or a wig or something, and put your hair up so they can't see it."

Howie didn't pick up on the advice. "You know, you should come with me next time, man. It would be good for you."

Glasser laughed again. "I'm a lawyer, Howie. I can't ride around Mexico in a van full of pot."

"I'm not talking about business, Lou, just a vacation. We'd drive down to Sonora and live with the Indians, take peyote and mushrooms and smoke weed under the night sky. It would change your view of reality."

"I like my view of reality." Glasser lit a cigarette, inhaling deeply and feeling his head spin. "And anyway, I've got cases stacked up every day for the next six months."

He said this with considerable pride. After law school he'd worked for another attorney, and then quickly went out on his own, but the next few years were rougher than he ever imagined possible. Renting an office in somebody else's suite, he'd spent most of his days in a clientless vacuum, reading the *Times* at a battered metal desk and scheming how to pay the bills. Afternoons, after prowling the halls in the court building, he took fitful naps in his chair, dreaming of all the different forms of failure. When the tiny office became unbearable he went up to Times Square, walking to save the subway token, then hid himself in one of the movie theaters that showed four films for a dollar. It was a point of honor—his one rule—that he did not go home before five-thirty, when his wife, Esther, got back from her secretarial job at Metropolitan Life.

Those years were too recent to be forgotten, and now that business was coming in, he made the most of it. The night before, he'd gone to the precinct to interview a client locked up in the pens, and the night before that he'd hunted down a judge to sign a bail order. And each time he was in court again by nine that morning, fueled by black coffee, cigarettes, and cheese Danish, eyes burning, with a load of ten or twelve cases on the calendar.

"You work too hard," said Silverman, shaking his head.

Glasser readily agreed. "I grew up during the Depression, Howie. Work is all anybody ever thought about."

"You've got to lay back a little, like the Indians, man. We've got so much to learn from them, you know." He seemed to remember something, and turned toward his entourage. "Hey, Randy, where'd we put that thing for Lou?"

"I got it right here, man." This was the thinnest and most stooped of the four kids, with a long scrawny neck and pinched face, floppy ears sticking out of his lank brown hair. Yet the sum total of his features was anything but comical. Though he was as stoned as the others, there was an air of wariness about him, a hardness to his bloodshot eyes.

"Here it is," said the kid—Randy—as he reached into the bag on his shoulder and pulled out some kind of Indian artifact, then lifted the thing for Glasser to see. The object was a heavy clay pipe, maybe half a foot long, with some simple carvings on the bowl.

"It's a present," said Howie, beaming. "We got it in Sonora."

"Gee, thanks," said Glasser, taking the pipe from Randy's grimy fingers. He held it up in the palm of his hand, unsure what to do with it.

"It's got heavy religious meaning," said Randy, smiling to show a mouthful of bad teeth. "Right, Howie?"

Silverman spoke directly to Glasser. "Randy made the trip with me to Mexico, man. I needed some help with the driving."

"It was great," said Randy, nodding loosely. "It's a magic place, man."

Glasser thought of this scrawny kid sitting in the van as the customs agents knocked around for the hidden compartment, and he felt a dull pang. There was nothing he could do about it, of course— he had no real influence over Howie or any of his other clients—but some things made him less happy than others. He lifted the pipe up to eye level for careful inspection, pretending to be delighted with the gift. "This is beautiful, Howie. If I ever start smoking peyote, I'll definitely do it in this."

Randy Schotts surfaced again a month or so later, trailing behind yet another of Glasser's clients, a street hustler named Richie

Dunbar. "We were in the neighborhood," said Dunbar, not very convincingly. "Thought we'd stop in, you know, hang out for a few minutes."

It was noon on the dot, lunchtime, and Dunbar often did this, knowing Glasser would feed him. In frayed dungarees and dirty tennis sneakers, an old lumberman's jacket too light for the November weather, he looked half-frozen, a stray caught out in the cold.

"You're in luck," said Glasser, sticking to their little ritual. "I was just about to order up some lunch." There was never any strain to Glasser's generosity, and in any case Dunbar was a likable guy— an acidhead autodidact, full of theories and arcane information, his pockets crammed with the crumbling paperbacks he stole from used-book stores. Glasser would sit him down in the waiting room and sometimes Dunbar would spend the entire day there, talking to the other clients, reading aloud passages from whatever he happened to have with him—*The Doors of Perception*, say, or *Confessions of an English Opium-Eater*.

"Cool," said Dunbar, grinning through his ragged black beard. "You know my man Randy Schotts?"

"The kid with the pipe," said Glasser, making the connection back to that afternoon with Howie. "How're you doing, Randy?"

"Groovy, man." Randy tried to smile, but he was in even worse shape than Dunbar. Dressed in a flannel shirt and a jeans jacket, he had his hands thrust deep in his pants pockets and his bony shoulders hiked up around his ears for warmth. Glasser could see that the last few weeks had been hard on the boy: Randy was even thinner than before, and much, much dirtier, his clothes shiny with grime. But the biggest difference was in his face: the wary, calculating expression was gone, replaced by a look of barely suppressed panic.

There was no point in asking what had happened, Glasser knew, because Randy would never say. Glasser had seen hundreds of kids just like him, runaways drifting at the fringes of the New York drug culture. They slept in parks and abandoned buildings, sold dope on St. Marks or peddled their asses on the docks. Draped in dirty tie-dye and famished for drugs, they were the dark underbelly of the counterculture: devoid of Eastern mysticism and radical politics, so free they didn't have to bother with a philosophy of freedom. As far as Glasser could tell, most of them stayed on the scene a short while, then disappeared. They drifted elsewhere or went home, or they ended up dead.

"Cold out, huh?" said Glasser, lighting a cigarette.

"Yeah, it's pretty cold."

Glasser ordered up sandwiches from the delicatessen downstairs and the three of them ate in his office, the two hippies seated on the couch, Glasser at his desk. Randy ate with absolute absorption, rocking slightly as he chewed, his fingers and chin glistening with grease. It was an arresting sight, private and sad. Glasser ordered the boy another and watched him devour that one too when it came, only half listening as Dunbar talked in the usual stoned circles.

"I'm reading about Buddhism now," said Dunbar, contentedly licking salt from his fingers. He lifted one thin haunch to pull a yellowed paperback from his rear pocket, began delicately turning the pages. "This part here is the Heart Sutra, man, which is, like, the most important—the key to it all, you know."

Give him soup and a sandwich and Dunbar snapped back within minutes, as if nothing had ever been wrong. Thumbing through his book, he seemed genuinely unconcerned about the weather, or that he'd be outside again in just an hour or two. Small and shriveled-looking, like a piece of beef jerky, he was probably deep into middle age, but his shoulder-length hair was still jet black and his creased face looked strangely timeless, like an old pair of work boots that will not fall apart. He made his living selling loose joints in Washington Square Park, crashed in an abandoned building on Avenue D. He dropped acid and stole books, and though he was infinitely flexible on all points, these two things seemed to be the sum total of his ambitions.

Dunbar emptied a packet of sugar into his mouth, then went back to his book. "The Buddha said all five senses are empty, man. That means they're real but they're not, you know. I was trying to tell Randy that, Lou. The cold is real but it's an illusion. Like a real illusion, you know."

Glasser nodded, not really listening anymore. He had been up most of the night preparing a case for trial, and his mind had now returned to the fine points of his opening statement—that and the hundred other things he'd have to take care of before walking into court the next morning. Finishing his own lunch, he went back to work, making calls from his desk while the two hippies continued to eat. Every once in a while, put on hold, he would try casually tossing a question at Randy. "So where are you staying these days?"

"Crashing at Dunbar's pad."

Dunbar looked up from his book. "We're painting the place, Lou, whenever we can find a can of paint, you know. Pink and red and yellow. It looks really cool."

Glasser had actually been to Dunbar's squat the summer before, when the dealer had missed two court appointments and a bench warrant had been issued for his arrest. It was an old tenement, like the one Glasser had grown up in, but long abandoned, the bottom floor boarded up with plywood. The wood over the doorway had been pulpy and soft, and Glasser had pulled it back without effort, like a tent flap. Inside, there was a faint fruity smell of dampness and garbage, overlaid with chalky plaster dust. He had found Dunbar in an otherwise empty room on the second floor, wrapped in blankets on a bare mattress and shivering with fever.

Glasser looked at the boy. "How do you like it?"

"It's cool."

"Have you seen Howie?" Glasser thought the kid would have a much better chance if he stuck around Silverman. Howie lived on Sixth Street, in an apartment with heat and electricity, full of souvenirs from his smuggling trips—Mexican folk art and Turkish rugs.

"Nah, he's disappeared," said Randy. "Somebody told me he's in Thailand, but I don't know."

Just then Glasser's party came back on the line and he had to return his attention to the phone. When he finally hung up, Dunbar rose from the couch, saying he had to pick up a package across town. "Duty calls again. God bless you." He thrust his book into his back pocket, then put his dirty palms together in the Indian gesture for thanks.

"Yeah, thanks, man," said Randy, reluctantly getting up to follow.

"Wait a second." Glasser picked up his new winter coat and held it out to the kid. "Try this on." Made of beautiful green loden and imported from Austria, it was the single most expensive piece of clothing he'd ever bought, a reward to himself for months of grueling labor.

"You're kidding," said Randy, running a hand over the soft sleeve.

"I wish I were. But it's supposed to snow tonight."

Randy put it on over his jeans jacket, not overeager but obedient, his face filled with a sudden, spooky sweetness. The arms were a little too short and the waist much too big, but the shoulders almost fit, and the whole thing hung well enough to keep the cold out.

"Take it," said Glasser. "I've got others." He meant the old duffle coat he'd worn since law school.

"Far out." Randy smiled in a way that caught Glasser's attention: not an expression of thanks so much as one of childlike pleasure in himself, in his own extraordinariness, the thing in him which made coats materialize on his back as soon as the weather got cold.

Randy showed up again about six months later, in the summer of 1967. He stood in the doorway to Glasser's private office, smiling like a kid about to spring a surprise, and it seemed only to increase his pleasure that Glasser didn't recognize him. "Remember me?" he asked. "With the coat?"

"Coat?" Glasser looked up from the papers spread over his desk, a lit cigarette dangling from his mouth. He had motions to submit by the end of the day, and he'd barely started.

"Yeah, man. You gave me your green winter coat."

"I did? That was dumb."

"Yeah, it really was."

Glasser looked him over, squinting through the tobacco smoke. The boy had changed again, this time for the better. He was relatively clean, for one, in a purple T-shirt and cutoff jeans, sandals on his feet; and he looked healthier too, with some color in his face and a little muscle on his bare arms. The panic of that winter day was gone from his eyes, as was the wariness of the time before, and in their place was a brashness that could pass for confidence or pride. He had obviously come to show Glasser how well he was doing, and the point was a fair one. If he wasn't exactly thriving, he'd lasted longer than most other runaways, and that in itself was an achievement.

"I remember now," said Glasser, and then added, "I was just about to order up some lunch," though in fact he'd already eaten.

"Cool. We can talk about my case."

As it turned out, Randy's visit was professional. He had been arrested three days before, for selling dime bags of pot in Washington Square Park, and had spent a day at Rikers Island before a friend bailed him out. "Definitely uncool," he said, a trace of real fear still evident beneath the affectation of unconcern. He ate as he talked, stuffing french fries in his mouth.

It wasn't much of a case; some phone calls over the next few weeks and Glasser had cut a deal with the district attorney for six months' probation, no jail time. That was no surprise; the really amazing thing was that Randy paid him his fee—all at once, five hundred dollars in dirty fives and ones, wrapped in a paper bag—taking evident pleasure in Glasser's surprise, as if the pile of dollars were a birthday present and not money he owed.

"You're an honorable man," said Glasser, counting the bills on his desk. It was a ritual of his and he did it with relish, the same relish whether it was a wad of ones or hundreds.

"I pay my debts," said Randy.

"Good policy." Glasser counted as he spoke, his head nodding slightly with the rhythm of the passing bills. "Now listen to me, probation is a serious thing. Get caught in the park again and you go to jail." He looked up to drive the point home. "So stay cool for a while, okay?"

"How long?"

"Six months. You got six months' probation."

Randy looked blank for a second and then gave an empty smile. "Yeah, sure. I hear you."

Glasser had felt obligated to give the warning, though he knew there was no chance the kid would stop selling pot for six hours, let alone six months—it was, after all, his livelihood. "You could work for me," he said. "I could use an assistant here."

"What would I do?"

Glasser never gave much thought to the details of his chaotic operation. "All sorts of things, I guess. Whatever we need done."

Randy shook his head, the long lank hair hiding his face. "No way, man. I'm not made for an office job."

Glasser had to admit the truth of this. "Well, probably not."

But Randy made it through probation anyway, and in a few years he was out of the park and working for himself, servicing his own steady clientele. It wasn't much different from any other kind of sales work, actually: he went to concerts, parties, nightclubs, met people, got friendly, casually let them know what line of business he was in. It required a veneer of sociability, an aura of cool, enough sophistication to get invited to the right places, where the good customers hung out. Glasser watched as Randy—the runaway, the street urchin—began to get some polish. The boy was really clean now, down to the white crescents of his fingernails, dressed in a tutti-frutti-colored dashiki and orange hip huggers, or an embroidered shirt from India with little round mirrors the size of pennies sewn into the design. He became a regular at the office, sitting in the waiting room, talking to whoever was around or reading magazines, joining Glasser for lunch or dinner, part of the swirl of clients and hangers-on that filled the place.

For Glasser's business had been growing too, and by the end of the decade he had three lawyers working for him, as well as a secretary, two clerks, and an assortment of helpers who came and went, culled from the ranks of his clientele. The phones were always ringing, the typewriters pounding, the delivery man back with another order of food. He was a success now, and being a success meant not only money but love and attention—a full waiting room, and all the phone lines lit all the time.

In 1970, Randy was arrested for attempted sale of fifty hits of LSD. He made bail but came out shaken by the night he'd spent behind bars, scared of having to go back. The charge was serious—conviction could mean up to five years in prison—and Glasser had to tell him that the situation didn't look good. The U.S. Attorney's Office wasn't offering much in the way of a plea bargain—a lesser charge worth three years in the slammer. This meant the feds were confident they could win at trial, and the facts seemed to justify this view: Randy had been caught red-handed selling to two undercover agents, and they had tapes of the phone conversations leading up to the deal. Still, there was always a chance, a crack in even the most impregnable-seeming wall of evidence; Glasser knew it was a matter of looking for the weak spot—with a magnifying glass if he had to—and then chipping away till a hairline fracture became a chasm large enough to walk through. He had done it before. But it would mean a lot of work, and that would be costly; his fee would be six thousand dollars. "More if it goes longer," he said, turning pages in the complaint the U.S. Attorney's Office had sent.

"This is my life, Lou. I'll get the money. You just get me off, man."

"Randy, lawyers don't give guarantees."

It was about the tenth time they'd been over it. Just one night in jail had stripped away the thin layer of smart-alecky sophistication; the only thing left was a shivering kid with a runny nose and chattering teeth.

"There's a chance," said Glasser. "There's always a chance. They're not offering much of a deal, so you don't risk anything by going to trial."

"What are the odds?"

"Of an out-and-out acquittal? Small." Glasser watched Randy's eyes drift in blind fright.

"How small?"

"Maybe ten percent. Maybe twenty."

Late that night Glasser got a call, waking him from a shallow, fitful sleep. That was how he slept in those days—tense and overtired, pulled awake three nights out of five by another client in trouble. The calls made Esther furious; she would change their unlisted number every few months, hoping for some peace, but Glasser always gave the new number out to anyone who asked. The truth was, he liked the calls. They were better than the swirl of thoughts in his head, keeping him awake and tossing, or the sudden panics that left him with his heart racing and his eyes frozen open, staring at the ceiling. An emergency meant something to do.

This time it was Randy. "I need to talk to you. There's been shit going down, man."

"What kind of shit?"

There was a long pause. "Shit shit."

They met at a coffee shop. Randy was already there, sitting in a booth by the window. It was two A.M., but there were customers scattered at the tables, night-shift workers and insomniacs with that suspended, displaced look, hunched over cups of coffee and copies of the *Post*. Glasser and Randy sat together in distracted silence, Randy chain-smoking while Glasser ate an odd assortment of foods chosen more for color than taste: lemon meringue pie, raspberry Jell-O, Black Forest chocolate cake.

Randy spoke first. "I can't go to jail." He blew a cloud of smoke, white as the meringue on Glasser's pie. "I'm going to run, I've decided."

Despite the early hour, a little warning light went off in Glasser's head. This was a tricky situation, and in order to protect his own position, he must not say or do anything to help Randy evade justice. "As an officer of the court I have to advise you against it."

Randy seemed a little hurt by Glasser's official tone. "Yeah, why?"

"Because it's against the law."

The boy gave a bitter laugh. "It's a little late to worry about that."

"Besides, you'll lose your bail money."

"Fuck the money. I wouldn't survive a month in there. I'd hang myself."

"Running isn't easy. Most people get caught sooner or later."

"I know how to disappear." Bravado, of course; the kid was shaking.

"You're sure about this?" asked Glasser.

Randy nodded, about to light yet another cigarette. "I can't go to jail."

"Okay then, a word of advice: pay the bail bondsman what you owe him." He lowered his voice, leaning forward over the table. "If you don't, he'll hire a bounty hunter to find you, and that's something you don't want."

Glasser knew he shouldn't have said this, but his bent was ultimately pragmatic: if Randy was going to run, it was better that he didn't get caught, because he'd end up with another couple of years tacked onto his sentence. Besides, Glasser did a lot of business with the bail bondsman in question, and he didn't want to see him out ten thousand dollars; if a single Glasser client burned the man, he'd be less willing to underwrite bonds for the others. It was that simple.

Randy nodded at the soundness of the suggestion. "Okay, I'll pay him." He stood up, working his way out of the booth. "I'm going now," he said, eyes on the door. But he didn't move. He looked like a boy trying to steel himself into jumping from the high diving board.

Glasser had the feeling the kid wanted to tell him something more—his plans, his destination, as if saying them out loud might make them real. "Don't tell me anything," Glasser said. "You don't want me to know."

"I'm going now," repeated Randy. And this time he really did go, with a stiff self-conscious walk, out the glass door to the street.

That was the last Glasser saw of Randy Schotts, until a day in January 1975—Howie Silverman's funeral. Glasser stood at the edge of the open grave, staring down at the coffin lid, which was sprinkled with earth the color of cigarette ash. The ceremony, such as it was, had ended: a thin young woman, shivering in a cloth coat, had read from a book of poetry, intoning the lines in a reedy, singsong voice. The eulogy had been given by a man with a fiery red beard, a self-proclaimed priest in what he called the Present-Day Church of Joy. He wore a thrift-shop overcoat and a fur cap with the earflaps sticking up, and it gave him a cockeyed, rambunctious look, like a puppy dog. But he rambled on for almost an hour, and Glasser noticed some of the mourners wandering off to the shelter of a little granite mausoleum maybe thirty yards away. When the icy wind blew from that direction, he caught the incongruously tropical odor of marijuana.

The Present-Day Church of Joy? Howie Silverman had barely reached thirty. Once a world traveler, a hippie aristocrat bedecked with Indian jewelry, he had died a dope fiend, with brown needle marks in the webbing between his fingers.

"Death isn't real, Lou." Richie Dunbar had come up beside him while he was staring down at the grave.

"It looks real to me."

Dunbar shook his head. His hair was completely gray now, but otherwise he was much the same—shriveled and strangely indestructible. He walked with a limp, the result of a beating he'd taken in the park. "It's an illusion, Lou. We're born again and again. K-k-karma, you know?" Under stress, he would sometimes break into stuttering. This had worked in his favor on the witness stand; choking on his testimony, he had endeared himself to the jurors.

"Well, I hope you're right." Stepping back from the grave, Glasser noticed a figure off by himself, so far away that he seemed to be in the orbit of another, much larger funeral nearby. Too well dressed for one of Howie's friends, in a dark green overcoat and black muffler, the man was clearly intent on Silverman's mourners. "Know that guy?" Glasser asked Dunbar, gesturing with his chin.

Dunbar squinted. "Nah."

They walked over to where the other mourners stood, by the paved road that led to the parking lot. The group looked aimless and despondent, a dozen or so young people with their hands thrust in their pockets, shifting from foot to foot as if waiting to be dismissed. Most of them were drunk or stoned, with a rubbery, loose-limbed gait, a slackness to their faces in spite of the cold. When Glasser joined them, they started to move down the road.

In the sixties they had been startling creatures, full of outlandish stories of their adventures in Turkey, Nepal, and the Himalayas. Dressed in djellabas or sarongs, giggly and irreverent, they had radiated the rock star's air of glamour without the rock or the stardom. But then they got into heroin or cocaine or pills, and after a while their faces were no longer placid and dreamy but visibly preoccupied with obtaining their next fix. Their skin took on a dull waxy look, and their teeth turned brown. In a little while the last of their money was gone, and Glasser was representing them for petty larceny, purse snatching, possession of a hypodermic syringe—the kinds of things for which junkies get arrested.

In the parking lot, six of them piled into Glasser's car for the ride back to Manhattan, sitting on each others' laps. The cemetery was in Queens, by a freeway, and the most inspiring thing about the place was the view from this road: a nearly endless expanse of headstones on the left, with the skyscrapers of Wall Street straight ahead like a mountain range.

"Look at that," said someone in the tangle of bodies. His voice had the gee-whiz tone of the very high. "Those are some tall buildings, man. They are *tall*. They are way up there."

"I hate funerals," said someone else. "A total downer, you know? And it was fucking cold."

The voices began to mix, not really amounting to a conversation. "We should celebrate life, man, not death. That's what it's really about."

"Howie loved life. That guy really *lived*."

"Life and death are both, like, illusions, man." That one was Dunbar. "Howie isn't dead, man, he's been transformed."

"Transformed?"

"Like a ca-ca-caterpillar into a butterfly, man."

"He owed me money."

"*You* owe me money, man. Seven bucks."

"Those are some motherfucking tall buildings, and we're heading straight for 'em."

Glasser dropped them off outside his office. They unfolded slowly in the cold, not quite stretching to full height, hands in their pockets. Their hippie finery was gone, replaced by secondhand overcoats and mismatched gloves. For a moment they stood blinking in the weak afternoon sun, looking as if they'd somehow been transported to a foreign city without map or currency. But then suddenly they all flew apart, like a rack of pool balls on the break, no one turning to look back or say good-bye.

Glasser parked, then headed up to the office. The waiting room was crowded when he walked in, clients springing up to shake his hand, slap his back, but the attention didn't please him as much as it once had. In the corridor leading to his private office, Rainbow gave him his phone messages. "Poor Howie," she said. She had come to work for Glasser in '72 and had witnessed Silverman's decline.

Glasser shuffled through the wad of pink memo slips. "All they do is talk about reincarnation, but he was a Jew, not a Hindu. I'm not sure they understand he's really dead."

"They understand, Lou. They just can't take it." She gave a shrug of her practical shoulders. "Don't forget Paul's due at four."

"Oh, yeah, good." Glasser perked up a little. Paul Moreno was a new client, a coke dealer facing indictment for conspiracy, and Glasser stood to make more on this one case than he'd made in over a decade representing Howie Silverman.

Seated in Glasser's office, Paul Moreno crossed one meaty leg over another, gently swinging a patent-leather boot. He talked slowly, a deliberate progression of self-conscious sentences uttered in a quiet voice. Thick liquid indolence hid an intense watchfulness. He smiled often, but it was a cold, lazy smile, all light but no heat, like winter sunshine. "I don't want to talk to them if they're not being up-front with us."

"The U.S. attorney's playing hardball because he knows you won't cooperate," said Glasser.

Moreno nodded gravely. His polyester shirt was as clingy as Saran Wrap, with a wild blue-and-green geometric pattern stretched tight over his chest and belly. "He's got it right. I'm no snitch, Lou."

"He knows that. He knows your rep." This was just a little bit of strategic flattery. Dealers like Moreno liked to think of themselves as "stand-up guys," but Glasser knew they all rolled when they had to, and he wanted to plant the thought now, so it would be there when the time came to start real negotiations. "Still, you never know. They might try to make an offer."

"I want to beat it in court. No deals."

Glasser backtracked. "Absolutely. That's what I like to hear."

The subject switched to one of Moreno's co-conspirators who was already cooperating with the government. "That dirty lowlife scum." Moreno's voice kept the same even tone as always, as if discussing the weather or baseball. "Somebody's going to end up putting a bullet in his face."

Glasser tried to laugh this off, holding up a hand to stop the flow of words. "Hey, I don't want to hear that stuff."

"I didn't mean *me,* Lou. I meant *somebody,* you know." Moreno gave the slightest shrug to his heavy shoulders, then reflexively checked his watch. "People get upset, I can't control them."

Later, after Moreno had gone, Glasser sat in his chair, staring out the window. For the first time in his career he was finding one of his clients a little hard to love, and the experience was confusing. Professional without apologies, brutally violent, there was no innocence in Moreno, not even of the childish, self-deluded sort the hippies specialized in. But the small-time pot dealers were gone now; coke was the new boom drug, and by 1975 it was already big business, generating staggering legal fees.

He was thinking about going home when Rainbow buzzed. Less polished in those days, she mumbled into the receiver so as not to be overheard. "Lou, a guy here says he wants to see you."

"Appointment?" Glasser never turned away business, but that evening he was on the verge.

"No appointment, never been here, but says he knows Richie Dunbar."

Rainbow escorted in a tall, bony young man of twenty-five or -six, a forest green overcoat and black cashmere scarf draped over his arm. His voice was soft, an unhurried drawl, but he punctuated his rambling talk with a smile like the crash of cymbals—two rows of perfect white teeth gleaming like bathroom tile. It took Glasser a while to realize that they were capped, like a movie actor's. And that was not the only source of his confusion. There was something familiar about this kid in his black velvet jacket and white jeans. "What did you say your name is?"

"Brianson. Brian Brianson." The young man smiled, raising his eyebrows like quotation marks.

"You don't know a kid by the name of Randy Schotts, do you?"

"Scotts?"

"Schotts. A client of mine."

"Doesn't sound familiar."

Brianson wanted help with a commercial lease for a clothing store he was opening in the Village. It was an unusual request for a lawyer who specialized in criminal work, but it was also very simple—Glasser would give it to one of the paralegals to do. Besides, Brianson didn't look like an ordinary store owner. A small retail store is just the kind of legitimate business a drug dealer needs to launder the money he makes elsewhere.

The next time Glasser met Brianson, some weeks later, he watched him carefully. Now that he knew what he was looking for, it was obvious the man was Randy: the sharp features and the small black eyes lit with intelligent calculation, the paradoxically naked smile, overwhelming in its need to be loved. And then the fake smile that usually followed, numb as an advertising jingle.

"Is that yours?" Brianson asked, pointing to a photo on Glasser's desk—Glasser standing next to his little airplane, a single-prop Cessna.

Glasser watched him reach over to pick up the photo, suddenly touched at this runaway's version of a homing instinct. Some memory of warmth had brought him back to this office, even with a fake identity. But Glasser knew he had to be careful. Randy was still a fugitive, and though Glasser wasn't legally obligated to turn him in, he must not do anything to help him evade the police.

"I've always wanted to learn to fly," Brian said, looking at the photo. "There's something about flying in a little plane, that feeling of perfect freedom, like you've got wings on your back." He gave his real smile this time. "You think maybe I could go up with you one day?"

"Of course," said Glasser. "Whenever you want."

"Cool." Brian put the picture back on the desk. "I think I have a case for you. A criminal case."

This was to be one of the benefits of their charade. As long as Brian Brianson didn't directly confess to Glasser that he was actually Randy Schotts, a fugitive, there was nothing to keep them from picking up where they'd left off, six years before.

Brian stroked his long chin. "A friend of mine's in some trouble."

Brian's friend was really an employee, with the bad luck to be mentioned in somebody else's wiretapped phone conversations, and Glasser had her come into the office the next afternoon: a pale, middle-aged New England woman with the incongruous name of Bunny. Looking forlorn and strangely puritanical in her peasant skirt, her lips the same faded color as her face, Bunny sat with her hands folded in her lap. She seemed to have been building up to this disaster for years, was not so much scared as exhausted, like a runner after a marathon. Bunny. The name conjured an Easter egg hunt, but here she was looking at ten years in prison. Glasser could only marvel at what happened to people, the places they ended up, like a piece of paper somebody lets drop on Wall Street, only to be deposited by the wind in the Bronx.

The case was almost hopeless. The D.A.'s Office was more interested in her friends than in Bunny herself, but she wouldn't negotiate, just clamped her pale lips shut and stared ahead with granite determination. This didn't surprise Glasser, who assumed that Brian was paying her legal fees with the understanding that she'd leave him out of it. And though Glasser did his best at the trial, pulling his hair and sobbing in front of the jury box, it didn't add up to much. Bunny, that bleached presence, got the full ten years.

The Saturday following Bunny's conviction, Glasser drove Brian out to the tiny airport in New Jersey where he kept his plane. There were three runways, a control tower, a row of metal hangars, a terminal building with an orange windsock riding at the top of a flagpole. Between these things stretched hundreds of yards of weeds and weather-cracked asphalt, enough empty space to make the hangars look small from the terminal, the control tower appear tiny from the runway. Only the sky seemed close to everything, a white cloudless tarpaulin stretched tight over the marshes. From somewhere unseen came the sound of propeller planes, like the amplified buzzing of insects.

"This is great," said Brian, his face lit with excitement. "It's so wide open. I feel like I could touch the sky."

Standing in front of the terminal building, they watched a twin-engine Piper Apache shoot down the runway, then start to rise as if lifted by wires, finally shrinking to nothingness in the glare. Squinting after it, Brian turned sober. "I think of Bunny locked up in that place there, Bedford Hills, and it makes me feel terrible. I can hardly bear to visit her like that, to see her caged like a zoo animal. And she's going to be in there for ten years. I couldn't last ten days without my freedom, without all this—" He swept his arm over the scene before them. "The possibilities, the choices."

Glasser decided to stay neutral. He had recommended cutting a deal, and she had turned him down; his professional responsibilities had been adequately acquitted. "It was a hard case to win at trial. The tapes were devastating."

"I'm not criticizing you, Lou. I know you did a fantastic job for her. It's just such a shame, you know."

Later, flying over the Jersey landscape in Glasser's plane, Brian seemed to cheer up. Eyes glued to the scenery below, he talked excitedly over the noise of the engine, jumping from topic to topic: Bunny's case and the D.A.'s Office, the marijuana business and the new drug laws. Then he went on to Eastern mysticism, reincarnation, Zen Buddhism, the Chinese *Book of Changes*—a little bit of Dunbar still in him somewhere. "You see it so clearly from up here." He gestured down at the pattern of suburban streets spread out like a diorama. "This is what Indian philosophy calls *maya*, Lou. Illusion. Those little houses down there seem real to the people who live in them, but from up here we can see what they *really* are—just dollhouses. Jesus, a man can waste his life paying the mortgage on a dollhouse. Isn't that crazy?"

After so many months spent with Paul Moreno and the coke dealers, this kind of talk sounded almost civilized. Glasser let it wash over him, not really paying attention. He looked out his Plexiglas windshield at the sky, which was white like soapy water, and then down at the houses below—the dollhouses—breaking up into open fields the color and texture of a burlap sack. There were real people in those houses, he knew—not illusions but actual flesh and blood—only they were tiny now, just inches tall, and if they were to look up from their business at Glasser's plane they would see nothing but a speck, hardly bigger than a bird.

Glasser didn't need to be told that things were relative; the shifting nature of appearances was his stock-in-trade. As a trial lawyer, the main part of his job was the invention of plausible stories, and this activity wasn't untruthful so much as eerily truthless. Glasser had to get up and tell the jury that appearances are deceiving, that more than one interpretation can fit the facts; he had to teach them how to doubt. Playing the kindly professor or the indignant citizen or a half dozen other dramatic roles, he walked them through the prosecution's case, pointing up chips and cracks in the evidence like a building inspector searching for fire hazards. Blurry surveillance photographs, garbled audiotapes, conflicting eyewitness accounts, missing pieces of evidence: Glasser seized on these things with the glee of a card player unmasking a cheat. See! he cried. The government lies! The police lie! Photos lie! Facts lie!

This was a game, and the laws of the land were merely the rules of this game. Guilt and innocence were not irrelevant, of course, but they were complex, amorphous things, here and then gone like a shadow glimpsed from the corner of one's eye. After so many years of this, Glasser found himself alone in the white space between fact and interpretation, frightened by the way truth dissolved into doubt, like sugar into tea. He was scared by his own ability to manipulate appearances, scared too of his need to play the game; and he was terrified of the way the stakes had climbed now that people like Paul Moreno were sitting at the table.

It was only a game, but Bunny got ten years. It was only a game, but Howie Silverman was dead. "You know," said Glasser, breaking into Brianson's monologue, "Howie died."

Brianson's eyes fluttered slightly at the news. "Doesn't ring a bell." For a moment he looked out the window blankly. "Listen, man, I've got another case for you."

It was only a game, but he was flying with someone who was pretending to be somebody else. "I'm always ready for another case."

4

FUCK THE PIGS

After returning from McDonald's, Glasser slept badly. He woke late, exhausted, his hands clenched in fists, his jaws locked together, aching. The events of the night before were vivid in his mind but slightly unreal. Had Brian really fired them? Could there really be a rumor going around that the partners were being targeted by the Feds? And if so, could it possibly be true?

This last question was too frightening to consider. Blinking in the light of day, Glasser decided that the simplest explanation was the most likely: there was a rumor—there were always rumors. Frightened about his case, high on drugs, the dealer had panicked and fired the lawyers without stopping to think; he would regret it as soon as he woke up. Indeed, Glasser remembered how Brianson's face changed the moment he, Glasser, jumped up to go. Suddenly it was brimming with disappointment, loneliness, a childlike need for comfort. The bloodshot eyes had grown soft and round, the eyebrows arched, the forehead wrinkled.

This was the image that stuck in Glasser's mind, the one that allowed him to ignore his misgivings. He understood the calculus of need, and he was used to being needed; it was his main professional tool, the source of his power. On the most elemental human level, he realized, Brianson needed him—they needed each other. All Glasser had to do was remind him of this fact, and they could take up where they had left off, lawyer and client just as before.

He phoned Brianson four times before shaving, but got no answer—not surprising, he told himself, since the smuggler rarely woke before noon. Esther was already gone, so he breakfasted on odds and ends culled from the refrigerator: a piece of gefilte fish, the heel of a rye bread, a small bag of chopped walnuts meant for baking. He tied his tie in the cab downtown and by ten-thirty was walking through the dim filthy lobby of the criminal court building on Centre Street, late for a hearing on Auerbach's obscenity case. He found the pornographer pacing in front of the ancient padded-leather doors to Part 50.

"Where have you been?" cried Auerbach. He was dressed in the suit he always wore to court appearances, misfitting dark blue serge, a little too short in the leg. "I called the office ten times but nobody's answering the phones."

"Not answering the phones?" Alarmed, Glasser stopped short, his hand on the door. "Listen, I'm going to adjourn this thing."

"Adjourn? Why?"

"Because it's better for us," he lied, dropping his voice. "Berkowitz"—he meant the judge—"just got back from prostate surgery. He's in a vicious mood."

Auerbach's eyes went big with dread. "Will they let us?"

"I'll tell them I've got a toothache. Kean won't mind, he's got a stack of cases on his hands."

A.D.A. Kean was in fact more than happy for the delay, still hoping Auerbach might take a plea. All Glasser had to do was get the case called and move for an adjournment. This turned out to be a problem, however. With more than a hundred cases a day on his calendar, Judge Berkowitz cared about nothing more than his schedule, and Glasser had arrived late—was chronically late, in fact, and prone to just this kind of sudden toothache. Feeling vengeful, Berkowitz gave his bailiff the high sign, and the bailiff moved Glasser to the bottom of the list for that morning. Moaning about his emergency dental appointment proved useless with this bureaucrat. Glasser sat in one of the well-worn benches with Auerbach or ran out to the greasy pay phone in the hall, alternately calling Brianson and the office. Neither answered.

It was nearly one when the case was called and the postponement arranged. Glasser ran out of the courtroom, Auerbach clutching his sleeve as they hurried down the hall. "Can we change judges?" the pornographer asked under his breath.

"What for?" His mind racing ahead, Glasser had already forgotten his excuse about the adjournment. He stopped at a pay phone by the elevators and dialed the office, listened for a long time to the ringing on the other end.

"A man without a prostate shouldn't be judging a case like this," said Auerbach. He whispered passionately, a lofty look in his eye, as if arguing a question of constitutional justice. "It's not right, it's unnatural."

Twenty rings, no answer. Glasser hung up the receiver. "Listen, Henry, I've got to go upstairs to the court clerk." The truth was that he needed to ditch the pornographer so he could get to the office, alone.

"I'll go with you."

"You go home, I'll call you tonight."

Auerbach was about to protest, but Glasser prodded him into one of the waiting elevators, waving good-bye. When the door closed, the lawyer hurried down the hall to the elevator bank on the other side of the building. He knew he could reach the office in five minutes, but on the ground floor, darting toward a side exit, he ran into a further delay: Petruccio.

"Lou!" cried the other lawyer, an unlit Nat Sherman hanging from the corner of his mouth. The cigarette was lime green, to match his silk tie and pocket square, the pinstripe in his cream-colored suit. Who else but Petruccio would dress like a Miami gambler in the middle of a dismal fall in New York, where the sky is the color of a steel cooking pot?

"I'm in a rush, Rocco."

But Petruccio's small eyes were alight, his face veiled with the mock seriousness that indicated, in him, suppressed exultation. He had information, something to tell, and so Glasser allowed himself to be steered into a particularly dark and fetid corner, where the marble walls smelled of stale urine.

"I've got a pal in the U.S. Attorney's Office over in Newark, and he says the accountant has definitely cut a deal." Petruccio whispered, more for dramatic effect than secrecy; barely five feet tall, he liked to make other men stoop to listen.

Obediently, Glasser lowered his head. "How does he know?"

"The accountant's been dialing for dirt." Petruccio meant the Feds had Leon making what are termed "consensual calls," a time-honored procedure that involves phoning associates and getting them down on tape as they incriminate themselves. "Has he called your guy yet?"

"I've warned him to be careful." Then Glasser let slip something he hadn't intended to mention. "You know, my guy's barely mentioned in the complaint. Twice in thirty pages."

A flicker of curiosity traveled over Petruccio's face, quickly suppressed. "Is that so?"

Glasser hadn't realized till now how much this fact bothered him. "Yeah, the case looked so weak, the judge granted bail."

The ends of Petruccio's lips curled into a slight smile, making the Nat Sherman bob. "So he's cooperating, huh?"

"No, he's not." But Glasser could see that it was a logical conclusion to draw: Brianson, the ringleader, hardly appearing in the complaint, let out on bail despite a previous charge of bail jumping. Without another word, he turned and headed for the exit.

He reached the office by one-thirty, only to find the place in a kind of moving-day tumult. The big double doors to the suite were propped open and the waiting room crammed full of neatly taped boxes, U.S. GOVERNMENT stamped on their tops and sides. Where were the clients, the staff? Where were Feldman and Rainbow? He stood for what seemed like an hour, trying to make sense of the noises coming from inside. And then he took out his confusion on one of the boxes, tearing the soft skin of his fingers as he savaged the cardboard flaps.

The box was full of papers from his desk: legal pads covered with jottings and faint brown coffee rings; his court calendar with its pulpy, water-stained cover; a paper napkin with a phone number but no name. He reached in and pulled out an old file, its manila jacket tattooed with a cartoon he'd done of Feldman dressed as a Nazi storm trooper, the words "Pay up!" in a balloon over his head.

"Hey, you can't do that. Put that down." A young man came out, pushing a hand truck. He was a fresh-looking kid in his late twenties, dressed in a dark blue windbreaker and matching baseball cap. They stood watching each other for a moment, and when Glasser made no move to replace the file, the kid marched up and tore it from his hands, leaving behind a whiff of cheap citrus aftershave.

"These files are private," said Glasser. "They're protected by attorney-client privilege."

"You're just making extra work for everybody." The kid picked up the open box and Glasser saw the yellow letters on the back of his jacket: DEA. Drug Enforcement Agency.

Glasser plunged past him, into the offices. The usual sounds of the workday had been replaced with the commotion of packing and sorting, the squeal of tape pulled from the roll. He maneuvered through the hallway, between boxes and loitering DEA agents, and though he was certainly noticed nobody made a move to stop him. He was simply irrelevant.

Sticking his head into Rainbow's room, he watched a group of agents browsing through the open drawers of the file cabinets, pulling out folders and dropping them into boxes. In their windbreakers and baseball caps, they resembled a troop of suburban Little League coaches, and they bent to their tasks with the bland grace of former athletes—high school ballplayers become accountants.

"Get out of those files," Glasser yelled. "They don't belong to you."

The DEA agents looked up, not to answer but to stare—curious, bemused, openly contemptuous. In that brief moment, Glasser could see the calculation pass through their smooth, clean-shaven faces, their stolidly blinking eyes: the shyster made in a month what they made in four or five; he drove a Jag while they tooled around in Plymouths and Chevys. And now he belonged to them. And they would right the balance.

Shyster. Mouthpiece. Fat man. Jew lawyer. Glasser staggered under their collective gaze. He lifted the sleeve of his suit jacket to his forehead, and it came back glistening wet.

"Lou! Thank God you're here!" It was Rainbow, seated in a corner opposite the cabinets, her voluminous skirt draped over the swivel chair like a parachute. The chair was on caster wheels, and instead of getting up she rolled herself over toward him. "Look what they're doing. Look at this."

His voice came out as a croak. "Why hasn't anybody been answering the phones?"

She gave him an odd, exasperated look. "What was I going to say?"

"Somebody's got to do something," he said, then continued down the hall.

The agent in charge was named Barrels, and he stood in Glasser's private office, surveying the changes his troops had wrought. Glasser came in and stood beside him, cowed into silence by the emptiness of the place. The files that had sat on the windowsill were gone, as were the court transcripts he'd kept piled by the couch. Worst of all, his desk had been stripped bare. The once-massive piece of furniture looked shrunken and humiliated, left with only a phone.

Barrels wore the self-satisfied look of a homeowner who'd gotten up early to clean out the attic. "Needs a dusting," he said to Glasser, gesturing with his clipboard to the desk.

The dust made a pattern of ashy lines on the dark wooden surface—an imprint of the objects now gone. Glasser walked around to his big leather chair. The drawers were all open, empty except for the bottommost layer that such drawers always carry—a thick mulch of paper clips and rubberbands and plastic coffee stirrers.

Barrels nodded appreciatively. "Nice piece of furniture, though."

"Mahogany," said Glasser, as if to himself. "Nineteen thirty-nine." He sat down in his chair carefully, as if testing the fit, then leaned forward to brace his hands against the beveled edge of the desktop. From this spot he had negotiated men's freedom, bargained for their lives. He had saved people from jail and been paid money for it—more money than he'd ever imagined possible.

"Must've cost a fortune," said Barrels.

"It did." He pushed away from the desk, letting his chair roll back. "I'm Louis Glasser."

It seemed to make no difference to the DEA agent; perhaps he already knew. "We should be out of your hair pretty soon now, Louie."

The first name was a jab, but Glasser did not react. "You have a warrant, I guess."

"Your partner's got a copy. What's his name, Farbstein."

That too was a jab. Glasser nodded, wondering where Feldman might be hiding. "Can you tell me what this is about?"

Barrels smiled coyly. "Hey, I'm just a working stiff."

"Well, who's the assistant?" Glasser meant the assistant U.S. attorney in charge of the investigation.

"The assistant is Anna Freeburg."

"Freeburg?" The prosecutor on Brian's case, the one who wore a little blue suit and pearls to the dealer's arraignment—the Our Crowd type with her nose in the air.

"Know her?" asked Barrels, catching the look on Glasser's face. It clearly amused him, the irony of launching one lawyer against another—the working stiff's strategy of divide and conquer. "She's a tough one, Louie. We call her the Human Barracuda."

Glasser found Jerry Feldman in the conference room, surrounded by their employees. Feldman was sprawled in a chair, tie open and shirt undone, his broad, fatty chest rising up and down with ragged concentration. The two young law associates, Lipkin and Samuels, were in attendance by his side, each with a Styrofoam cup of water. Lipkin's free hand supported Feldman's large head, with its unruly black curls, while Samuels gripped the stricken lawyer's chubby hand.

"It's his asthma," said Samuels. "He was arguing with them, and then he got an attack."

"He was a lion," said Lipkin. "He tried to keep them out of the files."

Glasser bent down to look at his partner. "Do you need to go to the hospital?"

Feldman shook his head no. His round face was pale and sweaty, his eyes grim with the effort of just breathing. "If I die," he gasped, "sue them." Unable to say anything more, he lifted his free hand to show a crumpled piece of paper—the search warrant.

Glasser took the document in both hands. Search warrants aren't much help usually; they name the place to be ransacked and the things to be seized, never the target or purpose of the investigation. Reading quickly, he found this one even more opaque than usual. Utterly indiscriminate in its appetite for paper, the warrant betrayed no trace of a specific subject of inquiry. Rolodexes, wall calendars, scratch pads were all listed, and just in case anything had been forgotten it ended with a broad greedy grope: "and all books, records, files, and documents pertaining to the functioning of said legal offices."

"They're taking everything but the furniture," said Glasser. "They're shutting us down."

"The warrant's way too broad," said Samuels, sounding like the A student he'd been just a few years before. "It'll never hold up in court."

"We'll get it all back," added Lipkin, though the look on his face said he didn't actually believe this.

Glasser wasn't consoled. "It'll take weeks, they'll have photo-copied everything by then."

He let the warrant drop to the floor, then turned to look at the rest of his staff, sitting around the big rectangular table with exhausted, stricken faces. Grown men and women, lawyers some of them, they drooped like guilty children trying to guess at the punishment to come, eyes fixed on their own hands. Around them were piled their personal effects—jackets, pocketbooks, briefcases gathered from their offices. They looked like refugees in a train station, wondering if they would be stopped at the border, if their counterfeit papers would stand up under inspection.

One of the paralegals began to sniffle. "Are we going to jail?" She was a young woman just out of college, and her fingers worked nervously, shredding an empty Styrofoam cup into fake snow.

"Absolutely not," said Glasser. "This is a law office. Nobody here's done anything wrong."

"If we're going to be arrested, I should call my parents."

"Stop saying that." They were criminal lawyers, not *criminals.* Lawyers went to court; they argued with prosecutors and reasoned with judges; they hammed it up in front of juries. They wore suits and carried briefcases full of important documents they were too busy to read. It was the clients who got the handcuffs and the fingerprints and the mug shots, the jailhouse lunch of Kool-Aid and baloney sandwiches.

"This is barbaric," said Lipkin. "Absolutely barbaric." He was mopping Feldman's forehead with a handkerchief now. "They could've killed him."

Suddenly too tired to stand, Glasser fell into an empty chair. The men out there, pawing through his confidential files, were committing a fundamental breach of decorum. The legal system was adversarial by design; the defense fought the prosecution with everything it could get its hands on, including tears, sarcasm, ridicule, and innuendo. But at the end of the day the game was over; you shook hands and went home. What was happening out there wasn't part of the game.

Then what was it? He could not untangle his thoughts. He sat like the others and listened to the agents lugging boxes out to the elevator, till finally the last of the noise disappeared and Rainbow stood in the conference room doorway. He'd forgotten she was out there with them.

"They're gone." Her ponytail had come undone, and wiry black hair spilled over her back and shoulders. "Look what I got," she said, holding up a shabby green ledger. "I stuck it under my skirt when the pigs came in."

With a rush of excitement, Glasser recognized the logbook in which she took down his phone messages. "You sat on it?" he asked.

"I couldn't get out of my chair to pee."

It was a good move. Filled with names and numbers, the log would have given the Feds a more or less complete map of Glasser's life over the last few months: the clients he spoke to, the dates and times they called, the messages they left.

He bolted up to hug her. "Rainbow, you're a genius!"

"I am a legal genius!" The two of them swayed in an awkward victory dance, bumping into chairs as Rainbow waved the ledger in the air. "Fuck the pigs!" she crowed. "Fuck the pigs!"

Glasser's eyes glistened with tears. "You get a raise! Everybody gets a raise!"

"Fuck the pigs!"

There was a burst of nervous laughter, clapping, and hoots. Lipkin pounded the conference table and Samuels threw shreds of Styrofoam cup in the air like flower petals at a wedding. Even Feldman sat up in his chair. It was giddy and loud, but it lasted only a minute, because the pent-up energy, the relief, and the defiance were almost immediately spent. And when silence returned it felt worse than before, an admission of defeat. A dozen people stood frozen in place, eyeing each other for a sign as to what might come next.

Somber now, Glasser gestured to the phone log in Rainbow's hands. "How far back does that go, anyway?"

She flipped the cover open, ran her finger over the first page. "About two months."

"And the others?" The old logs had been too useful to throw out, a repository of contact numbers for clients who never spent more than a few weeks in any one place.

Her face began to fall. "Lou, this was the only one I could reach. It was right by the phone."

"Yeah." He said it very softly, averting his eyes. "I just wanted to check."

"There wasn't enough time."

"It doesn't matter. You did good. You did a brave thing." He patted her on the shoulder.

How many of those old ledgers had they kept piled by the copying machine? Six? Ten? The DEA had them all now, packed in a box.

"They know I haven't done anything," he said out loud, as if someone had asked.

"Of course you haven't," said Rainbow.

Samuels was quick to jump in. "It's not you they want, it's one of the clients."

Glasser shook his head. "When they want you, they can get you. You don't have to be guilty of anything."

"It's not *you*," said Rainbow, resorting to the tone of voice she used to settle arguments.

"Whatever they're looking for, they're not going to find it," croaked Feldman, his face ashen white as he rose from his seat. He looked over at Glasser, a private locking of eyes. "Nothing's going to happen."

They left the conference room tentatively, like survivors emerging from hiding, and wandered slowly from room to room, all twelve of them sticking as close together as space would allow. The suite had a ruined feeling to it, dust and stray pieces of paper littering the carpet, desk and cabinet drawers hanging open, confessing their emptiness. A telephone rang, but nobody moved to answer it. Lipkin bent down to pick up a roll of packing tape forgotten in the hall; as if in response the others began to bend too, fingers raking the carpet for string, paper clips, a felt-tip marker.

The sight was too much for Glasser. "Forget it, everybody go home and get some sleep. Be here by nine tomorrow."

They stood, cupping the detritus in their hands, clearly disturbed by the thought of returning the next day.

"I don't want anybody calling in sick either," said Feldman, his voice ending in a thin asthmatic wheeze. "We've lost the battle, but we'll win the war."

Afterward, the two partners stood in the waiting room, watching as their employees filed out toward the elevator. Rainbow was the last to go, tying a bright yellow kerchief over her head. "You sure you don't need help locking up?"

"We're fine," said Glasser. "You're the hero today, so we'll take care of it." He pushed her gently through the door.

Alone, the partners went from room to room, shutting desk drawers and file cabinets, turning off lights. Darkness was a relief; it hid the empty bookshelves and the litter on the floor, hid the two lawyers from each other. It was not even six, but it could have been midnight, and they moved on tiptoe, reluctant to break the silence. The office suite seemed to have fallen into the heavy sleep of the sick.

"How are you feeling?" asked Glasser, barely above a whisper. They were in the soft dark of the waiting room now, getting ready to leave, and though he could hear Feldman's ragged breathing he could not actually see him.

"Scared."

Glasser had meant the asthma, actually. Disconcerted, he took some time fishing the keys from his pocket, then spoke again. "What happened here, Jerry?"

"*Kristallnacht.*"

At home, Glasser told Esther what had happened. Giddy with nervous exhaustion, he narrated the story like one of his courtroom anecdotes, playing it up for laughs. "I walk into the conference room and it's like a wake where the corpse won't be quiet. Jerry is laid out on the table, croaking, 'Sue them! Sue the bastards!' and everyone else is crying."

He wore a broad smile but eyed his wife warily, testing her reaction. They were seated at opposite ends of the dining-room table, an enormous claw-footed antique piled high with old newspapers, junk mail, and unopened bills—as rich in paper flora as his desk was now barren.

Her face was hard to read: watchful, serious, grimly patient—her crisis mode. She sat with her hands in her lap, shoulders squared.

"One of the DEA agents offered me a hundred bucks for my desk." He took a long swallow from the cup of coffee in his hand, which trembled. "I got him up to two-fifty, but then he had to leave."

"With all your files."

Glasser waved the point away. "I never write anything down. The files are worthless."

"But *they* don't know that. They're looking for something."

"So let them look."

"What is it they want, Lou?"

He answered truthfully, as truthfully as he could bear while staring into her tightly composed face. "They're on a hunting expedition, looking for something they can use. But they're not going to find anything, believe me."

"It's serious, isn't it?"

Glasser heard himself speeding up, rushing to take refuge in the big picture. "The country's turning into a police state, Esther. People have sold their civil rights to keep the junkies and muggers off the street. The warrant was illegally broad, they took hundreds of files that are protected under attorney-client privilege. I'm thinking of calling up some reporters I know—"

Suddenly she was angry. "Goddammit," she said, slapping her palm down on the table. "I wish you'd just stop it."

"Stop what?"

"Whatever it is you do—getting into trouble—and making jokes about it."

"There isn't going to be any trouble. The whole thing'll blow over soon, I promise you."

She seemed to think about this for a moment. "Just don't tell Jason, I don't want him to know unless he has to. Let him finish his last year in peace. Promise me that."

"Not a word."

Unable to sleep, Glasser went out for a walk sometime past midnight. He started west, worked his way over to the side streets of Chelsea, then turned south, toward the meatpacking district. Every few blocks he stopped at a phone booth to try Brianson, without success. By two A.M. he was shivering with cold, looking for a taxi among the warehouses on Washington Street, far downtown. It was then that he recognized a particularly eccentric building—a stucco facade in a neighborhood of brick—and realized he was just a block away from Purgatory, the disco run by his brother, Eddy. The place was new, hardly a month old, and Glasser hadn't seen it yet. He started walking.

What neolithic memory is it that makes people want to socialize in a cave? Purgatory's lobby was low and wide as a parking garage, the lighting a frigid neon blue; the concrete walls looked slick, as if wetted by an underground stream. Though the dance floor was out of sight in another room, the entire structure vibrated to the music like a bunker under artillery fire, and Glasser had the urge to anchor himself around a pillar. But there was nothing to hold on to, neither furniture nor ornament, and he stuck his hands deep into the pockets of his coat, watching the flow of people around him. The patrons had a searching, dissatisfied look to them. Glancing over their shoulders as they walked, they came together in knots of two or three, then split apart again, wandering in different directions.

Glasser didn't notice Eddy until he was halfway across the floor, waving: a small, dapper man in sports coat and slacks, shiny shoes, his shirt open halfway down his chest. Two years older than Glasser, he was nearly fifty pounds slimmer, a weekend tennis player vain about his physique.

"Where have you been?" asked Glasser. "I sent one of the bouncers looking for you."

"I was on the roof." This was just like Eddy, to start a business selling noise—a disco—and then disappear somewhere quiet, to study the cityscape in peace. "Come on, I'll show you around."

"I came to talk, actually."

Glasser surprised himself with this statement, and not only because he'd arrived by accident. There had been some tension between the brothers for a while now, and they hadn't met face-to-face in nearly four months.

The problem had started in May, Glasser sitting at a picnic table in Riis Park one Sunday, watching four pounds of cold cuts turn greasy in the sun while Eddy pushed him to buy into the disco project.

"I don't have any money," Glasser had said. It was the truth, though he didn't expect Eddy to believe it.

"Don't lie to me, Lou. I'm your brother."

"I'm not lying. And anyway it's too dangerous."

This was a reference to Eddy's partners: men who wore fur coats and pinky rings, who double-parked their big Lincolns and tore up the tickets. It didn't take a genius to see the thievery that was sure to break out among these hoodlums, and Glasser knew the project would end in disaster: a suspicious fire and a contested insurance claim, then maybe some indictments. "It's a setup, Eddy, designed to go bust."

His brother had simply lifted one hand to his forehead, shading his eyes against the glare. "You worry too much, Lou. That's why you never have any fun."

"This isn't fun, it's a free-for-all."

Eddy reached for a slice of turkey breast, dipped it into the open jar of mustard on the picnic table. "I know all the tricks they know, and a few they don't."

Glasser could see that arguing would only tangle him further in this question of tricks, the value of Eddy's cunning. Though he didn't have any money himself, he introduced his brother to Brianson, who had excess cash flooding out of trash bags and was always looking for investment opportunities, usually of the most incautious and wasteful kind. Let the two of them scheme each other into the madhouse, thought Glasser, as long as they leave me out of it. It was a natural fit, actually: the drug dealer was perfectly happy taking a loss, as long as the remainder of his money came back clean, documented with a receipt. He and Eddy were doing business within an afternoon.

But this didn't get Glasser off the hook. Eddy remained bitter. A dollar wasn't simply an abstract unit of value, interchangeable with other dollars. Eddy had wanted his brother's money, not Brianson's, and his brother had said no.

Now, four months later, both men appeared chastened. Even in the dim blue light, Glasser could see the bags under his brother's eyes, the new furrows in his forehead.

"We can talk in the VIP room," Eddy said. "It's not open yet." He led Glasser across the lobby to a metal door set in a rough concrete wall, then took out what looked like a credit card. "We're going to give these to VIPs. Sort of a club within a club—real exclusive." He stuck the card in its slot and punched in a code on the keypad below. "State-of-the-art security."

Moving from the lobby to the VIP room was like slipping into a lake at night. The room was silent and dark and entirely mirrored. Pinpoint lights in the mirrored ceiling twinkled like stars, multiplying in the mirrored walls. Glasser made a circuit of the room, watching himself move through the mirrors, a chorus line of fat men free-floating in a deep, star-filled space. Behind them followed a string of Eddys, beaming, their arms open like hammy magicians milking the audience for applause.

"Classy or what? Cost us a fortune." Eddy made his way over to the bar in the corner, circled behind the black slate counter, and went into the refrigerator. He pulled out a couple of diet sodas, then turned on an overhead lamp.

Glasser studied his brother in the new light. "What happened to your hair?"

A set of curls sat atop Eddy's head, like a handful of little soap bubbles. "This?" He stuck a finger in one of the ringlets. "I got a perm is all."

"You get a dye job too?" Once an ashy gray, his brother's hair was now a strange sort of reddish blond, a mixture of shades that shifted in the light like sharkskin.

"Staying young. You might start thinking about it." Eddy reached across the counter and gave a gentle pat to Glasser's belly.

In truth, his brother looked worn-out. He seemed genuinely glad that Glasser had come, but after smiling, his expression went back to a sort of private mourning. Glasser perched on one of the leather barstools and opened his soda, trying to keep the suspicion out of his voice. "Well, the business looks okay."

"You should have bought in when you had the chance. This place is going to be a gold mine. And this"—Eddy slapped the counter—"this room is going to make it famous."

"It's amazing, it really is."

Eddy looked suddenly aggrieved, letting his large brown eyes sink into their pouches. "You embarrassed me in front of my partners, Lou."

Glasser had surmised that his brother was under pressure to pull him in. There had been delays with the liquor license, construction-cost overruns—no doubt he'd promised the hoodlums more capital. "I didn't have any money, Eddy. I still don't. I'm six weeks behind on the mortgage and double that on the office rent. I'm getting final notices on the phone bill—*the phone bill.*"

"All right, I've forgiven you." Eddy aimed the Glasser family eyes at him, those two perfect tools of recrimination and guilt. "What hurt was the lack of trust. You thought I was trying to push you into some kind of scam."

"I never thought that."

"You did! You thought I couldn't handle the other guys!" Eddy had stiffened, holding his head up as if he were chin-high in water—a small man's posture of defiance.

"Nobody can handle them, Eddy, that's my point. They're crooks. Crooks are my business, I know them when I see them."

"No, ever since Kosher Tiki, you've had this attitude. Twenty fucking years I've lived under this shadow, and I'm sick of it."

Sweet and feckless, a passionate financial schemer, Eddy had a near-religious belief in the big score. In the mid-sixties he bought a nightclub on Long Island—Kosher Polynesian, with dinner theater and doo-wop acts, the waitresses in grass skirts. The place did well, but he grew bored, blowing his money on a scheme to produce Hong Kong knockoffs of Cartier watches, an idea cooked up by one of his busboys, who had relatives out there. For a while he flew back and forth between New York and Macao in a state of high excitement, handing out business cards to just about everyone, even the skycaps at Kennedy. *Glasser International, Edward P. Glasser, President.*

Perhaps it was a breakdown of sorts. Glasser remembered rushing out to meet him at the airport after a particularly distressing phone call, Eddy slurring his words with impatience. In a dark airport bar, one of those places tingling with transience, they ate Reuben sandwiches by the light of an overhead TV. Usually so dapper, Eddy was unshaven, bleary-eyed. And he was supposed to hop another plane to Macao. His briefcase was bulging with plans, contracts, organizational charts—so much so that the locks wouldn't snap closed. He kept it shut with a length of rope.

"I need another three thousand," he said, spearing a french fry with a toothpick. "That's why I called. Without it the deal can't go through. The Chinese will cancel on me."

"I can get it for you, no problem," said Glasser, who didn't have a hundred bucks to his name back then. "But I'll need a few days. Cancel your flight."

The idea was to keep him in New York, maybe get him to a doctor, but Eddy gave Glasser the slip, hiding out in a stall in the men's room. He crouched atop the toilet seat so his legs wouldn't show, the heavy briefcase cradled in his arms, then took a later flight on a different airline. Neglected, Kosher Tiki began to crumble. Steaks, pots, cases of whiskey disappeared from the kitchen. A plumbing problem flooded the dining room, leaving a damp sulfurous smell in its wake. The rabbi who certified the operation kosher was nabbed at a porno theater, and the police turned up a warrant for his arrest on a bad-check charge. A professional con man, he wasn't a rabbi, wasn't even Jewish. A year later, Kosher Tiki, long dark, was seized by the government for back taxes.

And now, twenty years later, Eddy was running a disco backed by gangsters, hiding out on the roof or in a VIP room silent as a vault, while the rest of the building shook with violent dance music.

"The Cartier thing could've happened to anyone," said Glasser. "I never blamed you for that."

Eddy snorted bitterly. "Ten trips to Macao in a single year? Two thousand engraved business cards? Come on, that's a prize fool."

They lapsed into a charged silence, Glasser watching his brother: a man of sixty, with gray hair on his chest, bottle-blond curls above a pushcart peddler's weathered face. Ridiculous, yes, but they were all that was left to each other of childhood and youth, a past that had slipped through their hands like water from the tap—gone before they could drink.

"What if I told you it was my turn now," said Glasser. "My turn to fuck up."

"What?" Eddy's eyes were on the mirrored wall to his left, his face full of his own thoughts.

"We were raided by the DEA yesterday."

His brother turned to look at him, confused. "You were raided? Why?"

Why? Glasser was beginning to hate that word. He let it go with a shrug and a wave of his hand, too tired now to elaborate. "They came and took everything. Who knows why."

"Are you okay?"

"I'm surviving. Have you seen Brianson?"

"Brianson?" Eddy's voice took a jump. "Why Brianson?"

"I need to talk to him."

"Is he involved?"

Watching his brother's eyes grow round and panicky, Glasser began to recognize a new complication: Eddy's business arrangement with Brianson. The lawyer had absented himself from the negotiations, but whatever the nature of the deal, a money trail from the smuggler to the disco meant that Eddy was vulnerable too.

Glasser felt a wave of cold misery move through his body. "Don't worry," he said quickly. "Everything's all right, I promise you."

Eddy wasn't soothed. The words came rushing out, something between confession and denial. "I paid him off in August and haven't seen him since. It was just a short-term loan to cover the sound system, the lights. Nothing more."

"Do you have a number for him? The one I've got isn't working."

Eddy shook his head no. "He always called me. We only met twice." In a moment's time his delicate brown eyes had sunk deep into his face, the fleshy pouches underneath them darkened and sagged. "This is bad, Lou. My partners are going to be very upset."

"You didn't do anything illegal. The Feds can't expect you to know where the man's money comes from."

"It's not just that. We can't have the cops coming around here, sticking their noses into everything. The plumbing, the wiring, everything was done without permits. And what about our liquor license? Christ, my partners—"

"It's not going to come to that, Eddy."

"You brought him here."

It was true, of course: Glasser had introduced Brianson as a substitute for himself. And perhaps there had been some malice in that; in a moment of anger he'd hoped the two men would scheme each other into the insane asylum. But he'd never expected anything like this. "You said you needed the money."

"I did need the money." Eyes closed, Eddy began massaging his temples with his small manicured fingers. His eyelids were pale and yellowish, like old window shades drawn down against the light. "This place is my big chance, Lou. You don't get many more at my age."

"We haven't done anything wrong."

Eddy opened his eyes and began to laugh quietly. It was the Glasser family laugh, instantly recognizable: bittersweet, satirical, gently self-mocking. "Just like Papa, the two of us." He meant their father, Morris Glasser, unemployed bricklayer and small-time gambler, dead for almost fifty years.

"This is different," said Glasser, annoyed by the comparison. "Completely different."

5

EVERYTHING FOR THIRTY-FIVE DOLLARS

Louis Glasser's father, Morris, died in 1940—was killed, rather, beaten to death by a bookie's goons. He disappeared one night in December, and a day later the body was found in an alley off Christie Street. The funeral was held in a light rain that made the cemetery mud suck at Louis's shoes.

No suspects were located and no arrests made. Many years later, when Glasser was in law school, an uncle told him that it was probably an accident: the enforcers had meant to lean on Morris—break something, maybe, as a warning to pay up—and had gone too far.

"Small-timers," his uncle said. "Like your father, like all of us. It was still the Depression, you know, money was scarce even for the crooks. They'd smash your hand with a hammer for a hundred bucks—I know because it almost happened to me too." He looked at Louis with the enormous, sad eyes that were the Glasser family's primary inheritance, eyes that seemed to expect things to be wasteful and pointless. "But they didn't kill you for that kind of money. Not even back then." His face sagged with the memory.

Louis was eleven when his father was killed. Alive, Morris had been a dark, recessive presence, inviting approach only to retreat in coolness and shadow, like cellar stairs. Shy round eyes, a slight, vaguely pained smile. He was bulky, with a thick chest and a big, almost square torso, but he moved with a wonderful delicacy, as if it were three A.M. and he didn't want to wake anyone. Forty-seven years later—older now than his father ever was—Louis remembered him primarily as the soft snoring behind a Yiddish newspaper: the newsprint a grayish paper tent, the lettering an abstract design like the intertwining of bare tree branches. Morris carried an unmistakable male fragrance, an incense lit by sleep and compounded of newsprint, hair oil, damp wool clothing, sweat, and tobacco.

Morris worked as a bricklayer till the company went under in 1935. He drove a dump truck for a few months after that, but by '36 he was out of work again, more or less permanently, and the Glassers were on relief. Of course, this was a common story during the Depression, but 1936 was also the year that Morris's gambling flew out of control. The shy, worried smile never left his face, but something else lurked beneath. He would bet on anything: horses, baseball, football. Working odd jobs, borrowing from friends and relatives, he scraped together whatever cash he could, only to blow it all on the next sure thing.

The Glassers lived on Manhattan's Lower East Side, a square mile of Jewish streets dark and narrow as subway tunnels, lined by tenements, swarming with people, traffic, pushcart peddlers hawking their wares. In the winter of 1940 they had two rooms on the top floor of a house on Ludlow Street, with a bathtub in the kitchen and a communal toilet in the hall. Forty-seven years later, Louis still remembered the fury with which his mother scrubbed those rooms. Cleanliness was her harsh religion. She practiced it on her knees, scrubbing as if scrubbing were an act of atonement. Louis hated watching her at it, the brush in her red chapped hand, her face just inches above the soapy floorboards. It was pointless, a ritual drained of all meaning other than self-punishment. There was no way to remove the smell that came up from the walls like somebody's sour breath, a mixture of boiled cabbage and rotten potatoes. The building was alive, and the tenants were the least important part of it. Cockroaches crawled out from impossible places—the light fixtures, the doorknobs—and moved like evil thoughts across the ceiling. Mice slipped out of the stove with the grace of swimmers rising from water, their eyes inhumanly serene.

On the last day of his father's life, Louis came home from school to find Morris alone in the apartment, standing in the little front room with his coat buttoned to the chin. The heat was off, as it usually was, and the place was feathery with the cold, a bare cube filled with icy light. Dust spun in the air like the fine, dry snow filtering outside on the street.

Morris had a startled expression on his face, a look of exquisite guilt, like a burglar caught in the synagogue at night, reveling in his own shame. His breath came in excited little puffs as if he'd been running, and it hung in the air like smoke. "I thought you were someone else."

It was then that Louis noticed the family radio tucked under his father's arm like a loaf of bread. "Do you have to?" he asked, his voice taking on the plaintive tone his mother so often used. The radio was the last good thing they owned: an oblong case of dark wood, the front upholstered in a nubby cloth the color of straw.

Morris looked pained. "It's broken," he said finally, squinting as if the words were written on Louis's forehead and he was only reading a script. "I'm going to get it fixed."

"Don't do it."

Morris's face began to undergo a complex evolution: from self-loathing to simple irritation at the delay Louis was causing. By the end it wore a mask of beleaguered reasonableness, hooded eyes and twitchy, impatient cheeks. But the shame remained present somewhere below. "I'll get you another one. I promise."

"You won't." Louis felt the tears starting, a wet heat in his throat. "You can't."

"I'm in a jam, Louie. I owe some people dough."

"Take something else."

"There isn't anything else." Morris said it blankly, as if the fact justified his position. And it was more or less true. Their possessions had been disappearing for some time now, a gradual emptying like the darkening of a winter afternoon.

Louis wanted to run at his father headfirst, knock him down, and take the radio, but he threw his schoolbooks instead, watching them skid across the floorboards and spread at his father's feet.

"Louie," said his father, looking down at the books. He had a shy man's sadness at display.

"I'm hungry," said Louis, and the words were their own realization. He was hungry, unbearably hungry. His radio was going to disappear, his mother wasn't home, his after-school snack wasn't ready. "Where's Ma? I want my snack."

"Hmm," said Morris, in something like a sigh. There was no telling what he meant by this, but it always sounded intensely sympathetic. It was his favorite expression, a space where the words should be.

Looking back forty-seven years later, Louis could see his father as a Depression-era type: penny-ante operator and small-time chiseler, gonif, and schnorrer. But it was only a trick of perception that allowed him to view Morris this way, as if he were observing a stranger through a telescope, the distance not one of feet but years and whatever it is that separates the living from the dead. The real picture of Morris remained the child's: an exquisitely gentle, moon-faced man, with a laugh as quiet as a whisper, and breath the flavor of sour pickles and tobacco.

"I'm hungry," Louis repeated, in the angry tone of an accusation. He felt good saying it. The phrase meant so much in the Glasser household; it expressed such a voluptuous fear. Despite poverty, the Glassers were nervous, constant eaters, as if it were necessary to reassure themselves that they would indeed have dinner by first having two lunches. Among themselves they spoke the language of food.

"We'll get you something on the way." It was an invitation to come along, of course. No doubt Morris wanted to clear out before Louis's mother came home, but there was more to it than that: he was offering him some compensation for the loss of the radio.

"What?" demanded Louis.

"Something good."

True to his word, Morris took him to a delicatessen on Delancey. It was hard to remember now what a thrill that had been—thrill enough to make the eleven-year-old Louis almost forget that he was about to lose his radio. The Glassers, though they did not go hungry, did not usually have the money for restaurants either. Louis had passed this particular delicatessen hundreds of times but had never once been inside.

"You have money?" he asked his father. They were standing outside by the glass door, about to go in. The glass was opaque with steam, water beads speckling the interior surface.

"Hmm" said Morris vaguely, giving his sigh again, that expanding gray space where anything could be true. He pulled open the door.

It was warm inside, a wet steam heat like the Russian baths or the indoor pool on Henry Street. Salamis hung from the ceiling, their dark varnished skins wrinkled like fingers too long in water. Chains of orange-brown frankfurters ran in loops like bunting, ready to be cooked. A long glass case stood near the door, filled with heavy pieces of meat: pastrami and corned beef, rose-colored tongue. Round loaves of pumpernickel and rye, dusty with flour, waited on a shelf against the wall.

Louis and his father sat at the counter on round swivel stools, breathing in the beefy fragrance of hot dogs on the grill. Morris held up the radio to show the counterman, as if an explanation were necessary before they could be served. "Broken," he said, lifting it in both hands as if presenting a baby. "Going to get it fixed. With the kid."

The counterman shrugged noncommittally. "Things break," he said, wiping up some crumbs with the edge of his hand, then popping them into his mouth.

Apparently satisfied with these preliminaries, Morris placed the radio on the floor by his feet, then ordered a cup of coffee.

"What can I have?" whispered Louis.

"Anything you want."

Louis ordered a corned beef sandwich and french fries—corned beef, a tremendous delicacy. At home they ate potatoes and kasha, stews made with things other people wouldn't touch: brains, hearts, kidneys, lungs, stomach. These were the vital organs, the butcher's leftovers, secret and dirty—poor people's food. *Ess,* his mother would say, *eat,* and Louis wolfed it down, but always with a faint sense of shame. He was slapped if he resisted, if he did not swallow seconds, thirds; it was stuffed in his mouth like a gag. But it was rare that he refused to eat. He was hungry, they all were, starving in a way they could not understand but could feel, the way a coal cellar is starving for light. And the more they ate, the bigger this hunger got.

Louis finished the corned beef and fried potatoes and immediately wanted more. He rubbed his finger over the plate, wiping up the salty grease from the potatoes, and watched his father. Morris sat with his elbows on the counter, the tips of all ten of his thick stubby fingers perched delicately on the rim of his empty coffee cup. He stared into space as if he were gazing out of a rain-streaked window.

"Mmmm," tried Louis. "That was good. That was the best corned beef I ever had." No response. "Thanks, Pa. I could eat ten of those." Again, nothing.

Morris wasn't listening. He sat absolutely still, frozen in his odd pose, fingers resting lightly on the coffee cup. Suddenly he stood up and pulled from his pocket a big handful of bills—more money than Louis had ever seen—then peeled off a dollar for the check and bent down to retrieve the radio. He wasn't ignoring Louis; the blank look on his face made it clear he had simply forgotten him. He walked off without looking back; Louis scurried after.

They seemed to meet again on the street outside, Morris accepting his son's reappearance with bland equanimity, then started walking east on Delancey. Louis asked, "If you have so much money, why are you taking the radio?"

Morris took his hand and gave one of those answers he specialized in, that seemed to fit some other question in his own mind. "Don't worry," he said. "Everything will be A-o.k."

The pawnshop was in a storefront on East Broadway, near the blackened stone arch of the Manhattan Bridge. Three brass balls hung like grapefruits above a window full of watches and saxophones. While his father stood reading the price tags attached to the merchandise, Louis went back and forth, looking at the neat rows of bracelets and wedding rings laid out on a dusty black velveteen cloth.

The Lower East Side was full of pawnshops just like this one, and Louis often studied the things in their windows. They were his equivalent of the great department store windows uptown: Macy's, Gimbel's—museum displays containing all the treasures of the world, known and unknown. Louis would stand in front of pawnshops gazing longingly at the guitars and cigarette cases, not really wanting the things themselves but captured by a kind of abstract desire, a wanting *for* things, vague yet achingly real too. After all, what could an eleven-year-old boy do with a wedding ring, a giant pocket watch, a silver hip flask? Nothing. They drew him precisely because they were adult accoutrements, beyond the sphere of his own personal desire.

He loved the neatness of their display too, the long, even rows, each object with its little white price tag, everything grouped by category, wedding rings with wedding rings, wristwatches separate from pocket watches. And he loved the basic sameness of the objects: twenty flat, square cigarette cases, one after another—the voluptuous monotony as you moved down the row. The plenitude this implied: a world with twenty million cigarette cases! It was soothing to think of this riot of desire, of ownership and loss tamed into precise silence behind glass.

Louis wondered if he'd find something that had once belonged to the Glassers. He knew from listening to his parents fight that his father pawned things, though he'd never gone with him before and didn't know if this was his usual shop. Everything in the window had the scars of past ownership: monograms, inscriptions, the traces of wear, of damage well or clumsily repaired. Louis stared at the gold cover of a locket, crosshatched by fine hairlike scratches; then the brass body of a saxophone, darkened around the valves by years of handling. These things had been wanted, captured, used, finally released; they had outlived their owners' ability to keep them; but they were marked by this history.

"Uhhm," sighed Morris, moving toward the door.

The air inside was stuffy with steam heat, the dusty-water smell of a leaky radiator. On all four sides were glass display cases, and behind them were shelves with appliances: phonographs, hot plates. There were two shelves of radios. A man in a white shirt and yarmulke stood by the cash register reading a Yiddish newspaper.

He had a bushy gray beard with streaks of black in it like licorice, and glasses on a string that hung from his neck. Morris stepped toward him, holding the radio in that way he had, as if showing off a baby.

Only then did the man look up. He had huge black eyes molded over with angry boredom like the gray caul that grows on rotten fruit. Do not tell me what happened, these eyes seemed to say; do not tell me who's sick or how much you need. I am bored by that. As if warning Morris not to expect too much, he pointed at the two shelves behind him, their radios lined up in a hodgepodge of deco shapes like the skyline of Wall Street.

"Ahh," said Morris, nodding his head in anxious understanding.

The pawnbroker took the radio and disappeared beneath the counter, no doubt plugging it into a wall socket, because suddenly Louis heard the voice of his radio calling out to him, a hammer blow of big band music replaced by a woman's singing voice and then a slice of newscast as the tuning dial spun.

The broker reappeared with the radio, his thin black eyebrows raised. "Three," he said.

"But it's almost new," said Morris. Actually, they'd had it ever since Louis could remember, but it was the one thing they owned that wasn't beaten up and scratched from the constant moving.

"Three," repeated the broker.

As if in answer, Morris reached into his overcoat pocket, laying out a gold locket, a bracelet, a set of earrings, some rings. Louis dimly recognized these as belonging to his mother, things he had seen only very rarely, when she went to a wedding or bar mitzvah.

The broker looked at each carefully, opening the locket and peering in as if it were the shell of a walnut he'd just cracked open, running the links of the bracelet through his thick fingers. For one of the rings, which had a red stone, he screwed a jeweler's glass into his eye and examined it under a lamp at the other end of the counter. "Twenty-five," he said.

"For what," asked Morris, "the ring?"

"For all of them."

"That's a ruby." Morris's voice was quiet, as always.

"It's a piece of glass."

"I'd give you everything for thirty-five," said Morris.

The broker put the ring down. "It's worth what it's worth. I don't bargain."

Morris tapped the countertop with the nails of his hand, a sound like mice make scrambling over tile. Then he removed his wristwatch and put it with the jewelry. The broker picked it up and rubbed at the crystal with the flat of his thumb, as if trying to remove a smudge. His thumbnail was a thick wedge of black. "Thirty-two for everything."

Morris filled his cheeks with air, then slowly blew them flat again; it was an infrequent gesture, the closest he ever got to showing disappointment. "What about this overcoat?" He thrust his sleeve at the broker. "I got it last winter." In truth, he'd had it a lot longer than that, but it was good quality, bought at an Orchard Street tailor when Morris still worked for the construction company.

The broker didn't move to touch. He looked off past Morris, at the front door, as if hoping another, better customer might come in to rescue him. "What am I, a ragpicker now?"

When they left the pawnshop five minutes later Morris was coatless, in a gray jacket, baggy and shapeless from overwear. "Warm," he said, as if to himself but clearly for Louis's benefit. "Warm."

The wind was picking up. Louis assumed they'd head back now, but they wandered aimlessly, first toward and then away from Ludlow Street. This made him nervous: it was getting dark, and his mother was probably home, wondering where they were—neither he nor his father ever missed dinner. Morris stopped to get him a pretzel, a roasted potato, an onion roll, a bag of chestnuts, a knish. Louis didn't have to ask; if they passed a food vendor, his father automatically reached into his pocket, paying from his big wad of bills. It was a strange situation: they had more money than Louis had ever seen and were spending it more freely; yet he knew that it wasn't enough. He could feel the lack in his father, as palpable as the cold, the double of his own hunger. They needed more, and that's why they couldn't go home.

Then Morris seemed to reach some kind of decision. He changed directions again, taking Louis's hand to hurry him, and in a few minutes brought them to a tenement on a street Louis did not recognize, with a hallway so narrow they had to walk single file through light as brown and crepuscular as rusty water. The walls were the color of pea soup, and the paint blistered in damp pockets. Their breath made cold steam as they went.

Morris knocked at a door from which most of the paint had peeled off, stood and listened till it opened a crack. "Morris," he whispered softly, as if the feeling in his voice might determine the possibility of entry. "Morris."

A man widened the crack, blocking the space with his body. He wore a fedora, long underwear, work boots with the laces undone. "No," he said. "No and no and no." Then he glanced down at Louis, who had positioned himself behind his father. "Aw, for crying out loud," he moaned, and quickly shut the door.

They went to four other apartments, all in different tenements, on Rivington, Hester, Pitt, Catherine. The same thing happened at each: Morris fidgeted while the man at the door scolded him; and then father and son were back on the street, crunching veins of old snow as they walked, skidding over patches of ice. It was completely dark now and felt eerily late, as if they'd reached a part of night Louis had never yet known, beyond the measure of clocks. Though he was with his father, in his own neighborhood, this sense of lateness changed everything, and he had the unshakable feeling that they were lost and becoming more so, as if tangling themselves up in string.

The last place they went to was on Norfolk, near Stanton. The man who opened the door wore a sleeveless undershirt despite the cold but had a woolen muffler wrapped around his neck. He was fat, with one of those big stomachs that jut out aggressively to a blunt point. He looked at Morris with sad, pouchy eyes, then looked down at Louis and grimaced. An air of weary resignation hung about him, as if he knew that what he was about to do was pointless, but he couldn't help doing it. His voice was stuffed up and nasal. "Hello, Morris," he said.

"I guess you've heard," said Morris.

The man shrugged in response, then stepped aside to let them in. He told Louis to stay in the front room and then disappeared with Morris into the back. The tiny room was lit by a single small lamp that threw crazy shadows over everything. As best as Louis could make out, the place was full of furniture, so full that chairs stood against the walls, stacked one on top of the other as in a warehouse. Louis stood listening to the murmur of voices in the other room, but his father's was soft and difficult to distinguish from the other man's.

It was only then that he spotted an old woman sitting on one of the sofas, in the shadows. She was staring at him, working her jaws up and down, and her black eyes glittered.

After leaving, they went back to that same delicatessen on Delancey. Louis had a brisket sandwich, mashed potatoes, endless amounts of pickles and sauerkraut and cole slaw, two pieces of cherry pie, and a large chunk of halvah.

"Did you get it?" asked Louis.

"Another ten," answered Morris. Then, as if realizing he'd spoken too fast: "Sure, I got it. We're all set." He drank his coffee, watching Louis with an absentminded expression.

At the door to their building on Ludlow Street, Morris sent Louis up alone. "Go on up," he said. "Your mother will be worried. Tell her I have to take care of something."

"You're not coming?"

"Umm," his father sighed, and headed down the block.

6

ANIMALS

It was late afternoon, the day after the raid, and Glasser and Feldman were riding in an elevator as ornate as an old Pullman car, complete with wood paneling and a heavy brass rail, carpeting of a vaguely Oriental design. They were on their way to the forty-first floor for a three o'clock meeting with Corman Hayes, partner in the Wall Street law firm of Sedgewick & Ashberry.

Glasser wasn't feeling half bad, considering it was his second night without sleep. His eyes burned, but his mind seemed deceptively clear, charged with a strange, giddy optimism. He had a strategy now, and with him that usually meant success.

Feldman wasn't nearly so confident, however. Standing on the other side of the car, he looked seasick, dark rings under both eyes, his inhaler gripped in one chubby hand. He was still uncertain about their choice of lawyer. "I don't know about this, Lou. Ray O'Donnel might've been better." He meant the Mafia lawyer, the one who appeared on TV news shows, providing expert commentary on mob killings.

"You know what Petruccio said, O'Donnel's under investigation, they've got his office bugged. He's the last thing we need."

"Yeah, but he's a tough infighter."

"A barbarian," sniffed Glasser.

"A deterrent. If Freeburg's looking for an easy kill, he'd scare her off." Despite the tough talk, Feldman's eyes were childlike, wide with fear.

Glasser understood. O'Donnel was flashy and vain, he wore wide-shouldered suits and cuff links the size of doorknobs, and his broad bony forehead looked like a battering ram. He was, in short, a grown-up version of the playground toughs Feldman had fended off thirty-five years before, as a kid in Flatbush. Back then, the young Feldman had learned to defend himself with humor and guile, the qualities that would later define him as a lawyer. But now, losing his nerve, he reverted to what must have been his deepest childhood wish: he wanted to buy a bully.

Glasser shook his head. "It's the wrong approach, Jerry. A guy like O'Donnel would turn this into a shooting war. What we want is a peace treaty. That takes somebody Freeburg will listen to—an insider." Hayes was most definitely that: once high up in the U.S. Attorney's Office, he'd been Anna Freeburg's boss.

"Hayes doesn't have experience with this kind of thing," said Feldman. "He handles crooked stockbrokers, bankers caught in the vault."

"So what? He's got access—*access*." Glasser lingered on the word. "He can put his arm around Freeburg's shoulder and say, Look, you've made a mistake, these guys are clean. She'll listen to him because he's her rabbi, he's guided her career." Glasser lowered his voice for emphasis. "They say there was even a little office romance, you know." This last from Petruccio, who claimed to have arcane sources of information in the U.S. Attorney's Office.

"That could backfire," said Feldman.

"Maybe, maybe not."

Feldman took a quick shot on his inhaler, steadying himself against the brass handrail. "We're small fry to him, Lou. I mean, look at this." He waved a hand at the wood paneling, the Persian carpet. "This is just the elevator, for godsake."

"Hey, my money is as green as anyone else's."

That was the end of the discussion. The doors rolled open, and they began the long silent walk to the reception desk.

A few minutes later they were seated in Hayes's office, Feldman outlining the reason for their visit.

"Yes, I see, I see." Corman Hayes nodded as he listened, his pale blue eyes studiously reserved. He was a thin, precise man, somewhere in his early forties, with ash-blond hair and a waxy complexion, pink around the nose and cheekbones.

Glasser's eyes wandered from Hayes's long, handsome face to the bookcases, the signed photos of mayors and governors. Maybe the lack of sleep was beginning to tell; he felt disoriented, out of place. He was used to being on the other side of the desk, sipping a Coke or smoking while the clients rehearsed their rambling, frightened stories. He had always loved those hours, sorting out the lies, the mangled facts, calculating the possible courses of action. When the clients hunched forward, hungry for reassurance, he could see his own calm authority mirrored back in their adoring, trusting faces. It was a kind of love. He had been loved.

But now Hayes was behind the desk—and it was a vast desk of some burnished and powerful wood, glowing darkly. Transplanted to the visitor's chair, Glasser felt a terrible need rising in him, demanding to be answered. Solace, comfort, protection, absolution: he wanted them all, wanted them right now. He could hear himself talking over his partner, veering crazily from topic to topic, expounding at length. "Look at this, look at this," he said now, waving the copy of the search warrant he had saved. "Nothing is specified. This is absolutely illegal. A travesty, a farce."

"Lou—" said Feldman, putting a hand on his arm.

"They wrecked our offices, thousands of dollars of damage. And what about the stain on our reputations? After we get the files back, we're going to sue—"

Hayes cut in. "And you think this may have something to do with the Brianson case you mentioned?" Used to bankers and business executives, he was beginning to wilt under this much passionate digression.

"Sure, they want to knock us off the case. We've beaten them four, five times in the last couple of years—big cases. With us gone, they think they've got a free hand."

"We feel they may be talking with Brianson behind our backs," said Feldman, "pressuring him to implicate us in something dirty."

"He won't do it," said Glasser, turning to his partner. "Believe me, I know how he thinks."

"He may already be doing it," said Feldman. "How else did he get out on bail like that? How else could he have known about the investigation?"

Hayes put up a finger. "What about the situation with the alias?" He meant Glasser's representation of both Schotts and Brianson.

"It's a joke," said Glasser. "How could I know that Brianson was an alias? Somebody says his name is *Pisher,* why should I say it isn't? How do you know my name is really Glasser?"

"Lou—" said Feldman.

Hayes shot a glance at his watch, looking like he'd reached the end of his patience. It was time to wrap this up, but with a flourish, something to preface his fee. "Gentlemen, why don't we just put out a feeler right now. I happen to know Anna Freeburg quite well—"

The two lawyers fell silent. They knew this already, of course; it was the reason they were there.

"So let me give her a call and see what she can tell me." He reached for the phone, lifted it slowly to his ear. It was a grand, solemn gesture, a pointed reminder of the thing he possessed, the thing that was his to sell: access.

After thirty years as a lawyer, Glasser understood that Hayes was acting a part, but this awareness counted for nothing. Watching Hayes dial, he felt a tumult of emotion filling his breast: gratitude, relief. He listened with rapt concentration as Hayes chatted casually with their mysterious nemesis, the woman who had ransacked the offices of Glasser & Feldman—the woman whom Agent Barrels called the Human Barracuda.

"Anna, it's Corman, how are you? Fine, fine. Listen, I have two gentlemen in my office right now." His glance flickered up at Glasser and Feldman. "A Mr. Louis Glasser and—yes, yes. A preliminary consultation, see how the matter stands. If I may. Good. Aha." Next came a long series of opaque yesses, Hayes taking a line or two of notes with a fat black fountain pen. "Yess, yess. I see. Yess. Yess." And then suddenly he was saying his good-byes.

"Thank you, Anna. We'll have to get together soon—tennis, lunch. Good, yes, call, bye."

Hayes turned somber after hanging up. He looked at his notes for a moment, then seemed to actually grow larger in his chair. "Well, she can't say anything that might compromise her informants, you understand."

"Of course," murmured Glasser.

"And she can't identify any other possible targets, naturally."

"Naturally," said Feldman, nodding. He took a deep breath on his inhaler.

"That means we're working without specifics right now. But she can confirm that her office is running an investigation, and that the raid on your offices was part of that investigation. The possible charges are serious."

"Serious?" asked Glasser.

"They include acting as house counsel—"

This meant a variety of things, including giving legal advice prior to the commission of a crime and representing a number of individual members in the same criminal organization.

"That's absurd," said Glasser.

"Aiding and abetting a fugitive—"

Glasser half rose from his seat, indignant. "The woman is crazy, some kind of nut."

"Tax evasion—"

"I'm not even going to dignify that—"

"Money laundering."

"Ridiculous," Glasser sputtered, but his voice was growing weak.

"And conspiracy to transport and sell narcotics."

This last was too much. Glasser slumped in his chair, silent. He glanced over at Feldman, but his partner's eyes were closed, his face twisted with pain. He gripped his inhaler to his chest like a child's toy.

Hayes spoke into the silence, his voice measured and calm. "Now there's the matter of our fee. I'm going to ask you for fifty thousand dollars as a retainer against four hundred dollars an hour."

When Glasser spoke it was barely above a whisper. "I'll have it for you by the end of the week."

The partners spent the rest of the day dashing from bank to bank. Glasser had nearly a dozen accounts scattered around the city, and almost as many safe-deposit boxes, but emptying all of them netted only twenty-nine hundred dollars. Feldman's financial empire was less far-flung but equally shaky: a finicky man, neat in his habits, he was nevertheless as liberal as his partner when it came to spending money. His contribution to the defense fund: seventeen hundred and fifty-six dollars, eight-two cents.

By two o'clock they found themselves in a cab, fighting the downtown traffic on Park Avenue. "What about your credit cards?" asked Feldman. The car's heater was malfunctioning, and it was cold inside, but he wiped the sweat from his face with a handkerchief. "What about a cash advance?"

Glasser watched the flow of cars—cabs and limos, mostly, with a sprinkling of sleek foreign machines. It occurred to him that he was now two payments behind on his Jaguar. "They're threatening to take them away."

"Well, you own your apartment, don't you? You could get a mortgage."

"I've got two mortgages already." Come to think of it, the only thing he actually owned was his airplane, a beautiful twin-engined craft capable of flying to Miami in six hours without a stop for refueling. He wished he were in it now, far above the traffic and the banks.

"We can borrow somewhere, can't we?" asked Feldman.

Glasser rested his forehead against the icy windowpane. "Who would lend to us, besides a juice man?"

The two lawyers ended their trek at the old limestone bank on Broadway and Canal, where they kept the firm's business account. Slipping in just before closing, they found a balance of ten thousand bucks, with three thousand more in a safe-deposit box. Thirteen thousand total—but the money was earmarked for salaries.

They argued about this in the anteroom to the safe-deposit vault, a hushed marble space without tables or chairs, uncomfortably reminiscent of a mortuary. "We could give them all a bonus next time, to make up for it," said Feldman, his round face looking prematurely guilty in the dim light.

"Rainbow's got a daughter in private school, and Samuels's wife is in the hospital. They need their checks."

"They won't be getting any checks if we're both in jail."

Glasser shook his head no. "It's not enough anyway. We have to collect some of the money people owe us."

"Not by the end of the week," said Feldman. "Not by the end of the month either." He was right, of course. Clients were quick with the retainer, because the lawyers would not commit to a case otherwise. But afterward the balance came in drips and drabs, if at all. Normally, Rainbow used the phone logs to track down delinquents and hound them into paying, but it was a long, tedious process, and those old ledgers were gone now—locked away in a sub-subbasement of the U.S. Attorney's Office.

"There's Brian," said Glasser. "If we could just get his case back, convince him to put down a retainer—"

Feldman looked grim. "Stay away from him, Lou."

"We don't actually know that he's cooperating. If I could just talk to him—"

"We can't take the chance."

They stood facing each other, eyes averted, silently reviewing the possibilities. Finally Glasser took a deep breath. "There's my airplane."

"What about it?" Feldman hated the thing. He had gone up with Glasser only once, at the very beginning of their partnership, a sort of honeymoon voyage over the Poconos, and he'd come down whitefaced, gasping for air.

"It's worth a lot of money, Jerry. I bought it new for four hundred thousand, and I've hardly used it. I could still get three, no problem."

"Three hundred thousand?" Feldman's eyes turned soft with gratitude. "The firm will buy you another one, Lou. As soon as this is over, I promise. A goddamn jet fighter if you want it."

Glasser only shrugged, and the next day he drove out to the dealership in New Jersey. He sold the plane back to the exact same salesman who had sold it to him, a soft young man with an indolent nonchalance that had once elicited in Glasser the paradoxical hunger to spend.

"Trading up?" asked the salesman. He was sprawled in a chair in the cramped office, his short, pudgy legs stretched out before him on the orange shag rug. "We have some real deals right now. Ever flown a helicopter?"

"Maybe later," said Glasser, fidgeting with the paper cup of coffee he'd been given. "I'm getting out of flying for a while."

"The helicopter comes with flight training."

Glasser sought for an explanation as to why he was passing up such a bargain, something that would be intelligible to this well-fed young man. "I need the liquidity—for a business opportunity."

"I see." But it was hard to tell what the salesman was thinking, or if he was thinking anything at all. He sat back even farther in his chair, putting his hands behind his head, and his face took on the blankly organic look of pleasure that a cow might have while digesting an especially good lunch. Unlike most of the salesmen Glasser dealt with, he was in no rush, perfectly comfortable with silence. That was his professional secret, of course: he was at peace in the presence of need.

Glasser drank coffee to fill up the space, glanced at his watch. "Well, what can you do for me?"

"I think we can help you out."

In the end the young salesman deftly squeezed him, without getting up out of his chair or raising his voice, and Glasser walked away with two hundred thousand, not three. Even so, two hundred grand was an awful lot of money, far more money than Glasser's father, Morris, had made in a lifetime of passionate struggle, building brick walls and handicapping ponies.

On the ride back to New York, Glasser kept touching his shirt pocket, where the dealership's check lay nestled, folded in thirds. He felt his optimism returning, and in response his foot pressed harder on the gas. The Jaguar didn't so much jump as stretch out, happy to be released, and Glasser felt the onset of something like rapture. The autumn sky was a thin blue, full of light, and the landscape strangely beautiful despite generations of cruel use. To either side were long stretches of marshland, oil tanks, scrap-metal yards, abandoned railroad sidings. Factory canals siphoned water the luminous green of mouthwash. So what if he'd just lost his airplane:

he would get a bigger one when this was over. So what if he was two payments behind on the car: he was still at the wheel, doing a hundred in the straightaway, the blood roaring through his veins.

He had money now.

But money could only do so much, and at particularly frustrating moments over the next few months, Glasser was reminded of an ancient piece of graffiti in one of the criminal court bathrooms: *The wheels of justice are slow, and those of injustice even slower.* The scrawl had been there for nearly a decade—eye-level above a urinal—and during those years he had read it a thousand times without any real feeling. But that was before he underwent the transition from lawyer to client. In a moment's time the law had been transformed from a thing of books, paperwork, and court appearances to a form of slow-motion torture: insomnia, phone calls to Hayes, and a steadily dropping bank account, the balance of which he checked almost daily.

Hayes got most of their files back—everything unconnected to Brianson—and he had a meeting with Freeburg, though their one conclusion was to talk further. That talk did not seem imminent. In the meantime, word of the raid on Glasser's offices had begun to spread, and soon his law practice was sliding toward ruin. New cases stopped coming in, and old clients stopped paying what they owed. Why should they, if Glasser was going out of business? What use was he then? Instead of sending money, they sent flunkies over to pick up their files. Henry Auerbach, the pornographer, came in person.

Glasser tried to plead his cause. "I'm still the best there is, Henry. I know the case backwards and forwards." He had been caught in the middle of an unlawyerly game of solitaire and had half a deck of cards in his hand, the rest spread over his otherwise empty desktop in uneven, melancholy rows.

Auerbach glanced at the card game, then averted his eyes. "I don't give a shit what you are. I want my money back."

"Lawyers don't give money back, Henry."

Glasser meant this as a joke, but Auerbach started to shiver with rage, his large narrow head thrust forward, inches from Glasser's face. "I said I want my money back, Lou. I want it back."

Glasser knew it was fear that made Auerbach wild, and he tried to put an arm around the pornographer's thin shoulders. "Henry, how long have we known each other?"

Auerbach shook free. "Don't give me that Henry shit, you fucking chiseler. Just pay me what you owe me so I can get a lawyer."

"I am your lawyer."

"Not anymore."

"Henry," said Glasser. "What are we, animals? Just give me a chance—"

"That's it," shrieked Auerbach. "Animals! We're animals. Animals! I do what's right for me. I don't give a shit about you." He sounded as if he were trying to convince himself of this. Glasser could see the doubt flicker in his black eyes, followed by fear, like the thunder that comes after lightning.

"Trust me, Henry, please. You're not going to jail."

"I am, and I know it." Exhausted, Auerbach fell from rage to self-pity. He collapsed in an armchair, panting for breath. "You won't give me back my money, and I can't afford another lawyer. They'll crucify me just to get you. I'm finished."

"Don't be ridiculous. We're both going to come out fine." The words sounded hollow even to Glasser.

Auerbach shook his head back and forth in a kind of mourning prayer, his hands squeezed together in his lap. There was nothing Glasser could do for the man but watch, making vague soothing noises. The truth was, he couldn't have returned the pornographer's money even if he'd wanted to. The cash from the airplane had lasted four months but was now almost completely gone.

"It'll be all right," said Glasser. "Believe me."

Auerbach looked up, a strange, bitter smile revealing the pink tip of his tongue amidst the gray of his shaggy goatee. "I'm stuck with you, Lou, and I hate you for it. I want you to know that."

Glasser walked over to the window looking down on Broadway, fighting the urge to beg Auerbach's forgiveness. He felt the need for forgiveness a lot these days. The government's investigation was having its effect, he thought: soon he'd be confessing to anything, just for the sweet security of absolution. "I'll do the best I can for you, Henry. I promise."

It was late when Auerbach left, and Glasser sat in his office with the lights off, letting the evening shadows fill the room like water in a jar. The last of his staff had quit weeks ago, all except Rainbow, and she and Feldman had both gone home before Auerbach even appeared. There was absolutely nothing for Glasser to do, no reason to stay, but leaving would have been like abandoning a dying man, and he could not bring himself to do it.

When the phone began to ring he reached for the receiver. In the old days he wouldn't have; a compulsive promise-maker, he had too many people to dodge. But now that calls had become a rarity, each one represented some undefined hope.

"Lou, is that you? It's me, Paul. Paul Moreno, man."

Paul Moreno, the coke dealer with the tight disco shirts and the smile like winter sunshine—light bouncing off ice. Glasser had represented him through the late seventies, had gotten him surprise acquittals on charges of importation and sale. In '81, Moreno had been shot in the back six times and had ended up confined to a wheelchair, his once meaty legs withered to sticks. Glasser hadn't seen him since then, though he'd heard he was still in the coke trade—doing better than ever, actually. But why was he calling now after so many years?

"How are you, Paul?"

"I'm all right for a gimp, man."

It was impossible to imagine the old Moreno saying something like that. In the seventies, before the shooting, he had sat in Glasser's office with a heavy, princely malevolence, and each word had been uttered like a royal decree. Now the voice was higher, softer, a little breathy and rushed. The air of threat had been transformed into middle-aged self-mockery.

"Well, it's good to hear from you," said Glasser. This was true, strangely. The lawyer had never been comfortable with the big coke dealers, their thuggish self-importance, their temper tantrums. He had been almost relieved, in fact, when Moreno stopped bringing his business around, despite the tremendous fees involved. Now, however, he welcomed any connection to the past.

"Yeah, me too," said the dealer. "The good old days." There was a scratchy pause—the line was not the best. "Listen, Lou, I'm in trouble, and I need some advice."

Advice? Glasser sensed the possibility of a new case, and his pulse quickened. "Advice is my business, Paul."

"You remember that first case I had with you, the one in 'seventy-five?"

"How could I forget? Conspiracy to import twenty kilos, a brilliant acquittal. The jury was out six days."

Moreno seemed less inclined to nostalgia. "Yeah, well, you remember that guy, the snitch you told me to get rid of?"

"Snitch?" Glasser's whole body clenched.

"You know, Porfirio—the snitch. You told me to get rid of him, remember?"

You told me to get rid of him. The lawyer's heart had begun to pound, like a fist drumming on a locked door. After three decades of practicing criminal defense he recognized what was happening: it was a setup, obviously, a consensual call. There was a tape machine attached to Moreno's phone, and every word was being recorded. The coke dealer was trying to tangle him up in something dirty.

When Glasser spoke, his voice was hoarse with fear. "You're crazy, I never told you anything like that."

"It's too late for that, man. They're asking questions about what happened to him. They found his, um, skull. Out in Jamaica Bay."

Glasser remembered this Porfirio vaguely. One of Moreno's co-defendants in '75, he was a small wiry man with deep-set eyes and a sickly pigeon-chest, dirt packed under the fingernails. Porfirio had disappeared suddenly while Glasser was preparing Moreno's case for trial, but the lawyer had been busy reading transcripts and had no energy to spare for curiosity. In the simplified terms of win-or-lose, Porfirio's disappearance was nothing more than a lucky break: there was no doubt that Moreno's case was much the stronger for his pal's absence.

Now Glasser remembered that Moreno had threatened the other dealer while sitting in this very office. Not knowing what to do, Glasser had made a weak joke, tried to laugh it off. Moreno threatened everybody, he'd reasoned back then, even the delivery boy from the deli downstairs. And anyway, what business was it of Glasser's, as long as the predators preyed on one another and left innocent people alone? Who cared if the lion ate the wolf?

Of course there was an underlying assumption: Glasser was a lawyer, a citizen, a family man. He was separated from the world of his clients by an invisible barrier, the kind of clear plastic partition that one peered through when examining the snakes in the reptile house at the zoo. With that partition came the possibility of curiosity, sympathy, bemusement. Profit. But now that partition was gone.

"Leave me alone, Paul. Please."

"Wait a second, man. I'm trying to help you here."

"I know what you're trying to do."

"Lou, they're going to take me in for questioning. We've got to get our stories straight now, while we have a chance."

"Stories? I'm not interested in stories. I've got nothing to do with this." It didn't matter that he had no connection to the killing, of course; if he helped Moreno construct some kind of alibi, the Feds would have him on a whole battery of new charges, from obstructing justice to suborning perjury.

"Well, if they ask me about you, what should I say?"

Glasser took a deep breath. "Tell the truth, Paul. Just tell the truth."

Glasser hung up on Moreno, then sat gripping the armrests of his chair. The room was largely dark by now, with stray gleams of light reflecting off the metal objects on his desk—a chromium paperweight, a gold pen. The only sound was his breathing, rapid and panicked, a dry heaving that hurt the muscles in his chest. He tried to stand, but his legs wobbled, and he flopped back into his seat, exhausted.

Suddenly the phone was ringing again. He stared with horror at the little light flickering on his console. His first impulse was to run, hide, but he didn't have the strength to get up, and he found himself grabbing the receiver just to stop the noise. In truth, he was too frightened *not* to answer.

"Thank god you're there, I thought maybe you'd gone home."

Glasser recognized the voice, and his fear began to shrivel into sadness. He had expected Moreno again, but it was Richie Dunbar instead, calling from Attica, where he was eight years into a twenty-year stretch for carrying smack into the country from Hong Kong. The ill-fated trip had been his very first job as a "mule"—a cut-rate courier, fee payable on delivery—and out of necessity Glasser had represented him for free. They talked on the phone fairly often, and the lawyer sent a little money every month so Dunbar could buy things at the prison store.

Dunbar was grateful for all this, Glasser knew, but gratitude went only so far. With twelve years left to go on his sentence, only the Feds could get him early parole. That was simple fact.

"Richie, what do you want?" Glasser spoke warily, but he was distracted by his own sense of grief. Moreno was a predator, with the simple instincts of a predator, even in a wheelchair. Dunbar was a more complicated creature, however: weak, yes, but open to the full range of human emotion, capable of gratitude. To be betrayed by him after all these years—it made the lawyer feel suddenly hopeless.

"Lou, listen, there's a long line for the ph-ph-phone, so I can't talk too long." Dunbar was stuttering, as he usually did under stress. "The F-F-Feds have been here to see me, man. They wanted to know stuff about you."

"Yeah? So tell them whatever you want, I've got nothing to hide." That was for the tape.

But Dunbar scuttled off in an unexpected direction. "They said they'd ge-get me early parole if I helped them, you know. And it's not just me, man. They've seen six other guys in here, looking for dirt on you."

This was strange stuff for a consensual call. Glasser waited for the bait to appear, some sign of the hook. "You say they're talking to my clients, offering parole deals?"

"Yeah, and they threatened me, Lou. They said that if I didn't cooperate they'd block my parole each time it came up. I'd have to serve the full twenty."

Indignation overcame suspicion. "That's disgusting."

"Yeah, man. And they've done it at Sing Sing too, somebody told me."

Glasser's heart surged. This wasn't the kind of thing that would play well on a government tape; whatever Dunbar was doing, it wasn't a phone setup. But then what was it? "Richie, I appreciate the tip, but I don't know why you're telling me these things."

"What do you mean why?" Dunbar sounded confused. "I'm ca-ca-calling to warn you, man. They're out for your ass."

"But you're cooperating, aren't you?"

"Cooperating?" The inflection was heart-wrenching, compounded of hurt and surprise. "Lou, I thought you trusted me."

"I do, but—"

"You've hurt my feelings now."

There was a long pause as Glasser tried to gain control of his own emotions. "Listen, Richie, I understand how things are. Twenty years is a long time." He wasn't exactly sure what he was trying to say. For the last thirty years he'd been the one other people thanked, and that was the arrangement he understood. Besides, he wasn't quite sure he wanted this sacrifice, twelve years of another man's life. "Think it over. If you change your mind—"

"Forget it, man. I'm sixty-four years old and I'm going to die in this place. I know that." He said it matter-of-factly, without bitterness. "And what's the difference really? It's warm in the winter, dry when it rains, and I get three meals a day."

"Don't talk like that."

There was shouting in the background. "I gotta go, man, they want the phone, and you don't argue with these people."

"I'll send some dough." He meant money for Dunbar's commissary. The old hippie had bad teeth and liked to buy Milky Way bars because they were soft and easy to chew.

"Thanks, man. Remember to watch your back."

The next morning Glasser sat on the living-room couch in his boxer shorts and black socks, too afraid to pull on his pants and go to work. The Feds were trying to entrap him, and their malevolence seemed to have permeated even the late winter light outside. After chain-smoking an entire pack of cigarettes, he realized that he was not only out of money but everything else too: hope, energy, fight, sanity.

The telephone began to ring and he gripped the couch with both hands, bracing himself against the noise. He was certain it was Moreno or someone else like him, a serpent hired to hiss in his ear. But it was Feldman's voice that finally rose from the answering machine, urgent and familiar: Corman Hayes had asked them to meet at Sedgewick & Ashberry as soon as possible. He had important news.

An hour later, Glasser found himself seated once again in Hayes's office, facing that dark ocean liner of a desk. In the four months since he'd first sat in the visitor's chair, it had come to seem his natural place. He was a client now, with all the thoughts and feelings of a client, a client's petulant need for reassurance and love. He leaned forward, and his big brown eyes examined Hayes anxiously, trying to divine his mood.

Hayes seemed more than usually pleased with himself. "Gentlemen, I have some good news." He swiveled in his high-backed chair to single out Feldman. "Anna has informed me that Jerry is no longer a subject of the investigation."

There was a pause. "You mean I've been cleared?" asked Feldman.

"They couldn't build a substantive case."

Feldman closed his eyes, and his delicate black eyebrows arched, his nostrils quivered. "I don't think I could've taken it one more day. I was ready to crack."

"So we've had a success," said Hayes, and then primly swiveled to focus on Glasser. "Now I also have some news for Lou. Anna is interested in offering him a deal."

"A deal?"

"Complete immunity for cooperation."

"Against who?"

"Unspecified clients, past and present. If you're interested, we can start hammering out the details."

"Why are they dropping Jerry and not me?"

Hayes put up a dry palm. "Don't answer now, just think about it. You've got a couple of days. But if you don't take the deal, she says she's going to the grand jury."

Glasser knew what this meant. Grand juries were for the most part just rubber stamps, doing whatever the prosecution preferred.

If Freeburg wanted an indictment, the grand jury would give it to her, and Glasser would face a trial.

He squirmed in his chair, furious. "That woman has destroyed my business. She's had clients try to entrap me on tape. She's pressured them to testify against me—"

"Anna's a tough cookie, no doubt about it." Hayes stared back coolly, the picture of weary reasonableness.

"You were supposed to talk to her."

"In my opinion, total immunity is a very good deal—an excellent deal. It would put an end to this thing once and for all, with no further risk to you."

"I'd be a snitch."

"You'd be a cooperating witness. And a free man."

After leaving Hayes, the partners had lunch at a Chinese-Polynesian place on Beaver Street. The restaurant was down a flight of stairs, cool and dark, with soft reed matting on the walls and palm fronds separating the bamboo tables. It was past two, and there were only a few diners left. Muzak lapped like water against the silence.

Giddy with relief, Feldman insisted on ordering for both of them from the tropical-drinks menu—sweet, fruity things with alliterative names. When the cocktails came, he lifted his glass in a toast, then took a long lusty sip through the straw, sighing his satisfaction. "I feel good, I feel like a new man." He took another sip and then his eyes caught on Glasser's, shining in the candlelight. "I'm sorry, Lou, it's just—" His soft expressive face was torn, a complicated mix of celebration and guilt.

"You have a right to be happy."

"I wish it were the both of us, that's all."

Glasser tried to force a smile. "I'll be free of this thing soon enough." He sipped his cocktail. It had a sweet milky coconut taste, followed by a sharp alcoholic bite that was vaguely medicinal. Never much of a drinker, he downed it thirstily, eager to reach the pineapple chunks at the bottom.

He ordered another, and it came with their food, the pu-pu platter for four. The platter itself was in the shape of an outrigger canoe, with pontoons on either side. Up at the bow were ketchupy spareribs on a bed of crushed pineapple, followed by jumbo shrimp, fried wontons, and chicken nuggets skewered on toothpicks. At the stern was a mountain of sweet-and-sour pork, glazed like candied apples.

Glasser filled his plate. "Did you know my brother once owned a Polynesian place? About twenty years ago—he lost it to back taxes." He began to gnaw on a sparerib. "Whatever people have they just throw away."

"You know, Lou, Hayes isn't wrong. It's a good deal, you can't do better than total immunity."

Good or bad wasn't the point, so Glasser filled his mouth with pineapple chunks and began to eat. The real point was that any deal at all would put him on a level with the Paul Morenos, the rats and backstabbers, the animals.

"They would all do it to you if they had to," said Feldman, trying to read his thoughts. "Every one of them."

"But I'm not *them.*"

"You want to go to trial?"

"Why not?" asked Glasser, picking up a sparerib. "They don't have anything on me."

"Innocence isn't everything, Lou. You know that."

"I mean they've got no *evidence.*" Glasser looked like his old self suddenly—shrewd, the grizzled veteran of thousands of cases. "Think about it, Jerry. Why else are they making Paul Moreno dial for dirt? Why are they going through the prisons, offering deals to my clients?"

"They're scumbags, that's how they operate."

"It's because they haven't got anything solid." Glasser was excited now. He leaned forward, and the little candle lit his face from beneath, giving it an orange glow. "Right now their whole case rests on Brian, and he's a lousy witness—a fugitive with a record. My bet is that they don't even trust him to get on the stand, they're afraid he'll disappear. And that's why, after a four-month investigation, they're suddenly offering me full immunity."

"If you lose you'll be disbarred."

"If I take that deal I'm finished anyway." True, of course: no one would ever hire a lawyer who had testified against his own clients.

"But there's the other thing too," said Feldman. He meant jail.

"I'm innocent, Jerry."

The two men seemed to have reached some kind of plateau. They ate in troubled silence, unburdening the outrigger of chicken and shrimp and glistening sweet-and-sour pork, emptying their drinks till nothing was left but the pineapple chunks at the bottom. Glasser's head spun in tipsy circles, but the dizziness was a help, leading his thoughts to the difficult place they had to go. Hayes and Feldman were both useless, and anyway it wasn't their asses on the line. He would have to save himself.

With the food mostly gone, Feldman sat back. "Hayes will want a big piece of change for a trial."

Glasser looked up from his plate. He knew what his partner was telling him, that there was only a few thousand left in the firm's account. But he had already come up with a plan to work around their financial limitations. "Forget about money. The case will never make it to trial anyway. She won't even get the indictment."

"Lou, that's a pipe dream."

"They won't indict, because I'm going to testify," said Glasser.

Feldman was half out of his seat, aghast. "That's crazy. Hayes won't let you. *I* won't let you."

Glasser rather enjoyed Feldman's reaction. It seemed to prove the audacity of his plan, and in his experience the audacious thing was almost always the right thing. True, at the moment he couldn't remember a single instance when he'd let a client testify in front of a grand jury. The grand jury hearing belongs to the prosecution, which gets to present its case without challenge from the defense— defense lawyers aren't even allowed in the room. It would have been foolhardy to send a client to answer questions, under oath, in a room where Glasser couldn't protect him.

But Glasser wasn't a client. He was himself, Louis Glasser, and he still believed in his ability to persuade. If he could connect with the jurors, wrest them away from Freeburg, there was a possibility that they might not indict.

"It's suicide," said Feldman.

"It's a chance, and that's all anyone can ask for." Glasser was almost giddy, feeling confident for the first time in months. "Now let's celebrate with some dessert."

7

TWO VISITORS

Walking across Harvard Yard, Jason Glasser passed a stream of seniors headed for the on-campus job interviews being held at the Science Center. As a group, they looked eager and purposeful in their topcoats and suits, with their hair carefully moussed, and for a moment he yearned to be among them, safely hidden in the midst of the pack. Watching them march by, he had to remind himself that he was eager and purposeful too, busy with his own urgent life preparations—that tapes eleven and twelve of *Japanese Like a Native* were even now waiting for him at the language lab.

At the language lab he picked out his favorite carrel—the one in the corner, farthest from the door—and then put the bulbous headphones over his ears. For the next two hours he ran through acrobatic grammar drills, listening to the sharply enunciating voice and repeating after the beep, his throat constricted with the earnest eagerness to do right, to speak like a native. It was maddening labor, like running an obstacle course or tightrope-walking with a plate balanced on his head. But he pushed till his voice cracked and his lips went numb, till even the roof of his mouth had begun to ache.

At six o'clock he headed back to the dorm. It was dinnertime, and, more important, he was anxious about the mail. An answer from the K-T Fellowship was now days overdue.

Jason lived in Winthrop House, a sprawling, elegant, slightly seedy red-brick pile about six or seven blocks from the Yard, just across Mem. Drive from the Charles River. The Winthrop lobby was gloomy—a lot of marble but no lightbulbs—and he stood in the semi-dark as he searched his mailbox, a small brass door with a little glass window, one of dozens that lined the wall. Sticking his arm in up to the elbow, he came up with an unusually plentiful catch: three letters for his roommate, Norm; a phone bill; yet another flyer from Hillel House about Israeli folk dancing . . .

And *it*, from the K-T Fellowship.

For one prolonged moment Jason held *it* in his hand, measuring, weighing, assessing. And then his fingers began to work, tearing the envelope open, unfolding the sheet of stiff letterhead. In the lobby's twilight he had to hold the letter up to his nose in order to see the print. *Dear Mr. Glasser . . .* His eyes scanned the page twice, three times, but he was too excited to get more than a blurred impression: his own name and a short paragraph beneath, hardly more than a couple of lines. *It is with great regret that we must inform you that you were not among those selected . . .*

It dawned on him slowly, a feeling of not-rightness at the edge of his consciousness, as if he'd somehow put on his underwear backward or walked out with his left shoe on his right foot. *Not among those selected . . .* But why? He struggled with the question as with an impossible math problem, recalculating from every direction. The interview had gone well, extremely well, in spite of the pinstriped body armor his father had forced him to wear. A very nice Japanese gentleman in a baggy blue suit had ushered him into his office, offered him a seat, nodded a great deal while Jason talked. Indeed, Jason could not remember the last time he had felt so deeply, truly listened to. He had talked a lot, and the man had nodded a lot . . . it had all seemed so utterly *harmonious*, just as he'd imagined a Japanese interview should be.

Not among those selected to receive . . . He stuffed the rejection letter deep inside his coat pocket and then stood for a while, uncertain what to do next. Finally he began walking toward the dining hall.

The cafeteria was full of seniors back from their job interviews. Standing on the food line, he watched them laughing and shouting and banging the tables like Vikings at a banquet, giddy with relief and after-the-fact bravado. He could see on their faces how they felt: they had been scared half to death and now they were safe— till the next time, anyway.

Tray in hand, he found Norm at a table by the coffee machine, still dressed in his interview suit and dabbing a stain on his tie with a wet napkin. "Hey, it's Prince Genji," said Norm. "Welcome, honorable prince."

Jason eased himself into a free chair and began removing dishes from his tray: broccoli-cheese pasta, freeze-dried mashed potatoes, pale gray peas. The fabled Harvard endowment did not get wasted on food.

"How was the interview?" he asked, eager to forestall any questions about himself. He had already decided to forget the letter for the rest of the night, to pretend it had never arrived.

Norm counterfeited a free-and-easy shrug. "The guy from Merrill Lynch didn't like me. Two minutes and I was out. I've been sitting here drinking coffee since four-thirty."

The whole table must have heard this; as if a switch had been flipped, the noise suddenly gave way to anxious circular questioning. Two seats over, Chaz Howell began describing his own interview line by line, from the handshake on. A varsity fullback, he downed his third glass of milk, and his eyes narrowed. "So the guy leaned back in his chair and put his feet up on the desk, and he looked at me and said, If interest rates keep climbing, what happens to gold futures?"

Norm started at this. "He put his feet up? What kind of shoes was he wearing?"

"Tasseled loafers."

"Christ, my adviser told me cap-toed only."

General head nodding around the table, murmurs of agreement. "Not even wingtips," added Norm, looking grave.

"Well, maybe it's different when you're a junior V.P.," said Howell, shrugging his enormous bison shoulders. "Anyway, I crossed my legs very slowly, and then I said, All things being equal, gold goes down, because it's an inflation hedge. And he said—"

"Wait a second, aren't you thinking of silver?" asked Norm.

There was a fraught pause. "Silver?" Howell's face fell. "Jesus Christ, are you telling me it's silver?"

Unable to eat, Jason put down his fork. What would he do now that he wasn't going to Japan? Sign up for some interviews? The thought terrified him. He imagined the representative from Bear Sterns staring at him from across a desk, ursine and heavy, with a meaty neck and a carnivore's jaws. He would give Jason the once over and see immediately that the boy couldn't tell where supply met demand or what the market would bear, that he was too uncertain of himself to hustle, too frightened to fight, too weak to hold his own, that he wanted only to hide.

J ason spent the rest of the evening lying on the couch, trying to forget about the letter. This wasn't easy, since there was nothing else he wanted to think about, and the effort left him stupefied, unable to do anything but stare at the cracks in the ceiling. He wouldn't have gotten up at all if there hadn't been a knock on the door.

"Brian!"

Brian Brianson was standing in the hall, his vicuña overcoat thrown open to show an angora scarf and a black cashmere jacket, a shimmering gray silk shirt. "Hey, stranger." He grinned as he stepped inside, clearly pleased with the look of surprise on Jason's face.

In truth, Jason felt something like gratitude, glad to be free of the rejection letter. "How'd you find me?" he asked, a touch of awe in his voice. That was how he felt, *found*.

"I stopped by University Police. They had a directory." Despite the big smile, Brian seemed nervous. He moved about the room, inspecting books and magazines, picking through Norm's tape collection. It was a three-room suite, and though the bedrooms were closet-sized, the living room was genuinely grand, equipped with big windows that faced out on the courtyard three flights below. He finally settled at one of these, peering out with his nose to the glass. "I was in town on some business. I finished up early and I thought, Why spend the evening with a bunch of criminals? Why not drop in on my old pal Jason, the Harvard man?"

"I heard you were in some kind of trouble."

Brian straightened, a cautious smile on his lips. "Heard? What did you hear?"

"Well, I was at the office the day you were arrested. I walked with Dad to MCC."

"Oh?" The dealer became preoccupied, doodling something on the windowpane with his finger, then erasing it with his palm. "What else have you heard?"

"Nothing, I guess."

"You haven't talked to Lou?"

"Haven't heard from him much lately. Guess he's busy."

Brian seemed to brighten at this. He turned from the window and rubbed his hands together with renewed spirit. "I'm starved," he said. "Let's get some dinner."

After broccoli-cheese pasta, a second dinner was very welcome. Jason took Brian to the Kowloon, a Chinese joint in Harvard Square that was something of a student hangout and therefore the best place to show off his distinguished guest. The Kowloon's decor was a hybrid, with walls and ceilings painted a dusty black and synthesized techno-pop blaring over the tinny stereo. But it also sported the more traditional accoutrements, including bead curtains, paper lanterns, and tropical drinks. The drink of choice among the college cognoscenti was the Piranha Bowl, a large rum-and-fruit punch that came in a glass fishbowl large enough to be shared. Sipping through his straw, Jason peered around the room, as excited as if he were at a party. The other diners were almost all students, and he recognized a few. They had seen him, he knew, and were already wondering who Brian was, a grown-up and an outsider, dressed in silk and cashmere.

But for conversational material he was drawn back to the one topic on his mind, and between sips of the Piranha Bowl he told Brian about his disappointment over the K-T. "I don't know what I'm going to do now. I've made no plans."

Brian shrugged. "I never bother with plans anyway. You got to let it flow."

Of course, Brian's business was all planning, really, the organization of many minute particulars into a single coherent whole. Need to ship four hundred pounds of pot from Florida to Maine? Brian could find the boat and crew and the trucks to meet it, the warehouse to store it in. He could buy off the Coast Guard and the sheriff's office if necessary, and he could hire a local fishing captain to act as pilot up the craggy Maine coastline. But in his own mind this wasn't planning; it was dramatic improvisation, sleight of hand, a natural expression of character.

Jason simply took him at his word. "Everyone here has plans. They're all going to med school or law school or working for a senator in Washington. The ones who say they don't have them really have them anyway. They're going trekking in Borneo or riding camelback over the Silk Road to China. They've worked out sponsorship agreements with National Geographic."

"So?"

"So I'll end up working for Dad."

Brian laughed, shaking his head, and then took a long sip of the Piranha Bowl through his straw. The question, when it came, seemed to slip quietly through a space in the music. "Have you ever dropped acid, Jason?"

"Acid?"

The dealer was solemn now. "What you need is an eye-opener, something to give you a little perspective."

"I seem narrow to you?" Narrow was bad; the Harvard ethos stressed diversity and well-roundedness.

"I'm telling you as a friend, man. You've got to broaden your point of view." Brian pulled out a little brown glass bottle, the kind that would carry something like eye drops, held it in the light of the candle for Jason to see. "Absolutely pure and unadulterated, you can't get better than this."

Jason took a quick glance around the room to see who might be watching, then stared at the bottle, fascinated. "I thought it was a sixties sort of thing."

Brian unscrewed the top and pulled out the dropper, the hint of a liquid droplet quivering at its tip. "Hallucinogens have been sacred for thousands of years."

"It's a liquid?" asked Jason.

"Here, keep your eye open. Look up at the ceiling."

"You're going to put it in my eye?"

"It's like a fairy tale, man. Just one touch of the magic wand and you will see the great big world, everything you've been taught to ignore or filter out since you learned to think. And all the man-made things you thought were so real, the rules and religion and plans, the slave morality—all of it just evaporates like a mirage."

Jason giggled nervously. No graduation, no need to work, no plans; it sounded pretty good.

Brian moved along the circular banquette till his thigh was hard against Jason's. "It's worth a lot more than a trip to Japan, believe me."

Jason teetered on the edge of a decision, his heart drumming in his chest. He was scared, but the fear was different from the one he'd borne since the letter arrived—graduation fear—and it felt good, sharp and rejuvenating. He felt the hard grip of Brian's hand on the back of his neck, steadying his head, and the slightly sour heat of Brian's breath on his face. Looking up as instructed, he saw the dull glow of a paper lantern like a full moon against the black of the ceiling, and then the glass stem of the dropper, big as a turkey baster. He stifled the impulse to flinch, and a single drop fell into the corner of his eye, a cold blurriness that made him blink.

Brian released his head, and he looked around, a little disoriented. "Am I going to start seeing things? Visions?" Why was he only sorting out the consequences now, when it was too late? For a cautious kid, there was something reckless in him.

"It's not like going to the movies, man." Brian moved back along the banquette to his original seat, where he gave himself two drops, one in each eye, as careless as if it were Visine.

They talked of other things after that—movies, music, his father—but Jason hardly paid attention, wondering when he would start to see the effects. The thump of his heart mixed with the dance beat over the stereo, becoming something like the amplified tick of a clock. He started to wonder if he'd made a mistake. Should he get up and run to the emergency room? What would they do in a case like this? Pump his stomach? *But the stuff had gone in his eye.* He resisted looking at his watch but noticed the crowd in the restaurant thinning out little by little, like sand through an hourglass.

"Relax," said Brian. He slurped up the last of their Piranha Bowl. "These things take time. And we've still got to eat."

"What if I have a bad trip?"

"No such thing."

"You're telling me no one's ever had a bad trip?"

"Listen to me, Jason, I've been dropping acid since before you were born, and I've done it with all the greats too—Leary, Ginsberg, Hendrix, Jerry Garcia. I know for a fact that every trip is a good trip."

Jason was momentarily derailed by the list of names. "You knew those people?"

"In my business you get around."

It would never have occurred to Jason to question the truth of this assertion, and in any case the waiter had just arrived with their dinner. Brian's days as a vegetarian were over, and they had ordered liberally: chicken chunks on a bed of broccoli, beef mixed with baby corn, something called Kowloon Krazy Shrimp, glazed a beautiful Chinese red. Filling his plate, Jason found his fears suddenly evaporating, and then just as suddenly he was overcome with a strange rush of emotion—joy, gratitude so intense he felt the tears start to his eyes. Wasn't this the perfect meal, a sign that he was indeed embarking on a beautiful journey? Lifting his chopsticks to begin, he lost himself, staring at the mound of glistening chicken chunks. It seemed to be breathing, inhaling and exhaling, then inhaling again, lit from within by a warm illumination.

"I think something's happening," he announced.

"You're feeling something?"

"Our dinner is beating like a heart."

Brian laughed. "Yeah, it's working, all right."

After that, the conversation died away—too many important things to do. Jason's sense of time stretched like a piece of caramel, giving him the space he needed to observe in minutest detail the glowing, gemlike surface of the shrimp pincered between the tips of his chopsticks, the salt shaker with its millions of tiny glittering crystals, the candle in its bulbous red holder. Later, after dinner, he exercised the same intense scrutiny on the Kowloon's front door. Indeed, there was so much sensory information to sort through that he didn't realize at first that he had crossed Mass. Ave. and entered Harvard Yard. Down the path to the right was the immense broad back of Widener Library, and straight ahead was the Yard itself, an open rectangle of winter mud bordered by gentle red-brick buildings—dorms mostly. The dorms seemed to be breathing with the slow rhythm of sleepers, their facades bellying outward as they inhaled the night air.

Jason saw Brian a few feet ahead, walking toward University Hall. He felt strangely free of his body, separate from it, as if he were just a pair of big eyes being carried piggyback. "Everything is filled with light," he reported, running up, breathless. But what he really meant was *life*; light and life were one and the same.

Brian sauntered along with his hands in his pockets, an old pro at this sort of thing. "It's what the Buddhists call the dharma-body, man. Pure being."

"Sure, I get it now. Everything is suffused with this powerful— this powerful—" He struggled for the word, opening and closing his fists as if grasping at the air. "This *power* of being. You can't control what happens, you can only *be*."

"Be yourself, man. That's right."

He laughed, cutting through the late-night quiet of the Yard. "Fuck the K-T, who needs it. I'm free."

"Liberated," said Brian. "Hey, look at that." He had stopped in front of the bronze statue of John Harvard, founding father of the university.

Jason drew up alongside and saw immediately. "It looks like you."

"God, it does."

Jason had never paid the statue much attention before, though he passed it two or three times a day on his way to classes. Beardless, disconcertingly young and handsome, John Harvard had always looked to him more like a matinee idol than the founder of what was originally a Puritan seminary. But now he examined the long straight nose, the high bony forehead, and he was stunned by the likeness to Brian. It was as if the dealer were sitting in that massive bronze armchair, suddenly grown two times bigger than life. "You're everywhere," he whispered, genuinely awed.

Brian nodded, as if this were simple fact. "You remember that time we went to Ratner's and I got you stoned?"

"Another first," said Jason.

"Remember that cane I used to carry around, the shotgun cane?"

"How could I forget?"

"You were going to blow Petie away. Or at least give him an ass full of bird shot." He laughed, clearly taken with the memory. "I mean, what good is bird shot against a motherfucker like that? But you didn't know."

"He was going to attack you."

"We were just arguing. We always argued, but we still did business together. He cheated me, and I cheated him back." Brian lit a cigarette, watching fascinated as the smoke coiled into the night air. "But I admired what you did—it took guts and a lot of heart. Somebody like that could work for me."

He turned to peer at Jason, and it was clear from his smile that he expected an immediate yes to this sideways invitation, that no other possibility had occurred to him. "Well, what do you say?"

"*Work* for you?" Disconcerted, Jason stumbled on the words. "Is this an acid trip or a job interview?"

"I'm offering you a real opportunity to learn the business, man."

"Come on, I can't do that." Going along on a lark was one thing, but getting paid was quite another. He was a Glasser, not a client; Brian of all people should know the difference.

But the dealer only looked puzzled. "Why not?"

"Because I'm a college student, not a criminal."

This seemed to upset him. Brian gathered himself up to full height, smoking in grand wounded silence. "Thanks for pointing that out," he said finally. "I get it now, I really do. I'm a freak to you, an amusing exotic."

"It's not that, it's just—"

"Just what? My business too dirty? I've had dinner with the president of Mexico, man. I'm a figure in world diplomacy. I party with Dennis Hopper."

"Brian—"

"Forget it." He waved away any protests. "Lou's been good to me over the years, and I figured I owed him something, that's all. To make amends."

"Amends for what?"

Brian stubbed out his cigarette butt on John Harvard's shoe, looking intensely peeved. "Wrong word," he said.

"I doubt it would make him all that happy anyway."

"Maybe not."

They started walking again, back out the way they came, then through the narrow streets toward Winthrop. But instead of heading inside they crossed Mem. Drive and strolled along the Charles for a while. They ended up on a footbridge that spanned the river, sitting on the wide stone railing and dangling their legs over the water.

"It's got nothing to do with Lou, really," said Brian. He lit another cigarette and then dropped the match into the water—a little spark consumed in blackness. "You know, I don't really have a family of my own. What I need is somebody I can trust, and in my business that's hard to find."

"You can trust me."

"I know that." Brian gave him a sideways glance. "The job's in Amsterdam, Jason."

"Amsterdam?" Now, that was interesting. If Japan was out, Amsterdam might make an acceptable substitute.

"Hippest place in the world. Great women, and everyone speaks English. Hash on the menu in cafés, perfectly legal. On the production side, it's the center of developments in hydroponic gardening and the new seed strains. I go every year just to stay current."

"You're getting into growing?"

"Pot is the biggest cash crop in America now, ahead of corn and wheat."

"What would I do for you?"

"Research the new growing technologies, the new plant strains, keep me abreast of developments. If some new piece of equipment or some new type of seed looks good, I might want you to send it to me. A crash course in agronomy. Nothing illegal in that."

"Nothing illegal?"

"Absolutely legit."

Jason felt himself waver. "I don't know, Dad wouldn't go for it."

"Why not? I mean, how's it all that different from what he does for me?"

"You know the difference. He's a lawyer, he has a constitutional role to perform, defending people in court. The whole criminal justice system depends on that."

"The criminal justice system?" Brian snorted with theatrical disdain. "It's a joke."

"You aren't afraid of going to jail then?"

"I've been in this business for almost two decades, made millions of dollars, and I've spent a grand total of eleven days in jail. I'm way too smart for them."

"That doesn't surprise me."

"Jason, say yes to me."

They were not on the bridge anymore; they were up in the Lowell House belfry, little more than a crow's nest stuck in a cutting breeze amid the washed-out salmon pinks of dawn. Crowded above Jason's head were the great inert bells, looking like giant pears about to fall. He stepped over to the railing and gazed out over the sleeping streets. Kirkland and Eliot Houses were to his right, his own house, Winthrop, straight ahead by Mem. Drive.

"Say yes to what?" he asked.

"To the job in Amsterdam."

Jason gripped the wooden railing and bent over to look down at the sidewalk. "I could get expelled for this." The belfry was strictly off-limits; they had busted the lock to get in.

"Fuck it, who cares." Brian laughed, and then lightly began to climb onto the railing, one arm wrapped around one of the wooden posts. His movements were graceful, and in a moment he was at full height, his thin Italian loafers with their slippery leather soles bending slightly to match the curve of the rail. He reached out with his free arm, stretching so far that Jason thought he would keep going and going, unraveling like a spool of black thread.

"Say yes to freedom," said Brian, his shout almost lost in the wind, the flapping of his coat.

Jason watched with utter delight. There was no possibility of falling because there was nowhere to fall to. Brian was tied firmly by threads of light to everything, to the railing, the clouds, the sidewalk—to Jason himself. The whole world was a single organism, and freedom was the law by which it breathed. But it took bravery to admit that you were in fact a part of it, that you weren't separate and alone.

"Say yes to me," said Brian.

"Yes," said Jason, feeling an enormous door open inside himself, light pouring in to fill his body. "Yes."

They had breakfast at the Mug and Muffin on Mass. Ave. and then Brian got a cab—to where he wouldn't say. Jason wandered the Yard feeling bewildered and aimless, numb with exhaustion. When Lamont Library opened up he was first inside, moving through the uninhabited reading rooms to a couch he knew on the third floor. When he woke it was evening and the library was closing. He dragged himself back to the dorm, as tired as if he'd been up for three days straight. But opening the door to the room, he was immediately taken by a fresh surprise: his father sat sprawled in the chair by Jason's desk, hands in his coat pockets and legs stretched out in front of him, as if waiting for a bus.

Jason had scared himself with Brian the night before, and the sight of his father came as a tremendous relief. He ran over and hugged him like a little boy, breathing in the familiar smell of cigarettes and wool and aftershave, feeling the warmth radiating from his body. "What are you doing here?"

"I had a case in Boston."

"Brian?" He said this cautiously, testing to see if the dealer had told his father that he intended to stop by.

Glasser gave him a veiled look. "Something else."

Just as well; better to leave the visit alone for now. And then he noticed his roommate, Norm, sitting at his own desk on the other side of the room, tapping a pencil on the bare wooden top and looking annoyed.

"I found him standing outside when I got home," said Norm.

"You should've called," Jason said to Glasser.

"It was a last-minute thing," said Glasser. "I decided to stay over and take you gentlemen out to dinner."

Suddenly Jason was aware of a certain tension in the room. His father and Norm looked like strangers in a bus station who had argued over a seat and were trying to ignore each other. There was an awkward pause, and then Glasser said, "I was just telling this fine young man about that case I had last month. You know, the necrophiliac."

This was his father's favorite trumped-up crime story, one of a bunch he liked to trot out to test the credulity of his listeners. But the usual playful manner was gone, and instead he radiated a sort of deep manic gloom. He was grinning, but it was the sort of scary grin that would make a little kid burst into tears: lips and eyes wide open, as if torn by a blast of wind.

"Your father's some storyteller," said Norm. He stood up, grabbed his coat and bookbag. "Well, I've got to get to dinner before they lock the slop away."

"You're not coming with us?" asked Jason, greatly relieved.

"Got to study. Thanks for the advice, Mr. Glasser." He directed this last to Jason too, as if the son were supposed to translate into whatever exotic language the father spoke.

They listened to Norm's steps retreating down the hallway stairs. "Got a real stick up his ass," Glasser said.

"That's true, he's a real square." But this was exactly what Jason liked about him: his stupid beer-bottle collection, his subscription to *Sports Illustrated,* his membership in a touchingly earnest group called Young Entrepreneurs of Harvard. Norm was a live-in example of *norm*ality. "What advice did you give him?"

"Women, grades, the career of law."

"Norm's not going to law school. Why would he be interested in law?"

Glasser only blinked. "Let's go to dinner. You've got your credit card?"

In the cab, Jason told his father about the letter. "I didn't get the K-T."

"The what?"

"The K-T Fellowship. Japan, Dad."

Glasser gave a distracted shrug, and Jason rushed in to fill the vacuum, providing both sides of the conversation. He described how well the interview had gone, how it was a mystery he'd been turned down. The effort was pointless, though, because Glasser wasn't listening. It looked as if he were staring at the passing scenery—Storrow Drive, the Charles—but in fact he was gazing at his own reflection in the darkened window, making faces at himself like a bored little boy: hideous comic smiling faces like the one he'd made in the room; then surprised faces, eyes popping, mouth puckered in an Oh!-type gasp of horror. In between the masks his features fell slack and exhausted, like an actor coming offstage.

"Are you listening to me?" Jason snapped. Even a lecture about law school would have been welcome at this point.

"What?"

"Are you— Forget it." The man was clearly in one of his moods, worrying about a case gone wrong or a debt he couldn't pay. But then he was always in one of those moods, wasn't he? It would serve him right if Jason ended up in the pot trade in Amsterdam. Then they could at least talk business.

The restaurant was in a big hotel in downtown Boston, near the Commons, and it was just the kind of place his father loved, meaning the sort of stuffy businessmen's restaurant where neither one of them actually fit in. Jason categorized the decor as The Robber Baron's Boardroom, with dark wood paneling on the walls and a deep crimson carpet on the floor, so plush he had to check his feet to make sure he was really walking. Glancing down at his jeans and workboots, he felt naked.

The maître d' was one of those men described as "brutally handsome," with a big square jaw and a chin like the business end of a sledgehammer. A failed actor, probably; in any case, his rendition of maître d' seemed to have borrowed something from the old gangster movies—an air of dignified menace, amplified by a tuxedo and plenty of hair pomade. "Reservations?"

Glasser looked into the dining room, bounced on his toes. "Glasser. Louis Glasser."

Jason was surprised by this, as to his knowledge his father hadn't reserved ahead for anything in his entire life—hotel, plane, or rent-a-car, let alone a table at a restaurant. Living in the eternal present, the elder Glasser just couldn't think that far into the future. Sure enough, the maître d' checked his book but couldn't find any Glassers.

"Oh dear," said Glasser, not overly flustered by this sudden revelation. "That's very strange. My secretary made the call."

"I'm sorry, sir."

"But we've come all this way." Glasser turned his mournful brown eyes on the man.

"We're booked solid. Perhaps another night—"

Glasser listened, nodded with the utmost reasonableness. "No doubt it's my secretary's mistake, and I'll have to speak to her. But in the meantime—" He leaned forward, lowered his voice. "My son, you see, it's his birthday. He goes to Harvard, and I'm in town this one night only. It will ruin everything . . ."

Birthday? Jason took a big step back, feeling his face turn hot with embarrassment. The maître d' glanced at him, and he smiled weakly, trying to melt into the hardwood paneling of the wall.

"I wish I could accommodate you, sir, but I can't," said the maître d'.

"Can't?" Glasser seemed genuinely surprised. "Can't? I don't think you understand." Suddenly he turned surly in a way Jason had never seen before. "You fuck up our reservations, and now you won't seat us? Is that what you're telling me?"

The maître d's face turned professionally blank, like a metal shutter coming down on a store window. "What I'm telling you is that all the tables are taken. Of course, if you'd care to wait at the bar, something might open up eventually."

"Wait at the bar?" Glasser looked like he wanted to use his great bulk to slam past the man and his reservation book, but then his attitude abruptly changed. The air rushed out of him, and in the next moment he looked too exhausted to stand. "Okay then, we'll wait."

Yet another surprise. Always rushing out of places, cutting lines, his father never had the patience to wait for anything, most especially a meal. Normally they would have stormed out and jumped into a cab, making the driver run the red lights on their way to the next restaurant. But this time his father only shrugged.

They sat at one of the small tables near the bar. Glasser huddled in his coat, hands in his pockets, but it was hot, and Jason took his off. Their waiter came over with news of a dress code; jacket and tie were required, and Jason was outfitted with some castoffs from the cloakroom: a lime-green polyester sports coat, the sleeves of which stretched past his fingertips, and a black clip-on tie as wide as a bib. Glasser ordered a piña colada.

"You know," Jason said to him, "it's not my birthday."

"What's the difference?" He looked over Jason's head, obviously thinking of something else.

"Let's go somewhere else to eat. I'm paying for it, I should decide."

"I said I'd pay you back. Have I ever *not* paid you back?"

"Look what they've put me in." He tugged at the enormous lapels of his sports coat. "It's a clown suit. I can't eat in this."

Glasser's piña colada sat before him in a glass shaped like a pineapple, complete with paper umbrella. Hands in his pockets, he bent his head down to sip through the straw. "You're a college senior," he said between sips. "You should dress like an adult. What do I give you an allowance for?"

They waited a long time. Glasser had another piña colada, sucking it through his straw as if it were a malted. He didn't seem drunk exactly, but his face became redder and redder, and the sweat stood out in milky white beads on his forehead. The muffled noise of the restaurant fell away, and it began to feel very late somehow; if the clock over the bar hadn't said 9:15 Jason would have sworn it was midnight. Glasser ran his finger over the inside of his empty pineapple glass, scraping up the last of his piña colada as if it were cake batter in a mixing bowl.

"They're making us wait on purpose," said Jason. "They're hoping we'll just get up and leave." He tapped on the table, trying to get a response. "Well?"

"What?" Glasser looked up, listening for the first time. His index finger glistened with the last of the piña colada.

If it was a war of attrition they were fighting, the Glassers were the winners, however, because the maître d' finally came over to tell them a table was ready. Glasser looked up and blinked with a genuine lack of recognition—he seemed to have no memory of the battle over reservations. Standing up, he took the empty pineapple glass with him, and Jason followed behind, holding in the voluminous waist of his lime-green sports coat. The walk to the back of the dining room seemed endless, taking them past a dozen empty booths till they reached their own small table, strategically placed between kitchen and bathroom for maximum discomfort.

"Would you care to check your coat?" the maître d' hinted.

"That's okay," Glasser said simply. He left his coat buttoned to the chin, and when the waiter arrived he ordered another piña colada. "And your biggest steak," he said. "Well-done. Two baked potatoes."

"Same," said Jason, waving away the menu. The sooner this is over, the better, he told himself, and the waiter seemed to think so too; the steaks came within minutes.

But Jason was too busy watching his father to start on his own food. Of course, they'd sat across the dinner table thousands of times over the years, but Jason began to observe him in a different way now, as if he were looking though the eyes of a stranger, somebody like the maître d'. He watched how awkwardly his father held his knife and fork in his fists as he cut his meat—big pieces of steak that could hardly fit in his mouth, that he could barely chew before swallowing. Juice from the meat spread to his hands; his fingers began to glisten; his mouth and chin glistened. The sleeves of his overcoat dipped into the plate, came up brown at the edges. Grease splattered his chest. His eyes wandered unfocused, unconnected to the action of his hands. He ate faster and faster, drank while his mouth was still packed with food. He dropped his fork and lifted the remaining steak in his fingers, tore at the meat till the last of it was gone. The look on his face, private and naked, was not of hunger or abandon or pleasure or gluttony but of the deepest sadness.

Jason despised his father for the display, hated himself for having seen it—seen it through the eyes of the maître d', whom he also hated. Oblivious, Glasser called for the check. He seemed woozy but impatient to go. "Got your credit card?" he asked. "I'll get the tip."

Jason handed him the card and then started on his steak. He ate with exaggerated precision, careful with the knife and fork, careful not to drip. But he ate quickly too, because he knew his father would jump up as soon as he'd paid. The elder Glasser was dopey with food and when he left he would not even turn around to see if Jason were behind.

The boy was almost finished by the time the waiter came back with the receipt, on which Glasser scrawled *Jason Glasser.* "Hold on," he said to the waiter, and then reached into his coat pocket. He pulled out a dollar bill that had been crumpled into a ball, unfurled it, and placed it in the waiter's open hand. "Wait a sec," he said, and then began pulling from both pockets, extracting wrinkled dollar bills, loose change a coin at a time, piling it in the waiter's palm.

Back in Harvard Square, Jason was both saddened and relieved when his father said he was taking the last shuttle flight home. Saddened because the man seemed always to be teetering on the edge of some terrible disaster; relieved because he didn't want to take care of him anymore—which saddened him further, till the anxiety of parting became nearly unbearable. "You'll need a cab to the airport. Do you have enough money?"

"I've still got a little time. Let's take a walk."

The Yard was empty and dark except for a few widely spaced street lamps, and they walked for a while in silence, Glasser trailing slightly behind. "Remember when we got that letter, saying you'd gotten in?" said Glasser. "Fourteen thousand a year, tuition alone."

"I can tell you they're not spending it on the cafeteria."

But his father was serious. "You did your part, and I made a promise that I would see you through."

"I don't remember any promise." In truth, the cost of the place hadn't ever occurred to Jason. He had never seen a contradiction between the stacks of past-due bills and the assumption that the Glasser family had an endless source of cash. Didn't they own a Jaguar and an airplane? Hadn't they just finished a hundred-dollar steak dinner? Sure, his father had appropriated his credit card, had tipped the waiter in nickels and quarters, but that was the way he did things.

"I keep my promises," said Glasser now, and then walked right past him, toward University Hall and the statue of John Harvard. Jason hurried after him.

"What's going on?" He drew alongside his father, who now stood in front of the statue, examining it with the keen absorption of someone who does not want to make eye contact. Jason followed his gaze. John Harvard's resemblance to Brian had completely washed away with the effects of the acid, like dust in the rain. It was dull and inert once more, a lifeless piece of kitsch.

"I don't want you to worry," said Glasser. "But there's been some trouble. Some legal trouble. Stupid stuff."

"Legal trouble?" Nothing special about that: legal trouble was his father's business, wasn't it?

"Your mother and I, we haven't really done you a favor by sheltering you like we have."

"You know, going out to dinner with you is not my idea of being sheltered."

"Maybe not." Glasser stared hard at John Harvard, and Jason watched his eyes move over the dark bronze. He seemed to be considering what he was about to say. "Criminal law is a game, Jason, like football or baseball, no different. The government comes up with a new offense, then lawyers invent a new defense. Both sides will do anything to win. And when the government can't get the crooks anymore, they go after the lawyers. Win a few big cases and the Feds start to watch you. They tap your phones, bug your office. They get your clients to rat on you."

Jason glanced over at his father but then fixed his eyes on the statue again, unable to look at the distress on the elder Glasser's face. He realized now that the legal trouble was *theirs*. "What's this about?"

"Nothing, probably. All I know is that it has something to do with Brian."

Jason felt a shock travel through his body. He was about to blurt out that Brian had just been there, but he stopped himself, unwilling to tell the rest. "What's he got to do with it?"

"I don't know yet. I need to sit down with him and talk it out, make sure we're thinking the same way. But whatever happens, I haven't done anything illegal, and I think that still matters. The Feds will see there's nothing there, and they'll move on. What I want to tell you is that they will start saying things. You will hear things."

"Things?" Jason reached out to touch John Harvard's metal foot. The cold was sharp and strangely soothing. Brian must have known all about this. Why hadn't he said something?

"You can depend on me for the truth, Jason. I am your dad and always will be. I am the same."

"What happens next?"

"Next?" Glasser gave a weak laugh. "I'm going in front of the grand jury."

Jason nodded, trying to absorb, to think. A dim voice in the back of his head told him that things were more serious than his father wanted to admit. "Isn't that a little unusual? I mean, you never let your clients—"

"I'm innocent, and I want to clear my name. You believe I'm innocent, don't you?"

"Yes," he said, and did, absolutely.

8

INSIDE OUT

Jason woke up late the next day and immediately wandered over to his desk, trying to think things through. It was a difficult, slippery process. Losing the K-T Fellowship obviously meant nothing next to his father's legal problems, yet the boy was having trouble distinguishing the one crisis from the other. They seemed linked in some way. He replayed every moment of their walk through the Yard again and again, and his mind darted from pity for his father to anger at his persecutors to fear for himself—and then to a sudden fury at his father too, which surprised him and made him feel guilty. But the man was always causing problems, always getting into trouble, always needing something, whether it was a cold drink or a tissue or an extra pillow or the important file he had misplaced. He took up all the light and air in a room until there was nothing left for other people.

These thoughts were followed by a wave of shame. Something had to be done—something. When his father had hidden that credit-card bill from his mother, seven new suits from Saks accruing twenty-one percent interest, Jason had forced him to tell her, and she had paid it. The man needed direction, and more often than not it was Jason who gave it to him.

He was still at his desk when Norm walked in, his bookbag slung over one shoulder. Norm's cheeks were red from the cold and he was smiling the way he did when he wanted to pick an argument—upper lip curled to show his two front teeth. "Have a good dinner?" he asked. He put his bag down and started rearranging the books inside. "I've been up since six, did three hours in the library after breakfast."

Jason put his hands to his mouth like a megaphone. "Hooray for Superwonk!"

Norm gave a little shrug, then sat down at his own desk and began straightening some loose papers. For Norm, it was not good enough that his papers were neatly stacked; the edge of the stack had to be aligned with the edge of his desk, and he did this with little pats of his palm. "God, your father's a funny guy. Were those jokes he was telling?"

Suddenly Jason had no heart for the fight. "He likes putting people on," he said, softening his voice. "I know it can be annoying."

Norm started rooting through one of his desk drawers. "That stuff about the necrophiliac? Pretty gross. Talk about bad taste."

"You didn't have to sit with him if you didn't want to. You could've gone to the library or whatever."

Norm looked up for a moment. "You never said he was coming."

"I didn't *know* he was coming."

"Well, a little notice would help next time." He banged shut the drawer and opened the one below it. Jason could hear him rearranging things in there, stacking little boxes of something.

"Come on, Norm, this is just plain stupid."

"It's not stupid. The man's telling sicko jokes about some client who does it with dead people—"

Jason shrugged. "That story happens to be true, by the way, just a little exaggerated."

"Yeah? And what about that other one, the one about the client who wants to marry the horse?"

"Okay, so you don't like his sense of humor. You were offended, and I'm sorry. Are we finished?"

Norm looked up from his drawer, grinning slyly as if he held some big dirty secret. "You know, I had the weird feeling he was trying to impress me or something. All those stupid jokes, and then the man-to-man stuff, the fatherly advice."

Jason felt himself growing angry. "My father is a very successful criminal attorney, Norm, and I seriously doubt he gives a fuck what a pimply college geek thinks of him."

"*My* father is the biggest plastic surgeon in La Jolla."

"Okay, he takes big Jewish noses and makes them little, he takes little boobs and makes them big. So what?"

"There's nothing wrong with cosmetic surgery, if that's what you're implying. And it's a lot better than getting murderers and rapists off on technicalities, or putting drug dealers back on the streets."

"Technicalities? Due process? The Bill of Rights? The presumption of innocence? Those aren't technicalities, Norm, they're democracy." Jason was standing now, gripping the back of his desk chair, and his knees were shaking, but he couldn't stop the rush of words. "The criminal lawyer performs a constitutional function. He's required by law to give his client the best representation possible, and he makes no moral judgments, because that would prevent him from doing his job."

He recognized this speech only after he'd finished: it was his father's, more or less, the one he used to defend his profession. But the elder Glasser gave it a cool, statesmanlike delivery, and it sounded a lot less persuasive to Jason in his own strangled falsetto.

"No moral judgments?" Norm asked. "How convenient." He was smiling again. "It seems to me that if you defend someone you know is guilty you're almost as bad as he is."

"Who can decide guilt or innocence just like that?"

"I can, you can. It's obvious."

"People have reasons for what they do, you can't always know why."

"You don't have to know why. If you break the law you should be punished. It's as simple as that."

"Thank you, Norm, for finally revealing yourself as the smug, self-righteous, totalitarian neo-fascist that you really are." Jason sat back down, eyes on the floor.

Norm looked worried and a little dazed. "Going to lunch?"

"Maybe later."

Instead, Jason got his coat and his bookbag and headed for South Station, where Amtrak left for New York. From a pay phone by the ticket window he stopped to call Brian, but there was no answer, not even the machine. It was impossible for him to say what this meant—he told himself it meant nothing at all—but the ringing on the other end was enough to make him buy a ticket home. There was nearly an hour till the next departure, and he spent it alternately pacing in front of the information board and trying Brian's number, wild thoughts flying through his head: Brian was back in jail; Brian had been killed; his father was in danger. By the time he got on the train he had scared himself into a state of nervous exhaustion. Hungering for a dose of normalcy, he reached into his bag and pulled out *Japanese Like a Native,* the textbook that accompanied the tapes. He began the dialogue for chapter thirteen.

Ms. Hata: As you can see, Kamakura is very beautiful.
Mr. Tanaka: Yes, I must thank you for bringing me here.

But it was no good. He was too agitated to read, and anyway the silly dialogue no longer had a purpose—Japan was gone. He spent the entire ride staring out the window as the train crept through weedy lots, past junkyards and asphalt plants, stretches of marshy coastline. The air smelled of franks cooking in the dining car. A baby wailed. He didn't reach Penn Station till six, didn't get home till six-thirty, and by then the muscles in his legs were knotted tight. He was nearly bursting with a pent-up fury for action, any action at all. Instead of knocking he used his key, rushing inside to tackle the problem like a football player, to crush it then and there.

He found his parents frozen in postures of surprise. They were sitting at the big table in the dining room, an excited, guilty air about them. But there was nothing particularly incriminating in sight—only a disorderly swirl of papers on the table, stacks crumbling into other stacks. In a glance he took in bank statements, canceled checks, credit card bills, legal files.

"What is this?" asked his mother. "Has something happened?" She started to straighten some bills, then discreetly covered them with a manila folder.

"I'm here," said Jason.

"I can see that."

And then suddenly he was tired—very tired, and at a complete loss as to what should come next. "Tell me what I need to do," he said.

"Do?" She glanced suspiciously at his father. "There's nothing here for you to do. You should be at school."

"I know everything, Mom."

"Somehow I really doubt that." And then turning toward Glasser: "You told him?"

Glasser's mouth worked up and down, a look of appeal on his large sensitive face. Jason intervened. "You need me, I can help."

"We're the parents, Jason. Let us handle it for once."

But he could tell she was secretly glad he'd come. She looked tired and frail in her nightgown, with her reading glasses slipping down her nose. He took a seat at the table and watched as they sorted through bills and brokerage account statements and pass-books, but it was hard to tell what they were after—they themselves didn't seem particularly sure. They vacillated between figuring out how much money they had, calculating how much they owed, and estimating how much they could borrow, and his mother had a personal agenda too, which his father didn't share—tracking down where it had all been spent.

"Look at this," she said, brandishing a pink receipt. "Six hundred dollars at Tiffany's."

"Not mine," said his father, becoming very interested in the bank statement in front of him.

"It's your signature."

"I don't remember."

"It's from last month."

He looked up, and his face was frankly pleading, the exquisite brown eyes big with regret. "I was depressed, I thought it would cheer me up." And then a look of faint hope. "It was the cheapest thing in the store."

"Just four weeks ago, with the lawyer bills and everything else?" She stopped suddenly, struggling to master herself, but Jason could see the fury rising in her eyes. When she spoke again her voice came out low and strangled, as if there were a noose around her neck. "What was it?"

"Cuff links."

"Can they be returned?"

"I lost one."

That did it. She slammed the bill down on the table. "I don't know why you're doing this to me," she wailed and ran from the room.

There was a moment of charged silence, father and son left together at the table before a mound of papers. Then Glasser whispered the obvious. "She's upset. She's a good woman, but she's upset." He seemed to think about this for a while. "All I need is a new case, one new case, and then the money won't be an issue. She doesn't understand that. It's just temporary."

"Dad, what's happening here?"

"They picked up one of Brianson's boats down south. There was a rat and wiretaps and surveillance photos, a lot of people got arrested."

"I thought Brian was always so careful."

"He's gotten sloppy. It happens to all of them, too many drugs, too much money, they start to think they're god."

"But what's it got to do with you?"

"Nothing, absolutely nothing." His voice was strident, as if addressing a jury, and he chopped the air with his open hand. But then he went back to his earlier mode, an embarrassed half-whisper. "My guess is they look at him and figure he's too crazy to be running things himself. I'm supposed to be the puppetmaster pulling his strings. He says they're squeezing him to testify."

"Against you?"

"Against me, against a whole bunch of people. I saw him up in Boston, briefly. It's been hard to make contact."

Up in Boston, of course. The two men had been there to see each other, not him. And this simple realization seemed to stand everything on its head, as if he were no longer at the reliable center of his own life. "He wouldn't turn on you," said Jason, trying to dispel a sudden doubt.

His father's reaction to the idea was vehement. "He'd never do that. Never. And they can't force him, because they don't have much of a case against him—no leverage. But even if he did, what could he tell them? I'm a lawyer, not a drug dealer. Nothing can change that."

That night, in his old bedroom, Jason found it impossible to sleep. His mind wandered through memory after memory, trying to put things back in order, back as they should be, but nothing fell into the right spot anymore. He remembered waking up once in that very same room when he was six or seven. He had heard something interesting going on in the living room—lowered voices, suppressed laughter. Light had come through his half-open door. He had gotten out of bed and padded into the hallway, careful not to make any noise. His parents were standing by the coffee table, facing each other, a shopping bag on the floor between them. His mother had her hands on her hips, and she was smiling. His father was still in his overcoat, snowflakes glittering on his shoulders. *He's brought me a present,* thought Jason, *it's in the shopping bag.*

Sometimes his parents were angry when he woke up like this, other times glad. He knew the first moment was crucial, so he tried to be crafty. He took a step into the living room and waited to be noticed.

"Hey," his father said, "look who's here. It's Jason."

"Want to hear a joke?" asked Jason. But it wasn't necessary; his parents were smiling. It was one of the glad nights.

"Come get a load of this," his father said, pointing into the shopping bag. "Your dad's been busy tonight."

My present, thought Jason, but before he could move, his father had turned the shopping bag upside down over the coffee table and something unexpected had fallen out. "Money," said Jason.

"You got that one right."

The bills were divided into rubber-banded packets, and the packets made a shaggy pile on the table. Jason was confused; he couldn't figure out why his father was giving him money when he must know the boy wanted a toy. "This is your college education," his father said, "right here on the table."

"The first year of it, anyway," said his mother. She was staring at the money, and there was something like awe in her voice.

"Harvard," said his father.

"Yale," said his mother.

Jason was beginning to understand that the money wasn't for him, that there was no present for him, and he could feel himself getting angry. "I want a toy," he said.

"We should count it." His father bent over the coffee table and divided the money into two separate piles. His mother sat down on the couch, arranged her pile into a neat stack, took the rubber band from a packet, and began moving the bills through her fingers. His father sat down beside her and did the same.

"Where's my toy," said Jason, afraid of being left out. "I want my toy."

But he couldn't get much force behind it now; he was too busy watching his parents. They were silent, but their lips moved, their heads bobbed. They were moving together, working together, and he had never seen them in such harmony before. When his father finished counting the last packet in his pile, he took a deep breath. "My half's exact," said his father. "Ten thousand."

"Same," said his mother. She lurched up from the couch, wide-eyed and out of breath. "Snack?" she asked and then ran to the kitchen before anyone could answer.

His father turned to him. The snowflakes had disappeared from the shoulders of his overcoat, leaving dark speckles. "You're one lucky kid, Jason. Your dad is rich."

Rich, thought Jason, and for the first time he understood what that meant. With the money on the table he could buy anything he needed, all the missing pieces: laughter, excitement, even the mysterious accord he'd just witnessed between his parents. He was tired and his eyes were scratchy, he was half-sinking back into sleep, but he could feel an electricity that made his legs twitch. Something good had happened to them.

"How about a banzai?" his father asked. "Banzai!" they yelled, throwing their arms up like in the old war movies, Jason's little voice mixing with his father's amazingly deep grown-up one. "Banzai! Banzai!" And he could hear his mother in the kitchen too, calling out like an echo, "Banzai! Banzai! Banzai!"

The next morning Jason came out of his room to find his father sitting on the couch in the living room. Red-eyed and unshaven, a cigarette dangling from his mouth, his father was in his boxer shorts, and his stomach looked enormous. For as long as Jason could remember, he had measured the turmoil in their lives by the size of this belly: smaller in the more tranquil periods, bigger in hard times. Now it was as big as he'd ever seen it.

"Better get dressed. We've got an appointment with the lawyer at ten-thirty."

"The lawyer?" He noticed there was no mention of his going back to Boston.

His father lifted himself slowly and walked over to the armchair where his clothes were piled. "He used to work in the U.S. Attorney's Office. In fact, he used to be the boss of the woman handling our investigation." He began pulling on a blue dress shirt. "In a situation like this you need an insider, somebody who can nip it in the bud."

"Nip it how?"

"He can reason with them, tell them the facts. They'll listen because he's one of the club."

His father struggled to button a pair of gray wool pants, which looked ready to split. "This prosecutor, Freeburg, is a real ball buster," he continued, trying to draw in his stomach. "You don't want to get into a spitting match with her. That's why I'm going in front of the grand jury, to show her I've got nothing to hide. I want to come across as fully cooperative."

"What's your lawyer think?"

"He's bringing her around slowly. She's young and ambitious, and she thinks hanging me is going to make her the next U.S. attorney for the Southern District." He managed to get the pants closed with a sharp intake of breath. "But it doesn't make any sense. I mean, who am I? A nobody. Not like Ray O'Donnel, preening on television."

"What kind of evidence—"

"That's just my point. No evidence, none." He became thunderous, all moderation gone. "Put up or shut up, I told her, but she thinks she doesn't have to. Evidence? They don't need evidence, they're the U.S. Government." He began tugging on a blue blazer, skintight. "Aren't you hungry?" he asked finally, giving Jason a beseeching look—obviously hunting for an excuse for a second breakfast.

They took a cab down to Sedgewick & Ashberry, the elder Glasser talking nervously all the while. "They call them white-shoe law firms because they're so WASPy. Don't ask me why. Maybe the WASPs wear white shoes." He checked his watch, clearly worried about being late—a man who had never been on time for anything. "They're expensive as all hell, but they've got clout. You know, Hayes used to be Freeburg's boss."

"You told me already, but I don't see why it's such a big deal." There was something about his father's eagerness to believe that made Jason angry.

"I know you're not as naive as you want to sound." His father looked over at him. "There are insiders and there are outsiders, and you should be glad you've never had to figure out the difference."

"What's that supposed to mean?"

"It means you've got a dad who can buy you things."

"Well, if this guy's such an insider, why should he care about you?"

"Because I'm paying him to."

They rode in silence for a while. I know the difference between inside and outside, thought Jason. I am inside this body, and I am looking out through my eyes at cars, buildings, sunlight. We are inside this family, the Glasser family, and everyone else is outside, a stranger. We are inside this cab, and the world is outside, flowing around us like water. "Which am I?" he asked.

"You go to Harvard. You're in like Flynn."

It was the answer he had expected—even wanted—but it didn't make him feel any better, especially if his father was left standing on the outside. "Inside what?" he asked sharply.

The cab pulled up to the curb before his father could answer. The building was of cold gray stone, towering over a narrow strip of sidewalk. Jerry Feldman was waiting inside the lobby, looking nervous and fat, much fatter than Jason had ever seen him before. "Where were you? You're late," he said to Glasser.

Glasser kept walking toward the elevators, looking at his watch. "We've got five minutes," he said. "What are you doing down here anyway?"

"I didn't want to wait up there by myself." From the expression on Feldman's face Jason could tell this was true; the partners were both intimidated by the place.

To Jason, Sedgewick & Ashberry's reception area looked as big as his father's whole office. Corman Hayes's secretary came out to meet them, then led them through a maze of corridors and cubicles to a conference room, where they waited. The room was impressive: an enormous rectangular table, thick red carpeting, heavy leather chairs, floor-to-ceiling shelves full of law books. They milled around, touching things. When Jason was a kid, he used to think his father was the biggest lawyer in the world, the richest man ever; he could do anything, buy anything—toys and cars and airplanes. At twenty-two, he still found it a little shocking to be reminded this wasn't so.

"A firm like this has over a hundred lawyers," said Glasser, rubbing the leather back of a chair.

"One hundred and twenty-nine," said Feldman. "I read an article."

"It's like a factory."

"Lone wolves like us are an endangered species." Feldman began buffing the shiny conference table with the sleeve of his suit jacket, then tried looking at his reflection.

"They're picking on us because we're small," Glasser said. "They think they can get away with it."

"The big firms never get in trouble, and they're dirtier than anybody. They're up to their eyeballs in dirt."

Glasser moved down a row of law books, running his finger over their spines like a kid pulling a stick over the spokes of an iron fence. "Everybody gets a little dirty. You get splashed."

"There's a difference between that and really dirty," said Feldman. "Only a fool doesn't know the difference."

Glasser walked back slowly, examining the carpet. "What we need is some carpeting like this," he said. "This is really plush."

Feldman picked up a heavy glass ashtray, tapped it with a fingernail. "One thing at a time, Lou."

Corman Hayes came in a few minutes later. He was a thin, precise man, a good fifteen years younger than Jason's father. Jason checked for the white shoes, but his footwear was a glossy black.

"Gentlemen," said Hayes, "good to see you again." He shook hands with Glasser, Feldman, and then Jason. It was a dry hand, with blond hair and freckles on the back. Glasser made the introduction.

"Corman, you went to Harvard, didn't you?"

"College and Law School, yes."

Jason tightened, knowing full well what his father was up to. He hated being trotted out for display, and it was worse this time, because he knew there was a secret message meant for him, something about insiders and outsiders. In his father's simple formulation, Hayes went to Harvard and he was an insider, so Jason could be one too. What the elder Glasser didn't know was that there were many different Harvards. There was the old-money Harvard of prep-school grads, who wore faded chinos and Top-Siders without socks, who were living in dorms their fathers and grandfathers had lived in. Jason saw them on the streets late at night, dressed in black-tie and drinking from champagne bottles as they stumbled home from the finals clubs to which he would never have been "punched." And there was the jet-set Harvard, the children of Italian financiers and Indian movie moguls. They had been to school together in England or Switzerland and now spent Christmas with one another at St. Barts or Gstaad, places he had never heard of before arriving in Cambridge. And there was the famous Harvard, the children of politicians and Nobel Prize winners, who knew the professors by their first names—professors who were themselves celebrities, consulted by senators and CEOs, and who therefore had no time to talk to Jason after class.

But there was no saying this now. Glasser beamed at Hayes like a poker player laying a royal flush on the table. "Jason is a senior this year."

Hayes smiled politely, and his face broke into a series of dry cracks—sun damage from years of tennis or golf. "Wonderful," he said, and then turned to Jason. "Sportsman or scholar?"

"Neither, probably."

"Ah, yes." Hayes looked a little blank.

"Jason's a lover," said Feldman.

The boy cringed, but he could see that it was only going to get worse. Indeed, his father immediately launched into one of his jokes. "There are these two lawyers, Pinsky and Klein," said the elder Glasser. "They've been in practice together over thirty years, the last ten without a single day's vacation. So one day Klein turns to Pinsky and suggests they take the day off. It's a slow day, no clients coming in, nothing on the calendar."

"Dad," said Jason, trying to reroute him. *"Dad."*

But his father was too wrapped up in his performance to notice. He gripped Hayes's immaculate gray sleeve in a you-don't-want-to-miss-this gesture, and Hayes responded with a chilly little smile that translated into something like *Unhand me, please.* But Glasser went on, undeterred. "Pinsky is reluctant, but Klein eventually talks him into riding the train up to Yankee Stadium. The two lawyers sit in the bleachers in their suits, each with a hot dog and a beer, trying to relax and enjoy the game. Suddenly Pinsky sits bolt upright in his seat, he turns to Klein, and he's very upset. Oh my god, he says, something terrible has happened, we've got to get back to the office right away."

Hayes looked blank behind his smile, probably wondering if he would have to delay his next appointment, and Feldman laughed nervously, sensing that Hayes wasn't with the spirit of the thing. But Glasser was locked on course, his voice booming, filling the enormous conference room with the rest of his joke.

"What is it? asks Klein, jumping out of his seat. Tell me what's wrong. Near tears, wringing his hands, Pinsky confesses the truth—I just remembered I was in such a rush I left the door to the safe wide open. Is that it? asks Klein, and instead of running for the exit he settles back in his seat and takes a bite of his hot dog, completely unconcerned. So the safe is open, he says, so what? We're both here."

Glasser started to laugh, and Feldman joined him, a look of relief in his eyes now that it was over. Jason smiled hard, trying to do his part too.

"Marvelous," said Hayes. Vigorous nodding of the head seemed meant to substitute for laughter. "Now let's get to work." He turned and asked Jason to wait outside in the reception area.

"But he's my right-hand man," Glasser said, looking genuinely disturbed at the idea.

"We've got some serious stuff to talk about, Lou."

"It's okay," said Glasser. "We have no secrets."

This was true, in a sense. Law was the family business, and as a little boy Jason had gone with his father to court and had sat on his lap while he talked to clients. He had learned the language of lawyers and drug dealers and had heard all about the mechanics of crime. But it had always been like a movie or a comic book to him back then—exciting but safe—and now he wondered whether he had ever really understood any of it.

They sat down at one end of the table, Hayes at the head, Jason next to his father, Feldman across from them. "Gentlemen, are we ready?" Hayes began asking questions about Brian, the sort that were sure to come up in the grand jury room: how Glasser had first met him, how their relationship had developed, how Brian had become a client. The broad outline was familiar enough—Jason had been on the scene, after all—and there was certainly nothing startling in the details, so far as he could make them out. This was a little difficult, however, as his father gave long elliptical answers, full of jokes and unrelated anecdotes, a grab bag of whatever came to mind. Feldman cut in sometimes, meaning to add or clarify, but his interjections became rambling. Hayes sat very straight, taking notes on a yellow legal pad—fewer and fewer as time went on.

"Thirty years in the practice of law," said Glasser. "Never any problems. A spotless reputation. We can get letters."

"Letters?" asked Hayes, looking dubious.

"From judges. Or an assemblyman. Jerry's active in the Mott Street Democratic Club."

Hayes glanced at his watch. "It's a little early for something like that. We're just worried about the grand jury now, since you insist on going through with it." It sounded like Hayes didn't like the idea either.

"This woman, Freeburg, is some kind of nut. She's delusional."

"Definitely," said Feldman, nodding vigorously. "Out of her mind."

It was not a great performance—and that's what it seemed like, a performance, with Hayes as audience and critic. Jason could see that the partners were trying to convince Hayes of things, and the harder they worked at it, the more skeptical he became.

"What about fees?" Hayes asked, checking his watch again. "They'll be interested in the money."

"Sure, we got paid," Glasser said, indignant. "What about it? Are we supposed to work for free now?"

"Do we have a problem with undeclared cash?"

Glasser shrugged. "Who gives the tax man more than he has to?"

"What about checks? Did Brianson ever pay by check? Did he sign himself Brianson?"

"We never knew anything about an alias, if that's what you mean."

"But you remember this other client they're talking about?" asked Hayes. "This Randy Schotts?"

"Corman, it's more than seventeen years ago. The court record says I represented him, so I must have, but I can't remember that far back. I had him on exactly two cases, and the first was a minor marijuana charge, the kind of thing I got five hundred bucks for back then. The second one, he jumped bail halfway through, and I never saw him again. There was never any reason to remember him."

"So you had no suspicion that Brian Brianson, when he first appeared in your office, was actually this same Randy Schotts?"

Jason stiffened in his chair, finally getting the point: Brian was not really Brian, he was someone else, and this someone else had merely called himself Brian. A fake name. A fake.

Glasser seemed pained by the question. "Of course I had no suspicion. It was years later, and I was running a very busy practice by then. I *still* can't believe it."

"That's the thing, she won't listen to reason," said Feldman, referring to Freeburg. "She gets her government salary every week, paid by the taxpayers, and she has no idea of the pressures we work under in private practice."

"Ask Jason," said Glasser, turning to his son. "He was there, he used to come to the office all the time. Jason, have you ever heard of a guy by the name of Randy Schotts?"

"No," said Jason, unhappy to be pulled into the show. He was beginning to get the sick, dizzy feeling of someone who has been spun around too much.

"Did you know that Brian Brianson was an alias?"

"No."

"Neither did I," said Glasser, a look of vindication on his face.

Jason glanced over at Hayes and saw that his eyes had glazed over. He watched as the lawyer put down his pencil and leaned back in his chair, even as the partners talked on and on, too swept up to notice the loss of their audience. Hayes made an elaborate show of looking at his watch, and when that had no effect he just stood up. "Gentlemen," he said. "I'm afraid I've got another appointment. We'll have to continue later."

"So how's it look?" Glasser gazed up with an expression full of worry and trust, as if Hayes were a judge in black robes, there to decide his case—and not the lawyer he'd hired, at four hundred dollars an hour, to listen to his jokes.

"Fine so far." Hayes moved toward the door.

"With you on our side we'll be okay," said Feldman, smiling ferociously. "We can't lose."

Out on the street, it had turned bright and cold. They stood together against the granite face of the building, uncertain what to do next, afraid to step into the rush of pedestrian traffic. "Fine lawyer," said Glasser, looking a little giddy with relief now that the meeting was over. "Harvard puts out a good product."

"Sharp," said Feldman. "Very sharp."

Jason refrained from comment. The news about Brian had left him feeling disoriented and vaguely stupid—a dupe of some kind. And that made him angry. "Christ, why didn't you tell me?" he asked his father.

"About Brian? I thought I had."

"When did *you* find out?"

"When *they* told me." His father managed a smile, full of counterfeit confidence. "You see now, there's nothing to worry about, everything's under control."

But Jason could tell this was just the beginning.

9

THE FACTS

On the day of his testimony Glasser waited in the hallway outside the grand jury room. It was a long hallway that led to half a dozen different courtrooms, and he had walked it thousands of times over the years—as a lawyer, not a client. They all stood there, leaning against the filthy brown walls like kids pulled out of class and told to wait for the principal: Esther, Hayes, Glasser, and Feldman. They shuffled their feet, whispered, coughed, the atmosphere hushed, as if they'd been commanded to silence. Glasser and Feldman stood next to each other, whispering in short, jagged bits—not quite a conversation, but an intermittent volley of random thoughts, non sequiturs.

"They could sweep the halls," noted Glasser.

"The whole country's falling apart," said Feldman, who would be testifying right after his partner. "It's past saving."

Each glanced at the other only long enough to conclude that he looked sick with fright, then fixed his eyes elsewhere. Their need for each other was overwhelming, yet neither of them could address this fact directly. As a result they were overcome with shyness and a sentimental gratitude for each other's presence that brought them both to the edge of tears.

"You'll be fine," said Feldman.

"I know it." Emotion-choked, Glasser's voice came out like the squawk of a bird.

Feldman kept his eyes focused on the floor. "Just stick to the facts. Tell it straight."

"The truth," said Glasser. "We'll be okay."

Feldman nodded, his round face glistening with nervous sweat. "That's all you need to do."

Esther was at Glasser's other side, her eyes large and flat as silver dollars. Shrunken with misery, she stood lopsided in high-heeled boots, her thick, powdery makeup unable to hide the deep circles under her eyes, even in the dim light of the courthouse. Hayes had told her to dress simply. "Plain, dull, honest, no jewelry," he'd said. "Humble like a pilgrim."

She had meant to follow his instructions, but before she knew it her nerves had led her the other way: fur coat and a towering fur hat, large earrings, necklaces and rings, a gold chain belt, a pocketbook the size of a small suitcase that she kept putting down and picking up, switching from shoulder to shoulder. A middle-aged woman in animal skins and gold: it was the finery of a primitive, a tribeswoman from the Central Asian steppes, meant to frighten and intimidate; but it left her looking overwhelmed and choked, fragile to the point of breaking.

Hayes was clearly annoyed. "You look lovely today, Esther. All that marvelous fur."

Too far gone to catch the sarcasm, she peered up at him from beneath her big hat with a terrified gaze. "Why isn't it starting?"

"You know the courts. The wheels of justice are slow." He gave a thin, debonair smile. "Especially after lunch."

"I wish it would start already."

"It will."

And then it did. There was a commotion, people passing in and out, the heavy padded doors swinging. The bailiff stuck his head into the hall, looked briefly at Glasser, spoke to Hayes. Glasser winced: he recognized the officer's red, paunchy face, knew the man remembered him too.

"Keep to the facts," said Feldman, staring doggedly at the ground, his eyes red and swollen. "You can't go wrong."

"Take a deep breath," said Hayes. "I'll be here if you have any questions." He was required to wait in the hall; Glasser would be on his own inside the grand jury room.

But their voices were already a distant echo in Glasser's ears. Everything was a jumble now, a mix of thought and bodily sensation. There was the pressure of the door against his shoulder as he entered the grand jury room, and the brighter light of that room filling his eyes. And there was the sound of his own breathing, the crash of his heart against the walls of his chest. Looking back, he caught a last glimpse of Esther in the hallway before the door swung closed: beautiful, frightened Esther, absurd in her bulky furs. The expression on her face was terrible, as if she were watching a car crash from the curb.

Light-headed, wobbly, Glasser looked around but saw little: dirty, peeling walls, rows of wooden tables littered with open boxes of doughnuts and coffee containers—the kind of room in which he had spent years of his life, happily negotiating the misery of others. Up ahead, a pair of figures huddled over some documents, whispering, coughing. He recognized one of them as Freeburg and glanced away. The court stenographer busied herself adjusting the tripod of her stenographic machine. It was all so familiar, the atmosphere of bureaucratic ritual, boredom, and impatience, the hurry-up-and-wait of the justice system. Yet it was utterly changed now too, a sinister fever dream. He looked at the members of the grand jury, the ones who would decide his fate. They sat at the tables facing forward, an amalgam of people as random as you'd find in a subway car—but all with a weary, coffee-tense look, their eyes on Glasser as he passed.

He knew what they saw: a fat man in a cashmere coat; a fat man bathed in sweat, so frightened he could barely walk. He knew they watched as he stopped to remove the coat, an endless task he performed in self-conscious slow motion, unable to maneuver his bloated body. He had eaten himself so big in the last month, his roomiest suit was skintight, the jacket impossible to button. Dressing him at home, Esther had been forced to close his pants with a safety pin.

The court officer swore him in by the witness stand, slurring as they always did; Glasser had heard the same elided phrases ten thousand times, but now the words crumbled to their constituent syllables. He answered "I do," no longer sure what promise this entailed or what sorrow it would bring him. His mouth was chalky.

The questions began. Freeburg stood before him, crisply professional in a blue suit, a yellow legal pad in her hands. She began to walk him through the preliminaries, building her case from the bottom up. In a grand jury hearing, the jurors can ask questions of the witness directly, but the prosecutor remains the dominant presence, controlling the direction in which things move. "Mr. Glasser, you are an attorney?"

"Yes."

This was only their second meeting in person. She was smaller than he remembered, fine-boned, almost delicate. He felt not anger but a deep desire to persuade, to be liked, to be known. To tell everything, all of it, the good and the bad.

"Do you know the name Randy Schotts?"

"Yes."

He shifted in his seat. Yes, he knew the name; there was no harm in admitting that. But he realized now that he did not ever know the person behind it: the runaway, the street urchin, the angry young man so disgusted with his own eagerness to please. Glasser had been attracted to something in him—a combination of sorrow and ambition, perhaps, or simple loneliness. But he had not wanted to *know* him. He hadn't the time.

"Was he ever a client of yours?"

"Yes."

Freeburg continued with a series of questions mapping the history of Glasser's professional relationship with Schotts. She stood rigidly still, flipping pages on her yellow pad, a slight hunch to her shoulders. Glasser had no choice but to follow her lead, a prisoner of the ritual. The way she asked her questions determined the form of his answers: yes or no, a few dry words at most. Frustrated, he had to swallow his urge to equivocate, to backtrack. He tried to provide details when he could—dates, the names of judges—but the effort was unnecessary. Well prepared, she clearly had them all in her notes.

"You don't remember this particular court date?" Her face was a professional blank, frightening in its chilly neutrality.

"It's over seventeen years ago." He tried to keep the shake out of his voice. His memory had become atrocious. He was just fifty-nine, but his mind was already an old man's jumble of bric-a-brac, a collection of empty drawers and locked cabinets.

"That's all right," said Freeburg. "I have the date right here."

"Thank you." He wiped the sweat from his eyes with a finger, listening as a whole period of his life was reduced to a few names and dates. Try as he might to remain focused, his mind wandered, hungry for escape from this dilapidated courtroom, this relentless woman and her questions, her catalog of facts. He watched the stenographer's fingers at work on their cramped keyboard, recording his every tentative utterance, fixing it forever on paper in stark black-and-white.

Freeburg flipped a page on her pad. "Now Mr. Glasser, I'd like to draw your attention to a meeting you had with Mr. Schotts in June of nineteen seventy. June fifteenth, around two in the morning, at the Spartacus Coffee Shop on Third Avenue. Do you recall this particular meeting?"

He twisted in his seat, embarrassed to come up blank again. "I'm not sure."

"You're not sure if you recall?"

He tried to smile, but it felt as if his face were cracking. "I'm not sure which meeting you're referring to."

She glanced over at the jury, allowing herself a momentary smirk of complicity. Glasser saw it, the message to those earnest, tired faces at the tables: trust me, the good stuff is coming. She was gaining confidence, loosening up. "Let me refresh your memory. Mr. Schotts was out on bail at the time, awaiting trial. He called you some time near one A.M., saying he had to meet with you, and you met him in the coffee shop, where he advised you of his decision to jump bail and become a fugitive. Does this help your recollection?"

"Yes, I remember now."

Glasser felt a flutter of panicky grief, because the story of that meeting could only have come from Brian himself. Months ago, the dealer had assured him that he would not cooperate with the Feds against Glasser, and Glasser had chosen to believe him, though it flew in the face of everything he'd learned in thirty years as a criminal lawyer. Now he saw just how deluded he had been.

"Do you remember him telling you that he intended to jump bail?" asked Freeburg.

"Yes."

"Mr. Glasser, is it true that you advised Mr. Schotts to pay his bail bondsman? That if he didn't pay him the bail bondsman would come looking for him? And that this would be a bigger problem for him than the police?"

Glasser hesitated, looking not at Freeburg standing before him but at the white doughy fingers of the stenographer, poised to record his answer. Yes, he remembered this piece of advice. Advice offered in pity, from an insomniac lawyer to a teenage runaway, given at two in the morning in the melancholy shelter of an all-night coffee shop. He had meant only to give the kid a fighting chance, and to protect the bail bondsman from a big loss—Manny Lopez, a good-hearted man he had done business with for years. But out of context, Freeburg would misconstrue it as help in evading the law—aiding and abetting a fugitive. "First I advised him as to the seriousness of his intentions. I advised him against jumping bail."

"But once he made his decision clear, did you tell him to pay his bail bondsman?"

Afraid to look into Freeburg's face, Glasser watched the stenographer's fingers tapping on their keys. "I reminded him that he had an obligation. I didn't want the bail bondsman to lose his money."

Keep to the facts. Tell it straight. Outside in the hall, Feldman had insisted on the facts, the facts, the facts—as if they were a collection of magic words, a spell to ward off evil. Truth would be the bedrock they stood on, the armor they wore, the shield nobody could break. But the facts shimmered and blinked, shifting like lights in the fog. And what was truth? Truth was an atmosphere, a glance, a certain way of sipping coffee, a moment of pity in an all-night diner. Truth was the way all those facts felt when you lived them, so different from when you recited them again seventeen years later in a dingy courtroom. Feldman was wrong: there was no straight way to tell the story. The words themselves twisted and snaked as they left your mouth. If you were really honest, you could offer only your uncertainty, your fear.

But do that and they would pounce on you. Glasser tried to explain himself instead. "A bail jumper ruins it for everyone. If

Schotts didn't pay, it would've been hard for my other clients to get a bondsman later."

"Did you know that Schotts paid before fleeing?"

"Manny Lopez—the bail bondsman—told me. But I never spoke to Schotts after that."

Freeburg did not stop to gloat; flipping pages, she moved quickly to 1975 and Glasser's first meeting with Brian Brianson, the new Randy Schotts. Question followed question in rapid succession, Freeburg trying to take advantage of her momentum to push Glasser off balance. "Mr. Glasser, when did you first realize that Brian Brianson was in fact Randy Schotts?"

"Never." Glasser tried to be as emphatic as possible, given the dreamy syrup of exhaustion through which his thoughts now moved. "I had no reason to believe that the two were related in any way."

One of the jurors interjected. "You had seen Schotts what, five years before?" He was an elderly man with unkempt white hair and piercing eyes, a Styrofoam cup of coffee smoking between his wrinkled hands.

"Yes."

"But you didn't recognize him?"

Glasser turned in his chair, remembering that it was better to make eye contact. "No, I didn't recognize him. He was just a boy when he jumped bail. They change fast."

A middle-aged woman seated at the other side of the room spoke up. She had a pointed, hawklike face and an elaborately ruffled blouse. "Nothing alerted you to the possibility that the name Brianson might have been an alias?"

Glasser turned in his seat to face her. "I had a very busy practice back then. Hundreds of people passed through my office every month." He decided to try a little charm. "I'm ashamed to say it, but conditions in the office were chaotic, a mess. I was so busy, sometimes I couldn't remember my own name."

That was true enough: crisis after crisis, a hundred things going wrong, always in debt, borrowing more, late for court, the lights on the phone blinking. He had not given Randy's reappearance the importance he should have; he had assumed it was enough that neither of them said anything outright, that his suspicions were never directly confirmed. And then he had simply stopped thinking about it.

Freeburg stood silently as the jurors followed up on her line of questioning, and when they were done she picked up where she had left off. "Did you draft a commercial lease for Schotts, under his alias of Brian Brianson?" She looked down to read from her notes. "I'm referring to a lease for a store on MacDougal Street, between the One thirty-six MacDougal Street Corporation and Monique Boutique, Incorporated, dated February second, nineteen seventy-five."

Brian's store. Glasser knew the seriousness of this: helping a fugitive from justice conduct business—even legitimate business—under a false name. To do so knowingly would be a felony. "One of my paralegals did the work on that. But it wasn't for Schotts. We knew our client only as Brian Brianson."

How could he begin to make her understand the truth? Tell a real-life story and there were a hundred stories beneath it. Before he could explain about Randy Schotts he would have to tell her about winter mornings on the Lower East Side, after his father's funeral: getting out of bed and walking across the floor in his bare feet, his soles burning with the cold as if it were fire. He would need to show her the way ice looked on the windowpane—glistening crystalline structures like the leaves of a tree, blue in the morning light. And the bubbles and whorls in those imperfect panes of glass too. He would have to make her see every minute of every day of his life, because without the smallest details nothing made sense.

It wasn't possible, of course. Question followed question for what seemed like hours, but they got no closer to what Glasser could recognize as the truth. Names, dates, numbers, money, cases—the length of his relationship with Brianson. He answered mechanically till Freeburg and the jurors ran out of things to ask. She said, "Do you have anything you wish to add, Mr. Glasser?"

"Add?" He wanted to tell her she was making a lot of noise about nothing, that these were ordinary events in the world of criminal law. He wanted to tell her that real life required compromises, and only a prig or a hypocrite would ruin a man for what everybody else was doing anyway. "Yes, I have a statement."

He reached into his pocket for the statement he had prepared the day before with Hayes and Feldman. The sheets of paper shook slightly in his hands, but he read in a modest, well-practiced voice, a smooth recounting of events from his point of view, polished clean of both anger and uncertainty, full of cautious, lawyerly phrases like "At that time" and "To the best of my knowledge." And after a few minutes he just stopped listening to himself. The flow of names and dates sounded so similar to Freeburg's—equally irrelevant.

There were no questions afterward, and the examination ended politely enough. Freeburg thanked him for his time and then quickly turned toward the prosecution table, where her files sat. It was over for her, a piece of work well done. But Glasser continued to sit in the witness chair, stunned into immobility, his hands on his knees, trembling. It was just beginning for him, he realized, and it would never be over, never. Unsure whether he had the strength to get up, Glasser stared at the jurors, wide-eyed and frightened by his own helplessness, like an infant stranded in his high chair. What were these people to him? What did they know about him? Yet he wanted them to love him, in his weakness, and this desire kept him bound to the chair.

Freeburg looked up from the file she had opened, her face flat and emotionless. "That's all, Mr. Glasser. You may step down now."

In the hallway Glasser found the others where he had left them, standing by the door. "How did it go?" asked Feldman, searching Glasser's face.

Glasser tried to smile but couldn't. He had never been so tired before, wanted only to sit down before his legs gave out. Esther gave him her arm, and he gripped the wonderful, plush fur of her sleeve for support. "Okay, I guess."

"The next round is up to you," said Hayes, turning to Feldman, putting one of his big, immaculate hands on Feldman's shoulder.

Feldman nodded grimly. Barely suppressed terror had turned his face into a mask—everything but the eyes, which looked at Glasser sadly, with longing, as if the separation might be permanent. "I think I might piss myself." He managed a horrendous, death's head smile, and the effect was oddly brave.

"Just stick to the facts," said Glasser, his voice quiet. "It worked for me."

"Give me a second, I'll make a few up." He took his inhaler out of his coat pocket and put it to his mouth, breathed in deeply as the device made its hissing noise. When he spoke again his voice was tight. "Okay, it's now or never."

After Feldman disappeared through the padded doors, Glasser and Esther left Hayes for a bench down the hall. They sat without speaking, Glasser sunk deep in a kind of temporary senility, gripping Esther's arm like a favorite toy. Thoughts came and went; watching them was like watching drifting clouds, strange evocative shapes, curious but miles distant. He thought of the years he had spent walking through the halls of the criminal court building, rushing from courtroom to courtroom, always late, always a client in tow—sometimes a string of them. He had moved through the halls as if he owned them, in love with the hustle, untouched by the filth and misery they housed. It had been fun, really, to be king among the junkies and pushers and pimps and thugs, the heavyset women in stretch pants come to find their incarcerated husbands, infants in their arms and children running about their feet, wild and dirty as a pack of dogs.

For thirty years he had watched the criminal justice system at work. He had seen judges in the old Bronx Courthouse presiding from behind Plexiglas screens like the subway clerk in a token booth, afraid of bricks and bottles lobbed from the benches. He had seen defendants sitting a year or more in Rikers because they couldn't afford five hundred dollars' bail, and convicts transferred from prison to prison until they were completely lost in the computers, untraceable. And what about the daily irrationality of plea bargaining? The D.A. offered you attempted murder, you held out for grievous bodily harm, and the two of you compromised at assault with a deadly weapon. As long as you played by the unwritten rules everybody benefited: your client got five years instead of ten, the D.A. got his conviction, the judge cleared the case from his calendar, all without the time and expense of a trial. It was a game, a big complicated game, and the defendants were nothing but chips to be wagered and traded.

Which was fine as long as Glasser was a player, safe inside his protective booth. He had never thought it possible he would end up a chip.

"So," said Esther, her tone measured and careful, "it was a success."

Glasser emerged from his reverie. "It went okay."

"Just okay." She nodded, considering the meaning of the words. "How okay?"

"The most humiliating experience of my life."

But their conversation was cut short by a commotion at the other end of the hall. Turning to look, Glasser saw an ambulance team, two men rolling a stretcher from the elevator, a third carrying equipment of some kind, all of it clattering as they race-walked toward the grand jury room. The court officer was holding the padded doors open for them, and Hayes stood off to the side, looking patrician and useless, a disgruntled expression on his face.

"Oh, my god," said Esther.

"It's Jerry," said Glasser, trying to rise. A man of Feldman's over-generous proportions, his sensitive nerves and fatty appetites, not to mention that inhaler he was always sucking on—Glasser assumed it could only be a heart attack. Poor Feldman, devoted to his elderly parents in Flatbush, taking them to bingo on Thursday nights; a cunning lawyer but with a child's sense of cunning, so eager to please that fear of a scolding might actually have killed him. Ten years before, Glasser had gone partners with the younger man because he couldn't stand the pressure of single practice anymore. Instead, they had egged each other on, juggling cases and court dates, vying to devise the most outlandish, reckless defenses, eating two dinners a night. They compared their indigestion and insomnia and bowel troubles, the scaly white patches of psoriasis that bloomed on their elbows and knuckles as the tension mounted.

And now this had happened. Glasser heaved himself up with Esther's help, and the two of them headed toward Hayes, who stood waiting for them outside the padded doors. "Something with his breathing," he told them.

"A heart attack," said Esther.

"I don't think so. He was sucking on that thing, that device he uses—"

"The inhaler," said Glasser. "He has asthma."

"I think he got a little upset on the stand." Hayes seemed genuinely shaken, but he spoke with an air of disapproval, running a hand over his limp yellow hair, as if to make the argument for self-control.

Yes, thought Glasser, too much emotion, too unruly to be contained. And then there was Feldman's love of high drama; in his own nervous way he had a real feeling for the grand gesture, could not resist it. And maybe he was right. If they are bombarding you with questions you can't answer, suffocating you, why not let them know it?

Ten minutes later, Glasser was crouched over his stricken law partner, holding Feldman's hand as he lay strapped in the stretcher. A small crowd had formed around them—Esther and Hayes, the ambulance crew, four or five court officers—but it kept a respectful distance, eyes focused on the two men. It was their show. "How are you feeling?" asked Glasser softly. "Are you comfortable?"

Feldman could only nod and roll his eyes; a clear plastic oxygen mask covered his mouth. He had been magnificent; a passionate opera fan, he had played his scene to the hilt, like a preening tenor, reducing everyone else in the room to a supporting role. Even Freeburg had been silenced, relegated to holding Feldman's discarded suit jacket. But now he was tired. The paramedics had given him an injection of adrenaline and the attack was subsiding; jacket and tie gone, shirt unbuttoned, he lay waiting for the elevator to take him down to the ambulance.

And yet it was not merely theater; as with all good performers, the emotion was real. Glasser could see the fright in his partner's eyes—real terror, naked and childlike. The elevator doors opened and Glasser followed alongside the stretcher, still holding Feldman's hand. "It's all over," he kept saying. "It's all over."

It wasn't, of course; Feldman's testimony would be rescheduled, and the questions would be no easier to answer the second time around. The whole episode had been pointless. Only, Glasser found himself strangely jealous too. His law partner had found something to *do* with his fear: he could at least choke on it.

Glasser and Esther accompanied Feldman to the hospital, and after his discharge a few hours later, they saw him home. He was tired and subdued, gripping his inhaler in his hand as the three of them bounced together in the back of the cab. "Well, I fucked up big-time." His voice was barely above a whisper.

"Don't even think about it," said Esther, seated in the middle, her fur hat squashed up against the low ceiling of the car. "You get into bed and take the medicine the doctor gave you."

Feldman nodded. He was a devotee of medicines of all kind, a passionate self-medicator; there was no chance he would forget.

"It'll be over soon," said Glasser, trying to reassure him. "Then life goes back to normal."

"I hope so." Feldman held the inhaler to his chest, turning to stare out the window.

Glasser did the same. It had rained briefly while they were in the hospital, and the streets had the glistening, patent-leather look that New York gets at night, elegant and expensive. At one time, the sight had made him frantic with longing. The city had challenged him to step beyond himself, to merge, to be the kind of man it needed, somebody equal to its beauty. *Buy me,* it had whispered. *Buy me.* And he had wanted to, knowing full well that it was impossible, that it would take all the money in the world.

10

A LAWYER'S NIGHTMARE

A week later, Glasser was indicted. The document arrived at Hayes's office, and the two partners went over to Sedgewick & Ashberry to read it. Flipping the pages of his copy, Glasser felt the air rush out of him and the room begin to spin. It was all there, in heavy bold letters: conspiracy, importation, sale, money laundering, tax evasion, aiding and abetting a fugitive.

Wild-eyed, Feldman tried to talk it all away. "It's meaningless, Lou, a classic example of overindictment." He meant the practice by which prosecutors pile on unsubstantiated charges to intimidate a defendant into cooperation or plea bargaining.

Glasser wasn't listening, however. "Why?" he sputtered. "Why is she doing this to me?"

"I've scheduled the arraignment for tomorrow," said Hayes, coming from around his desk. "I think it's healthier to get it over with." He wore a look of professional empathy, but he was clearly eager to avoid one of the partners' melodramatic scenes.

Standing now, Glasser gripped Feldman's arm for support. "Not guilty," he said, indicating the plea he would enter the next day in court. His head shook, and his voice was clotted with passion. "Not guilty!"

"Will he need to post bail?" asked Feldman.

Hayes shook his head. "They'll let him out on his own recognizance, I'm sure of it."

The next day, at his arraignment, Glasser looked around as if he'd never seen a courtroom before. Towering ceilings and great arched windows, heavy wooden pews and dim brown light—the place was like an old-time railroad station. It had that same feeling too, of the communal and impersonal, of transience and wrenching departure. A sad place: Glasser had never realized how sad. In front, the magistrate's upper half seemed to rise directly from the polished wooden platform called the judge's bench—a torso without legs, like a bust on a pedestal. The magistrate leafed through documents, took notes on a pad, used a finger to push up his glasses, but the specific features of his face were lost above the severe ecclesiastical blackness of his robe.

Glasser stood beside Hayes as Hayes gave the not-guilty plea. Normally, the positions would have been reversed, Glasser doing the talking on behalf of a client, his appointment book in one hand so that he could jot down the dates for motions. But his hands were empty now, dangling at his sides. He could hear the low buzz of spectators coming from the benches behind him—lawyers whispering, families talking among themselves. He could feel their eyes resting idly on his back. They were here for their own cases, but they had to wait for him to finish, and so they watched with desultory interest, like people staring at the TV in a bar, marking time.

Freeburg stepped forward. She looked much as she had at the grand jury hearing—blue suit, white blouse, legal pad in one hand, blankly, almost grimly professional. It didn't sit well with her youth. In the fifties, when Glasser had started out, criminal law was still the province of night-school graduates. There had been lots of Petruccios back then, little guys who routinely matched pastel shirt, tie, and pocket square, who didn't, in fact, dress much differently from their clients. This wasn't surprising, since they had grown up on the same streets, played on the same baseball teams. Their style was irreverent and they were ready to improvise. They could put an arm around the other lawyer and hammer out a solution in the hall.

But that was the past. The new breed of criminal lawyers were much the same as their corporate brethren—staid, careful about the rules. Freeburg, Glasser had learned recently, was a graduate of Yale Law.

"Your Honor," said Freeburg, gazing down at her notes. "On the matter of bail, we ask that bond be set at five hundred thousand dollars."

Glasser gave out a little exhalation of surprise. He glanced at Hayes, who arched his eyebrows.

"Your Honor," said Hayes, "my client is a prominent member of the defense bar of this city. There's absolutely no risk of flight."

But Freeburg clearly meant business. "The indictment contains extremely serious charges, Your Honor. The defendant possesses a current United States passport, and we have reason to suspect substantial hidden assets overseas. Taken together, these factors make him a fugitive risk, and we feel bail is warranted to ensure his appearance at subsequent court dates."

Glasser couldn't suppress a grimace of pain. After spending the past six months destroying his legal practice she must have known he had nothing left, nothing to sell or mortgage. With bail like that, he'd have to sit in MCC for a year, waiting for trial. And what was the point of that? It was vindictive and cruel, and he could think of only one rationale: Freeburg was trying to change his mind about turning down the immunity deal.

Hayes looked perturbed. "Mr. Glasser is fifty-nine years old and a lifetime resident of this city. That statement about hidden assets is completely untrue, and the U.S. Attorney's Office is offering no proof whatsoever."

"Your Honor, tracing foreign assets takes considerable time."

"In point of fact, Mr. Glasser has been made destitute by legal bills and the loss of his legal practice. He is heavily in debt."

"All the more reason to flee, Your Honor."

It went on like this, the arguments circling around Glasser's head. Did Freeburg really think he had Swiss bank accounts, a secret stash in the Cayman Islands? Or was it just a story cooked up to sway the magistrate? Was she a naive, deluded crusader, a zealot? Or a cynical old pro who thought a taste of jail would make him cooperate? He couldn't decide which it was. She could be either or perhaps both, and all he knew was that he wanted to strangle her—that or get on his knees and beg for mercy, because it was clear that Hayes's patrician dignity was no match for her.

"Your Honor, this is absurd—" said Hayes.

But Freeburg didn't budge. "The defendant represents a continuing danger to the community, Your Honor."

In the end, the magistrate grew visibly bored, cleaning his glasses on the sleeve of his robe. He struck a compromise, letting Glasser sign a PRB, a Personal Recognizance Bond, for three hundred thousand. The PRB was essentially an IOU, and it would be forfeit if Glasser missed a court appearance. But it didn't require any collateral, and so it was perfect for a man who was in fact broke. Afterward, signing the paperwork in the clerk's office, Glasser got a small bit of satisfaction from this point, that the bond was essentially meaningless. If he skipped town the Feds could search his sock drawer for any spare change they might find.

Hayes gathered up his briefcase. "Listen, Lou, I've got an appointment back at the office. Can you do the rest by yourself?" He meant the processing in the U.S. Marshal's Office downstairs.

Glasser nodded. Hayes knew he was broke and was giving him second-class service—the surprising thing was how lonely this made him feel. "I know where it is."

Still, his legs felt weak as he walked down the marble stairway. He sat in the marshal's office for over an hour until he was taken in back, where he was fingerprinted and then photographed, front and profile. For the photos he stood in front of a big Polaroid on a tripod, the kind used to take passport and I.D. shots. Everything felt strangely ordinary, except for the rectangular board they made him hold to his chest. It had U.S. MARSHAL'S OFFICE printed on it, followed by a long line of digits—his arrest number.

Afterward, not wanting to go home, Glasser went back to the office. As he strode through the door, Rainbow looked up from the book in her lap. Since there was no work to do, she spent her days reading Hermann Hesse novels in paperback. "How did it go?" she asked.

He waved away the question with his ink-stained fingers and headed into his private office. He wanted only to be alone, to sit at his desk and eat a stupefying, thought-obliterating lunch: two cheeseburgers, a Reuben sandwich, a chocolate shake, a solid wedge of Black Forest cake, french fries and coleslaw and macaroons. He was dialing the deli downstairs when Feldman came in, a look of sheepish concern on his face.

"Lou, is everything okay?"

Glasser put down the phone. "Freeburg tried to get bail set at half a million. I'm lucky I'm not sitting in MCC right now."

"The bitch." Feldman seated himself on the couch and shook his head. "I don't know why, but she's got a real hard-on for you." It was a common phrase around the courts, and he used it without irony. For whatever reason—misplaced zeal or excessive malice—this prosecutor wanted Glasser.

"Hayes asked for another hundred thousand."

"Well, we expected that."

Glasser began to massage his temples. "How am I going to pay him?"

There was a long, empty silence, the two men staring off in separate directions, and then Feldman sat forward, dropping his voice. "Lou, I know it's a bad time, but we've got to do something about Rainbow."

"Rainbow?" But of course Glasser knew what he meant. Rainbow hadn't gotten a check in four weeks, a fact that pained him whenever he stole a glance at her somber face—so much so that he had lately taken to sneaking by her on the way to his office, eyes fixed on the carpet. For the last few months she had tried to cheer up the partners, chattering about anything that came to mind— movies, the winning lottery number. The act had been a strain on all three of them, and she had been forced to give it up. Now she slumped flat-footed in her swivel chair, all attempt at pretense gone. She looked like she was sitting shivah, waiting with a mixture of sadness and boredom for the prescribed period of mourning to end.

"It's the only decent thing," said Feldman, whispering. "We can't even pay her anymore."

"She's been with me over fifteen years."

"We owe her four weeks already," said Feldman. "It's not fair to her."

"We'll get the money," Glasser said, but his tone of voice acknowledged otherwise.

Feldman took a deep breath. "I'll take care of it." And so he did, shifting from foot to foot in the hall as he told her the bad news, with Glasser hovering in his doorway, watching. "So you see maybe later, when this thing's cleared up and the office is back to normal—"

Rainbow seemed neither hurt nor surprised by what she was hearing. "Will you be all right without a secretary?"

"There isn't much to do," said Feldman, clearly grateful that she wasn't making it harder on him.

"And will you be okay?" She looked at Glasser with real concern in her eyes.

"I'm sorry," he said, finding it easier to apologize than face the question. "I wish there were some way I could—"

"We'll be fine," said Feldman.

Rainbow stared at an empty spot between the two men, a look of concentration on her face as if listening to complicated instructions. From where he stood, Glasser noted the two long furrows on her forehead, the way they deepened when she was thinking about something. It was a familiar expression, and it saddened him to see it, so much so that he had to fight the impulse to shut himself in his office once more. They had grown old together, their lives entwined for the last sixteen years. He had watched her change from a twenty-five-year-old druggie to a middle-aged woman with a careful, measured walk, and in the process he had come to know her face, her gestures, as intimately as he knew Esther's or his own. Yet he knew almost nothing about Rainbow's life outside the office— how she spent her weekends, whether she had money in the bank— and only now did the true fragility of their connection become clear to him. Tomorrow she would be gone.

After his arraignment, Glasser started coming into the office less and less frequently. There was just no point. When he did come in, he spent hours playing solitaire or leafing through the old magazines piled in the waiting room, spent whole days staring out his window. He and Feldman wandered the empty suite of five offices like addled brothers in a forgotten mansion—calling to each other from different rooms, occasionally crossing paths, but keeping their distance. They had become wary of each other, pained and embarrassed by the disaster they shared, each tired of seeing his panic mirrored in his partner's blanched features. Yet they could not really part either. Down the long corridor they batted ideas back and forth like tennis balls—fragments of hope, fantasies, absurd schemes and wishful thinking.

And then one day Feldman came rushing into Glasser's office, clearly excited. "I've just been on the phone with Ray O'Donnel. Guess who Brianson's new lawyer is?"

"Who?" This was painful news for Glasser: his biggest client, now represented by somebody else.

Feldman's eyes glittered strangely. "Petruccio."

"Petruccio? That's impossible." Brianson was way out of his league.

"Apparently not," said Feldman, pulling Petruccio's card from the Rolodex. "Here, call him, set up a meeting. He can help us with Brianson, at least give us some idea what's going on."

"That's privileged information, Jerry."

"He'll do it, he owes us big time."

"I don't think it's a good idea." Glasser wanted to say something more, but Feldman was already punching in the number, and in a moment Rocco's voice was coming over the line.

"Louis Glasser, how are you, you old bastard? Long time no see." Petruccio's voice was complicated: sarcastic and gloating, a little nervous beneath the mock friendly tone. But Glasser thought he detected something else too, a hint of melancholy or guilt, a streak of real sympathy.

His own voice, when he answered, was hard to control. "Fine, Rocco, fine."

"Lou, I'm just on my way out."

Glasser felt himself wince. It didn't help that Petruccio sounded halfhearted about giving him the brush-off. He could imagine Rocco on the other end, his clear blue eyes with their nervous, sarcastic squint, a baby-blue Nat Sherman still unlit between his childlike fingers. Glasser decided to get to the point. "I know you've heard about our problem."

"Heard what? What have I heard?" Petruccio was not very convincing, did not try to be.

"I can't talk about it over the phone, I was hoping we could get together face-to-face."

"This week is really terrible for me, Lou."

"Half an hour is all I need. Fifteen minutes."

There was silence, Petruccio clearly struggling to say no, but in the end it proved too much for him. "Okay, all right, I'll meet you at Albini's." Albini's was an Italian place frequented by civil servants from the Municipal Building and the city offices on Church Street. Criminal lawyers didn't go there.

"Albini's it is."

The appointment was for nine, but the partners were standing at the bar by eight-thirty, pensively sipping Cokes and eating peanuts. Rocco marched in at ten, a look of determined self-mastery on his face. "Can't stay long," he said, waving a twenty to get the bartender's attention. "I'm parked at a hydrant." He ordered a double scotch and drank half of it down in a gulp. It was clear he knew what Glasser was going to ask him.

"We thought maybe you'd want some dinner," said Glasser, trying to smile.

Petruccio checked his watch. "Got an appointment."

Glasser wasn't sure how to start, and not just because he wanted Petruccio to do something dirty. The truth was, he didn't like asking for something when there was a chance he might be turned down. In the old days it had always been Glasser offering assistance, spreading largesse, and that was the role he preferred. "You know we've always considered you a friend, Rocco."

"Same here," said Petruccio, without much enthusiasm. He took another slug of his drink.

"We go back what, twelve, fourteen years?"

"That long?"

Petruccio's look was surprisingly bitter, but Glasser was too wrapped up in his own internal struggle to notice. "Longer maybe. Good, productive years."

"Well, maybe it's been long enough."

Glasser gave a little laugh, like a dog's yelp. "We've referred you a ton of business, Rocco."

"I've always given you your third."

"That's not what I meant. The point is, there'll be plenty more once this problem is solved." He glanced over at Feldman for help, but his partner had a look of pained disbelief on his face.

"I haven't gotten a case from you in months, Lou."

The tone was openly sarcastic, but Glasser found himself apologizing. "We haven't had anything to send you." He had his eye on the door now, wanted only to disentangle himself and leave.

But Petruccio had begun unburdening himself, and there was no breaking away. "So maybe I'm no Clarence Darrow," he said, pulling out an orange Nat Sherman, the same color as his tie. "My clients are shoplifters and pimps and whores. So what? I drive a new Cadillac every year and my house is paid for." He lit the cigarette, letting out a long curl of smoke.

Glasser had observed him piloting these cars through the narrow alley behind the court building: heaped with chrome and massive as a pharaoh's pleasure barge, Petruccio's black toupee barely visible above the steering wheel. The sight was ridiculous but strangely regal too, and Glasser's heart had gone out to the man. The delusions of grandeur required to bring a car like that into the overcrowded streets of Chinatown every day! The sheer act of will! Even now, Glasser wanted to call out to him: Rocco, I *know* you, I've seen the inside of your heart. You know how to dream big. Rise to the occasion and help me now—dignify us both!

But he could not find the words. "Rocco, there's been some kind of misunderstanding."

"No misunderstanding, Lou. I know every inch of that court building, and I know everybody in it. I know all the judges and all the file clerks—I see them in the hall and I wave hello, I run over and tell them a dirty joke. I keep my pockets stuffed full of candy bars for the court officers. You know what that means? It means I walk in and my case gets called first, while all the big-shot lawyers are sitting around cooling their heels."

"All I wanted to ask—"

But Petruccio would not stop. "You think I like playing the clown for you, telling you jokes, running your errands, picking up your scraps? Well, get this surprise, I don't like playing the clown. For twenty-five years I've worked like a fucking mule. I'm in court almost every night at two, three in the morning bailing out the whores, their stinking titties in my face. I deserve this break, I'm ready for it."

"You mean Brianson?" asked Glasser.

"Yeah, I mean Brianson."

Glasser's voice dropped to a whisper. "We're just asking for some help. Nothing that would compromise you in any way."

"Compromise? Lou, you are under indictment. I shouldn't even be seen here with you."

"I thought we were friends."

Petruccio dropped his Nat Sherman on the floor, grinding it out with the toe of a small, delicately shod foot. "We are friends. But don't call me till this is over."

After that drink with Petruccio, Glasser stopped going into the office altogether. He spent whole days in his underwear, eating whatever was in the refrigerator, lying on his back on the living-room floor, and blowing cigarette smoke up at the ceiling. He gave up shaving, stopped combing his hair, wouldn't bathe; a grimy film spread over him like mold. At night, while Esther snored lightly in the bedroom, Glasser emptied the refrigerator of bowls, bottles, scraps, gorging till morning, when a strip of blue light in the window made it possible to stretch out on the couch for a few hours' rest. But he woke when Esther did, seven A.M., watching dizzy and bloated as she rushed to get dressed for her new job in the billing department of a large insurance company.

"You could at least make me some coffee," she snapped, checking her makeup one more time in the living-room mirror. After years as a housewife, she was struggling to retool for today's marketplace, as she kept saying, borrowing a phrase from the night course she was taking. The effort showed on her face as she went through her morning ritual, pulling at her dress, cinching her belt tighter—all in an attempt to look younger, more energetic.

Glasser curled tighter, as if the couch were a raft and he was afraid of tipping it. "I don't feel good."

"Oh," she said, taking off one heavy gold brooch and putting on another just like it. "You're impossible."

"Bring back some cigarettes," said Glasser.

She was buttoning her coat, her pocketbook slung over one shoulder. Her clothes were expensive, even elegant, but there was something vaguely martial to her appearance, like a foot soldier dressed for the battlefield—false bravado and a whiff of fear. "You've got two legs. Get your own."

"I'm out of money."

"Then you're out of luck."

She was steeling herself, practicing how to be tough, but cruelty seeped into the mixture. Ever since Glasser's business collapsed, she had been in charge of their finances, scurrying around collecting the little bit of money that was still left to them, cash he had hidden away in safe-deposit boxes and a few small, forgotten bank accounts. From this she paid the mortgage on their condo and just enough to their creditors to keep them out of court. To Glasser she gave a few dollars now and then, for cigarettes and an occasional box of doughnuts, but she was fickle toward him, and her generosity depended on her mood.

"It's my money," said Glasser weakly.

She finished tying a kerchief over her head and started for the door. "And aren't you lucky I'm watching it for you?"

Later in the day, with Esther gone, he dozed in the yellow afternoon sunlight, moving so frequently between a thin fitful sleep and wakefulness that the two states seemed to merge. The smallest task took hours to perform, his limbs heavy as if he were moving through water. Lighting a cigarette, his mind wandered, and moments later he noticed the tobacco still unlit between his lips, the lighter gripped between his fingers, its long yellow flame quivering.

At some point in the afternoon Glasser looked up from the TV and saw Feldman standing over him in a suit and raincoat, like an apparition materialized without sound.

"I rang," said Feldman, "but nobody answered. And the door was open." He peered down at Glasser uncomfortably.

"Didn't hear," said Glasser, making no move to get up.

"I've tried calling. I've spoken to Esther."

Glasser shrugged, reached for his cigarettes. He felt no particular shame at being seen like this, in his underwear, with empty food cartons spread on the floor around him. He didn't feel much of anything—*that* only came at night. "Sorry," he said, meaning the opposite.

"Nothing to be sorry about." Feldman glanced around at the disorder of the room. "It's just we have some decisions to make now, Lou, and they can't wait any longer."

"Decisions," echoed Glasser, as if it were a word from a foreign language. Feldman had an air of unreality to him, like a memory or photograph, a figure seen through a car window. None of his decisions could be of any importance, Glasser knew—none would make a difference.

Feldman rubbed his chin nervously. "We owe three months' rent, but I have a plan to keep the office open." He paused, then went on when Glasser failed to respond. "I want to sublet the empty rooms. If we can get four guys in there, our own rent is covered."

Four guys? There were only five offices in the suite. "What about my office?" he asked.

"You and I can share."

"I see."

"And now here's the hard part, Lou, but just hear me out. I want to take down the shingle." He meant the brass plaque on the door, the one that said GLASSER & FELDMAN, ATTORNEYS-AT-LAW. "I'll put up my name instead, till things quiet down."

"Your name?"

"But everything will be just the same. We'll split whatever I make fifty-fifty."

Glasser was the senior partner; the clients, contacts, reputation were all his—and the split had always been sixty-forty. "Don't bullshit me, Jerry."

Feldman stiffened. "It's not what you think."

"I know when I'm getting fucked."

"Lou, listen to me. This can work, we can still save the practice. Everything you spent years building up."

"Fuck the practice. You can have it."

"All I'm asking is an even split. I'm doing all the work." Jerry had a heartsick look on his face, clearly torn between ambition and loyalty. The advantage was all his, and the fact seemed to make him sad and guilty. "You understand, Lou, I'd feel like a chump if I didn't get my fair share. That's all it is. We're not talking about a lot of money here."

That was certainly true. And the figure of Feldman, standing there sweating penitently in his raincoat, was nothing if not poignant. Glasser watched his junior partner struggling against the bonds of loyalty and affection, trying to reconcile his deepest inclinations with his pride. He understood Feldman's dilemma: the younger man would have to think less of himself if he didn't grab more now that he could—even if he didn't *want* more; even if there was no profit in it. By the logic of their profession, more of nothing was still *more*.

Glasser dropped his cigarette butt into an empty herring jar. "The pathetic thing is that you've come here to ask my permission." He had no intention of letting Feldman off the hook; he wanted to see him squirm.

True to form, Feldman's eyes grew big with misery. "I'm trying to save us both, and you're only making it harder."

"I don't need any saving." Feigning unconcern, Glasser turned back to the TV.

Glasser shot awake an hour later, his heart pounding, his chest so tight he could barely breathe. He had dozed off in front of the TV, dreaming a series of short, terrible dreams: that he was twisted in plastic wrap; that he was running in mud; that he had met his father, Morris, on the street. "How do you get to the El?" asked Morris, no sign on his sad, attentive face that he recognized his son.

"They've knocked it down," answered Glasser, and it had seemed like a cruel, dishonest thing to say.

Pushing himself upright, he looked around for Feldman, but his partner—ex-partner—was long gone. He sat for a while, panicked and confused, and the conversation with Feldman began to blur with the dream he'd just finished, till it was somehow Morris kicking him out of his office, changing the brass nameplate on the door, even though Glasser knew this wasn't correct. He argued with himself, shamefaced at his own choking rage. How can you be angry at a poor dead man who did no harm to anyone but himself? A man who was twenty years younger than you are now when he was murdered? He found one last cigarette in the pack, but his hands shook too much to light it. Hungering for the cigarette, he knew suddenly that he would never make it to trial—a trial he couldn't pay for and would probably lose. He would crack up first. He was cracking up now.

End it, he told himself, and his mind flashed on all the ways of cutting short his misery. He could throw himself out the window or turn on the gas or jump in front of a car or take Freeburg's deal—which was a kind of death too, a soul death. Or he could just plead guilty. This last actually made him chuckle, imagining the look of surprise on Freeburg's face. Why not plead guilty? His law practice was gone, his money gone, thirty years of work all gone. Tell Eddy, he said to himself. The thought of his brother's cavernous disco was deeply soothing, a dark, safe place without windows from which to jump.

He got up and dressed himself in an old track suit, the only thing that still fit him after weeks of all-night gorging. His initial plan was to take a cab, but a search of his pockets turned up only eighty-nine cents, which meant that even the subway was out of the question. It was a long walk downtown, and Glasser hurried, the agitation moving from his heart to his legs, till his breath came in sharp, painful spurts and his face was bathed in sweat. By Fourteenth Street there was a stabbing pain in the center of his chest, and he felt light-headed, weak in the knees. On Tenth he actually stumbled and fell, but he got up quickly. A heart attack, he thought, almost gleeful at the idea of a clean white hospital bed. But then, no such luck—the pain was subsiding, his breath coming back. The Glassers were built like Sherman tanks, unfortunately; they would keep rolling, taking punishment long after their minds were gone.

He crossed the street to a phone booth and called Eddy's private line at the disco. About twenty minutes later, leaning against the side of a building, he saw his brother's enormous Lincoln pull up to the curb.

Usually immaculate, Eddy looked rumpled and exhausted, his heavy cheeks prickly with white razor stubble. He drove in silence, methodical but vicious, brandishing the Lincoln as if it were a weapon—wedging it between taxicabs, tailgating a phone-company van—yet never once blowing his horn. Glasser spread out in the passenger seat, enjoying the show, secretly hoping for a pileup. He wanted the sound of glass shattering.

They didn't speak till they were back at the disco, locked in Eddy's VIP lounge. Despite the mirrors, the soft semi-dark, and the twinkling lights, it had the feeling of a bunker under siege. There was a blanket crumpled on a couch and clothing stacked on one of the chairs. Eddy seemed to be using the bar as an office: open ledgers lined the countertop, along with an adding machine and a textbook—*Concepts in Accounting*. The book was glossy-new, the price tag still on it. A shoebox full of receipts sat nearby.

The two brothers stood facing each other in the middle of the floor, a yard apart, strangely formal. Eddy was the first to speak. "They're killing me, Lou, my fucking partners."

"Yeah, welcome to the club."

Eddy chuckled. "The Glassers are a hard-luck family, all right. Starting with Papa." He ran both hands back over his hair, but it did little good; misery was making his perm act up, popping springs like an old mattress. "That man knew how to pick his partners, same as the ponies. I don't think he had a winner once."

"People took advantage of him, and when he needed help they slammed the door in his face."

Eddy shrugged. "I'm not asking anybody for anything." He went around the bar to the refrigerator and came back with two Cokes. "So you're going to take the immunity deal?"

Glasser accepted one of the sodas and pressed it to his forehead like a cold compress. "Should I?"

"Well, it's a good one, isn't it?" Eddy seemed to consider his brother's face. "You don't owe those people anything, Lou." He meant the clients, the people Glasser would be forced to testify against.

"Yeah? What if they want me to testify against you?" To be truthful, Glasser wasn't sure if this was an issue anymore. The investigation had been running more than half a year, and there had been no mention of the money Brianson had invested in the disco. But if Glasser took a plea he wanted it to be for someone, and right now that someone would have to be Eddy.

Eddy's whole body sagged with tiredness. This was clearly just one of a long list of disasters to consider, perhaps not even the worst. "You do what you have to, I can take it."

"I'm not going to live like that. Like an animal."

"You going to trial then?"

"With what? How can I pay for it?"

"If I had any money, Lou, you know I'd— But it's all sunk in this." He waved his Coke to indicate the VIP room.

"I'm going to cop a plea."

His brother's eyes went big. "What are they offering?"

"I don't know, but I'm saving her from a trial with Brianson as her witness. That's got to be worth something."

"But pleading out—are you sure?"

"You think I have a choice?" Glasser was breathing hard suddenly, the anger pressing up through his chest into his throat, filling his head. The soda slipped from his hand, and as foam spread across the gray carpet, he began to move around the room, kicking at the low-slung furniture—big booming kicks, all of his great weight behind them, making the cushions jump. He saw Eddy's shocked face only in passing, reflected in one of the mirrors: a ghostly white sliver, old and tired, floating like the moon under a galaxy of little electric lights.

While he kicked he yelled. "If they want me to be guilty, I'll be guilty! I'll do anything they want! What the fuck difference does it make! I'm guilty! Let me be guilty! I'm fucking guilty!"

Freeburg was surprised when Hayes phoned to open plea negotiations; in fact, she offered the immunity deal again.

"No good," said Hayes. "My client won't take it."

"Is he crazy?" It was lunchtime, and Freeburg was munching a sandwich while she talked.

"Well, yes, I think he might be. A breakdown of some kind. He just wants out, and so do I."

"If he wants out, he'll have to pay the exit fee." More munching. "Tell you what, I can give you import of a controlled substance, how's that?"

Not a serious offer. At the amounts of pot given in the indictment, import would get Glasser forty years. Hayes let out an amused, slightly weary sigh. "Please, Anna, don't make this harder than it has to be."

On the other end, Freeburg slurped her soda. She always made a point of playing lowbrow to his highbrow; it was part of the fun. Once she'd gotten firmly in character she could dicker all day, like a rug merchant in a souk. "Sorry, Corman, that was a special offer, just for you. If you take a look at the indictment you see money laundering, racketeering, harboring a fugitive . . ." She let her voice trail off, as if there were too many charges to list.

"Do you really want to go to trial with this Brianson as a witness? He won't hold up on the stand—he may not even show up. We're offering you an honorable out."

She laughed again. "All right, you're twisting my arm. I can knock it down to a subsection four, but that's as low as I go. Take it or leave it."

Import, under fifty kilograms. It would get Glasser five years. "Not good enough. Call me back with something better."

Over the next few days they passed half a dozen phone calls back and forth, and when neither could be pushed any farther—when they both started to grow bored with the game—they quickly settled on concealing a person from arrest. Of all the charges in the indictment, it was potentially the easiest to prove, as the Feds had the commercial work—contracts, leases—Glasser had done for Randy Schotts under the alias of Brianson.

In the office the next day, Hayes tried to sell Glasser on the idea. "So what do you think, old fellow? Good, isn't it?" There was a self-conscious jollity in his voice, as if humoring a child. He had no doubt that his client had suffered a nervous breakdown, and though he was not without sympathy, actually dealing with the man made him uncomfortable.

Glasser sat on the edge of the seat cushion, too fat now to lean back in the narrow armchair. He was in his track suit, food stains up and down the front. "Concealing a person from arrest?" he asked, sounding uncertain.

"That's right." Hayes smiled indulgently. Indeed, he was in a particularly good mood despite the chore before him. Freshly scrubbed, pink-skinned, and vigorous, he was wearing an unusually snappy red tie. In a week or two he would be free of Glasser—a mistake, a terrible piece of deadweight—and, in addition, he had a new client coming in that afternoon with a very interesting stock-fraud problem. The stock case figured to be worth a million in fees, and it would put him in a very strong position when the firm's annual compensation meeting came around.

"I'll be disbarred," said Glasser.

"There's no way around that, I'm afraid."

Glasser rubbed his hands on his round thighs, nervous. "I just want this to be over."

Hayes remembered the advice his wife had given him the other night when he was complaining about the Glasser case: stick to the Wall Street criminals. Stay away from the *criminal* criminals. She was right; he would have to stop slumming. His division was growing, and he just couldn't afford the time anymore. So he decided to take this as a yes and proceed to the details. "The maximum sentence is a year, but the judge has wide latitude. I think you can expect a year of probation, which would include community service—church work or a hospital, cleaning bedpans, helping old people, that sort of thing."

"No jail, right?"

"Put you in with those beasts? I wouldn't think so." He laughed it away. "The U.S. attorney's sentencing report carries great weight with the judge. Freeburg has promised to go easy."

"I don't want to meet up with any old clients," said Glasser. He meant in jail.

Hayes nodded merrily. "Yes, of course, a lawyer's nightmare."

11

JUST SAVE HIM

It was nearly three A.M. when Jason woke from a troubled sleep, suddenly aware of the phone ringing in the other room. His heart started to pound. He sprang from bed and made it to the receiver before it could ring again.

It was his father on the line. "I want you to know I'm not guilty of anything." His voice was loud and accusatory, as if they were already mid-argument. "Not guilty of any willful wrongdoing."

"What? I never said you were."

"Okay," he said, "I confess. I *am* guilty."

There was a silence in which Jason's whole body stiffened. This was not what he wanted to hear.

"See?" said his father. "See what I mean? It's what you're thinking. And I *am* guilty too, guilty of swallowing all the lies they feed you. The American dream, what a crock of shit. Sure, make a little money, pay taxes. But don't win too many cases, don't make too much money, don't get uppity."

"Uppity?"

"The uppity Jew," he said. "The uppity Jew gets slapped down."

"Dad, this isn't a Jewish thing."

His father's voice took on a new kind of sarcastic clarity. "Is that so, Professor? Is that what they teach you up there?"

"Freeburg is Jewish."

"Sure, Freeburg is Jewish. My point exactly. She's a Jew like you, a white Jew, a Kapo. She goes to a fancy school, gets a degree, thinks she's one of them—just what they want her to think."

"Not everything's an anti-Semitic conspiracy."

"Oh, so what is it then, bad luck?" His voice was full of disdain. "My practice is ruined. They've scared all the clients away. That's thirty years of work down the fucking drain. They've destroyed my life."

"You're innocent, remember. All you need is a little sleep."

"I'm going to take a plea."

"You can't do that, you're not guilty."

"Guilty, not guilty, what's the difference anymore? If that's what they want from me, that's what I'll give them. I'll grovel, I'll beg for mercy, just the way they like it."

Jason could hear something ecstatic in his father's voice, a kind of masochistic joy, and it made him furious. "You can't just give up. You've got to fight back."

"There's nothing left to fight with, Jason. There's nothing left to fight *for*. I might as well lie down and get it over with. Hayes thinks he can cut them way down. I'd lose my license, but Freeburg would recommend probation."

"But you're not guilty."

"They've got Brianson. I don't know what lies he's been telling them, or whether a jury would believe him, but if they did I'd get forty years. Do you understand what that means? I'm fifty-nine years old, I'd die in prison."

Die in prison. It was like his father had suddenly switched into a foreign language—gibberish, words without meaning. And yet Jason felt a terrible pain rising inside him, the effect of those incomprehensible nonsense syllables. "He'd never testify against you, never."

"Brian's a rat, Jason. They're all rats. I've watched them rat on each other for three decades. But like a fool I thought I'd never get bitten."

"You're wrong about him." Brian was the bulwark, the last bulwark against disaster, and Jason would not abandon him without a fight. "You told me you met with him in Boston, he gave you his word."

"Yeah, sure, his *word*." His father let out a sharp angry laugh, like a spray of nails.

"Even assume he is ratting on you. If he lied on the stand it would be easy to prove. You'd win anyway."

"You poor deluded schmuck, are you really a lawyer's son?" That laugh again, full of scorn. "Conspiracy is like a swamp, it sucks everyone in. These cases are impossible to beat in the federal courts, the statutes are stacked against the defense. If you happen to have passed through the same public toilet on the same day you're a co-conspirator."

"But what about the truth?"

"Fuck the truth."

Fuck the truth.

Later, unable to sleep, Jason paced back and forth, thinking about those three words, scrambling them in every possible combination. The truth, the fucking truth, where had it gone? Where had Brian gone? Where had his father gone? He thought about all that he knew, and all that he did not know, and how the two categories of things mixed and swirled, till the feeling of knowing, knowing anything at all, seemed to disappear, no longer a part of his world.

Maybe his father *was* hiding something. He tested the idea like an inflamed tooth, prodding gently, exploring the potential for pain. There was no denying that his father had been evasive, leaving out choice bits of information, carefully shaping the picture he presented. He had failed to mention the fact that Brian had an alias, and it had taken him a long time to admit that he'd really come to Cambridge chasing after the dealer, not that horrible steak dinner. Jason had watched him run rings around his own lawyer in a frantic attempt to control what the man knew, as if he were hoping to snow Hayes so Hayes could then go and snow Freeburg.

But whatever he might be hiding, it wasn't anything big. Jason was certain it fit in the category of mistake, fuckup, shortcut gone bad. No drug smuggling, no money laundering, nothing that would transform him from father to criminal. The boy understood this as indisputable fact, the one remaining fact in his entire world, too precious to lose. Was Freeburg offering a deal? Jason didn't want a deal. He wanted his father, the truth of his father, his kind brown eyes, his smell of cigarettes and aftershave, and he paced back and forth trying to recapture them—till finally he was startled by the gray light of morning coming through the window. His eyes burned, but his mind was whirring like a generator.

The truth cannot be fucked.

Freeburg: Freeburg was the key. If he and she were both Kapos, white Jews—whatever those things were—then they could at least talk the same language. Inspired, he put on his pinstriped suit and a tie his mother had bought him freshman year, emblazoned with the Harvard crest, a shield with three open books and the Latin tag *veritas*, truth. Silly, but a potentially useful prop. He wrote out a note for Norm: *If my parents call, tell them I'm at the library.* Then he took the Red Line to South Station, where he got the train to New York.

Watching the early-morning scenery beyond the train window, he wondered about Freeburg, this woman who had changed his life so thoroughly in such a short span of time. He imagined her as a hag, a battle-ax, with cruel little eyes and thin pursed lips, a tight bun at the back of her head—the Mother Superior of legal torture. His father called her the Castrator, the Ball Buster, the Assistant U.S. Mohel. He said she was angling for a promotion, trying to make a reputation prosecuting lawyers, and that she would stop at nothing. Jason saw himself busting into her big shiny office, catching her plotting at her desk. Her eyes would widen with surprise as he began his speech, impassioned and articulate beyond his own wildest dreams. *You think you represent truth and justice, do you? Well, you're nothing but a smug, self-serving hypocrite.*

No, sharper than that, in a tone of dry, mocking disdain.

There is nothing more sickening, Ms. Freeburg, than the sight of a public servant cloaking her personal ambition in the rhetoric of duty.

It was a drizzly afternoon by the time he found himself in downtown Manhattan, standing outside the U.S. Attorney's Office. The building was right next to MCC, the jail in which Brian had been locked up. Not all that long ago Jason had stood near this same spot with his father, after they had bought the suit he was now wearing.

The Kiyomoto-Tate Fellowship had been in the bag back then, Japan just around the corner; he had felt pity for Brian, incarcerated somewhere behind those slit windows. Then everything had fallen apart.

It was a minute or two before he forced himself into the official-looking lobby. He stopped in front of a security desk manned by two uniformed policemen. "I want to talk to one of the assistant U.S. attorneys," he said. "About a case."

"You have an appointment?"

"No appointment, but I know she'll want to see me." He didn't know this at all, of course, but he gave Freeburg's name and one of the policemen dialed her extension, then waved him through.

He had expected sleek, efficient offices, the ominous hush befitting malice and treachery. Instead he found himself in a maze of desks and partitions, and within just a few seconds the din of typing and phones made him feel trapped and desperate. He stopped for directions, then followed the long outer wall, race-walking past stacks of legal files, secretaries, and paralegals with their arms full of documents. He grew frantic with the thought that his father was just one file among thousands—not even a particularly important one. This was worse than cool treachery, it was bureaucratic chaos, civil servants wading through an avalanche of paper, drinking bitter coffee from Styrofoam cups. Freeburg would have an in-box piled to the ceiling. She would not know who he was and would not care.

Her office, when he found it, was no better than what was outside. Small and dirty, it held a desk blanketed with papers, a beaten-up visitor's chair, case files stacked against the walls. A woman sat in the midst of this, holding a half-eaten sandwich over a paper bag.

"Ms. Freeburg?" He felt like he'd swallowed a rubber ball and it had lodged in his throat.

She put down the sandwich, using the bag to wipe her fingers. "What can I do for you, Mr. Glasser?"

It was hard to respond, because he was having trouble believing this was really Anna Freeburg, Assistant U.S. Mohel. She was surprisingly young, not much older than the teaching assistants at school, and definitely pretty, with long dark hair and big brown eyes, full lips.

It was a long moment before he could speak. "I'm here to talk about my father's case."

A flicker ran over her features, the look of someone steeling herself for an unpleasant duty. She gestured to the visitor's chair, and he entered the room and took a seat. Up close, he could see dark circles under her eyes, the greenish office pallor of the chronically overworked.

"What exactly would you like to discuss?" she asked.

He tried to fill his lungs with air, but it was no use. The speeches he had composed in his mind were gone, like breath from a windowpane, and he cursed himself for not writing them down. "Ms. Freeburg," he said, "my father is innocent."

She gave something like a sigh, looking at him wearily with her big brown eyes. "Does he know you're here, Mr. Glasser?"

"No," he said.

"What about his attorney, Mr. Hayes?"

"I've come on my own. That's the point."

"I see, yes, of course." She rubbed her eye with a knuckle. "This must be very hard on you, I understand that."

Suddenly he found himself wishing for the kind of woman he had imagined on the train, the Assistant U.S. Mohel, somebody who wouldn't care how he felt, somebody he could fight head on. "My father is innocent, Ms. Freeburg. I've known him all my life, and I know this for a fact."

She nodded slowly. "He's lucky to have a son like you. He must love you very much."

"He's a good, kind, generous man."

"Yes, that's what everyone says."

She seemed to mean this sincerely, and this left him confused. "Then why are you doing this?"

"Why am I prosecuting this case?" She looked pained by the question. "It's my job, it's what I have to do."

"You're destroying his life."

It took only a moment for her face to transform, from weary sympathy to a coolly distanced professionalism, and when she spoke again, her voice had a chilly authority. "My job is upholding the law, Mr. Glasser."

"You don't have any evidence."

"I won't discuss the facts of the case with you. Speak to Mr. Hayes if you have any questions."

"I'm not here to ask questions. I'm here to tell you that something terrible is happening. My father, who never hurt anyone, is going to plead to a crime he didn't commit."

He saw Freeburg catch herself before answering, and in the ensuing pause her face softened. "Please, Mr. Glasser, don't make this any harder on yourself than it has to be." She gave an exhausted smile, then gestured to the papers spread over her desk. "And don't make my day any worse than it already is."

"Why shouldn't I ruin your day? You're ruining my father's life."

She shook her head. "You've got the wrong villain. I'm just a lawyer, building a case on evidence."

"You're killing him," he said, listening to the warble that had entered his voice. There was a real danger he might burst into tears, and the thought mortified him.

Freeburg looked panicked at the possibility. "I know what you're feeling, believe me."

"No," he said, struck by the simple truth, "you've really got no idea."

It was overcast and gray when he stepped outside, and afternoon already felt like evening. He started walking uptown, past the criminal court building, past the old jail next to it, the Tombs. He should have known that pleading would be useless, that Freeburg would never listen. So why did he humiliate himself like that, nearly blubbering in her office, whining about innocence and justice? Because he was a child, a poor deluded schmuck, as his father had said. He had seized on a fantasy, and now there was nothing else for him to do but head back to Cambridge.

Yet everything in him resisted going back. He kept walking past the subway entrance, across Canal, through Little Italy and the East Village, up Third Avenue into the Twenties. He'd planned to cut west on Thirty-fourth Street for Penn Station, but instead he continued uptown, letting the momentum carry him onward. Dusk fell, a thickening of the grayness into that peculiar form of New York night: silvery at street level, pitch-black and starless above the skyscrapers. On Seventy-first he realized he was only a few blocks from Brian's place, a town house between Madison and Park. He'd tried to call the dealer a thousand times since the acid trip, but there was never any answer, and he assumed the house would be empty now. Still, he wanted to see it.

He crept up on it slowly, from the opposite side of the street, baffled by the row of lit windows on the top story. The building was as beautiful as ever: four stories, with a stately white limestone front and green copper mansard roof, every bit as elegant and sedate as its neighbors on the block, the property of bankers and CEOs. Jason remembered when the dealer had gotten it—almost four years before, his freshman year at Harvard. Glasser had muttered darkly about the ostentation of Roman emperors, about triggering a tax audit, but there had obviously been some jealousy intermixed in that. Brian had said simply that he was tired of living like a bum, that he wanted a break with the past. After a few weeks he was strolling with the silver-haired burghers who walked their poodles and shar-peis in the evening.

Was Brian cooperating with the Feds? Was he informing? Lying to shift the blame? It was impossible to believe this of the man who had led him through the Village when he was ten years old, fed him falafel from Mamoun's on Thompson Street, bought him Italian ices in Washington Square Park.

As he watched, a silhouette moved behind one of the windows. Jason rushed across the street to the brightly lit entrance and stopped at the red door with its ornamental horsehead knocker. He leaned on the buzzer for a long time, careful to stare up into the security camera perched above, so Brian would know it was him.

What would he find when the door opened? The man he had always known as Brian Brianson was really named something else. He had come to Harvard and offered Jason a job, and then he had disappeared when the boy needed him most. He had been missing for months, impossible to reach, even as Jason's father sank toward disaster. He might be the cause of that disaster. If he was, Jason could stop him, could talk him out of doing any more harm. And if he wasn't, they could work together to save Glasser before it was too late.

Brian opened the door, and there was a moment of silence between them. Then the dealer's head fell to one side, and the corners of his mouth stretched upward, though the smile never quite materialized. "What are you, a Jehovah's Witness now?"

"Where the fuck have you been?"

Brian gave a noncommittal shrug. "Difficult times." He was dressed in a Moroccan caftan of purple silk, with an elaborate design in gold thread. He led Jason through the darkened hall and then four flights up the twilit staircase, to the top floor, directly below the green copper roof. The boy had never actually been in this part of the house, and he was surprised by the room they entered. It looked something like the cabin of a sailing ship, with an improbably low ceiling and wood paneling on the walls. The deep bay windows, small and protruding from the roof, gave the feel of portholes. Books lay in piles by the couch and the armchair, and Jason noted not one but three different phones lined up on the coffee table. On a cabinet sat a bank of four small video monitors, clearly hooked up to security cameras around the building. On one screen he saw a grainy image of the front entrance, through which he had just passed.

They stood by the table, looking each other over. "Christ, did *he* buy you that?" asked Brian, eyeing the boy's suit. He gave a long throaty chuckle. "You look like a miniature Lou, man. Like somebody left Lou in the dryer too long."

Haberdashery wasn't what Jason wanted to talk about. "I need your help, Brian, that's why I'm here. I need—"

The dealer waved him silent. "First, a smoke." He reached into an ashtray and picked up a joint, lit it, and took a deep hit. The cannabis smell was overwhelming, a dense jungle odor that filled the room. "How are you feeling, by the way? Any flashbacks?"

"What do you mean?"

"You know, acid flashbacks."

The boys eyes went large with alarm. "You get them?"

"Only under stress." And then a crooked grin beneath the bloodshot dopey eyes. "I'm only kidding you, man. Lighten up." He offered the joint to Jason, and seemed a little miffed when the boy declined. A connoisseur, he was vain about his pot and wanted it appreciated. "I remember you in diapers, Jason. I was your babysitter, you know. We'd get stoned together—blow some smoke in your mouth, watch those little eyes cross."

"But I was ten when we met."

"Randy Schotts did some baby-sitting too." Brian took another toke, looking thoughtful now. "You had the strangest little baby smile. I don't know what you were thinking about, but it must've been something amazing." He looked at Jason with an earnest, heavy-lidded expression. "What do you think babies think about when they're stoned? Titty?"

Jason's mind seemed to wobble. He was sure—pretty sure—the story about baby-sitting was a fake, but how could he be completely certain? "I'm here about Dad. I just came from the prosecutor's office."

Brian broke into a sly smile. "Now, those are some nice titties. Tell me, you think I have a chance with her?" A glint appeared in his eye. "Or have you staked a claim? Because I wouldn't want to butt in if you've got something going." He took another long drag on the joint, smoke leaking out the sides of his mouth. "Hell, I don't even know if you've busted your cherry yet. I mean, are you a virgin, or what?" He looked at the boy as if expecting an answer.

"You know her?"

"Did I say I did?"

"Don't play games with me, this is too important."

"Hey, just because it's a game doesn't mean it isn't serious." Brian sat down on the couch, his long frame sinking into the cushions, his head rolling back as if he were suddenly very tired. "I've been reading about this thing called game theory. I've got lots of time for reading now." He lifted his head for a moment to look at Jason, then dropped it again. "They destroyed my operation, you know. Twenty fucking years of work down the drain. Do you know what that feels like?"

"Dad's going to take a plea, Brian, you've got to help me."

"That's what I'm talking about, man, I'm trying to help you. Game theory is about how people use information to make decisions." He picked up a book from the carpet by his bare feet and waved it at Jason. "Say you and I are partners and we're both arrested. They put me in one of those little rooms they've got, and they tell me, 'Hey, man, that pal of yours is spilling his guts, he's told us all about you.' "

"That's what they're saying about *you*, Brian."

The dealer stared up at the ceiling as if he hadn't heard, wrapped in his own thoughts. "They offer me a deal, man, a kind of either/or, you know. If I cooperate they'll cut me loose. And if I don't they'll give the deal to you instead, which means I do time for both of us."

Was this fact or fable? And if it was fact, why was the dealer telling it in this ridiculously indirect way? Jason felt he was being toyed with, but he didn't know to what end. "I trust you, Brian. Dad trusts you. That's why I came."

"Trust? That's exactly what I'm talking about here, man, the theoretical basis of trust. In this particular example there are two possibilities to consider. The first is they're lying to me and you aren't talking, in which case the best thing I can do is keep my mouth shut, right?"

"I know you wouldn't testify against him. You wouldn't do that. But he's in deep shit now—"

"The second is that you *are* talking, in which case I should cut my losses and take the deal."

"They offered him a deal, complete immunity, and he turned it down. You must know that already."

Brian examined him through half-closed lids, a schoolmaster watching to see if the lesson was seeping in. "Well, how do I decide what to do now? That's what game theory's about. I've got to assume they've told you the same shit they've told me, and I've got to consider how you might react to that."

"Brian, cut it out and listen to me—"

"Because if I'm going to base my choice on yours, I've got to consider that you're basing your choice on *mine,* you know. Maybe you aren't talking, and maybe you're betting I'm not talking either, but maybe you think *I* think you're talking. Get it? It's what they call a feedback loop."

Brian stretched, casually. The golden threads in his caftan caught the light. For a moment he looked as grand as he had when Jason was a boy, when he was the man Jason yearned to be, walking out the door with his father after dinner, the two of them heading into the city's mysterious night. The boy had begged to go along; his mother had held him so he wouldn't bolt into the elevator. But if he *had* followed them down the street and through the years he would have come to this, this awful, unreal moment.

There was silence for a while, Brian smoking his joint. "What we've got here are mirrors," said the dealer finally, "two mirrors facing each other across a room—reflecting each other's reflection."

Jason was shaking, a molten anger in his throat. "You used him."

"We used each other."

"But he never hurt you."

Brian reached over to the ashtray with a long thin arm, carefully stubbed out the remainder of the joint. "I'll admit it's a difficult situation."

"I'm going to tell Freeburg that you lied, that it's all lies." He was horrified by the sound of his own voice, a child's voice, a high-pitched squeal.

"Don't be stupid." Brian frowned, then leaned back on the couch. "Do you know what this is called, this little visit of yours? Tampering with a witness, a federal crime. One call to that cutie Freeburg and your ass is in jail." He watched Jason for a reaction. "I wouldn't, though, because I like you, man. Believe it or not, you're a lot tougher than Lou. Even when you were a kid you looked tough, like you were planning to buy the place and kick everybody out. But Lou's different, he expects to get caught."

"You did this to him."

"You're wrong there." A flash of anger, immediately covered over with a smile. "Sure, I promised Freeburg everything, man. I couldn't sit one more minute in that cage, like a zoo animal. But there are promises and then there are *promises*, you know what I mean? I'm just buying myself a little time till I can figure out my next move."

"Next move? What are you talking about?"

"You've got nothing to worry about, man. You're going to come out of this thing just fine." Brian stood up, rubbery on his long legs. "It's what they call a growth experience, you know."

"You've got some kind of plan—"

"I'm more worried about you, running around trying to save Lou's ass for him. Isn't it time you grew up? Isn't it time you got your own damn life? How are you going to do that with three hundred pounds of daddy dragging you down?" Brian leaned forward suddenly, picking up one of the phones on the coffee table. "Let me get you that ticket to Amsterdam, right now. Let me do that for you. Plus a two-month advance on salary. No, three months. You can tour Europe before you get to work, put this whole thing in perspective. By the time you're ready, I'll be back in business."

"Just save him, that's all I want."

"And how am I supposed to do that?"

"Do whatever you have to. Tell them you won't cooperate, tell them you lied. Turn somebody else in."

The dealer gave a rueful laugh. "There's nobody left."

"You just said you have a plan."

"I *said* I was keeping my options open. I suggest you do the same."

J ason ran from Brian's, ran the two long blocks to Central Park, then sprinted down Fifth. By the time he reached Grand Army Plaza he was stumbling like a drunk, gasping for air. He took a right on Central Park South and followed the dark edge of the park to Columbus Circle, where he turned downtown again. He wanted to hide somewhere, to close his eyes and forget, and the one place he could think of was Uncle Eddy's disco. If he found Uncle Eddy in the disco, he could go home with him in his big Lincoln Continental, over the Brooklyn Bridge, back to his bachelor pad in Brooklyn.

It was past eleven when he reached the disco. The entrance looked pretty forlorn: no line outside, no cabs waiting by the curb, not even a bouncer by the door, which was open, letting out a neon blue light. The lobby was nearly empty too, except for a few baffled men wandering in the blueness, trying to look purposeful—the kind of men deluded enough to be looking for women and fun in a place that obviously contained neither. A muffled bass beat thumped from behind the doors to the dance floor, adding to the sadness. The bartender, chin propped on his hands, looked resigned to it all. When Jason asked for Eddy he pointed to a door at the far end of the room. "His Majesty's in the VIP room," he said. Jason thanked him, and the bartender handed him a free beer.

The door was black, with a peephole and one of those high-tech locks that use a card instead of a key, but it was also slightly ajar, and he simply pushed it open a bit, peering into the semi-darkness inside. "Is Eddy Glasser here?" he called.

"He ain't here." High and strangled, the voice sounded a lot like Uncle Eddy holding his nose and trying to imitate a woman.

"Uncle Eddy? It's Jason."

"Jason who?"

"Your nephew."

When Uncle Eddy came to the door, he looked like a man in hiding. His hair was mussed, his jacket wrinkled, as if he'd been wedged in some tight corner. He glanced over Jason's shoulder, checking the lobby, then pulled him into the darkness of the VIP room. "What are you doing here?" It was his normal voice, sweet and a little sad.

"I was in the neighborhood," said Jason. "What's with the funny voice?"

"Didn't want to be bothered."

"Does it fool anyone?"

"Nah. But they leave me alone."

They walked slowly toward the back. There were strange shadows and glintings in the room, a feeling of endlessness, but as Jason's eyes adjusted to the dark he realized the walls were mirrored, and the shapes he'd been taking for furniture or even people were just reflections.

"What do you think?" Eddy seemed to be asking from habit rather than real interest.

"Nice," said Jason. "Spacious."

Eddy led him to a bar at the back, turned on a small lamp, and offered him a stool. At Eddy's spot there were already cigarettes, an empty glass, an overstuffed ashtray. "It's like that thing about a tree falling in the forest," he said, lighting a cigarette. "I mean, can you call it a VIP lounge without any VIPs lounging in it?"

"It's a weekday."

"The weekends are worse." Eddy glanced down at his glass. "Good thing you brought your own, because we're out." From the way he smelled, Jason guessed his uncle had finished it himself. They both stared straight ahead, gazing at each other in the mirror behind the bar, Uncle Eddy smoking, Jason drinking his beer. "So what's up?" Eddy asked finally.

Haggard as he looked, he seemed to deserve a direct answer. "I took the train in from school this morning. I saw the prosecutor, Freeburg."

"Your father know about this?"

"Nope." Jason punctuated his answer with a long gulp of beer. "It was pretty stupid, I guess."

"Pretty brave."

"She says it's nothing personal."

Eddy sighed, then drew deeply on his cigarette. "You don't have to worry about your father, Jason. The plea bargain is pretty good. They drop the drug stuff and the conspiracy, and he pleads out to that other thing, protecting Brianson from arrest. That's a nothing charge, like running a red light."

A nothing charge? The beer had started to make Jason's head swim. It was past midnight now, and he'd had neither lunch nor dinner. He felt weak and floaty, as if he were made of Styrofoam or balsa wood. "What if they send him to jail?"

"A fifty-nine-year-old man? A lawyer? He'll get probation, a slap on the wrist."

"If he went to trial he'd win, and Freeburg knows it. That's why she offered him immunity before, because she's got such a weak case. Brian would crumble on the stand. He's told her a shitload of lies, but she's in too deep to turn around." The thought of Brian filled him with rage now; he wanted to smash him, pulverize him for his betrayal of both father and son. "Dad should drop Hayes and get himself a real lawyer, a tough fighter like that guy on TV—"

"Ray O'Donnel? He's under indictment."

"Well, somebody else then. I'd work on his defense full-time. By the time we were through they'd have Freeburg *and* Brian in jail." He took a long drink of beer, trying to calm the shivers moving through him. "I'm going to tell him, I'm going to make him *see*."

"You shouldn't push him about this. He's made his decision."

"He's innocent, Eddy. That fucker Brian has victimized him. The truth has to count for something."

Eddy hunched low on the counter, smoking thoughtfully. "You think he's giving up, letting the other side win?"

"Well, yeah, I guess I do." Jason realized it sounded childish, but he couldn't escape the logic, or the image of Brian gloating in his purple caftan. "And then there's his self-respect. How is he going to live with himself if he lets them do this to him?"

"This is real life, Jason, not a football game. There are complications here you may not know about." Eddy lowered his voice to a confidential murmur. "Have a little trust."

"Trust?" Jason remembered Brian babbling about game theory and the theoretical basis of trust—that there was no basis, more or less. "I'm tired of that word."

"What I mean is sometimes things aren't exactly black and white, you know, the way we'd like them to be." Uncle Eddy had begun studying the bottom of his empty glass, turning it every which way to catch the light. "Your father's no criminal. He's a good man. But some of those charges might be hard to beat in court."

Jason felt a numbness move across his face. "I don't get it." He had already considered the possibility that his father might have slipped up somewhere—made a mistake—but hearing the thought spoken out loud transformed it into something horrible and real.

Eddy looked up, and their eyes met in the mirror. "Does it make a difference?"

"Well, yeah, I guess it does." Jason swallowed, trying to hold himself together. "It makes taking the plea sound like a good idea."

"I mean does it make a difference in the way you feel about your father?"

The numbness was complete; only Jason's eyes could move, from Eddy's reflection back to his own. "No," he said finally, more to himself than to his uncle. "It doesn't matter." Even as he spoke, he knew this was both true and not true, another layer of complication.

"He loves you more than anything, Jason. Whatever he does, he does for you and your mother. Remember that."

"Yes," said Jason flatly, suddenly feeling the full suffocating weight of that love. And then just as quickly trying to wiggle out from under it: "I never asked him to."

"That's got nothing to do with it." Uncle Eddy sagged forward, onto the bar. He seemed to be getting drunker somehow—without drinking anything—or maybe Jason hadn't noticed how drunk he was to begin with. He lay his head on his hands and his voice came out muffled. "I could shoot that bastard Brianson, or pay somebody to do it, and our troubles would be over. Believe me, it could be done."

Jason thought how he could've done it—gone into Brian's kitchen that afternoon, gotten a knife, and ended it right there. But it had never even occurred to him. "Maybe we should have," he said now.

"In the old days we were tough—you had to be. You made a buck any way you could. All the great fighters were Jewish—Barney Ross, Max Baer. You ever heard of these names? Of course not. Who remembers Jewish fighters anymore? And gangsters—the mob was Jewish too. Dutch Schultz, Louie Lepke, Murder, Inc. Now it's all doctors and accountants."

"So what do we do?"

Uncle Eddy seemed lost in his own thoughts. He got up from his stool, then stumbled off into the darkness behind Jason. His voice seemed to come from nowhere. "I'm turning on the lights," he said. "I want to show you something."

Jason braced himself for a sudden flash, but the light rose gently, like water filling a bowl. He could see himself in the mirror now, and Uncle Eddy a little ways behind him. He could see the other mirrored walls too, full of duplicate versions of the two of them, uncle and nephew. They seemed to be standing in the middle of the Milky Way, thousands of stars floating around their heads.

"Like Bugsy Siegel built Las Vegas, I built this," said Eddy. "And not a goddamn VIP in sight." He didn't sound bitter, only amazed at his own audacity.

"It's incredible," said Jason, really meaning it. The stars were wonderful in their silliness, and there was something good and true in the way they asked him to believe in them, the humblest sort of illusion. "It's like space. It's like we're walking in outer space."

Suddenly he was crying. He couldn't tell if Uncle Eddy was too drunk or starstruck to notice, or maybe just too polite, but Jason stood there all alone, looking in the mirror and letting the tears fall. When he turned around Eddy was stretched out on one of the black sofas, asleep or pretending to be. Jason lay down on another one, beneath the artificial stars.

12

PUNISHMENT

Glasser took the plea, and for the next few weeks Hayes was able to turn his attention to the clean, cerebral intricacies of stock fraud. Timothy Smithers, the new client, was exceptionally congenial: a neatly bearded, slightly built man equipped with a seemingly unshakable sense of calm. They had dinner at "21," drinks in the Oak Room; weekends, they played squash and chatted about their children. Smithers had made his fortune in computer arbitrage, and he had the philosophical, bemused gaze of a man used to navigating the higher reaches of mathematics. The avarice was all in his hands, delicate ivory instruments tipped with a beautiful manicure. They were always touching things—silverware, crystal—as if feeling out their shapes in the dark.

Hayes had just returned late from a Smithers lunch one day when he found Freeburg's sentencing report waiting on his desk. He was pleased, since this was the last formality left before actual sentencing, after which he would be officially free of the case. Of course, he would still have to figure out a way of collecting on the twenty thousand Glasser now owed him, but at least he wouldn't have him sitting in his waiting room in a filthy sweat suit, scaring the corporate clients. One of the older partners—Burton, from Trusts and Estates—had already complained to the Management Committee.

He picked up the phone, asked his secretary to dial Glasser, and while waiting for the connection began browsing through the report. The opening was standard, but then something caught his eye and he started reading in earnest. What he saw on page three made him slam down the receiver.

He punched in the number for Freeburg himself. "Anna, what do you mean by this?"

"The report is as easy as I can go, Corman."

"Easy? You call this easy?" He began flipping through pages, picking phrases to read. "How about this: 'The defendant, a close associate of major crime figures. . . .' Or this, 'The defendant's casual disregard for ethical standards. . . .' Or this old canard about offshore assets—"

"I wrote it, I know what it says. The report is accurate and fair."

"Maybe so, but it's not what we agreed on. With a report like this, he'll get the max."

"I said I would try my best, but there's a limit, you know that."

"Damn it, Anna, do you realize what you've done to me? I can't let this go. I'll have to move for a hearing, and I'm very busy right now. I can't afford the time on a case like this."

Freeburg gave a short sigh, the oral version of a shrug. "It makes no difference to me. We're on straight salary over here."

Hayes realized he had been trumped, that there was nothing to do but make the best of it. Expecting a scene, he had Glasser come in late that evening, when there would be fewer people around to hear. But the ex-lawyer surprised him. Glasser read the report in silence, an abstractedly melancholy expression on his large round face. He seemed to understand the legal consequences clearly enough, but he focused instead on the larger, philosophical issue involved—the why. "Why me?" he muttered. This is the question the deer asks the headlights, and the only answer is pain.

Sitting erect in his chair, Hayes drew on the dignity of his dark, frigatelike desk, of his wonderful double-breasted suit. "It would be a mistake to blow this out of proportion, Lou. The hearing will give us a chance to confront Brianson directly, and I think we'll come out ahead. Or at least not behind."

"How much time can I get?"

Hayes lightly traced the edge of his desk with his fingers, a gesture he had picked up from Timothy Smithers. "We have every reason to remain completely optimistic."

"Brianson will sink me."

"Nonsense, absolute nonsense."

Glasser closed his eyes. "Let's just get it over."

On the day of the sentencing hearing Glasser climbed the courthouse steps, Esther supporting him under one arm and Jason under the other. Those massive gray columns, the heavy stone roof seemed to weigh down upon him, crushing the air from his chest. He didn't have the strength to make it up on his own, didn't have the strength to look his son in the eye—wasn't strong enough to tell the kid he didn't want him there. He could not bear the inscrutable mask the boy wore, the distant, judging, assessing look in his face. "You hate me," he said. "I know."

"Don't be crazy," said Jason.

"I took the plea for you. I did it for you."

"You shouldn't have."

"Just ignore him," said Esther

Almost an hour early, they waited in the hall, pressing against the marble wall, neither speaking nor looking at one another. Feldman, Eddy, Rainbow appeared after a while, but Glasser ignored them, and they shied away from him also, talking quietly among themselves a few feet away. When the time came, the others went in to sit in the benches, but Glasser waited in the hall for Hayes, who hurried in late.

"Sorry, Lou, they've been running me ragged. You wouldn't believe my schedule. I've got this stock fraud thing, and—" Hayes waved his hand in the air, then headed straight for the door to the courtroom, signaling Glasser to follow.

They sat in silence at the defense table, rose when the magistrate entered. Patrick McCall was the man who would determine Glasser's sentence. Back in his office, weeks before, Hayes had professed satisfaction that he'd been assigned to preside over the hearing. "He's fair," he'd said then. "He's a skeptic, and he doesn't favor the prosecution. Also, he tends to be a little hard on lady lawyers, so our Anna may end up walking into some trouble." Then, out of nowhere, he'd suddenly added, "Real lace-curtain Irish. I know how to handle him. You have to lay on the respect."

But McCall didn't look like the kind to favor lace curtains. Vigorous white hair atop a meaty red face, with the squashed nose of a street fighter. He had the big, blocky body of a butcher or field hand, looming even bigger in his black judicial robes, and his pink hands were enormous and knuckley, thick fingers wrapped around a fountain pen. When the hearing began, he cocked an ear to listen as Freeburg spoke, his heavy lower lip drooping with the effort of concentration.

Glasser tried to listen too but couldn't because he was working so hard, repeating to himself all the things he was supposed to be feeling. He told himself that the hearing would end his nightmare. No more fighting, no more resistance, no more waiting, no more loneliness. Freeburg and McCall would do what they had to do to make him right again, punish and purify him, and he would help them do this. Then life could begin again.

At the same time he told himself it was bullshit, that he was only acting, his every gesture fabricated to match the part they put him in, and he took pleasure in thinking he was fooling them so completely. *Let them see what they want to see; I will be the cartoon they're looking for; I will blubber and wallow and beg for mercy.*

Yet the next moment he was back where he started. He thought of himself groveling, and the humiliation felt right and necessary to him, the first stage of his punishment, his cleansing. Because the act wasn't an act at all: it was real, a real fake act, and he believed in it absolutely, deep down in a place beyond words.

J ason sat between his mother and Uncle Eddy on one of the long wooden benches, two rows back from the front, watching as Freeburg started on her opening statement. She stood with her feet together, head bent over her notes—nervous. "Money is key," she said. "Defendant Glasser did what he did for money. He broke the law for personal gain. Your Honor, when lawyers knowingly flout the law, the justice system must be especially careful to see that they are punished to the fullest possible extent. The people must be reassured that the system doesn't try to hide or protect one of its own."

Glasser hunched over the defense table. He rested his weight on his elbows, shifted in his seat, mopped his face with his hand. Jason noticed the broad back of his suit jacket, stretched to its limit, and imagined how his father must look to the judge: guilty and annoyed at all the fuss over it, too preoccupied to pay attention to his own sentencing.

Hayes got up and talked about Glasser's long and honorable career. "Your Honor, the government's investigation effectively destroyed Mr. Glasser's legal practice before he was even indicted. His office has produced almost no income for nearly a year, and the cost of his defense has taken all his savings. He is fifty-nine years old and essentially destitute. Surely this is punishment enough."

Watching, Jason lost track of the passage of time. The scene took on a flat unreality, as if the courtroom were just a painted backdrop, the judge not a judge but somebody *playing* a judge—having trouble remembering his lines.

Then Freeburg called Brianson to the stand. Jason had hoped the dealer would not show up—for whatever deep strategic reason of his own, if not simply the spirit of perversity. But here he was, walking forward in a gray suit, glistening black wingtips, and a dark red paisley tie. It was hard to believe this could be the same man as the pale figure in a purple caftan, smoking dope and babbling about game theory. But Brian had always known how to play to his audience. Even now, he looked straight at Glasser and gave a conspiratorial wink. When Freeburg asked a question he paused, nodded as if acknowledging the importance of the topic. How would he characterize his relationship with Mr. Glasser? "We were very, very close. I was like a member of the family. I baby-sat Lou's son, Jason, when he was a little kid."

"So you were on intimate terms with Mr. Glasser and his family?"

"I came to New York as a runaway, I was sixteen and living in an abandoned building. To eat, I ran errands for drug dealers, sold loose joints in the park. Lou took me under his wing, he showed me how to survive in this business."

"And what business is that?"

Brian gave his most innocent, childlike smile. "The drug business."

"You jumped bail and became a fugitive. Did you seek out Mr. Glasser's advice before deciding to do that?"

"He said I didn't have much of a chance in court, that I'd better run if I didn't want to do time. He told me to pay my bail bondsman too, so I wouldn't end up with a bounty hunter on my tail. I think it's the best legal advice I ever got."

"So good that you eventually came back for more?"

"I was opening a clothing store and needed somebody to look at the lease."

"You came to Mr. Glasser using your real name, Randy Schotts?"

"No, I used my alias, but I could see that Lou recognized me right off. Later he took me for a ride in his private plane and said point-blank, 'Welcome home, Randy.' After that we dropped any pretense that I was somebody else."

"And you were still in the drug business?"

"I had three partners and a dozen people working for me. We were moving marijuana from Jamaica and Mexico, and each of the partners was clearing something over half a million dollars a year. I was twenty-six."

"And what was the nature of your relationship with Glasser during this period?"

"He handled a number of criminal cases involving people who worked for me."

"Who paid the fees for these cases?"

"I did. It was the arrangement I had with my people, that I'd pay for a lawyer if they got into trouble, and it was a good deal for me too. Lou kept me informed on the scope of the government's case, whether I might get drawn in, and he watched the defendant for me. His job was to get the best result possible without letting the defendant turn state's evidence."

Brian showed no discomfort about sitting on the witness stand, testifying against what he called his family. He was among new friends now, eager to please the pretty woman with the dark hair and yellow pad, the kindly old judge with the red face. *Isn't life strange?* his expression seemed to say. *I was there and now I'm here, in this nice courtroom.*

Jason lost track of the testimony for a while, all but the slow see-saw rhythm of question and answer. He knew that Brian's connection to his father, to his family, was something other than what the dealer claimed, something more distant and more complex, darker. Brian had been freedom and possibility beyond anything the Glassers could have managed on their own, both beautiful and frightening, the source of his father's power to spend without limit. Even as a kid he had sensed that the dealer made his parents giddy in a way they mistrusted, and that underneath it all they were wary and a little scared.

Freeburg finished her questioning, and Hayes got up to cross-examine, looking tired. He took a moment to glance around the room, and the expression on his face said that he'd already written this off as a bad day. *No, don't give up now,* thought Jason. *Destroy Brian. Chew him up like Dad would, pound at him. He's an acid-head and a drug dealer and a rat. In two minutes he'll be contradicting himself, and in ten he'll look like the psychopath he really is.*

But Hayes was dry and arch and exaggeratedly polite, and after maybe a dozen questions it was over. Suddenly Brian was getting up from the stand, walking with the bailiff back toward the door through which he first entered.

Hayes's summation attacked Brian's credibility. "Grandiose, paranoid, very possibly psychotic, his mind and memory undermined by years of admitted drug use. A career criminal and longtime fugitive, last arrested for conspiracy to import and sell a ton of marijuana—a crime for which he has received immunity in exchange for his cooperation in this and other cases. Randy Schotts's testimony is full of lies and exaggerations, of completely uncorroborated statements, and his self-serving motivation is obvious."

Then Glasser got up. From where Jason sat he could only see his father's back, the suit jacket riding up, no longer able to cover his backside. But from long experience in the courts the boy knew how his father must look: hands clasped together in front as if cuffed, shoulders sloped, body sagging at attention. It is a pose of submission, the stance all defendants take when standing before a judge, and it is automatic; there is no stopping the body from taking it. Esther gasped, tightened her grip on Jason's hand. This was real in a way the rest of the hearing had not been; the curve of his father's back was real. His father had crossed some line, impossible to describe but there all the same. The head tilted up to look at the judge, the hands clasped in front: that was what the clients do, the men with long hair, tattoos, and earrings, the men his father had escorted through a thousand courtrooms.

Glasser had stayed up all night writing his statement, had slept only a few hours toward morning. But when he woke and reread what he'd done, he found only half a page of fragmentary sentences—all false starts, all sounding like the opening line of something to come, messy block letters in pencil on a scrap of legal paper, a child's attempt at words. It was so hard to say what you needed to say, especially when you didn't know what that was. For thirty years he had stood in rooms like this one, watching defendants beg mercy from the court. They stood in front of the bench with their heads bowed, shaking as they repeated the formulas he had taught them. They had wives and children; they had made mistakes for which they were sorry, very sorry, and they would never break the law again; they were starting new lives. It was all completely true, and at the same time utterly false; real tears ran from their eyes, but the words were borrowed.

Glasser could use those stock phrases too, he knew them all by heart. But when he tried to apply them to himself, the words dissolved like vapor. He wanted to say that he had pleaded guilty to a crime he never noticed committing, even as he was committing it, that it had only felt like ordinary life, the things you do to fill your day. He wanted to say that Brian had never meant all that much to him, until this happened, and now they were bound together forever. He wanted to ask how this had happened. He wanted everybody to turn away and not look, because his heart was broken.

But what he had found written on the torn piece of paper now folded in his pocket was this:

Your Honor, I am standing here before etc. I went to the pawnshop with my father when I was eleven to pawn a radio and coat, and the next day he was dead. No arrests made. Justice was a thing in your head, an idea you used for comparison. An imperfect thing, my interest in law. He was a very quiet man, always kind to me and my brother, but it was the Depression and that made people hard. You do things in confusion, I know because. It feels like yesterday. What I'm trying to express: life is short. I deeply regret etc. etc. And somehow that has backfired.

The words circled in his head, scrambled and unscrambled as first Freeburg and then Hayes got up to give their summations. He watched them without listening, watched McCall on the bench, his ear cocked and face averted as if to deflect the force of their oratory. What do you say to a man like that, with a longshoreman's hands and a boxer's face? That I was weak? That I am sorry? That I won't do it again?

Struggling to his feet, Glasser could not shake his deep-felt surprise that the moment had really come, that it was happening to him, happening now, and that there was no way to stop it. He listened to the silence of the courtroom, trying to catch his balance on weak legs, leaning on the chair back for support. Bending over, Hayes whispered into his ear; he could feel his lawyer's damp breath on his neck but could not make out the words. The stillness of the room was a vacuum, an empty space into which Hayes was pushing him. For what? To ask forgiveness for something he didn't understand. To apologize for getting caught.

McCall looked at him from the bench with those small, piercing eyes set in the hard block of his face. Freeburg watched him from her chair, straight-backed and alert, still flushed with the effort of her summation. No longer nervous, she took a beginner's pleasure in her performance, but there was nothing personal in her gaze. For her, he was a victory, a job well done, a step in her career—nothing more.

Glasser stood before the bench and began to speak. His voice was soft and low, not the brassy rhetorical instrument he was used to using in court. The words came out one by one or in tight groups— found objects, unexamined, caught at the end of each long breath. He did not listen. He noticed that he had automatically assumed the usual posture, like everybody else: head bowed, hands folded in front. It just happens to you, he thought. That's why everybody does it. He heard himself saying, "I realize the terrible . . . mistake I made . . . and I am deeply . . . sorry . . . I have betrayed . . ." Another voice, in his head this time, screamed, Bullshit! Bullshit!

He was having trouble seeing because of the tears filling his eyes, fuzzing the light, making a milky aureole around the judge's head. The courtroom ceiling was a golden blur. He heard himself say, "The pain . . . of the last year has . . . shown me . . ."

Bullshit! Bullshit!

It was the usual formulas after all. Maybe it was just as well: they did not deserve to know what he could not say. Unspoken, it would remain with him forever, completely his. Numb with exhaustion, he sat down, waited in a kind of trance for his sentence.

J ason watched his father sit down. For a while there was nothing but the sound of his mother's rough breathing near his ear. His face stung, as if slapped. People shifted in their seats, whispered, till the judge put on a pair of glasses and began talking from his notes. His voice had a pleasant downward lilt, and it took a moment to realize that he was passing sentence.

"The court is grateful to counsel for their help in this task, which requires passing judgment on a member of the bar, and balancing his crime, his motivation, his suffering with the needs of society. The tragedy of this conviction derives from Glasser's status as an effective member of the bar of thirty years' standing." The judge readjusted his glasses on his nose, turned the page. The courtroom had grown hot. Jason felt a sudden desperate need for freedom, space, air. He tried to pull his hand from his mother's but couldn't break her grip.

"Whatever the motivation, Glasser's acts became significant because of his status as an attorney. The importance of the concept of justice creates a higher standard for those responsible for its operation. His undeniable suffering this past year, his painful self-realization, and his status as a first offender would have earned him probation if he were an ordinary defendant. But he is not."

Jason couldn't get enough air to fill his lungs. He tried to stand up, to go, but his mother had both her hands on his, pulling him down.

"Incarceration is punishment, pure and simple. It will signal others that crime by lawyers will not be condoned by courts. With this consideration in mind, I impose a jail term of one hundred and twenty days."

13

SURRENDER

A week later they were on the Henry Hudson Parkway, driving Glasser to a prison camp upstate. The Jaguar had been repossessed months before, and Esther had borrowed a car from one of her new friends at the insurance company. It was a battered little compact with hard narrow seats and dirty upholstery, and an engine that whined like a vacuum cleaner. Jason sat in back, alternately staring out at the passing trees and watching his mother's nervous, two-handed use of the steering wheel. He tried to avoid looking at his father, but it was impossible; Glasser overflowed the tiny passenger seat, filling the space in front with his hunched shoulders and broad fatty back.

His father had always been a car lover, and the miserable little compact seemed to be the last straw for him, indisputable proof that he was in fact going to jail. He had fallen deep into himself: eyes blank, face expressionless. It was a speechlessness more profound, more powerful than mere silence, and it negated the agreeable lie that had sprung up among the three of them back in the city: that this trip was just another task, to be carried out as quickly and neatly as possible—like moving furniture.

It was *not* just another task, obviously. Each exit took them farther and farther from the world of normal families and ordinary,
law-abiding fathers—fathers with jobs, fathers who came home at
night, fathers who had nothing to hide. Jason was desperate to turn
around and head back to the city before it was too late, before his
father was no longer his father, before all three of them were lost to
themselves. And yet he knew it was impossible to go back, that in
fact there was nothing to go back *to*. Their old lives were gone.

The little car made slow progress. His mother kept to the right
lane, never passing, never exceeding the speed limit. She and
Jason would bicker for a while, then lapse into a stunned, forgetful
silence, only to start the cycle over again a few miles down the road.
"What kind of shitty car is this anyway?" he whined, annoyed by
his own childishness. "Look at this, the stuffing's coming out." To
illustrate his point he began pulling at a rip in the upholstery.

His mother glanced at him in the rearview mirror. "You know,
you didn't have to come."

"You told me I did." He had taken the red-eye in from Boston,
had used the last fifty dollars in his bank account.

"I thought you could do that much for your father."

"I've done plenty for him, and for you too."

They kept this up for what seemed like hours, till the Henry
Hudson turned into the interstate, till they were both numb with
grief and exhaustion—so bleary they didn't even notice Glasser
eating from the lunch bag Esther had prepared that morning, to
save money on the road. By the time they realized what he was
doing it was too late and everything was gone—his lunch and theirs
too.

"Now look," said Esther, grabbing the empty bag from his lap,
then waving it in the air. Jason could tell she was furious: it was the
first time she'd taken a hand from the wheel except to shift. She
waved the bag in front of his father's face as if brandishing a
chewed-up shoe at a puppy, using that manner of speech reserved
for bad dogs—slow and loud. "You," she said, trying to get his
father's attention. "You ate this, didn't you?" But he wouldn't look
at her; he stared out the passenger window, chewing the last of a
cupcake.

"You. Are. Eating. Us. Alive," she hissed at him, one word at a time, then turned back to the road, steering with exaggerated concentration. She looked shocked and a little frightened at her own outburst.

In the backseat Jason felt a dark excitement move through him, swirling around those words: *Eating us alive.* He had been struck by a truth so immense, so obvious, that he couldn't believe he hadn't seen it before: his father was to blame for their situation; not Brianson, not Freeburg, not Hayes. His father.

They drove in silence for a while, till a rest stop appeared on the horizon and his mother took the turnoff. She sped down the long curving exit ramp and made the tires screech, then stopped at one end of the gigantic parking lot, leaving the little car straddling two spaces. Without a word or a glance she jumped out and started walking toward the low brick cafeteria building. She looked shattered, much older than she'd ever seemed before. It was as if she were trying to hold on to her anger just to keep herself from crumpling with exhaustion.

It took his father some time to struggle out of his seat, and even more to walk the fifty or so yards to the entrance, tottering under all the weight he now carried. Jason walked alongside, unable to tear himself away but unwilling to offer his arm or otherwise help. It was an ugly feeling, denying his father a hand, and it made him angry at all three of them in a deeply satisfying way. If his father had destroyed their lives, then perhaps they deserved it. They all deserved one another.

Inside, the cafeteria was noisy with the clang of silverware and plastic dishes. People sat alone at tables meant for eight, staring into cups of coffee, eyeing each other, checking on their cars from the window. An old woman in a brown uniform pushed her cart among the empty tables, picking up used trays, wiping off tabletops.

Jason joined his mother and began moving down the food line, reading the little cards that said what everything was and how much it cost. He picked a plate of red Jell-O for a dollar twenty-nine, a blindingly white piece of coconut cream cake for a dollar seventy. He picked fried clams on a bun for two eighty-five, complete with a paper cup of tartar sauce crusty from the yellow heat lamp under which it had been sitting. This was the food he wanted—fatty, salty, horribly sweet—the kind of food that confirmed his self-loathing. Five eighty-four of waste.

They stopped at the cashier. "What is that?" his mother said, looking over at his tray. "You can't eat that. Get a salad."

"It's what I want."

She shrugged with disgust, too tired to argue. Just then his father came up with a queer look on his face, one hand behind his back, sneaky like a little kid. When his mother put her head down, digging into her pocketbook, his father put a cellophane-wrapped sandwich on Jason's tray.

"I saw that." His mother looked up, pleased to have caught Glasser in the act. "You had lunch already. *Three* lunches. That's why we're here."

Jason felt too heartsick to watch. "Let him have it," he said to her. "I'll pay."

"If he's got money he can buy it himself. You're not paying for it and neither am I." She handed some bills to the cashier, then turned to face his father. "Put it back. Now."

His father hesitated, his hand on the sandwich. There was a masochistic gleam in his eye and a strange half smile on his face. He had the look of somebody proving something to himself, as if this were a test and he was pleased with the results. *Yes*, he seemed to be saying to himself, *this is what happens to you when you lose all your money and get sent to jail. This is how they treat you.*

"You can have some of my Jell-O," Jason said to him.

Glasser let him take the sandwich from under his fingers. The cellophane was warm and greasy and the sandwich had no weight at all. He took it back to its display case, picked up his tray, then joined his parents at a table by the window. Outside in the parking lot, people climbed from cars, looking startled at the sudden loss of motion. They stretched, blinked, shambled forward over the asphalt. For the first time in his life, Jason felt like he really understood the definition of a stranger: none of these people knew that his family was driving to a prison camp, that his father was going to jail.

He gave his father the red Jell-O and Glasser accepted it without a word, pursing his lips and slurping it straight from the dish as if it were water. Esther looked annoyed but too weary to stop him. She picked at her salad, turning over the wilted leaves with her fork. "If he wants to eat himself to death, there's nothing we can do about it," she said to Jason. "But we can't waste money like we used to."

"I'll be finished with school in another month," said Jason. "I guess that means I'll get a job."

She wasn't listening, however. "I'm the one who stays up nights worrying about money, then gets up at seven to go to work. I'm the one who has to deal with all the creditors."

There was no point in his saying anything, obviously, so he started on the piece of coconut cake, mashing the creamy filling against the roof of his mouth. The taste was so powerfully sweet it made his eyes water—a kind of sugary cascade, a pure whiteout of the senses.

But not quite. He could still hear his mother, like a disembodied voice calling through a blizzard. "How do you think I feel having to say no all the time? Do you think I like playing the penny-pinching ogre?"

"I haven't accused you of anything." The truth was he didn't want to hear about her feelings; he couldn't bear the idea of feeling sorry for her too.

"Look at me," she said. "I'm fifty-five years old and look what he's turned me into."

He bit into his clam sandwich. It was a mixture of something crunchy like sand and another thing soggy like dough, full of grease that spread to his hands and face and even smeared the tabletop. The intense saltiness came as a sort of sensual whiplash, like a hundred-and-eighty-degree turn in a speeding car. His eyes fluttered.

"Are you listening to me? Hello?" His mother rapped her knuckles on the table. "Does it matter to you what I feel?"

"Actually, I feel a little sick."

"That makes two of us."

It was only when they got up to go that he realized his father was gone. They walked outside, and as his mother headed to the car

Jason spotted Glasser standing by some garbage bins. He was staring off at the highway to their left, at the cars streaming by like
beads of water across glass. "C'mon, Dad, it's time to go."

His father looked at him with a weird expression on his face and
began walking—not in the direction of the car but away from it,
toward the highway entrance ramp. "Not that way. This way. *Dad*."

At that his father started to run. It was not running, really—he
was too heavy for that—but more like a slow stumbling forward. His
head bobbed and his arms pumped, but he covered little ground.
Jason watched him for a moment, stunned. He's trying to escape, he
realized. *From us.* He started to jog after him, and by the time he
caught up his father was barely moving, the highway still fifty yards
away. Jason grabbed his arm. "Let me go," his father wheezed.

"Dad—"

"Let me go."

What if we run away? thought Jason. What if we run away
together? He looked at his father, then at the no-man's-land beyond
the rest stop, a flat landscape of weeds and dusty shrubbery, dirt
lots and construction equipment. "Where?" he asked.

But his father wasn't really listening. "Let me go," he whispered
again, pulling against Jason's grip. But his eyes said, Take me back.

The last hour of the trip seemed to take years. Jason watched the
roadside scenery creep by his window—gravel pit, garbage dump,
Dairy Queen, gas station. He was not even bored, only intensely,
deeply numb, and for whole minutes at a time he forgot where they
were going and why. His father looked straight ahead, his lids half
closed, his face trancelike, an unlit cigarette forgotten between his
fingers.

They spent a great deal of time wandering up and down local
roads, till the sign saying Firnstil Federal Correctional Facility
appeared, standing in some shrubs. They turned off into a driveway
rutted with potholes, followed it to a gate with a little metal guard-
house that looked something like a tollbooth. There was a chain-
link fence spreading in either direction, topped with barbed wire,
but it was no more intimidating than what often circles a parking lot
or construction site. His mother handed his father's paperwork

through the car window and the guard looked it over, then bent down to give her directions.

Once inside, they parked by a long, low building much like the cafeteria in which they had eaten lunch. Firnstil looked like a big rest stop really, with small orange-brick buildings strung along the edges of a patchy lawn, connected by an asphalt walk. Jason and his mother helped his father out of the car, then supported him through the parking lot. His father put one foot slowly in front of the other, gulping air and talking to himself in a voice Jason had never heard before, low and scratchy. He seemed to be saying the same incomprehensible thing over and over again, chuckling. Something like, Farts in the wind, farts in the wind, yoohoo, yoohoo. Then he began to weep.

When Jason said good-bye his father looked straight through him, as if he didn't know who he was. "My blood pressure," said Glasser. "Explosive. I can feel it."

"Don't worry about us, we'll be okay."

His father looked up at the clouds. "What did I do? I must have done something." He looked at Jason again. "No, really, tell me, I want to know."

14

CLUB FED

Firnstil Correctional Camp was one of those so-called country-club prisons, and about a third of the inmates were white-collar: double-billing doctors, embezzling lawyers, fallen politicians, just about every type of fraudulent businessman imaginable. The remaining two-thirds were mostly petty criminals on short sentences: small-time dope dealers, con men, and check kiters. Only a few were serious felons, and these enjoyed a paradoxically elite status, walking about with an air of solemn dignity, hard men with nothing to prove. In reality they were weary and wanted no trouble. Having already served ten or fifteen years in the big medium-security facility down the road—Firnstil Senior, it was called—they had been transferred to Firnstil Junior, the country club, to finish out the last year or two before their release.

As it happened, Glasser had visited both places some years before, coming up to see two old clients in Firnstil Senior and then taking the opportunity to interview a new client at the country club. The difference had been striking. Firnstil Senior looked like a cross between a medieval castle and a steel factory: an enormous block of a building, streaked black with grime and circled by a thirty-foot granite wall, complete with guard towers and floodlights. The inmates there exercised in a dirt yard, watched from the parapets by guards shouldering shotguns.

Firnstil Junior had looked more like an army base, or a military school fallen on hard times. Standing in the parking lot, Glasser had seen a collection of small brick buildings, cheaply constructed and strung along a cracked asphalt path. The grounds themselves were spacious but poorly kept, the grass worn to dirt in places, the trees stunted and spindly. The visiting room in which he'd met his client was painted a forlorn shade of government-surplus orange and decorated with old travel posters proclaiming the joys of España and Italia. One wall had been covered with pen-pal letters from inmates in a correctional facility somewhere in Belgium, the result of a short-lived "sister-prisons" program.

On learning of his own assignment to Firnstil, Glasser was glad that this client had been released over a year before, that nobody would know him from his previous life as a lawyer. But now, after two full days as an inmate, he found himself wishing that he had somebody to explain things, perhaps even to watch out for him. Firnstil was a country-club prison, but it was still a prison; the atmosphere was not menacing or dangerous, but it was decidedly pissed off. In just forty-eight hours he had seen a shoving match over a place in line, a fistfight over a cigarette. There was a code of conduct among the inmates, clearly, but he had no idea what the specific rules of that code were. As a result, he worried about the implications of even the simplest acts, such as sitting down in the cafeteria. What if he sat in somebody else's seat? What if he chose the wrong group of people—a tough bunch looking for trouble?

On this, his third morning, Glasser followed the others into the dining hall, waited in the food line with his tray, then drifted over to one of the tables, already three-quarters full. There he hesitated, scanning the occupants. At first they were all blurrily similar, an effect of the khaki uniforms, the brown plastic cereal bowls, but after a moment he was able to draw some distinctions. Four Hispanic men occupied one end, chatting in Spanish, and a block of five or six middle-aged white men held the center. These last had the sullen, bewildered air of downsized executives contemplating their pink slips. They glanced up at Glasser through a haze of private distress, then went back to their food.

Glasser took a spot on the near end of the bench and huddled over his tray, careful not to make eye contact with his neighbors. He had loved his clients, but he had never forgotten that he was different from them, a lawyer. That distinction was gone now, but he still fought hard to hold the line. He was in jail, and the men around him were criminals, a word that he would not, could not, use in connection with himself, regardless of the guilty plea. He wanted nothing to do with their hard-luck stories, their family problems and money schemes, the things he overheard while lying on his bunk. He wanted to meet no one, speak to no one. He wanted Firnstil to flow over him like water, leaving no mark, no memory, no bruise.

He turned his attention to the food. Between his sentencing and his surrender at Firnstil, Glasser had eaten himself to the two-hundred-and-fifty-pound mark, a kind of penance through piggery, as if he'd meant to smother himself before reaching prison. In a sense, he had succeeded. His face was now swollen to the point of unrecognizability, a generic fat-man mask, and his frightened, angry eyes were all but invisible. His breathing came hard, and his voice when he bothered to talk was like wind whistling through shutters.

It had taken a lot of eating to get him to this point, but there were no between-meal snacks at Firnstil, and the meals themselves were an institutional horror, frightening even to a man acquainted with late-night mayonnaise sandwiches. Dinner the night before had been a single slice of meatloaf—more cereal than meat—and a mound of instant mashed potatoes, vaguely soapy. Breakfast this morning was the same as the two days previous, a bowl of gray oatmeal, thin and oily. Glasser was hungry all the time, hungry in a way he hadn't known since childhood: empty, with no hope of relief.

He gobbled his oatmeal in a panic of loss, cleaning the bowl with his finger to get the last slippery bits. When he looked up he saw someone he hadn't noticed before, watching him from across the table. It was a surprisingly elderly man, with white hair and wrinkled hands. "Want this?" the old man asked, pushing his untouched bowl toward Glasser.

"You don't?"

"This stuff?" The old man gave a disdainful wave of his fingers, then went back to his former occupation, dunking a tea bag in a cup of hot water. He had a long narrow face, dominated by a powerful nose and cold blue eyes, feathery white eyebrows. The overall effect was strangely pleasant, a mixture of cunning and—not kindness, perhaps, but detachment, a willingness to forgo harm.

Glasser hesitated, but in the end it was hunger that decided: he took the bowl and swallowed down the oatmeal, once again mopping up with his finger. The stuff was vile and did nothing to fill the emptiness in his gut, but the need to try was completely reflexive, like pulling a splinter from his foot.

The old man watched with a calm, proprietary interest, primly sipping his tea. He did not speak again till Glasser had finished. "Time for my morning walk," he said simply, and then, seeing Glasser hesitate: "I'll take your arm. It's wet out, and if I break a hip I'm finished."

This was a strange way to ask, but the ex-lawyer rose from the table, too uncertain to refuse. They left the cafeteria together, stopping for a while outside on the steps to the entrance. Glasser looked across the patchy brown lawn to the orange-brick Administration Building, the parking lot, and the front gate with its tiny guard box, no bigger than a phone booth. Firnstil was little changed from when he'd visited as a lawyer. It had that same air of institutional exhaustion, of a place slowly dying of apathy and boredom. There were tall weeds growing out of cracks in the walkway, stray pieces of litter in the grass. The new shrubs surrounding the cafeteria had already withered into a tangle of thwarted branches.

The old man looked around for a moment, then took a cigar from his breast pocket and lit it, letting out a cloud of rich smoke. In contrast to the seedy surroundings he cut a lean, almost elegant figure, vaguely military in his neatly pressed prison khakis, his severe white hair combed straight back with pomade. He took Glasser's arm in a surprisingly strong grip. "Okay, let's go."

The path was still slick from an early-morning rain, and the old man took cautious steps; the pace was slow even for Glasser, who could barely manage more than a shuffle. It was just six-thirty, and as work details did not begin till seven the camp was silent, the aggressive drabness of the place softened by the fresh May light. They passed the bunkhouses, a row of six identical brick boxes holding Firnstil's four hundred inmates, and then swung left around the gym, a large aluminum Quonset hut with a volleyball net strung on poles on the yellow lawn outside.

The old man talked between puffs on his cigar, gradually moving from subject to subject: the weather, vitamins, protein supplements. He introduced himself as Covington, without giving a first name, and Glasser would learn later that the whole camp—even the guards—addressed him simply as Mr. Covington. Yet the surname was obviously fake, or to put it more charitably, a later addition: Covington was clearly Jewish, perhaps even an immigrant; there were slight traces of a Middle European accent among his rough vowels.

Glasser did not ask, and Covington did not deny, though his round blue eyes seemed aware of the other's thoughts. Instead, he demanded that the younger man guess his age. "Seventy," said Glasser, shaving off four or five years in order to flatter him.

The old man gave a satisfied puff on his cigar. "Eighty-seven."

As he told it, he had run a savings and loan in Arizona that had gone under in the nationwide wave of bankruptcies, and in a subsequent criminal trial he'd gotten five years for fraud, malfeasance, tax evasion, and embezzlement. "More time than Charles Keating," he told Glasser, a glimmer of amusement in his sharp features. "They think I'll never make it, but believe me, I will. Thirteen days after my ninetieth birthday I'll be walking out of here. Look at this." He made a muscle with his free arm. "Weight training, every day."

"And then what?" Glasser was addressing himself, really. Broke, disbarred, he could see nothing in his own life worth returning to.

"I'm a rich man, Louis. I gave the government a hundred million dollars and they took ten years off my sentence, but I kept a bit too. I've got plans for when I get out."

"Well sure, with money it's different. You can retire in luxury."

"Retire? This is enough retirement for one life." He swung his free arm to indicate the camp. "I've got backers just waiting for me to get out, people who trust me with their money."

By now their path had drawn alongside the perimeter fence. Twelve feet high, chain-link, with a single roll of concertina wire at the top, it could be scaled in a few seconds by a limber adult, yet it was the only barrier separating Firnstil from the outside world. Glasser stopped to touch it with his free hand, thinking how strange it was that this flimsy thing managed to hold four hundred men captive.

"Forget about it," said Covington, blasé.

Beyond the chain-link Glasser could see only trees, well mannered and mossy, but he knew the road wasn't more than two hundred yards straight ahead. "No guard towers, no lights."

"The world doesn't work that way, Louis. Climb that fence and there's no place to go."

"But there is." Glasser was whispering now, embarrassed by his own excited tone. "Hitchhike up to Buffalo, buy a fake passport—I know how to do that. Then take a bus right over the border to Canada."

"Use a credit card, use an ATM, and they'll find you."

"I can get money, no strings attached."

Covington's feathery eyebrows rose, gently mocking. "Money without strings, that's a new one."

"People owe me," said Glasser, meaning his clients, the men he'd spent thirty years saving from just this fate. "They'd help."

"I see. So they'll just *give* you the money."

Glasser drew himself up, defensive. "That's right." But the doubt was now firmly lodged in his mind.

"And then what?"

"Fly to Europe, change airlines, fly to Israel. Immediate citizenship under the law of return."

"And what will you do there without money?"

"Work on a kibbutz. You don't need money then."

"A man of your age picking oranges?"

"At least I'd be free." He meant something more by this word: free of himself, of the wreckage of his past.

"Louis, it's all too much for a crappy four-month sentence. Just serve your time and get on with your life."

Glasser could only moan. "Shit," he said, rattling the chain-link. "Fuck." At two hundred and fifty pounds there was really no danger of him trying to scale the fence—the truth was, he could barely walk. But it made him furious that the prison authorities couldn't be bothered to supply him with walls and floodlights and shoot-to-kill orders, that they depended on his own common sense, his fat, and his despair to keep him inside, like an old house cat. And it made him even angrier that they were right, that they knew him so exactly. Each day felt like a weary lifetime, and yet the only way he was leaving was through the front gate, at the end of his sentence.

And if Esther didn't come to pick him up he might just stay on indefinitely, too demoralized to walk out or call a cab.

Firnstil was a psychological prison; most of its security resources went into making the inmates feel like prisoners in spite of the lack of walls. The process had started for Glasser on arrival, when he and five others were marched into a kind of storeroom, where they were ordered to strip naked and place their clothes in boxes. Goose-bumped and shivering with fright, Glasser focused his attention on the precise folding of his shirt and pants, smoothing out imaginary wrinkles. How many times had he been naked in front of other men? As a kid he'd gone with his father to the steam baths on Tenth Street, but other than the doctor's office, that was about it. He had never been an athlete and was unfamiliar with locker rooms. The male camaraderie he'd known had all taken place in restaurants and offices and the hallways of court buildings, where costumery, three-piece suits, ties and cuff links were an essential part of the ritual.

Clothes packed, he had stood at attention, shifting from foot to foot as if the floor were hot, his hands cupped over his genitals. The gray uniforms of the guards had had a terrible power then, and he had avoided the cold eyes, the grimly disgusted expressions.

"Gentle-mun, this is a cavity search," a bored, upstate country voice had bellowed. "Turn to the wall, bend over, and spread the but-tocks."

Bent over, Glasser had felt the blood rush to his head, dizziness mixing with shame. A man of his bulk was not made to hold such a pose; he was afraid he would pass out and fall. His eyes moved from wall to floor to the great curve of his belly, which hid his nether half, all but a set of ten long white toes, splayed and delicate. His vision shimmered, and his legs trembled.

Over the next two days, Glasser had learned that dispensing humiliation in the guise of security was in fact the guards' only function. The administration of Firnstil had grasped a fundamental precept of prison psychology: humiliate the inmates enough, often enough, and there was no need to watch the fence, because nobody would dare to think of escape. So the guards spent their days in spot checks and random searches, the more arbitrary the better. They could strip an inmate naked where he stood, in the cafeteria or the rec room, write him up for an infraction without the slightest proof. These citations could have a variety of consequences, from the loss of gym privileges to the loss of parole, from time in the bing—solitary confinement—to the most extreme and dreaded end: transfer up the road to Firnstil Senior.

Now, with the toe of his sneaker, Glasser started to scrape wistfully at the soft ground by the fence. "I bet you could dig under this real easy."

But Covington had lost patience. "Come on, forget about it. I've got an appointment I don't want to miss."

He led them to the rear of the cafeteria building. There was a loading dock, a large green Dumpster fruity with rotting garbage, a vent blowing hot air from the kitchen. He steered Glasser over to a metal door, giving it a set of sharp raps with his fist—surprising strength in those thin forearms.

"What are you doing?" asked Glasser, alarmed. He didn't want to get involved in any trouble.

"Relax and you'll see how an operator operates."

Glasser didn't have a chance to respond. The door swung open and a big burly man came out, face red and sweaty from the kitchen heat. He was dressed in a cook's white top and a long apron streaked with food stains, but his pants were prison khakis. He glanced at Covington, then gave a careful look both ways before hauling out a small brown shopping bag.

"Bruno, how are you?" Covington reached into his breast pocket and handed the man a cigar.

Bruno sniffed the thing with evident satisfaction, then passed Covington the bag. "Gotta run, Mr. Covington. Soup's on." He ducked back into the kitchen, closing the door behind him.

Covington carried the bag into the fragrant shadow of the Dumpster, then started emptying its contents into his various pockets: two carrots, a turnip, a green pepper, a tomato, an apple, a grapefruit, what Glasser took to be three hard-boiled eggs. Anything that wouldn't fit discreetly into his pockets he stuffed into his shirt, which began to bulge at the waist.

Glasser watched with hungry eyes. "You going to eat all that?"

"I have a healthy appetite, thank god." Covington took Glasser's arm once again, pointing him toward the path. "Okay, walk me to my bunk." He stuck close this time, using the ex-lawyer's great bulk to draw attention away from the bulge in his shirt. "So you see how it works here, Louis. Wherever there are human beings, there is a market. Bruno is a cigar fancier. I trade Bruno a cigar for some fresh vegetables, before they boil the hell out of them or cover them in oil."

"You can buy cigars in the commissary?" asked Glasser.

Covington looked amused. "You can't buy these in the entire country, Louis—they're Cuban, and I get them from a guy who gets them in Mexico. My daughter lives in Westchester, and she brings them when she visits."

"She smuggles them in?"

"My daughter? Of course not. She drops a box off with Ira, the night clerk at the motel down Route Twenty-nine, and then Mario goes to pick them up."

Glasser had already heard this name before. "You mean the guy in bunk three?"

"That's right, Mario, the nutty kid. You see, it's all right to go over the fence as long as you come back before the count." He meant the roll call held at 5:30 each morning. "Mario works for Gino in bunk four, bringing in stuff to sell or trade—liquor, drugs, dirty magazines. Anything you want, they take special orders."

"Chinese food?"

"For that you just ask one of the screws." He meant the guards. "Give him five bucks for his trouble."

"I don't have any money." Money was forbidden in the camp; Glasser had assumed that nobody had any. The only legitimate purchases to be made were at the commissary, where each prisoner had an account that could only be filled from outside. Esther had sent in a check for fifty dollars—the topmost limit—but the store sold little more than shaving cream, toothpaste, and cigarettes. Most important, it didn't sell food.

Covington shrugged off the money question. "Well, that's another story, but if you have any currency, hide it on the grounds, not on your body. Now a word of advice. Some of the guys go over the fence to meet their girlfriends at the motel. I don't recommend it, you understand. It's too much trouble, and for what?"

They stopped in front of Covington's bunkhouse. He took out yet another cigar and slipped it into Glasser's breast pocket. There was something old-fashioned in the gesture, like a big spender tipping the maître d' at El Morocco, and though Glasser felt he should be offended he just couldn't find it in him. The cigar would obviously be useful.

"Now listen to me," said Covington. "This is payment in advance, because I trust you. For one week you will take me on my morning walk just as you did today. If you want, you can trade the cigar to Bruno for some extra food, or you can make a deal with Carl in the laundry for some khakis that fit. Tell him I sent you."

Glasser looked himself over, the first time he'd thought to do so. His shirt was stretched to the ripping point, a six-inch swath of pale stomach showing where two of the buttons had already popped. His pants were even worse: he couldn't get them up to his waist, and he still had to leave them half unzipped in order to breathe. "These are the ones they gave me."

"It's up to you," said Covington. "All I ask is that if you choose to smoke the cigar, you light it with a match—a wooden match is best. Butane from a lighter poisons the flavor."

He started up the two steps into his building, arms crossed over the bulge in his shirt. "Oh yes, you don't have a job yet, do you?"

"No, not yet." Work was not required at Firnstil. Indeed, there weren't enough jobs to go around, and competition for the better ones was intense.

"Well, if you want a good one, come to me. I've got some pull."

Glasser went back to his own bunkhouse, number six, at the end of the row. His room was on the first of two floors, a narrow, low-ceilinged space crammed with twelve metal-frame bunk beds. It was here that he'd spent the last two nights, staring up with dry burning eyes at the stained underside of the mattress above as he listened to twenty-three strangers snore, snuffle, masturbate, and pass gas.

Glasser sat down on his bed, dreading the hours till lunch. Though the barracks were quiet now, they offered him no rest. The others had gone to work, but their possessions remained, screaming in his ear. Two footlockers under each bunk, two calendars on the wall, a hot plate, an electric fan, a blackened pot, a card table with an old manual typewriter.

The bed next to his had an upside-down orange crate that served as a nightstand; an ancient tape deck sat on top, next to a shoebox full of country-western cassettes. The cassettes were warped from overuse, and Glasser had spent the last two evenings listening with everyone else to the plaintive sounds, elongated like taffy, background music for circular conversations about family, finances, run-ins with the screws. Both evenings had had the deeply grooved feel of a routine that never varied. One man after another had gotten up to take his turn at the card table in the corner, and the snap of typewriter keys had melded with the music, a percussive accompaniment like castanets or tap dancing.

Glasser knew what his roommates were working on—he had glanced at the stack of boilerplate legal forms, the handful of old law books lined up in the space under the table. Over the years he had watched judges roll their eyes and snicker at these jailhouse appeals, with their eccentric reasoning, their sudden detours into autobiography and medical complaint, tales of marital woe.

He realized now that he had made a mistake telling Covington what he was in for; the word would go around that he was a lawyer—had once been a lawyer—and then they would all want his help on those doomed appeals. He was no longer interested in assisting others with their lies and evasions, their self-protective schemes. He had spent thirty years saving his clients from jail, and his reward had been betrayal and bankruptcy—and yes, jail. Of course he saw the self-delusion in what he had told Covington by the fence: there was no one he could call, even if he made it over the barbed wire without a heart attack. Auerbach? Feldman? Would either of them drive out of the city at midnight for him, clutching a paper bag of cash?

That kind of loyalty was gone from the world, if it had ever truly existed. He was alone, and he wanted only to be left alone, to wait out his sentence in peace. And yet the loneliness was terrible too. It was another type of hunger, an ache in his head just like the one in his stomach, and together the two pains tormented him. He had slept only a couple of hours toward daybreak, but he knew that he would not sleep now, that his mind would continue to spin and his body tremble with sick vertigo.

He got up and fled outside but came to a stop in the grass, uncertain where to go. Covington would be in the gym doing his calisthenics, his isometrics, lifting two-pound dumbbells with his thin hard arms, a cigar stuck in his mouth. Why go there? To be lectured by a crooked banker? The rec room contained a TV but it was always—always—tuned to some form of sports, badminton or croquet if nothing else was available. As for the library, it was really nothing more than a storeroom, without tables or chairs or even bookshelves. Water-spotted paperbacks, mysteries and thrillers, thrown together in a couple of cardboard boxes.

It was then that he remembered the cigar tucked in his breast pocket. Smoke it? Take it to Bruno in the kitchen? Carl in the laundry? And trade it for what? The sense of wanting was desperate, but the object of that wanting was still obscure. He knew only that the thing he needed was not a turnip or a can of beets or a shirt that fit. With a sudden flash of inspiration, he started for bunk three—Mario's bunkhouse.

Inside the front door, he walked into the first room he found. It was smaller than his own, six bunk beds lined up against the wall barracks-fashion, a couple of them neatly made, the others a tangle of sheets. The room was stuffy and warm, the atmosphere of too many people living in an enclosed space, full of concentrated male smells: cheap aftershave, cigarettes, sweat and dirty clothes, instant coffee. At first glance the place seemed unoccupied, but then Glasser noticed a single figure stretched out on one of the bottom bunks, eyes closed and legs crossed at the ankles, hands behind his head. The man was black, in a white undershirt and khaki pants, bare feet. Glasser started to back out of the doorway.

"I'm not asleep," said the man, his eyes still closed.

"Sorry," said Glasser. "I'm looking for Mario."

The man turned his head, eyes open now. "That's me."

Glasser hesitated. Half the camp was black, but he had been misled by the name into expecting an Italian, especially since he knew that Gino, Mario's boss, was an Italian from Bensonhurst. "Covington suggested I contact you. I'm interested in"—he dropped his voice—"you know."

"No, I don't know."

He lowered his voice still further, till he was barely whispering. "Placing an order."

Mario rose slowly to sitting position, rubbing his face with the palms of his hands. He was thirty-five, perhaps, or a little older, slightly built, with a boyish angular face and deep furrows in his forehead, a look of habitual brooding. His eyes were large and brown, but the whites were unhealthy, shot through with red veins. "I don't know you," he said.

"I've got this." Glasser pulled out the cigar.

Mario glanced at Covington's Cuban, then up at Glasser. "What are you looking for?"

Suddenly Glasser knew. "I want snack food, HoHos or Devil Dogs, something sweet."

Mario stared for a moment, then broke into a wet smoker's laugh. "Man, don't poison yourself with that shit. I can get you some 'ludes, how about that? We've got an overstock on 'ludes."

"Ring-Dings or Yodels," said Glasser, shaking his head. "I'm a man of simple tastes."

Mario laughed again, a private sort of chuckle this time, introverted and sour. He reached deep under his mattress and pulled out a small hip flask, unscrewed the top, and took a thirsty swig. It was only then that Glasser realized the man was in fact drunk, very drunk, though he held it with practiced ease.

"Eye opener?" asked Mario, offering the flask. It was barely eight A.M.

"Too early for me," said Glasser, wondering how this situation would affect their negotiations.

Mario simply shrugged and took another drink, and then another, and with each lift of the flask his face seemed to grow increasingly angular, as if his flesh were melting from the bone. "So you're new, huh?"

"Third day."

"Settling in?" he asked, eyes sweeping the barracks. The expression was meant to be theatrical and amusing but carried a load of real despair. He took another drink and then leveled a challenging stare at Glasser. "Can you believe I did this to myself?"

"Umm," said Glasser, hoping to forestall the story Mario was obviously preparing to tell. The only thing he wanted from this man was a little chocolate, nothing more—certainly nothing personal.

But it was too late. Mario had the same compulsion to talk that everyone at Firnstil shared, a compound of boredom and frustration and deep bewilderment. "I know what you're thinking, man, but I'm no criminal." He tapped his chest with the butt of the flask. "No criminal."

This was true, as it turned out: Mario was a draft dodger. He graduated high school in 1970, and a few months later his selective service number came up. A draft-resisters' organization helped pay his ticket to Sweden, and he worked in the group's Stockholm office for a couple of years, then managed a jazz club. "Tone-deaf," he said, taking another swig, "but I looked the part. Big Afro, dashiki—the Swedes loved me. And I loved standing behind the bar, watching all those blond heads bobbing so politely to the music. They were so goddamn polite, man, so *interested.*" He seemed rapt by the memory. "I was eighteen fucking years old, and in the space of a plane ride I'd gone from Detroit nigger to anti-imperialist peace hero. Anything was possible."

Glasser was sitting on the adjacent bed by this point, involved in spite of himself. He too could remember 1970 and that feeling of infinite possibility. In 1970, Jason was a little kid, and Howie Silverman was Glasser's biggest client, helping him build his practice among the East Village hippies, the pot dealers and acid freaks. Randy Schotts had jumped bail and disappeared underground—hardly more than a speck in Glasser's consciousness.

"Those were some good years," said Glasser.

Mario looked maudlin. "I loved Sweden."

"Then what are you doing here?"

"Six months." Mario snickered at his own joke, then took another sip from the flask. "The club folded back in 'eighty-three and I was out of work for almost two years. There ain't no jobs over there, man, even for Swedes. My old lady waited tables in a tourist joint—they made her wear a goddamn Viking helmet with horns. It gave her headaches. Finally I got something in a Saab factory. You ever work in a factory?"

Glasser shook his head. "Self-employed."

Something like contempt filled Mario's bloodshot eyes—he clearly felt himself superior on the scale of suffering. "Eight fucking hours a day, riveting truck bodies, just like my old man back in Detroit. If I hadn't hurt my back I would've gone insane." He broke into a clogged bronchial cough and the anger seemed to dissipate. "I don't know, after that the air just went out of me, like a leaky balloon. I got homesick, I drank, my marriage fell apart." He waved his hand weakly, as if shooing a fly. "The usual shit."

But the detail about Mario's back had caught Glasser's attention, making him worry about his sweets. "Wait a second: how do you get over the fence if you've got a bad back?"

Mario reached under the mattress again and pulled out a jumbo bottle of aspirin, three times bigger than the kind they carried in the commissary. With a what-the-heck gesture he popped the lid and swallowed a couple of tablets. But he seemed less interested in his back pain than in his failure as an exile. "I speak Swedish like a fucking native, man, but the words just roll out like somebody else is talking. For eighteen years I didn't understand a word I was saying."

"So you came back and they arrested you in the airport."

Mario gave a philosophical shrug, then lay back down in bed, closing his eyes. "Who can figure out the white man?"

There was a long silence, in which Glasser sat fidgeting. To a large extent it was self-interest: he was worried that Mario had forgotten his order. Leave? Come back later? He was about to get up when the draft dodger spoke. "I'd have to go to the convenience store on Route Twenty-nine. The screws gas up their cars there, but I know they've got Devil Dogs and shit like that. I can get you four boxes."

"Eight," said Glasser, certain that even this was too little. He was no aficionado, but he knew that Cubans were expensive, and that they were probably worth even more inside the camp. After all, a single cigar was a week's wages as Covington's paid companion.

"Six it is," said Mario, as if they had already agreed. "Three the first night, three the second. I can't carry too much at one time."

As the days passed, Glasser established a routine, eating breakfast with Covington—this ensured him two bowls of the oily oatmeal—then taking the ancient health fanatic on his morning walk, usually ending at the back door to the kitchen, where they met Bruno. Covington knew that Glasser had used his cigar to buy sweets from Mario, but this seemed to bother him less than the ex-lawyer's failure to get khakis that fit. "It looks sloppy," he said one morning, as they were strolling past the gym.

"I'm in jail," said Glasser. "Not the cocktail circuit."

"It's a question of self-respect, Louis, and it reflects badly on me too."

"It's got nothing to do with you." Glasser struggled to suppress his rising irritation. It was Monday, and he knew Covington was still recovering from Sunday, visiting day, a tough time for everyone at Firnstil. Covington's daughter had turned out to be a surprisingly tall, birdlike woman with nervous, sinewy fingers. The old man had bullied her the entire time, till her dark eyes sank visibly deeper into her face; but he had wept when she left.

As for Glasser, he had called Esther Saturday night and explicitly ordered her not to come. She had come anyway, as he knew she would, waiting in the visiting room with a look of grim martyrdom on her face, her presence a challenge and a rebuke to his fallen status—or so he felt. He had peeked at her through the doorway, just to make sure she was there, then slipped over to Mario's bunk, where he found the draft dodger stretched out on the hard floor, nursing his bad back. Eighteen years in Sweden without mailing a postcard, and Mario got no visitors.

Once they passed the gym, Covington and Glasser took the fork to their right, the one that led them along the perimeter fence and back to the cafeteria. Still brooding, the old man stumbled on a crack in the asphalt path, and Glasser steadied him. "And what about a job?" asked Covington, his voice increasingly querulous. "I thought you wanted a job."

"That's before I found out the going rate." Glasser had been horrified to learn that inmates got thirty-eight cents an hour for work inside the prison camp. Worse than insulting, the money was absurd, and it pointed up the essential absurdity of his situation. For thirty years he had punished himself with fourteen-hour days, at the mercy of the phone by his bedside, getting up at all hours to find a bail bondsman, attend a night arraignment. The result was that he was broke, busted, disbarred, jailed.

"Money's got nothing to do with it," snapped Covington. "You'll go crazy in here without a job."

"*You* don't have one."

"At eighty-seven years old my health is a full-time job." This was true, more or less; the old man spent his day steaming vegetables and doing yoga in the gym, a towel wrapped around his neck. Whatever time was left over he spent on the pay phone, talking long-distance to his accountant in something that sounded like code.

"Well, I'm pretty busy too," said Glasser. Indeed, since befriending Mario, he had realized that there were not enough hours in the day to savor all the anger he felt. He and the draft dodger sat in the bunk or a secluded spot on the prison grounds, Mario drinking from his hip flask while Glasser consumed the Devil Dogs he'd gotten with Covington's cigar. Together, they railed at the prosecutors who had persecuted them, the lawyers who had failed to defend them, the judges who had hypocritically passed sentence. Glasser told Mario about Brianson, and Mario returned the compliment with harrowing, X-rated stories about his estranged wife, Ingrid, whom he portrayed alternately as a sex-crazed dypsomaniac and a frigid, teetotaling, racist prude. Mouth stuffed with Devildogs, Glasser found both versions highly amusing, whatever the contradictions.

But Covington didn't approve. "That crazy kid Mario is going to get you in trouble," he said now.

"Mario? He's teaching me Swedish."

Covington gripped Glasser's arm tighter, stopping him by the perimeter fence. "Louis, you're like an idiot child. You say you were a lawyer and I don't doubt you, but how could anyone so naive practice law? Mario and Gino have been shorting the screws."

"What do you mean?"

"They haven't been paying the guards their percentage, and they are headed for trouble. Everybody knows this but you."

Glasser's ignorance was not surprising, since he avoided everyone besides Covington and Mario. The news hit him hard, but he managed to conceal it, finishing out the old man's walk before heading over to Mario's bunk for their daily rendezvous. He found the draft dodger in what had become his usual position, spread-eagled on the floor, the jumbo bottle of aspirin by his side and a pillow under his head.

"How's the back?" asked Glasser, sitting himself on the nearest bed.

"Fucking killing me," said Mario. "I could barely walk back after breakfast. Gino had to help me."

"If it hurts so bad, why don't you just give it up?" He meant climbing over the fence at night.

Mario gave him a suspicious look, as if wondering how Glasser had suddenly been transformed into such an intolerable square. "If I don't go, who's going to bring you back those yummy treats you like?"

Glasser hadn't thought of that. "But still—"

Mario gave an angry laugh. "Everybody's got a job to do." He lifted the ubiquitous hip flask and took a drink, then seemed to consider the question further. "I like going over the fence. I like walking through the woods at night. And I like my Kools too." He lifted the green pack of cigarettes by his side, a brand unavailable in the commissary. "Most of all, I like having them when I'm not supposed to."

"What if you slip a disc? You could do yourself some permanent damage."

Mario lit one of the cigarettes, then winced as a spasm passed through his lower back. "So? Who gives a shit?"

"Well, you're out of here in four more months, just like me. All you have to do is play it cool."

"Now you sound like Old Man Covetousness." He snickered at his nickname for Covington, then took a drag on his cigarette. "Forget about that shit, man. You may be broke and disbarred, or whatever they call it, but I am broke and black, and that's a whole lot worse. When I get out of here there's nowhere for me to go."

"That's not true—"

"Fuck yes, it's true. Back to Sweden? Ingrid has an order of protection against me. Back to Detroit? I haven't spoken to my family in eighteen years. I'm a goddamn Vietnam-era fossil, preserved like a bug in amber." He looked at the flask in his hand and then grinned at Glasser. "Or is it aquavit?"

It was the grin that upset Glasser more than anything; he decided to cut straight to the point. "Why didn't you tell me you and Gino were shorting the screws?"

Mario gave him a long stare, then took a deep drag on his cigarette. "Start to bug me, Lou, and you'll have to go elsewhere for your chocolate cakes. Get it?"

"Is Gino trying to make it up to them?"

This seemed to be the last straw for Mario. He tried to raise himself up on his elbows, only to fall back down, grimacing with pain. "Fuck Gino," he said through clenched teeth, staring up at the ceiling. "I ain't his nigger. And fuck the fucking screws. A man's got a right to make a living without kissing everybody's ass. Shit, it hurts."

"Maybe we should get you a doctor."

"What I need is a fucking divorce lawyer." From his place on the floor he pointed to his footlocker. "Take a look in there, she's served me with papers."

Glasser opened the lid and retrieved an official-looking document written in Swedish. "How long have you had this thing?"

"Couple of days, I guess. Who knows."

"Is there property involved?" He riffled the pages, trying to sound lawyerly, as in the old days. Of course, he had no idea what the document actually said.

Mario gave his usual self-disgusted snicker. "Are debts considered property?"

"Then you don't need a lawyer. Her lawyer will handle everything." He said this lightly, with a shrug, but was caught up short by the look of angry bereavement on the draft dodger's face.

"No, man, you don't understand, I'm going to fight it. I don't want a divorce." He took a long drink from the flask. "And neither does she." There was a hard stubborn gleam in his red-rimmed eyes.

Glasser nodded gently, putting the papers back in the open footlocker. Between the drink and the back pain, the Swedish divorce and the nocturnal trips over the fence, Mario had no mental energy left to consider the financial needs of the prison guards—that much was clear. Indeed, every time Glasser managed to maneuver him onto the subject, the draft dodger would sputter and rage for a minute, then loop back to Ingrid and his plans for reconciliation. Somehow, these plans all involved Glasser as ambassador or go-between, or as legal emissary to the wife's crooked lawyers in Sweden.

"But I don't speak Swedish," said Glasser, trying once again to broach the problem with the guards. "And I'm not a lawyer anymore, I've been disbarred."

"Doesn't matter. They all speak English over there, and they can't know about the other thing unless you tell them. You just go in there and lay down a little lawyer talk, that's all. I guarantee they'll shit in their pants."

"Mario, it's not that simple—"

"But it is. Sweden's the boondocks, man, the bush leagues of Europe. They've never seen a real Jew lawyer before. You just open your mouth and they'll give us whatever we goddamn want."

Glasser winced. "Don't you understand? The screws are going to come down hard on you."

"Why do you keep harping on that?" Mario gave him a furious look, but then his face turned sly and catlike. "Is it that you don't want to help me, Lou? Can't be bothered with a black man trying to save his marriage?"

"If you don't pay them off, they're going to search the bunk or some of your hiding places on the grounds. You'll lose your early parole."

"If they find my stuff, I'll know who told." He gave Glasser a frankly accusatory stare.

"They may not even bother with a search since they know your routine. Think about it. If they arrest you outside the fence, they've got you for attempted escape."

"That's ridiculous." Mario gave a snort of bitter amusement. "Everybody knows I've got nowhere to escape to."

"It doesn't matter to them. Escape is worth an extra five years up at Firnstil Senior."

There was a moment of silence, and then Mario rose up to his elbows, the pain evident in his taut face. "Get out. You and your fat white ass—"

"Mario, listen to me—"

"I said get out."

It was almost lunchtime anyway. Glasser got up and headed over to the cafeteria, where he got on line with the other early arrivals, waiting patiently for their plates of macaroni and powdered cheese mix. Faced with the prospect of another atrocious meal, Glasser's sympathy for Mario began to wane. To hell with the draft dodger, he told himself. If a man is bent on self-destruction, there's nothing you can do for him. Mario was rude, abusive, self-centered, manipulative—a real con artist. And that casual comment about Glasser being a Jew lawyer had continued to irritate. Is that how Mario saw him—as a Jew lawyer, a cartoon? Well, cartoons aren't much bothered by compassion.

But after lunch he found himself heading back toward Mario's bunk yet again, wondering if the draft dodger would need some help walking outside for the count, the thrice-daily roll call held on the lawn in front of the dorm buildings. Glasser intended to reason with the man once more, if only because he couldn't stand the stupidity, the waste. To spend six months in jail for draft dodging was bad enough, especially when the war in question had ended almost fifteen years before. But to add another five years for attempted escape was too ludicrous for even a bystander—Glasser—to bear without going insane.

"Mario!"

Still almost forty-five minutes till the count, but the draft dodger had left his spot on the floor. Glasser took a few steps forward and looked toward the back of the room, which was in shadow. The crowded space was silent, but he sensed a presence somewhere among the bunk beds. Mario was probably slumped in a corner behind a footlocker, too drunk to get up.

"Mario?"

Glasser took another step forward, hesitant now. From the corner of his eye he had noticed a bag of laundry hanging from the metal frame of the farthest bunk, by the wall. The drawstring was lashed to the top of the frame, and the bag hung heavily, a long bag, touching the floor.

He walked toward it and then stopped. The draft dodger had hanged himself with an extension cord, and as the bunk bed wasn't much over five feet high, his feet were planted on the floor, though his knees and hips now sagged, as if he had been caught in the act of sitting. Over his head he wore some kind of clear plastic sack, secured at the throat by the cord. Seen through the plastic, his face was a dark glossy blur.

He was still warm when Glasser lifted him up.

15

THREE HUNDRED BOTTLES

Uncle Eddy had been driving them to Firnstil every weekend for visiting day, but on this particular date he was unavailable, so Jason and his mother got up at five and took the train three and a half hours to Firnstil Station, where they waited for the shuttle bus to the prison camp. This was an old converted school bus, still wearing the remnants of a yellow paint job, but with wire mesh welded over the windows. Jason and Esther crowded in with the other families, squeezing into seats built for children, while the aisle filled with those who would have to stand the additional six miles to Club Fed.

Did they call Firnstil a white-collar country club? Those families came by car. The bus was for heavyset women in halter tops and spandex shorts, babies crying in their arms and three or four big-eyed kids in tow, eating cereal out of plastic baggies and spilling cans of soda. It was for uncles and cousins, sullen teenagers in tank tops and complicated sneakers, big radios tucked in their arms. It was for everyone so miserable and pissed off that they had to push and shove and argue and cry at the top of their lungs, oblivious to the others around them. Jason's mother looked shattered, as if it had finally dawned on her that her husband was in prison, that their lives were never going to be the same. The bus rattled and swayed on broken shocks, slowly filling with exhaust fumes.

The visits were always painful, but in a variety of different ways. His father refused to come out of his bunk sometimes, in which case they waited in the visiting area, on the off-chance he'd change his mind. One hour would stretch into two, two into three, Jason's mother wilting in a plastic chair, Uncle Eddy beside her, sipping resignedly at a Diet Pepsi as the other inmates and their families milled around, squabbling and eating lunch. Jason would imagine his father lying on his bed, snickering to himself at his little trick, the ease with which he could disappear again and again, yet keep them coming back for more. Look how I pull your puppet strings, he imagined him saying, Look how I leave you dangling in empty space! The Bureau of Prisons may control me, but I control you, you puny stupid schmuck!

But it was even worse when Glasser did appear. The sight of him bursting out of his ill-fitting khakis would put Jason into a dark, patricidal rage. Was this the man he had looked up to all his life, the man who had flown cross-country in his own airplane, whose booming courtroom oratory had saved men from a lifetime in prison? Jason would pace back and forth, feeling titanic forces moving through him, grief transfused by anger, anger driven out by guilt. Glasser looked like an old zoo animal now, ill-kempt and seedy, with his hair uncombed and the buttons missing from his shirt. His face was cunning and greedy, his eyes darting to the vending machines that lined one wall of the big open room—for visitors' use only. He dunned Esther for coins, then gorged on Twinkies and potato chips. Once the change was gone he tried to get away.

On this particular visit, however, Glasser was unusually communicative. He said he was fighting the administration about burial arrangements for an inmate. The prison wanted to ship the body to a stepsister in Detroit, but Glasser insisted they fly it back to the wife in Sweden. "Saving a couple of hundred bucks on a man's body," he muttered. "Like we're garbage." He had had a meeting with the assistant deputy warden—"not unpromising"—and was in daily contact with the warden's secretary. Uninterested in the vending machines for once, he paced up and down, eager to get back to the half-finished memo he was writing to the Bureau of Prisons. Jason noticed that his hair was combed.

Mother and son didn't get back home till close to midnight. Dazed and exhausted but utterly unable to sleep, they sat up for hours, staring at the TV set. "He looks better," said Jason, all the anger burnt out of him for now. "You see how he tried to tuck in his shirt?"

His mother kept her eyes locked on the TV screen. "He's going to get himself into trouble with that petition." And then: "Your father has made a mess of all our lives."

This was exactly how he felt, of course, but he could not accept it coming from her. "You can't blame him for everything."

"I can," she said, without a shred of humor. "I can and I do." She sat up straight in her chair, speaking very fast. "He made the decisions. He never consulted with me—never. Half the time I didn't know where he was, let alone what he was doing. The fool—I would've told him."

"Told him what?"

"Told him to be more careful."

"If you go along for the ride, then that's your choice. You liked it. And you liked the money too."

She looked genuinely surprised. "What's money got to do with it?"

In her version of events, Brian Brianson was just an example of his father's recklessness, the simple stupidity that ruined their lives; it had nothing to do with money, the money they all spent so freely. "Brian made us money," said Jason. "Obviously. A lot of money."

"I wasn't concerned with our finances. Your father took care of them."

"That's my point. That was a choice."

"Your father spent it, not me. Whatever he gave me, he spent double on himself. The airplane, the clothes—stupid toys."

"We spent it too."

"Some of it, yes. And why not?"

"I'm not blaming you for anything—I'm not even interested. I'm living my own life now." That sounded like a particularly hapless boast, but he lifted his chin and locked eyes with her, trying to carry it off. He had graduated from Harvard two weeks before, but the much-awaited event had passed almost unnoticed, overshadowed by the sight of his father in prison khakis. And now he was back home in New York, seemingly stripped of everything he had once counted on. No school, no fellowship, no Japan—no father.

Of course, his mother honed right in, gleefully. "Living your own life, huh? Then maybe you'd like to get a job while you're at it."

This was a sore point between them; the more she pushed, the harder it was for him to get started, or so he told himself. "I'm getting one," he snapped. "I've worked hard all year."

"So that makes two of us. Welcome to adulthood."

It seemed like the very next moment that she was standing by his bed in the morning light, shaking him by the shoulder. She was already dressed for work in a red jacket and skirt, a briefcase in her other hand.

"What's the matter?" Jason sat up and his head filled with a dull dry ache, the kind one gets after a few hours' interrupted sleep. "What time is it?"

"Time to get a job."

"Job? You kept me up all night."

"The want ads are on the table." She looked at him, then looked away, distracted by a thought. "We didn't do you a favor by coddling you. Maybe your father's tragedy"—that was her phrase for it, the one she always repeated—"your father's tragedy will force you to take some responsibility."

He blinked, eyes burning. "Responsibility for what?"

"There's coffee in the kitchen."

He got up, followed behind her as she walked to the front door. "A little anxiety is natural," she said, counting her change for the bus. "That's growing up."

"I don't want to grow up. I just want to sleep."

"Too bad."

Alone at the table he drank cup after cup of coffee, listening to the silence of the apartment, a staticky hum like a radio tuned between stations. Sleep was unthinkable now. By his elbow sat the Sunday *Times* Help Wanted section, a good two dozen pages of ads in a chaotic wilderness of type fonts. It took every ounce of strength he had not to get up and run, not to throw the paper out the window or shred it to kitty litter.

He glanced down. His eye caught on a headline howling JOBS JOBS JOBS and his heart started to slam to that same rhythm—JOBS JOBS JOBS—like a sledgehammer against concrete.

Are you a super-motivated self-starter? Do you thrive on a challenge? You must be focused, driven, organized to deal with this high-pressure, high-energy sales situation.

He could feel his breath accelerate with panic. What was a super-motivated self-starter? How did he self-start? What was he focused on and where was he driven to? What super-motivated him? Why was he none of those things? He ran his eyes down the page, but from column to column the phrases simply repeated: "high-pressure," "high-energy." He felt as if steel bands were being tightened around his head.

Are you a people-person? We're looking for someone with exceptional interpersonal communication skills to handle our demanding clientele. Must be warm, upbeat, and enthusiastic, with a winning smile. Heavy phone work. Light typing.

This is adulthood, he told himself with a wail of despair. He could forget about his father, with his airplane and his shopping bags full of money. This was the way *real* people lived: self-starting men who had no more than one lunch a day; highly motivated men who did not run out to meet clients at two A.M.; warm, upbeat men who thrived on a challenge but somehow, miraculously, did not end up in jail.

Jason's roommate, Norm, had gotten a job with a big commercial bank. Starting August first, he would sit at a desk and write reports and chat with his colleagues about football. But Jason had never figured out how to become like Norm, even after two years of close scrutiny, rooming together in Winthrop House. He truly understood only what he'd seen growing up—Glasser—and that meant the want ads were hopeless. But what were the alternatives? He could join the army, or maybe the French Foreign Legion. Or he could get a job at the disco.

He ran to the phone and dialed Uncle Eddy's number at home. "I need a job. I'll take anything, anything."

"Jason, is that you?" Eddy seemed groggy, as if he'd just woken up.

"Janitor, bouncer. Anything."

"How's your father?"

"He's fine." Considering he's in the slammer. "Busboy would be okay. Bookkeeper. I'm very good at figures."

"You're talking about a job?"

"Or I could be a go-go dancer. You know, I could dance in one of the cages."

Eddy coughed, a wet reedy sound. "Didn't your mother tell you?"

"Maybe I don't dance so great right now, but I could learn. I'm very coordinated."

"Jason, the disco closed last week."

It took a moment for the news to register. "Closed?"

"Closed as in broke." Eddy coughed again. "Sorry, kid."

There was a moment of silence in which Jason tried to shift attention from his own plight to Eddy's. "I'm sorry, I didn't know."

Eddy cleared his throat. "I'd like to help you, but I'm between things now."

"Forget about it. I understand." There was another silence, longer this time.

"You need something pretty bad," said Eddy—a statement, not a question.

"Probably not as bad as you."

"That's pretty bad. Meet me at the disco in two hours and we'll talk about it. I may have something for you that will help us both out."

The disco was locked when Jason got there; he stood by the door in the mild June warmth, squinting in the sun, watching people pass on the street. His panic was out of sight now but still present, like a fire engine that could be heard from blocks away, its siren reduced to a muted wail.

Eddy arrived a good half hour late, his big Lincoln looking like a parade float as it drifted to the curb, coming to a soft stop in front of a hydrant. Dull caramel brown and as rectangular as a brick, it was ostentatious only in its enormous stolidity.

Small-boned, with narrow shoulders, Eddy had to get his whole body behind the shove that slammed shut the massive door. He was wearing sunglasses and chinos and leather boat shoes without socks, and a pink polo shirt with the collar up. The collar formed a half funnel that framed his thin, wrinkled neck.

"You're at a hydrant," Jason told him.

"They know me," said Eddy, meaning the cops who ticketed the area. His paunch, round and hard as a basketball, pulled the pink shirt tight as he walked over.

"I'm sorry about the disco," said Jason.

"These things happen sometimes." Eddy began fishing for his keys in a little designer purse, the kind men used to carry in the seventies, when pants were too tight for pockets. His voice dropped. "I don't mind telling you it was my partners. They bled the place dry." He pulled out the keys and started struggling with the lock. "Now I'm afraid they'll try to burn it down."

"Burn it down?"

"For the insurance." His voice was barely above a whisper, winded from his struggle with the lock. "We'll all end up in jail."

"What kind of partners are these?"

"Scary ones." Eddy finally got the key to turn and pulled open the metal door. The interior of the club was dark. He hooked his sunglasses on the front of his polo shirt, then pulled a big gold lighter from his purse. "They've cut the power." He motioned for Jason to walk in first and he followed after, shutting the door. For a moment they were blind, then there was the faint glow of Eddy's lighter, giving a few feet of gray floor space.

"So how's Lou?" Eddy's eyes shone black in the orange glow of his lighter. They were the same eyes as Jason's father's, round and sad and maybe a little foolish. His narrow, handsome face looked unimportant in comparison, just a container for those eyes.

"Fine," said Jason, carefully smiling. The subject was too big for words, and he did not want to try.

Eddy had a complicated, bittersweet look on his face. The Glassers got this expression when they were sad—his father got it too, sometimes. Maybe it came from the satisfaction they took in assuming the worst about the world and turning out to be right. "It's a terrible thing," Eddy said softly.

"Yes," said Jason, trying not to sound annoyed.

Eddy's gaze shifted from Jason to the lobby, and he moved the lighter out to arm's length, then from left to right in a slow semicircle. A few chairs came into view, piled one on top of another and pushed against the wall, just a few feet away. This was the first time Jason had been there without the deep heartbeat thump of music from the dance floor, and somehow the silence made it seem darker.

"Jeez," said Eddy. "What a waste." He sounded tired.

"What are you going to do?"

He kept moving the lighter around, peering into the lobby as if he were studying his face in the bathroom mirror. "Stick close," he said, and then began walking cautiously toward the back.

"Is there someone else here?" whispered Jason, thinking he'd rather not be around when the partners came by with their cans of gasoline.

"Have you ever done sales, kid?"

"Sales? Like a salesman?"

Eddy stopped, then held the lighter out toward something big and gray and flat, a wall thrown up in the middle of the lobby. "Here it is," he said, taking another step forward, caressing the wall with his free hand. It made a dry sound, like paper or cardboard.

"What is it?" asked Jason.

"Your job."

Eddy swept his lighter over the surface, and for the first time Jason could see what was really there. "Boxes," said the boy, a little surprised. Roughly a foot square each, they were stacked like cinder blocks from floor to ceiling and, as best as he could make out, from one side of the lobby to the other.

"Five hundred of them," said Eddy. "Each containing sixty-four bottles."

It was an impressive sight, the way the solid block of boxes filled the lobby. It was grand, like a monument, and weird, like a truck parked in your living room—and oddly soothing too, like a hand on your forehead. It displaced the dark and muffled the silence; it was a weight to keep the empty disco from flying away.

"Bottles of what?" asked Jason.

Eddy ripped a flap open from the side and pulled out a small plastic container with a squeeze top. "Hold out your hand."

Jason did, and his uncle filled it with an oily custard, squeezed out in long coils. The smell was of cheap perfume: sweet and flowery and slightly metallic. "Lotion," said Jason.

"Hand cream, five ounces." Eddy held the bottle up, positioning the lighter for maximum illumination. Indeed, the label said exactly that: HAND CREAM, in utilitarian black letters.

"Where'd you get this stuff?" The cream had begun to melt, seeping into the cracks between Jason's fingers. He held the big glob in his outstretched palm, like one of those statues of the Buddha offering compassion to museum goers.

Eddy shrugged mysteriously. "A guy I know got stuck with no place to store them. Then he couldn't sell them either."

"Five hundred boxes?"

"Sixty-four bottles to a box," he said again.

"That's thirty-two thousand bottles," Jason calculated. "And at five ounces per bottle, that means something like a hundred and sixty thousand ounces of hand cream. One thousand two hundred and fifty gallons." He giggled at the image: enough lotion to fill the disco knee-deep.

Eddy seemed amused too. "There are a lot of chapped hands out there, Jason. A natural market." Just then his lighter began to sputter. "Damn, it's running out."

The flame had shrunk down to a yellow nub; they were sinking into a soft, velvety darkness. "And you want me to do *what* with this stuff?" asked Jason.

By the time Eddy answered, the flame was completely gone. His voice came out of a nowhere right by Jason's ear. "Sell it," he said softly. "Sell the shit out of it."

They had lunch at a coffee shop down the block. "I can't do it," Jason said, trying to wipe the greasy lotion from his hand with a paper napkin. "I'm not a salesman."

"Sure you are." Eddy stared at him from across the table, his eyes hidden behind round sunglasses, his arms spread across the top of the couchlike seat. With his long nose and pink shirt, he looked like a slightly deranged tropical bird. "You radiate warmth and sincerity, kid. People like you."

"But I don't know how to sell things."

"That *is* selling things."

"Not twelve hundred and fifty gallons of shitty hand cream."

"Let's try it at fifty cents a bottle. That's thirty-two dollars a box—sixteen thousand for all five hundred. You keep a third."

"Five thousand bucks?"

"But we've got to move it quick," Eddy said. "I don't know what's going to happen to that space."

"The partners?" asked Jason, miming someone striking a match.

"That or the landlord. He's trying to evict us."

Jason took up the little plastic bottle from where Eddy had put it down, alongside the salt and pepper. It was an ugly thing: milky white and only semi-opaque, with a ragged seam on one side. He could see the lotion still inside, a gray shadow line about one third of the way up from the bottom. And the label: no logo, no design, nothing but HAND CREAM spelled out in the kind of lettering more often used for words like RADIATION and TOXIC WASTE.

"This is going to be a hard sell." Jason tried to say it like he imagined a real salesman would, a hard-bitten professional. In spite of himself he was getting excited by the idea. It was a project at least, something to do; and five thousand dollars was a lot of money.

"Fifty cents is cheap," Eddy said, "about thirty percent less than name-brand stuff."

"But it's so ugly. Look at it." Jason gave the mostly empty bottle a squeeze and it made a short wet sputter, like an aborted Bronx cheer.

Eddy only grinned. "Why pay more for a fancy bottle?"

"If it's so easy to sell, why couldn't your friend get rid of it?"

"I didn't say it was easy."

Eddy's frankness left him momentarily speechless. When he resumed, most of the brassiness had left his voice. "So what am I supposed to do then?"

"Do?"

"I mean how do I sell them? Set up a table on the street?"

"Oh no, you can't do that, we don't have the time. You've got to sell them in big lots—fifty boxes, minimum. Discount drugstores, groceries, that kind of thing. Just walk in and speak to the manager. Show him the stuff and let him decide—simple."

After lunch they walked back to the disco. With the front door wide open, there was just enough light for Jason to trot over to the wall of boxes and fill his hands and pockets with bottles. They would be his sales tools, those ugly little things. Yet he was not unhappy: he felt like each bottle had a little bit of the disco in it, a little bit of whatever it was that doomed the Glassers to being themselves. It was only right that he should carry them with him into the world.

Eddy was waiting by the car, arms crossed over his narrow chest. "Give my love to your father," he said, reaching out to pinch Jason's cheek. Jason hadn't suffered that particular form of farewell since childhood, but for some reason the pressure of his uncle's fingers felt almost pleasant, reassuring. "And call me tomorrow night with some good news."

There were two parking tickets curled under his windshield wiper, like while-you-were-out memos.

It was only much later, back at home, that Jason remembered how much he despised salesmen. In the old days his father had always been surrounded by them. He would lead them on with sadistic pleasure, telling them to call back when he knew he'd be out, arranging meetings he couldn't or wouldn't keep, rescheduling again and again. Jason took their phone calls, so he knew what they went through. His father was such an enthusiastic listener at first, they were certain they had a sure sale—the boy could hear them salivate over the phone. But after a few weeks of the runaround, enthusiasm would turn to confusion, confusion to disappointment. "Where's Lou? He's supposed to be here, the diner on Eighth Avenue, right?"

"Maybe he got held up in court," Jason would say, his father sitting right next to him in fact, reading the paper in his boxer shorts.

Then they would empty out their hearts to him, a kid of ten—all the promises made and never kept, the appointments broken. They would try to wheedle out information about the elder Glasser's hours and whereabouts, his insurance needs. They would buddy up to the boy, pretending to be interested in what he was watching on TV, studying at school. Their voices shook with the strain of hiding their humiliation beneath mounds of gooey good humor.

There were other times, though, when the polarities were reversed and it was Jason's father who suddenly needed one of *them*. This would happen in a showroom usually, when father and son were whiling away a Saturday afternoon looking at some fantastically expensive new toy—a car or a motorcycle or a speedboat or maybe an airplane. The elder Glasser would display his knowledge like a teacher's pet, reeling off facts and figures, bragging about the model *he* had—always something better than what he actually owned. He would laugh when the salesman laughed, would use the man's name again and again, like a precious new-found object. "What do you think about those carbs, Ron?" or "I see it your way, Ron. You need the extra torque." He would glance into the man's face, searching for some reflection of his own feelings, and the salesman, if he was good, would pull back a little, turn slightly cool.

Jason would trail behind, forgotten and resentful, already plotting to tell his mother. There would be yelling and screaming at home that night, and his mother would call the showroom the very next day to cancel the order. His father would sulk on the couch, angry and humiliated but secretly relieved too, because he didn't really want the thing and couldn't afford it.

Was he really going to be one of them, a salesman? Jason sat at the dining-room table, making a list of potential customers from the Yellow Pages, filling a pad with names like Discount Dave, Drug-All, and More-for-Less. The bottles of lotion stood in a neat formation by his elbow, like a squad of toy soldiers, the only hint of purposefulness amid the teetering drifts of old magazines and dirty plates—the only hint of purpose in his entire life.

"Well?" his mother asked that evening, swinging her pocketbook onto the table and, without noticing, knocking down his bottles. They rolled helplessly, like bowling pins.

Jason knew she was going to be upset. "I got a job, if that's what you mean."

"So soon?" Her tone was startled and a little apologetic; she looked almost ready to be pleased. "That's great. What did you find?"

"I'm working for Uncle Eddy," he said, watching her face fall. "I'm a representative of his cosmetics company."

"Cosmetics? What does Eddy Glasser know about cosmetics?"

He searched for some way to explain: the black of the disco, and Eddy's eyes like two round pebbles made from that blackness. "We're starting with a hand cream. Test-marketing."

"How much is he paying you?"

He took a deep breath. "My cut comes to about five thousand dollars."

"Your cut? You mean you're not getting a salary?"

"I'm getting a third of the profits, Mom. I'm like a partner, see."

"And what if there are no profits?"

The thought had occurred to him. "Well then, that'll be my problem, I'll deal with it."

There was a moment of silence. "No," she said finally, shaking her head. "I'm not going to let you. It's as simple as that. I'm not going to let that man cheat you like this."

"He's not cheating me."

"I'm just too tired and too busy and too"—she searched for a way to end the sentence—"too sick of everything. I can't have another problem on my hands."

"I'm doing it anyway."

"You're not."

"I *am*." He grabbed one of the bottles from the table, placed it in his fist; at five ounces it was small enough for his fingers to completely cover the ugly label. "Give me your hand," he growled, snatching her arm.

His mother obediently stuck out her palm; she looked strangely frightened by the command, and for the first time in his life it occurred to him that he was bigger than her, that he might actually win in a fair fight. It was not a wholly good feeling, but it propelled him onward.

He put a dab of cream in her hand. "Rub it in," he said, and then watched her work one small red hand nervously over the other. By the time she'd finished, her face had recomposed itself, back to that look of bitter irony.

"How's that feel?" he asked.

"Oily." She lifted the back of her hand to her nose, as if trying to staunch a nosebleed. "And it smells cheap."

"It *is* cheap. We're aiming downscale."

Downscale—at that she became frankly pleading. "You're a Harvard graduate, for godsake, you speak Japanese. You could get a job with Sony or Mitsubishi, taking over the world."

"So?"

"So life is too short for this kind of idiocy, Jason. Look at your father."

"This has nothing to do with him. This is me."

He pushed open the door to Rock-Bottom Drugs, the first stop on his day's campaign. It was nine A.M. on a dazzlingly bright summer morning, but inside, the fluorescent lighting was an awful blue-green, like the water of an overchlorinated swimming pool. He stood uncertainly by the checkout counter, struggling with his feelings. The checkout girl stared at him with a bored fish eye, slouching as if she were at the end of her shift instead of just the beginning. Her upper lids drooped and her lower lids sagged; the effect was disconcerting, as if she were trying to peer out the bottoms of her eyes like they were granny glasses.

"Hi." He tried smiling, but she remained impassive. If the light was different from outside, the temperature was just the same—which was too bad, because today was the first really hot day of the season, and for want of a better idea, he was wearing his pinstriped suit. The whir of faulty air-conditioning made it feel even hotter, as if the controls were really stuck on Slow Bake. Sweat poured down his face.

"Yes?" The response came only after an eerily long pause, a length of time meant to show that any answer on her part was purely optional.

"Is the manager in?" The words were barely out before his heart started to slam. He felt a new crop of sweat sprouting on his scalp, between the hairs—little buds of fear.

The pause again. It was like she had to go all the way to aisle seven and back to bring him her answer. Her voice was heavy with the effort. "What you want him for?"

"I'm a cosmetics representative. I think he'll be interested." His voice sounded horrible—high, like the twanging of a metal wire.

She gave him another long look from the bottom of her eyes, then moved to a microphone sticking up beside the register. It had one of those flexible chromium stems, bent in a gentle arc like a space-age flower, and she leaned into it, almost touching the wire mesh head with her lips. "Abdulla," she whispered. "Salesman."

She returned to stare at him again, lazily, as if watching a fish in an aquarium, her mouth slightly open. He turned to face the back of the store, hopelessly trying to ready himself for the appearance of Abdulla from Rock-Bottom's inner recesses. He tried running through his sales pitch: Soft hands! And not at fancy prices!

He was so busy staring down aisle three, toward the back, that when Abdulla finally materialized by his side he was taken completely unaware. In fact, Abdulla had to tap him on the shoulder. Jason turned to see a tall, thin man with a pointy face and a shiny black beard, one of those bulky price-stamping machines in his knuckly hand, like a futuristic ray gun.

"What can I do for you, my friend?" Everything about Abdulla bespoke a barely contained rush. Even his clothes seemed built for speed: a black clip-on tie and sky-blue polyester shirt, dark polyester highwaters shimmering in the fluorescent light.

"Do for me?"

"You are selling something, yes?"

"Hand cream," Jason sputtered, remembering himself. "Hand cream." The words came off his tongue like boulders. It was like trying to talk after getting novocaine at the dentist.

"We have plenty of hand cream, my friend. Ten different kinds. Twenty."

"Yes, but look." Jason pulled a bottle of the stuff from his pocket, thrust it forward. It was not a good strategy, showing the ugly duckling right away, but he was stalling for time to clear his head.

"You must be kidding," said Abdulla, real disdain in his voice. "Nobody will buy that."

"But they will. The lotion inside is as good as the best. And the no-frills packaging makes it cheap. Besides, the five-ounce size is very convenient. Put it in your purse, your beach bag, the glove compartment of your car. Keep it in the locker at your gym."

Jason listened to himself with a little thrill of surprise. Glove compartment? Gym locker? It was all pure improvisation.

Abdulla looked skeptical. "Who makes it?"

"We do. Glasser International. We have a factory in Kuala Lumpur."

Abdulla took the bottle with his free hand, looked it over. "How much?"

"Forty cents per bottle, as many bottles as you want—one or a million, same-day delivery. Return any bottles you can't sell and we'll refund your money. So there's no risk to you."

All this was improv too, but of a more questionable kind. His very first sales call, and he'd already shaved twenty percent off the price; and if Eddy heard about the impromptu return policy, he'd scream. But getting Abdulla to say yes had become so important to Jason that he couldn't stop himself. He would have paid him to take the stuff, if he'd had more than a dollar in his pocket.

There was a moment when Abdulla seemed to be teetering on the brink. He stared at the label and his lips tightened in thought. But then he shook his head. "No, my friend. No. We do not have the shelf space for this."

"Shelf space?" Jason looked around. "You don't need shelf space. Put it in a big basket, like they do in supermarkets. Or put it right here on the counter. It's a good impulse buy."

"No, I am sorry." Abdulla offered the bottle back.

"Keep it," said Jason. "It's a present." The energy was leaking from him like air from an inflatable doll—he could feel his features collapsing in on themselves.

Abdulla shrugged, more burdened than grateful, his mind already shifting to other matters. He began to move away, price-stamper held high like a torch.

"Can I come by later?" Jason asked his retreating back, voice small as a pebble thrown against sheet metal. "You might change your mind."

"It will still be no. Thank you."

Shamefacedly, Jason glanced up at the checkout girl, who seemed not to have moved from when he'd last seen her. Her gaze had remained the same too: lethargic and incurious. "Thank you," he said, not sure what else might fit the occasion. There was only silence in return. He stumbled out the door.

It didn't even occur to him to try another place, though his list offered forty-nine more in lower Manhattan alone. He stumbled home instead, so deeply exhausted from his ten minutes at Rock-Bottom that he could barely work the key in the lock. His hands were shaking. Inside, he headed straight for his room, where he dropped his sodden suit in a pile, peeled off his sticky shirt and underwear. Naked, the only thing he could think to do was to wrap himself in the sheet from his bed, which he then wore into the living room. Clothed this way, he sat on the couch and turned on the TV. It was ten A.M.

He was still there when his mother got home from work in the evening. "Strike it rich yet?" She stood by the entrance to the room, leaning against the wall to take off her heels.

"Yes," he said, unable to lift his eyes from *Gilligan's Island.* "No." He gave her the choice.

She sat down at the other side of the couch and began massaging her feet, working her toes back and forth. "Are you going to a toga party?"

He grasped the sheet tight around his neck. "I think I have the flu. I feel awful."

When she spoke again her voice was gentle, tentative, as if she were trying something out. "It's not easy, is it?"

He glanced over at her. "No, it's not."

She sighed, heaving herself up from the couch. "It really isn't." She said this without rancor or sarcasm, walking out of the room in her stocking feet. Suddenly he missed her, with a deep aching love, as if she'd left for another continent, instead of just her bedroom.

Late that night Eddy called. Jason heard his mother chewing him out on the kitchen phone, and this made him oddly happy. He broke away from the late late movie and swished over, holding his sheet closed. "It's your uncle," she said, passing him the receiver, "the Great Tycoon." He took the phone, snickering with pleasure.

"Your mother's upset," Eddy said. He sounded a little rattled himself.

"Obviously."

"What about you?"

"I feel like I got hit with a sock full of quarters."

"That's sales for you." He gave a little laugh. "Do you want to quit?"

"No," said Jason. Then: "I don't know." Again, it was pick one.

"Because you can quit any time. You know that, kid. I'd rather throw out the five hundred boxes than give you a moment's pain."

Jason could sense something building, a con of some kind, and knew of course that he was doomed. The problem was that deep down he *wanted* to believe in Eddy's ugly little bottles and his own ability to sell them.

Still, he tried dragging his heels. "I'm not cut out for this, Eddy."

"Maybe so, but I feel like there's something here for you. A growth experience."

A growth experience—Brian Brianson had used the exact same phrase, hadn't he? Jason remembered him in his purple silk caftan, spread-eagled on the couch in that strange little room at the top of his mansion, an enormous joint burning between his fingers. Brian was a salesman too, of course, but of an entirely different class, better than Jason could ever be—better than all the Glassers put together.

"More like a humiliation experience," he told his uncle now.

"Because they said no? Where's the humiliation in that?"

"The humiliation is in going to a discount drugstore and begging the assistant manager, who is wearing a shiny black clip-on necktie, to buy your shitty cream. And *then* being told no."

"Who said anything about begging? You're not asking them for charity. You're offering them a business deal, a really good one. If they don't want it, fine—somebody else will."

But nobody else did. The next day Jason hit ten different stores and still came up with zero. Responses began falling into patterns: the manager was out or the manager was busy; only the owner made purchases and he was not in—was rarely in, was never in. At Chung's Pharmacy, however, Chung himself told him not in your life; at Angelo's Discount Drug World, Angelo's wife said forget it; at Pennywise Cosmetics, Penny personally showed him the door. He was actually grateful for these short, brutal encounters: at least something had happened.

He kept going, and one day quickly followed the next, till summer hit full force. Shod in leather-soled wingtips, his feet burned as if the street were a hot plate. His suit completely lost its shape, turned spongy with sweat till it looked like it was cut from thick insulating felt. The hand-cream bottles in his pocket drank up the heat, then radiated it back like stones in the sun. He switched to slacks and a shirt, added convenience stores and bodegas to his target list. The sales pitch itself remained an agony—usually he was treated like a cross between a giant cockroach and a holdup man as he stuttered out his lines. But the constant walking in the sun had a weird anal-gesic effect, like gas at the dentist's, making the whole experience increasingly distant and dreamlike. Soon there were long stretches of walking when he forgot what he was selling, or that he was selling anything at all. He became a speck drifting through the city, floating with the traffic, following one current and then another.

It was in just such a state that he shuffled into Kim's Kome In, a cavernous discount store on Chambers Street, near the court build-ings. The air-conditioning was frosty and the lights low, the very opposite of the boiling, sun-drenched streets outside. It was a little after one, and a lunchtime crowd browsed the long avenues of white metal shelving, taking refuge from the heat. He eyed the man at the register, a tough-looking Korean in a yellow aloha shirt, then ambled toward the back, putting off the inevitable.

A smaller place would have felt crowded with this many people, but there was room for everyone here, and they drifted among the shelves and bins with a dreamy self-absorption, examining the bar-gains—hot combs and flyswatters, ski mitts and hairspray. Jason ran his fingers through a barrel of quarter-inch wingnuts, then moved on to a crate of flame-retardant Christmas-tree ornaments, snowmen and reindeers and a strangely androgynous Santa that turned out, on examination, to be Mrs. Claus, looking just like her husband but without the big white beard.

Who picked up a half-pound of wingnuts on his way back to work? A pair of ski mitts in August? A flyswatter with GOTCHA!

printed on the business end? What Taiwanese manufacturing genius had bet everything on Mrs. Claus? Yet here they all were, in Kim's Kome In, and Jason knew that somebody must buy them.

Maybe there was hope for hand cream too.

He walked over to the register. The man in the aloha shirt was intimidating all right, middle-aged and husky, with a thick bull neck rising from his yellow collar. "Is the manager in?" asked Jason, vaguely aware that he should be more nervous than he was.

"What's the problem?"

"I'm selling wholesale cosmetics." He pulled out one of the little bottles. "Hand cream, five ounces. Is he around?"

The man eyed the bottle, then Jason, and Jason tried to keep things going. "I see you've got hairspray, Chapstick, nail-polish remover. This is a natural fit for you." No response. "People like small bottles, they're easy to carry." Still nothing. "Okay, I guess not. Thanks anyway."

He was about to leave when the man reached over wordlessly for the bottle. Jason gave it to him, then watched as he rubbed some of the lotion into his deeply creased skin. The man's hands were brown and swollen-looking, with fingers thick as cable. "How much?" he asked.

Though the partners had agreed on fifty cents a bottle back in June, Jason had gone as low as thirty since then, without eliciting a glimmer of interest. Even so, he now started high. "Sixty cents a bottle."

There was a long pause. "Forty."

"Excuse me?" After eight weeks of getting the boot, he couldn't quite accept what he was hearing—interest.

"Forty." The man said it as if it were a simple statement of fact: the bottles were forty cents, always had been, always would be.

Jason rubbed his palms on the sides of his pants, trying to slow down, to squeeze out the best deal he could. "With an order of five hundred, sure, I can do that."

"Two hundred."

Two hundred bottles at forty cents each was eighty dollars, eighty more than he'd made all summer. "We don't take orders for less than three hundred."

There was a long, long pause. "When can you deliver?"

16

DEAL ME OUT

The day before his release, Glasser stuck to his usual routine, taking the lawn mower out after breakfast. He had decided to cut the grass behind the Administration Building, a big piece of ground about a hundred yards long and fifty wide, reaching all the way back to the chain-link fence, Firnstil's outer perimeter. It was waste space, really, never used for anything, and there was no reason to mow it other than the fact that it would keep him busy till lunchtime. But that was reason enough. Ever since Mario's death, hard work had made it possible for Glasser to sleep in a cinder-block room with cement floors and twenty-three other snoring men. Hard work had kept him from thinking about Firnstil and the years that led up to it and, what was even worse, the world beyond it.

Glasser started at one end, pushing the mower back and forth between the orange-brick building and the fence. The shaggy grass was almost too much for the old machine. It burned oil, coughing greasy black smoke and complaining in a high insect-whine. He had to really push, and the muscles in his arms and back began to ache. But he kept at it. Nearly sixty, he had lost more than fifty pounds, was in better shape than at forty. He could work all day in the heat.

After an hour he stopped to rest by the fence, leaning on the metal handle of the mower and looking out at the woods that started on the other side. The sun was hot on his shoulders, but the woods were a cool sepia tone, cut by geometric figures of light, a smattering of stars where the leaf cover broke. The prison camp was all dusty lawns and asphalt walkways, rows of cinder-block bunkhouses—a little suburban township. But in the forest the earth looked soft, blanketed in things a lifelong city dweller could only guess at: pine needles and pieces of pulpy bark, fallen leaves and green prickly moss.

Glasser gave the fence a good shake with his hands. The single curl of concertina wire at the top looked more like a decoration than a deterrent, and he knew he could climb over in no time if he tried. He had thought about it a lot in the first month or so, especially after Mario's suicide, but the idea was as blatantly self-destructive as attacking a guard or trying to set fire to the Administration Building. Where would he have gone? How would he have lived? He could never have survived as a fugitive. And what was the point anyway, when he only had four months to serve? Instead of fence climbing he'd taken up mowing.

Now he wondered if there hadn't been another reason too. Deep down, the outside world scared him; he was frightened by what he might do with all that freedom, the damage he would cause, smashing into things like a drunk on a rampage. Firnstil offered a measure of safety, a place to hide. At moments he almost loved it for its drab, silent constriction, the fact that nothing ever happened.

Then again, he worried that prison might be all the living he could stand anymore.

Glasser went back to mowing, pushing harder than he should have, trying to erase the idea from his head. By mid-morning he was parched and exhausted, dizzy from the heat. Insects floated in the air like specks in a bottle of oil, and the strong scent of cut grass clung to his nostrils. He got a drink from the spigot at the side of the building, then walked over to the only source of shade, a small tree at the other end of the field. He sat down with his back to the trunk and dozed for a while, and when he opened his eyes he saw someone walking toward him. It was a lean figure in khakis, an inmate;

the sun flashed off the man's glasses, but when the face came into view Glasser recognized Winters Pettibone.

The prodigal son of southern gentry, Pettibone was barely forty-five, but he had a streak of prematurely white hair and a sullen, disappointed look until he got on the subject of art—which for him meant art forgery. Then his eye sharpened and he lost the gentleman's mumble. Hearing of Glasser's short sentence, he'd immediately tried to enlist the lawyer's help in a scheme to sell forged artwork on the outside. For weeks Glasser had nodded and smiled, saying little in answer but experiencing his usual difficulties with the word "no." He sympathized with Pettibone, sensing a struggle taking place behind the younger man's cool gray eyes.

Pettibone was just a few feet away now, fanning himself with a large manila envelope as he walked. "What are they paying you for this, Lou?"

"Thirty-eight cents an hour."

"Slave wages." Pettibone himself was one of those who refused to do anything, since work was optional at Firnstil. He spent the days stretched out in his bunk, watching the ceiling with a lizardlike patience that seemed to hide a private form of despair.

"It makes the time go," said Glasser. He knew he should get back to mowing before Pettibone started pressuring him about selling the forgeries. But he was utterly drained, too tired to stand.

Pettibone sat down beside him, a sour smile on his face. "Look at me, Lou: I do no work, I cost the taxpayers thirty thousand a year, and I like it that way. It seems only right they should suffer some too."

"Don't you get bored?"

"Bored? I'm way past bored."

Glasser turned to look at Pettibone's pale face, the small eyes caged behind steel-frame glasses. "You should set up an easel. Paint some original works and sign your own name. You'd probably get famous."

This must have been a sore spot, because Pettibone frowned suddenly, and his voice turned petulant, whiny as a child. "I can't paint in here, Lou. For godsake, it's all wrong, don't you see? I'm like a bird with clipped wings."

"Sorry."

They sat in silence for a while, the forger dabbing at his forehead with a white pocket handkerchief, looking perturbed. He was here about the artwork, obviously, but his attention had switched inward, and he was clearly struggling to get back on track. He attempted a ghastly smile, abandoned it, then simply opened the manila envelope and took out some photographs. "These are the paintings I was telling you about."

Glasser looked at the photos quickly, more polite than curious. For some reason he had expected Old Masters–type stuff, portraits of eighteenth-century gentlemen in powdered wigs, something befitting Pettibone's finicky, intellectual air. But the paintings turned out to be messy and expressionistic, and he had trouble deciphering the images. They were of meat, it seemed—big sides of beef hanging from hooks in a slaughterhouse. The canvases themselves looked bloody, the colors muddy reds and fatty yellows, the paint piled on thick as innards.

He couldn't keep the surprise from his voice. "What are these things?"

"They're by a man named Soutine, Lou. Chaim Soutine." In his soft southern accent, the name sounded like High Yam Soo Teen. "A Lithuanian Jew living in France, dead in 'forty-three. He did a number of large canvases set in butcher shops, but these are much smaller—studies, really."

Glasser looked with new interest at the carcasses on their vicious hooks. In '43 he had been living with his mother in an apartment on Rivington Street, collecting tin and rubber after school for the war effort. His father had been dead three years and Eddy was in boot camp, writing frightened letters home from Parris Island. The drill sergeants called him kike and hebe as he did pushups in the mud, and the other recruits hit him up for his pay. If he didn't lend them whatever he had in his pockets they called him a cheap Jew.

"You do great work, Winters."

"No, these are genuine. I've got all the documentation, and anyway the evidence is right there in the paintings. Look—" Pettibone took one of the photographs, pointing with a finger. "This brushwork here, Lou, the impasto technique is unmistakable. The blunt fury of it, the passion—it's pure Soutine. I know it can't be faked because I've tried."

Can't be faked? Pettibone's eyes were glittering. What the artist wanted to say, whether he knew it or not, was that the picture couldn't be a forgery because the emotion it expressed was genuine, dug from the same deep pit as Soutine's. What matter if the hand belonged to Winters Pettibone, Episcopalian, North Carolinian, graduate of St. Albans and the University of Virginia, inmate of a country-club prison? The painting itself was brutally alive.

"I can't help you, Winters."

"These paintings are worth a million dollars wholesale, Lou. I'm offering you ten percent to act as my agent."

"But I don't know anything about the art business."

"You don't *have* to know anything. All you have to do is drive down to my mother's house in North Carolina and bring the canvases back to New York. I'll tell you who to call and what to say. I'd do it myself, but I'm stuck here another two years."

Glasser looked at him, suddenly feeling the terrible loneliness of the man—unable to paint except in the guise of a Lithuanian Jew, dead before he was born. "I can't do it, I'm sorry."

"*A hundred thousand dollars.*" Pettibone made the words sound almost musical in his soft, lilting voice. "I know you need the money."

Glasser did need the money, but he shook his head no. "It would be a disaster for both of us."

Pettibone's usually laconic sentences started coming out fast and jumpy, veering between a lecture and a plea. "Lou, I'm asking you to be practical. I'm thinking of you as much as myself. You're not a lawyer anymore. How are you going to earn a living? Who's going to employ a sixty-year-old ex-con? Nobody, that's who. Can you wait tables, deliver pizzas?"

"If I have to."

"No, you can't." His voice turned peremptory, definitive. "You have too much pride. You're used to being a big shot and giving orders. It would kill you." He waved the photos for emphasis. "Are you going to let your wife earn the money? Are you going to live on her charity?"

"Of course not."

"That's the spirit." Pettibone's face softened to something like affection. "Now take this." He reached into the manila envelope for a slip of paper, handed it to Glasser. It had an address in North Carolina, with driving directions underneath, written in a neat looping script.

Glasser handed it back. "I can't, Winters, I'm sorry."

"But you just said yes."

"I said no." Glasser got up slowly, leaning on the tree trunk for support. His legs felt weak, but he was desperate to get away. "I've got to get back to work."

"You don't give a fuck, do you?" Pettibone said it in an offhand way, carefully sliding the photos back into the envelope, but his voice was clotted.

"That's not true."

"You're leaving tomorrow and I've got two more years here, two more fucking years looking up at the ceiling." He got up then, brushing the grass from the back of his pants. "It's killing me, I'll never make it." There were no histrionics in this last statement, only quiet certainty.

"You'll be all right."

"No, I won't."

Glasser had nothing left to say. If he tried to sell those pictures they'd both end up with another five years for forgery, and how would that help either of them?

He began walking toward the lawn mower, hoping the painter wouldn't follow. The sunlight was intense and he had to shade his eyes. Halfway there he turned to look for Pettibone, but the forger was already gone.

That evening, after dinner, Glasser lined up for one of the pay phones. He hated whatever it was that drove him to these stilted conversations with Esther, yet he could not prevent himself from calling. By the second or third word he was invariably silent. If he allowed himself to utter what he really felt there would be no going back; it would all pour out of him, like blood from an artery.

"We'll be there after lunch," said Esther, used to supplying both sides of the conversation. "You must be very excited." Her voice had taken on the impersonal, third-person cheerfulness of a practical nurse.

"Yeah."

She started to tell him about the promotion she had just gotten at the insurance company, to a new job processing claims. "Isn't it wonderful? It's such a relief. I can put a little more to the credit cards."

A relief? Who cared about the goddamn credit card companies? They could wait for their money. Glasser was taken with the long-range implications: controlling the money, she'd control him too. "How much?" he grunted.

"Salary? Well, twenty-one thousand, but I'm up for review in six months."

Twenty-one thousand—he used to make that much in five or six weeks. "Twelve hundred a month take-home." His voice said it all.

There was a pause on the other end. "How much will you be making, Lou?"

He'd be on probation for another eight months, which meant community service, ladling beans in a soup kitchen or wiping chins at a nursing home. Then he'd have to get his license back, which would require lawyers again, money.

Esther said, "You couldn't just be happy for me. You had to ruin everything."

Instead of denying it he hung up.

That night in the bunk they played poker as usual. Former bankers, CEOs, habitual high rollers, they now wagered cigarettes in a hesitant, lackluster game, more interested in filling the hours before bed than in winning—old predators ashamed of their fangs.

"Two pair," said Glasser, "kings high."

"You take it," said Covington, looking a little worried by Glasser's sudden streak of luck.

Glasser reached forward to claim the cigarettes, wishing he didn't have to. He'd won four hands in a row, and he knew the others were eyeing him nervously, afraid their mild-mannered game would devolve into a blood-letting.

"He's leaving tomorrow, he doesn't even need the goddamn cigarettes," said Peabody, the ex-stockbroker. In his early forties, Walter Peabody was thin and nervous, and his small, glittering eyes seemed to balance like pebbles on the points of his sharp cheekbones.

"I'll give them back when we're finished," said Glasser.

"No fucking way. You won them, you keep them, that's the game."

"But I don't need them."

"Then what the fuck are we playing for?"

Peabody was about to say something more when Covington cut in. "Forget it, just deal."

Gino Sganarelli, Mario's former partner in contraband, took the deck in his fine, neat hands and began to shuffle—slowly, as everything was done at Firnstil. The others watched in silence, listening to the snap of the cards. It was for this they played: for the soothing motions of the game, the ritual that allowed them to sit together without talking, without asking questions or attempting answers.

"Ah, shit," said Peabody, arranging the cards in his hand. "Look at this garbage." He was clearly having some trouble that night. They all were. "Twenty-two fucking months in this shithole, and now this."

Glasser looked at his cards: Three queens, a jack, and a six. He tried to consider what the others might have in their hands, but the effort was too much for him. There would be conflict, he knew. An air of doom had settled on the table.

Glasser put in his ante, a single Marlboro from his surprisingly large pile. He wasn't much of a card player; in fact, he had a long-standing aversion to betting games of all kinds. Glasser had a very distant memory of his father playing poker in his undershirt, cupping his cards in two hands like a man trying to keep an ember alive. Morris had sat absolutely still, his entire being focused on those cards, not so much calculating as hungering. Such a private man, but willing to let everyone see this thing he had trapped inside himself. Standing at the edge of the table, the four- or five-year-old Glasser had gotten one look at his father's face and burst into tears.

Yet hadn't Glasser inherited a taste for risk too? There was the airplane, the years of reckless spending. And there was the trial work, brutal and cruel and utterly exquisite. Why had he loved it so? Win, and he got nothing but a reprieve, permission to live on till the next trial. Lose, and he felt the life force leaking out of him as from a wound, would lie for days on the couch without speaking, wrapped in a blanket as if it were a shroud.

Whatever he had trapped inside himself, he couldn't bear it any-more, he had to let it go. But how?

Glasser kept the three queens and put in for two new cards, got, to his horror, a pair of fives—a full house. Covington began the bet-ting, tossing in a single cigarette, and everyone followed till it came to Peabody, who raised one. "I am so fucking tired of this game," he said. The others paused, glancing down at their cards with a kind of philosophical unease, as if considering the complexities of his statement.

"I'm out," said Glasser, placing his cards facedown on the table.

"What?" Peabody turned sharply toward him. "How can you be out?"

"I said I fold."

"Look at this, will you?" Addressing the group, Peabody pointed to Glasser's pile of cigarettes, neatly stacked like logs for the fire-place. "He has more than three packs sitting there, how can he just fold like that?"

Glasser shrugged, trying to hide his fright. "I don't have a hand, so I don't bet."

"Bullshit. You've won four in a row."

"It's junk, I can't bet on it." He pushed his cards facedown toward the deck, which sat by Gino.

"Don't touch those cards," snapped Peabody. "He's playing them."

"Jesus, Walter," said Gino, turning his sad, dark eyes on Peabody. "It's just cigarettes."

"I don't give a shit about cigarettes. It's the game, I don't want him throwing the game."

"Why would he throw the game?" Gino asked. But there was no need to answer, they all knew why. Glasser sat with a complicated expression on his face, tired and lonely and resigned, a stubborn old man in institutional khakis, hoarding cigarettes, bickering with strangers, afraid to play the winning card.

Covington broke the silence. "It's just a game, Peabody. A goddamn pastime."

"If it's just a game, why won't he play his hand?"

"I did," said Glasser. "I folded. That's how I played it, by folding."

Peabody seemed ready to explode. "You and your type are the reason I'm going out of my fucking mind here."

"You're always like this before visiting day," said Covington.

Peabody's wife came every week, a neat blond woman at least a decade younger than her husband, wearing Top-Siders and green slacks, an air of suburban serenity despite the surroundings. She invariably brought their daughter, a little girl of four or five, as composed as her mother—dressed like her mother too, down to the hairband and the pink Izod shirt worn with the collar up.

"Bullshit. All I'm worried about is the integrity of the fucking game." Peabody reached toward the cards Glasser had deposited by the deck. Glasser reached for them too, but he was too late to stop him from turning them faceup with an angry sweep of the hand. There they were, the full house, three queens and a pair of fives.

The next day, Glasser stood in front of a farewell contingent of bunkmates and friends. Dressed in the street clothes he'd come in four months before, he had to hold up the baggy pants with his left hand while he shook with his right, working his way down the line. Business types unused to expressing emotion, his bunkmates reached from a distance as if over a barrier, the skin of their palms dry like paper. It moved him to see these men, some of them older than he, still in their khakis. Covington, by far the oldest, would be ninety when he finally got out.

"You lucky fuck," said Peabody, smiling crookedly.

"Sorry," said Glasser. It was a foolish thing to say, and the embarrassment brought his emotion to a simmer. Tears came to his eyes.

"What's to be sorry about?" said Covington, smiling. "Just don't get caught next time."

"Is there something I can do for you out there? Calls I can make?"

They all shook their heads, uncomfortable with the offer, and Glasser felt a twinge, suspecting his own sincerity in making it. It was another foolish thing, making promises, as if the act of making them could lessen the fright of being alone. These men in khaki felt like the only brotherhood he'd ever known—a bitter, frightened, temporary one, a product of circumstances, but something real nevertheless. Still, he knew in his heart that once outside they would all mean nothing to one another. "I'll stay in touch," he said, unable to release the fiction of continuity quite yet.

Covington held Glasser's eye, and his clever old banker's face became grave, almost statesmanlike. "Forget about it, Louis. Go out and live."

17

THE CHECK

At Firnstil Glasser had maintained a series of simple rituals: the morning walk with Covington, followed by long hot days mowing grass, clipping hedges, watering trees. To mow the lawn, he had simply to push the mower in a straight line in one direction, and then back in the other. To eat lunch he had only to show up at the cafeteria at the appointed time, assured of his plate of spaghetti, his macaroni and cheese. After Mario's death, the cigars he got from Covington went to Bruno for oranges and grapefruits, and then to Carl for some khakis that really fit—a size forty by then, smaller than he'd worn in twenty years. Evenings he went to the gym with Covington to try his hand at light calisthenics, some jumping jacks, eventually coming within inches of actually touching his toes. Exhausted by nightfall, he slept deeply, free of dreams.

But those rituals were gone now, and he had nothing with which to replace them. Tired of hiding in the apartment, he went for a walk uptown, braving the busy streets like an invalid testing his legs. It was a mistake of course, both seductive and frightening. After the quiet of Firnstil, he found himself intimidated by the fast-moving crowds, the cars blasting their horns, the touts shoving paper flyers into his hands. ASPIRIN 49 CENTS OFF!! GIRLS! GIRLS! GIRLS! DISCOUNT

CARPET CLEANING! Vendors lined up at the curb, spreading blankets to display their wares, one eye out for the police. They hawked fake Cartier watches and counterfeit Chanel handbags, Gucci scarves with the signature altered to "Guci"—cheap Hong Kong knockoffs. Glasser shrank back, afraid of being trampled in the rush to buy and sell, to swindle and convince.

Up on Fifth Avenue, too tired to head back, he did some browsing, gazing into department store windows at the new fall merchandise: alligator calf boots and cashmere jodhpurs, a set of emerald cuff links in the shape of a dollar sign. What kind of city was this? The rich hungered for emeralds and the poor for green glass baubles, the derelicts for smack or a pint of Thunderbird. But it was the same hunger more or less, pursued with the same furious intensity, the same reckless disregard for others. What would become of him amid all this screaming need? He had a buck fifty-eight and half a pack of cigarettes in his pocket, and no idea how he was going to make a living now that he wasn't a lawyer. He would be trampled.

And yet it was too late to go back to his previous life. Even if they miraculously returned his law license, something inside him had worn through. At home again, he went straight to the big walk-in closet in his bedroom. The suits on either side of the aisle were glossy and dark, with wide padded shoulders and basting inside to shape the chests—body armor for the modern businessman. Who exactly did these belong to? Louis Glasser? He could barely remember the person who had worn them, but he could tell that the man had bought recklessly, with arrogant abandon. A dozen sky-blue shirts with white collars and cuffs, a dozen silk ties the color of flame. It was binge buying, obviously. He hesitated, then tried on one of the suits, furtive as a thief. The lustrous blue jacket wrapped around him like a bathrobe, and the pants kept falling down to mid-thigh.

Covington had given him a diet before he left Firnstil, written on notepaper in a wavering old-world script. Glasser carried it folded in his pocket and would sometimes pull it out to read, taking comfort in its eccentric prescriptions: honeydew but not pineapple, yams but absolutely no sweet potatoes. He followed it all with a nearly religious fervor, down to the weekly cupful of fava beans, but grew increasingly afraid he might falter. Late at night, restless, he would sometimes stick his head in the fridge just to stare at mayonnaise, ketchup, cole slaw, roast chicken draped in plastic wrap. Once he lifted the tinfoil off a wedge of chocolate layer cake, only to retreat quickly to the darkened living room, his hands trembling with fear. Becoming fat again meant fitting into those suits; it meant never getting enough and always being hungry. He was too tired to live that way anymore.

Instead of eating he chain-smoked, burning his mouth and numbing his tongue. But he was on a tight allowance from Esther, and to pay for extra cigarettes he had to steal from her pocketbook or borrow from Jason, who made a little money at whatever it was he was selling for Eddy, soap or mouthwash, Glasser wasn't sure. In general, he treated his wife and son as if they were strangers sharing the same compartment on a long train ride. He was polite, he smiled and nodded shyly, but kept his thoughts to himself. How could they possibly understand what he was going through, the feelings he was experiencing, when he didn't understand them himself?

The terms of his probation required him to perform a year of unpaid community service, and so he volunteered at a synagogue down on Pitt Street. It was an act of simple nostalgia—he had been bar mitzvahed at that temple over forty years before—but it soon darkened into something less comfortable. The Lower East Side had changed, the Jews mostly gone to the suburbs, and the synagogue had become a relic, as old and decrepit as the remnants of its congregation. The front doors were covered with Day-Glo graffiti, the first-story windows sealed with plywood as if to repel a siege. The rabbi, who drove in from Long Island, wore a metal brace on one leg and talked only about the last time he'd been mugged. When he found out that Glasser had once been a criminal lawyer, he started to sputter. "And you! You would get the bastards off!"

Glasser shrugged. "On a good day, yes." The truth was that he had never handled street punks—they couldn't afford his fees— but he was no longer interested in explaining himself.

He rode in a van that delivered meals to elderly shut-ins; it was his job to take the tray upstairs while the driver waited in the car. The tenements they visited were straight out of his childhood; he actually remembered some of them from when he was a boy. He climbed from landing to landing, a food tray balanced in his hands, and with each step his feelings changed, like notes on an ascending scale: claustrophobia, rage, bitterness, love, sorrow. He hated the dark crumbling halls, with their stink of garbage and plumbing, hated the cracked and broken stairs. And yet these were the relics of his childhood, of a world that was gone and would never be returned to him, and they seemed to mourn like he mourned.

The apartments themselves were hot and narrow, with mint-green walls and peeling linoleum floors, bric-a-brac and photos packed in everywhere, newspapers piled in a corner. The old folks were Covington's age but sickly and frightened, without his harsh self-confidence or his millions. The women dressed in nightgowns and bathrobes, the men in pajamas or ancient woolen suits, and they got about with the help of a cane or else by leaning on furniture. They had white cotton fluff for hair and big peevish eyes, clouded by loneliness and private obsession. They looked at Glasser dismissively, as if he were a figment of their imaginations, and at first their voices came from far away, weak with disuse. But once they were talking they seemed unable to stop, and their faces became sly, eager to hold their visitor as long as possible. They addressed Glasser in Yiddish and he answered back in a child's pidgin of that language, reactivating a vocabulary he'd forgotten he possessed. By way of chat, he asked them if they knew the people from his past, family or friends, and occasionally one or another would recall some neighborhood character everyone had known, a ward heeler or shopkeeper.

Until one of the old ladies claimed to remember Morris. To his own surprise, Glasser became tremendously excited. "You knew him? You knew Morris Glasser?"

"Morris Glasser, yes, a wonderful man," the woman said, her voice a reedy singsong. "So handsome he was, like a movie star."

He really had been handsome, thought Glasser, remembering through the eyes of an eleven-year-old: a big bulky man with a broad chest and stubbly chin, surprisingly delicate features. "When was this, can you tell me?"

She gave an airy wave of her hand. "Oh, whenever it was, after the war, yes." Her milky blue eyes examined Glasser shrewdly—despite her age, a woman reading a man. "You said he was a brick-layer, right?"

"Yes, a bricklayer." But Glasser's suspicions had been aroused, and the excitement was already seeping away. Morris had been killed in the winter of 1940, and he hadn't worked on a construction site for at least half a decade before that. It was possible she had accidentally scrambled the dates, but it was more likely she was inventing the connection based on what he'd already told her.

Indeed, her pale face had turned beatific, filled with innocent pleasure at having pleased him—and, more important, having got-ten him to stay a little longer. "Ach, but I was a young woman then. You should have seen me."

He couldn't blame her, considering that all she had for company was the TV. He stayed a few minutes longer, till the driver started honking downstairs, but his disappointment hung over him the rest of the afternoon, making the next series of hallways even darker, the garbage smells more rancid. Back home, he took off his shoes and sank onto the couch, pulling Covington's handwritten diet from his pocket. The news wasn't good here either: he had thought it was his chicken day, but according to the weekly chart, the night's din-ner was six ounces of steamed okra and a tall glass of soy milk. A cloud of greasy black despair rose in front of his eyes.

He was about to head for the refrigerator—just to look, not touch, he told himself, though he knew this was a lie—when the phone started to ring. It was a collect call from Walter Peabody, the stock-broker at Firnstil. "I'm sorry to be bothering you like this, Lou."

Salvation—Glasser felt his chest fill with gratitude. "You don't know how glad I am to hear your voice, Walter."

"Yeah, well, I wasn't sure. People usually like to forget this shit-hole. I don't blame them either."

"I'm not going to forget, believe me." He could hear Peabody laugh at this, cynical as always. But the sound was peculiar, some-thing between a snicker and a sob. "Walter, is something wrong?"

"Listen, I'm just calling because I thought you'd want to know. Mr. Covington died this morning."

"Died?"

"Heart attack in the gym—I was there. He was doing yoga and fell over in the middle of a Sun Salutation. The end came peacefully, within minutes."

Covington dead. A deep weariness spread through Glasser's body, forcing him to close his eyes. His mind wandered. He was struck by how formal the diction became when the subject was death. It had been the same—for a brief period anyway—when Mario killed himself. And when Morris died, the neighbors had crowded the Glassers' tiny apartment, murmuring about the "deceased" and the "departed." At eleven years old, Louis had found it hard to connect those words with his father.

"Lou?" said Peabody. "Are you there?"

Glasser cast around for something to say, but everything seemed suddenly irrelevant. "Did he have any pain?"

"Pain? No pain, thank god." Peabody hesitated. "Or at least I don't think so, he couldn't speak."

Well, of course, how could the stockbroker know, how could anyone? It was just simpler to assume the end had been painless, one of those needs the living impose upon the dead. Glasser imagined Covington lying on the floor of that squalid little Quonset hut, the Firnstil gym, with only a minute or two to reconcile himself to the fact that he'd be leaving jail early—in a hearse, not a limo.

"He got me my job on the grounds crew," said Glasser. "It's the best thing anybody ever did for me."

"Yeah, he was a greedy old bastard." Peabody's voice was full of emotion; he clearly meant this as a compliment of some kind. "He was sitting on fifty mil at least."

Startled, Glasser opened his eyes; he hadn't realized the amount was so large. "What happens to that?"

"I guess the daughter gets it now, if the accountant out in Phoenix doesn't steal it first."

And then Glasser heard a strange sound come over the line; it took him a while to realize it was weeping—male weeping, furtive and choked. "Walter, are you okay?" he asked.

"Yeah, sorry. I don't know why I'm so—"

"He was eighty-seven, he lived a long life."

"Yeah, sure. I guess I'm just all mixed up." There was a long pause. "I don't know who I'm crying for anymore."

Glasser was still seated on the couch when Jason came home. The boy passed by on the way to his bedroom, acknowledging his father with a hooded glance. This was their usual greeting, but it pained Glasser now—so much so that when Jason reemerged a few minutes later, Glasser startled himself by speaking. "How are you doing?" he asked.

Jason seemed equally surprised. "What?"

Glasser studied his son's face for what seemed like the first time in ages. It was a boy's face still, soft, and vulnerable, but with a man's features peeking through in unexpected places—the worried forehead, the thoughtful, overburdened eyes. He's trying to act like a grown-up, thought Glasser, but he doesn't have a clue. And he doesn't realize that nobody else has one either—not me, not anyone. We're all just faking it.

"How are you doing?" Glasser asked again, more softly this time.

"Fine, I guess."

"Good, good." There was an awkward pause, Glasser afraid the boy might leave. "How's the job going?"

"Okay." A careful nod, followed by a more complicated expression: pride, embarrassment, satisfaction, and self-mockery all mixed together. "Actually, I sold two more boxes today. To Pee Wee at Pee Wee's Bargain Barn."

Glasser laughed. "I bet Pee Wee's still wondering what hit him."

"I don't drive that hard a bargain. I pretty much take what they'll give me."

"I think you're a lot tougher than you know, Jason. Do you have a pitch?"

"A sales pitch? I used to. Now I see what the store's like first. The soft sell works better."

"Tell me what you say."

Jason gave an embarrassed squirm, like a ten-year-old. "Oh, come on, I can't do that—"

"Of course you can. Go ahead, pretend I'm Pee Wee." Glasser sat back, ready to listen. Morris was gone, Covington gone, but he and Jason were still here, and they were bound together by some fierce tie beyond wealth and poverty, failure and betrayal.

"I can't," said Jason, pleasure showing beneath his exasperation. "It's hand cream, for chrissake. It's ridiculous."

"It's not ridiculous." Since getting out of Firnstil, Glasser had spent his days agonizing over what he could do—what he could *be*. And now, suddenly, he had remembered he was already a father. "Go ahead," he said to the boy. "Knock my socks off."

That night, Jason went for a ride with his father and Eddy in Eddy's big Lincoln. The two older men sat in front, in the green glow of the instrument panel, and he sat in the rear, swallowed up by the black leather upholstery. No one spoke, but he found the silence peaceful: the faint whir of the air conditioner, the muffled car sounds. Eddy took a left on Park Avenue, pointing them south toward Union Square. The car felt huge, like a barge floating downriver with the current. It was a Saturday night in early September and the streets were still empty, but empty in a very particular way: like a parade had finished and gone, the crowds and music disappeared.

They swung with the traffic around Union Square Park, crossed Fourteenth Street into Broadway. At Houston they took a left, headed east, then south again, through the Lower East Side. It was different there, crowded, people spilling from the tenements onto the sidewalks. The women were in hot pants and halter tops, big hoop earrings, the men in sleeveless undershirts, gold chains around their necks. On the wider streets cars were double- and triple-parked, salsa music floating from their open windows. People sat on mattresses on the fire escapes, or stood leaning over the rails and looking down at the crowd, shouting to friends, drinking beer from quart bottles.

Eddy slowed them to a crawl, squeezing the Lincoln past Camaros with vanity plates, customized Chevys squatting high on balloon tires like animals about to spring. "It's all Puerto Rican now," he said. And then: "There—we used to live there, Two seventy-nine Orchard Street." He pointed to the right, hunching low against the steering wheel.

"And there." Glasser gestured left, to a brick building on the opposite corner. "Top floor. Almost a full year in 'thirty-nine." It was the first thing Jason had heard him say all evening, and it had come out so naturally, as if he'd simply forgotten to be silent.

"Sure, I remember that," said Eddy. He stopped the car in the middle of the street to stare out the window.

"And before that was the apartment on Allen Street," Glasser added. "Winter of 'thirty-eight."

Eddy nodded. "And before that the place on Rivington, the one with the broken stairs."

"Right," said Glasser. "You had to walk on boards."

A car drew up behind them, salsa pouring from its open windows. It honked, three musical notes in rising succession—a customized horn. Eddy started them moving again. "Do you remember the one on Hester Street?"

"Two-eleven Hester," said Glasser. "Sure. Fifth grade."

"Second floor, with the window boxes."

Jason leaned forward into the narrow space between the front seats, putting his hands over the seatbacks. That was how he had sat as a kid, eagerly watching the adult world up front by the dashboard. "You moved a lot," he said.

Eddy laughed. "Usually at night."

"Couldn't pay the rent," said Glasser. "Nobody could. It was the Depression."

"The Depression," agreed Eddy. They both said this word with soft pleasure, as if it were the absolution for whatever it was in their memories that was bothering them, the final release from a problem too complicated to solve.

They turned onto Delancey Street and then headed east onto the Williamsburg Bridge. The metal surface of the bridge grabbed hold of their tires, making a high insectlike buzzing noise, and the beams from their headlights slid up onto the metal structure, lighting up wires, cables, girders. Below, the East River shone slick and black as oil, two shades blacker than the night sky.

Brooklyn wasn't like Manhattan; it was deep and endless. They traveled down wide boulevards that seemed to stretch forever through neighborhoods of mounting desolation. They passed once-grand apartment buildings with crumbling facades, chain-link fences stretched over their art deco entrances, the sidewalks in front glittering with broken glass. Jason wasn't sure where they were exactly, but the scenery was all vaguely familiar, glimpsed out of car windows again and again for years on the way to visit Glasser relatives. And he knew where they were going: to Sheepshead Bay and the house where his father and Eddy had lived after the war, where his grandmother had lived till the end of her life.

It took nearly an hour, the last part a slow drift through a neighborhood of identical row houses. Jason had been to the house many times before, but he could still never distinguish it from any of its twins. He knew they had arrived only because the car stopped.

"Want to get out?" asked Eddy. Glasser only shook his head. The street was completely dark, without lights, the sidewalk bowered by gigantic shade trees.

It was almost midnight when they stopped at a diner on Emmons Avenue. They took a booth by a window, and Jason looked out at the fishing boats moored across the way. Sitting like this, across from water, docks, boats—it made him feel that they'd come to the end of something. End of the city, end of the drive, end of summer, end of a period in his life he couldn't yet define—all of those things, but something more too: something ending for his father, for Eddy.

Eddy talked and talked, a soothing patter that required no answer, that flowed around his father. "Remember Bucky Butler?" asked Eddy. "Sammy Cohen? Freddy Haims?" The list went on, words like pebbles down a well, faster and faster, a kind of chant. "Jerry Schwartz? Jimmy Johnson? Moe with the missing teeth?" Nothing else but the names. Eddy sounded as if he were calling out the contents of a bag he'd found at the back of the closet, forgotten for years—surprising himself. His father sat listening as to a song.

"The whole area was just empty lots," said Eddy. "Streets leading nowhere, built for houses that weren't built yet. The bricks sat in the middle of the grass in piles." He was looking at Jason now, including him in the story. "The houses were for the returning G.I.s. I got us a mortgage because I had the G.I. Bill. Otherwise we'd still be on Pitt Street."

He laughed, reached into the breast pocket of his pea-green sports jacket and pulled out a cigar wrapped in clear plastic. "You could say it was the war that got us out of the Lower East Side." He thought about this, then corrected himself. "Or you could say I got us out. I was sixteen when I went into the Marines." He slipped the wrapper off his cigar.

"Wasn't that young?" Jason asked.

"I lied about my age. I never did finish high school."

"Were you scared?"

"Sure, a little. But our home wasn't like yours. I wanted to get out."

"So Dad was left behind?"

"Yeah, I guess so, if you want to put it that way. He was just a little punk then."

"What was Morris like?" Jason did not know why he was asking that now, only that he'd wanted to ask it for a long time. He had never met his grandfather, and nobody ever mentioned him.

"My father?" asked Eddy, as if trying to clarify whose father Jason really meant. "He was dead before then."

"I know. I was just curious."

"He was a good man," Glasser said suddenly. "But it was the Depression."

"He was a bricklayer, but the construction company went out of business," Eddy added. "There was no work."

"It was the Depression," Glasser repeated.

"Sometimes I'd go over to where he sat reading the paper, and I'd ask him for a penny," Eddy said. "If he had it, he'd give it to me."

"He was generous," Glasser said.

"And if he didn't have it, he'd pretend not to hear me."

Glasser nodded. "There wasn't any work."

"Not working made him crazy," said Eddy. "He couldn't understand why this had happened to us. He thought it was a judgment." Eddy stopped, put the cigar in his mouth, then took it out again, the end dark with saliva. "I guess he had a lot of anger. Yeah, he was angry."

"But you can't blame him," said Glasser quickly. "He tried, but there was no work."

"Yeah." Eddy sounded tired of the subject now. "Papa did the best he knew how."

He lit his cigar, and the heavy smoke spread around them, the supreme male smell. The scent took Jason back to the occasional childhood visits, when Uncle Eddy lived on Eastern Parkway. The dark mulchy smell of the cigars had been out of place in that apartment, which was all windows and mirrors and blond furniture, the light pouring in everywhere. It was like he was keeping a zoo animal somewhere out of sight.

"Never judge," Glasser blurted out, as if he hadn't known he was going to say something till suddenly he was saying it. The syllables had a violent spin, like a wild pitch leaving his fingers too soon. He spoke to the Formica between himself and Eddy, but Jason knew the words were for him. "You can't know what another person is feeling," said his father. "You can't know why a person does what he does."

Suddenly Jason was overcome with a terrible, painful wave of love for this man, his father, and for his Uncle Eddy. It was a tight, constricting feeling, as if there were something big and heavy in his chest that shouldn't be there, something he had to hold in and not let out. And at the same time it was like he was rising above himself, above his table, looking down at the three of them sitting among their dirty dishes, their cups of coffee. He could see the fragility of this configuration—these three particular men sitting in a diner in Brooklyn in the summer of 1988—how it would never happen again, how it was just an insignificant speck in the flow of time. They themselves would forget this moment in a week or two weeks or a year. It would be gone, as if it had never happened. Jason would have gray hair one day, like his father's, and he would die and be forgotten too.

And yet this only served to make the love more intense, more painful—feeling it slip away, even as he tried to grab tighter, knowing it was useless, that the slipping was part of it. He knew he would never be a man like his father or Eddy, would never be a part of their world. He would never become a lawyer or own a disco, never cook up crazy money schemes or run out to do business at a McDonald's at midnight. He would never smoke cigars and drive a Lincoln, never go boom and then bust and then boom again, never count his bankroll.

He had spent the summer going from drugstore to bodega trying to sell Eddy's hand cream, and there was nothing more Glasser than that: a task half-silly and nearly hopeless. He'd gotten better at it too—he'd actually sold some—but it wasn't really in him, and he knew that.

When the check came he grabbed it from Eddy's blunt fingers. "It's mine tonight."

For a moment Eddy looked genuinely surprised, caught off guard, but then he collected himself and they began the adult ritual Jason had observed so many times from the sidelines. Eddy tried to grab the check back, mock angry. "What are you talking about? Give me that thing." With his other hand he drew out his wallet. "Lou, tell him."

His father watched sheepishly from his seat. In the old days he was always the one to pay, but now he didn't have any money. When Jason glanced over at him, he looked back impassively, as if nothing were happening—like Morris pretending he hadn't heard about the penny.

"Put it back," Jason said to Eddy, holding the check by his chest, then up in the air, out of reach of his uncle's exaggerated grabs. "Don't even try."

"All right then," said Eddy, role-playing defeat, "the Cosmetics King can get this one. I'll get the next one."

Cosmetics King. "Sounds fair," said Jason, laying down some bills—all his bills, actually, since the check was larger than he'd expected. "Plenty more where that comes from."

ACKNOWLEDGMENTS

I am rich in debts, and it is a pleasure to acknowledge them here, however briefly. The Fine Arts Work Center in Provincetown and the Michener-Copernicus Society provided very generous support during a difficult period. My agent, Amanda Urban, and my extraordinary editor, Jonathan Karp, both gave unstintingly of their faith and wise counsel. Lucy Rector and Margaret Mittelbach indulged my taste for self-promotion, Sean Siegel kept my spirits up, and Robert Cohen and Meg Wolitzer both provided soothing advice. Alyssa Haywoode, Holly Wiseman, Andrew Perchuk, John Kelly, Bob Welch, Jeremy Freeman, Sean Abbott, Stanley Siegel, Frances Silverglate Siegel, David Siegel, and Perrin Siegel all read with generosity and insight. The masterful Jennie Litt devoured numerous drafts, and her clear-eyed rigor set the standard I tried to reach. And most important, Karen Bender pondered every word with empathy and discernment; in the process, she taught me the essential lesson for both literature and life: that to know is to feel.

About the Author

ROBERT ANTHONY SIEGEL was born in New York City to a family of lawyers. He studied Japanese literature at Harvard and the University of Tokyo, then earned an M.F.A. at the Iowa Writers Workshop. In between, he spent a number of years working for a criminal law firm in New York. His fiction has appeared in *Story* magazine and he has won a Michener-Engle Fellowship and a Writing Fellowship at the Fine Arts Work Center in Provincetown. This is his first novel.

Robert Anthony Siegel can be reached by e-mail at louglasser@aol.com.